from
Pam xxx

FAST MOVIN' TRAIN

Pam Howes

Pam Howes
2023

FAST MOVIN' TRAIN

Published in 2016 by FeedARead.com Publishing

A CIP catalogue record for this title is available from the British Library.

Acknowledgements:

For my wonderful, supportive man, for bringing such pleasure to my life.
Always my inspiration and without whom there would be no story!

John Hudspith Editing Services

JD Smith Design for another fabulous cover.

Thanks to Restless Hearts for giving Rod and Mandy a song to remember.

CHAPTER ONE

MARCH 1994

Balanced on a plank fourteen feet above a polished wooden floor, arms laden with swags and tails, Mandy Radcliffe could think of better ways to spend a Monday morning. She drew a deep breath and edged slowly along to the girl poised on one of the stepladders supporting the plank, now wishing she'd hired a scaffolding platform.

'Ready, Sarah? Grab this tail and attach it to the end of the batten.'

'Don't know if I dare let go,' Sarah muttered, eyes wide, hands grasping the ladder so firmly, her knuckles were white.

'You'll be fine,' Mandy reassured, with more conviction than she felt. Why the hell had she told her client that height was no problem? 'I'll hold on to you while you press the Velcro in place. Whatever you do, don't look down. When we're finished I'll treat us to lunch at Brambles.'

She smiled as Sarah's face brightened. In spite of her recent engagement, Mandy knew her young assistant had a soft spot for the Brambles Italian waiter. Sarah secured the tail then Mandy positioned the swags, deftly curving and overlapping the plush red chenille as she worked her way along the wooden batten. She fastened up the right hand tail, tweaked it so the cream silk lining fell in soft contrasting pleats, and clambered down the ladder. She nodded with satisfaction. 'You can come down now. They're perfect. Let's hope Mrs Barn Conversion thinks so, too.'

Sarah joined her. 'Wow! They're fantastic.'

Mandy picked up the chunky plaited tie backs. She looped them around the floor length curtains and coaxed them to hang in neat folds. Red wasn't to everyone's taste, but her client had a passion for the sensual colour that featured in almost every room of the stunning mellow stone house.

The elegant lounge, with its solid oak floor, high ceiling and cathedral-style beams was a fantastic place for a party, if ever she saw one. The huge window, with its curved top, had been the entrance for hay wagons in the barn's previous life. It was the last one in the property to dress and by far the most challenging.

'Wonder if I'll ever be able to afford a place like this,' Sarah said, echoing Mandy's own thoughts.

'You might, if you win the pools.' Mandy packed her tools away. 'Right, let's get the car loaded. I'll leave the bill in Mrs B.C.'s office.'

Mandy waved goodbye to her client's cleaning lady and joined Sarah in the Range Rover. She drove down the rutted private lane and out onto the main street in the Derbyshire village of Rowarth. As they passed through the next village she silently counted the cottage windows she'd curtained in the last few years. Almost every dwelling in fact and some weekend retreats hidden away down country lanes.

*

Over a glass of house red and a dish of seafood pasta, Mandy reflected on the success of the morning. Not a window for the faint-hearted, but one that would pay for a week in Malta. A trip away might give her flagging marriage a boost. Not that Mike acknowledged it was flagging. He did his own thing and by and large, she did hers. Truth be told, she'd rather have a week in Rome or Paris with a couple of her mates, but she'd get pressure from the kids about being unfair to Dad if she went off for a girlie week and left him to his own devices. Not only that, the trip was supposedly to celebrate twenty-five years of marriage.

'Sup up, Sarah.' Mandy shared the last of the carafe between them. 'If we don't get back to the shop soon, Carol will be pacing the floor.'

Mandy settled the bill and the pair strolled through Pickford town centre. They stopped at Greggs to buy donuts for their afternoon break then headed towards the shop. Mandy looked up with pride at the red painted sign - Amanda Radcliffe Interiors - picked out in gold lettering. Her own business, built from scratch; first, by working from home out of the spare bedroom, and eventually renting the shop premises.

She'd developed her design skills during a short emigration to Canada where Mike had been offered a job in Calgary. He took the offer, too good to turn down, he told her. She'd disliked Calgary from the start. To combat the loneliness of being in a strange country she signed up for a soft furnishing course, discovered her talents, and began making drapes and cushions to sell.

She saw it as a way out and planned to earn enough money to go home and start again. Not to rely on Mike, who seemed to get a perverse kick from seeing her trapped and dependent on him. The rot set in, but they acknowledged each other for the sake of their three daughters. In 1982, after the third freezing-cold winter, she'd had enough and announced she was going home and taking their girls. Mike told her his contract was coming to an end and agreed to go with them.

They soon settled into their old lifestyle, reacquainted themselves with friends and bought another house. She put her business plan into action. Mike went back to his previous job and played bass guitar in his old band at weekends. To anyone observing them, Mandy knew they appeared to be a successful and happy family.

*

Carol, her middle-aged assistant, standing in the sales room with her coat on, handbag over her arm and lips pursed tighter than a cat's arse, was looking pointedly at her watch.

'Sorry we're late, Carol,' Mandy began. 'The job took longer than anticipated.'

'They always do,' Carol grumbled, hooking a straggly grey curl behind her ear. 'I've emptied the display area like you asked and given the window a damn good clean. It was proper mucky. You could hardly see through it.'

'I'll brew up,' Sarah said, disappearing into the tiny kitchen at the rear of the shop, but not before making faces at Carol behind her back.

Mandy stifled a grin. 'Thanks, Carol. We'll get cracking on another display this afternoon. I'll use some fabric from the new supplier.'

'Well - I'll be off then. I'm taking Mother to the podiatrist at two-thirty. I needed to get away a bit sooner really.'

'It's only half-one. You've plenty of time.'

Carol waddled towards the door. 'Oh, by the way,' she called over her shoulder, 'Rod Davies rang; said he'll call back later.'

Mandy watched as Carol left the shop. She felt a bit mean at times, always taking Sarah on the fittings. But

Carol couldn't stand heights. She was petrified of going any further than the second rung of a stepladder.

Sarah appeared with the coffee. 'You'd never think Carol's a similar age to you. She looks about sixty. You don't look a day over thirty-five. No one would ever guess you were a grandma.'

Mandy smiled, thinking of her two little grandsons. 'Carol and I were in the same class at school. She's nearly forty-six. She doesn't have much time for herself, with looking after her mother, and that older fellow she married. That's why she likes coming in here. It's a nice break for her, and she does a brilliant job, hand-finishing the curtains.'

*

The phone rang at three-thirty. Mandy climbed out of the window space to answer. Sarah was out sourcing silk flowers and baskets for the new display.

'Mandy, it's Rod,' a softly spoken male voice told her.

'Hi, you.' She smiled into the receiver. 'What's up?'

'Err, you free tonight by any chance?'

'I've some paperwork to do when I get home. I can be free around nine. Is that alright?'

'That's great. Is Mike going out?'

'Yep, he's rehearsing. Did you want to see him, too?'

'No,' he replied, 'just you.'

'Okay. Jenny coming with you?'

'No. I've, erm, got a bit of a problem. I need to talk to you - alone.'

'Is something wrong? With Jenny, I mean. She's not ill?'

'No, no, everything's fine. Well - not fine, but Jenny's okay. I'll explain tonight.'

'Sounds mysterious. See you later then.'

'You will. Bye.'

She hung up, frowning. Rod had sounded a bit agitated. Not his usual jokey self. And why did he want to see her alone? She hoped nothing *was* wrong with Jenny. Maybe she was ill and he didn't want to break the news over the phone. But then, surely he'd have wanted Mike to be there, too.

The shop bell interrupted her thoughts. Sarah waltzed in, her arms laden with flowers and wicker baskets, and two-hours later the window sported a fine display of the new spring stock.

Mandy went outside to take a look. The fabric lengths, draped at the back of the window, the piped and frilled cushions, set amongst baskets of silk flowers, looked lovely. Hopefully get her clients thinking about freshening up their conservatories.

*

Mandy pulled onto the drive of her Edwardian, semi-detached home, still wondering about Rod Davies's earlier call. Ah well, she'd find out what his problem was soon enough. She grabbed her briefcase and let herself in. Welcoming barks and clattering claws on the varnished hall floor greeted her. Two brindle Boxers leapt up and down. She fussed them and let them out at the kitchen door. 'Anyone home?' she yelled up the stairs. She could hear the strains of Wet, Wet, Wet's, Love Is All Around, so someone was in.

A door opened and a head popped over the balustrade, long, dark hair swinging.

'Hi, Mum,' Nicole called.

'Hi, love.'

Nicole ran downstairs. 'You look a bit flustered, Mum. Had a busy day?'

'I have. I'll take a quick bath then make dinner. Anyone else in to eat tonight?'

‘Just me. Louise is at her mate’s. Dad came home, loaded his gear and went out. Said he’ll eat at the pub before rehearsals. Actually, Mum, I’m not that hungry. I ate a huge lunch at college. I promised Becky I’d go round and help her bath the boys. Leave you alone to have a bit of peace.’

‘That’ll make a nice change,’ Mandy said with a smile. Becky, her eldest, lived a few streets away with her partner Andy and their sons. ‘There are sweeties in my handbag for the boys. Take them with you.’

*

Mandy lay back in the bubbles. She felt annoyed with Mike for not waiting until she came home before dashing out. His indifference got on her nerves at times. She wondered why she didn’t divorce him. After almost twenty-five years, things were unlikely to improve. Maybe she was expecting too much. Most long-term marriages probably ended up as stalemate. Couples - barely tolerant of each others’ needs - rubbing along because there was nothing else on the horizon. Divorce was expensive and soul-destroying. A case of better the devil you know for half of them. Mike was a good provider and a great dad. The girls adored him, he didn’t treat her badly. But she felt bored, trapped and not special anymore. She’d loved him at first, or at least she thought she had. They’d been quite passionate together, but once it wore off it stayed off. These days he hardly ever reached for her, or she for him, for that matter. She simply couldn’t be bothered anymore. What was love anyway? Just a word bandied around by singers, starry-eyed kids and Mills and Boon authors.

She thought again about the earlier strange conversation with Rod. She and Mike had been friends with Rod and his wife Jenny since their mid-teens. In fact, Rod asked her out a couple of times, but she’d been dating Chris, a boy she really liked, and had turned him down. Not that she didn't fancy Rod; she'd always had a soft spot for him. It was her that persuaded Rod to ask Jenny out when Chris complained he was sick of taking a gooseberry on their dates.

She recalled now how Rod had refused at first, saying they had nothing in common. But he asked her out eventually and Jenny accepted. The pair seemed happy enough. When she and Chris split up, Mandy began dating Rod's best mate Mike. They'd been a happy foursome. She and Mike were first to marry and Becky arrived six months later. Rod and Jenny followed suit. Their son James, and Becky, grew up like brother and sister. It seemed to Mandy that each time she announced another pregnancy, Jenny announced one shortly after. They had six children between them.

Mandy climbed out of the bath and towelled herself dry. She unclipped her long dark hair and ran her fingers through to remove the tangles. She dabbed concealer under her blue eyes to hide her tiredness, stroked blusher on her cheeks and slicked her lips with red gloss that matched her nails.

She pulled on black jeans, a red top with a V neckline and did a twirl in front of the mirror. Still slim, even after three kids, she was proud of her figure. A generous spray of her favourite perfume, Tocade by Rocha, and she was ready. Downstairs she made a cheese sandwich and opened a bottle of red wine. She ate half the sandwich, split the other half between the dogs, grabbed two wine glasses and carried them and her briefcase through to the lounge. Settling down on one of the sofas, she made a neat pile of invoices beside her. At exactly nine the doorbell rang and the dogs barked a welcome. She got up and shut them in the kitchen. Rod dithered nervously on the doorstep, his bright blue eyes not quite meeting hers.

'Come on in.' She took his leather coat, hung it on the hallstand and led the way into the lounge, gesturing to the cream sofas. 'Have a seat.'

'I don't want to disturb your work.' Rod sat down opposite her, stretching out denim-clad legs.

'I've finished what I needed to do.' She gathered up the invoices and stuffed them back into the briefcase. 'Fancy a drink?'

'Please.' He ran his hands through spiky brown hair, streaked with silver. Mandy thought it suited him. Very Rod Stewart, in fact. He took a swig of wine, sat back and half-smiled at her.

He looked tired, had dark circles beneath his eyes, and was subdued. Mandy frowned. She was used to seeing Rod bouncy and full of life. He always laughed a lot, a complete extrovert and the total opposite to Jenny who was quiet and took everything so seriously.

They made small talk for a while then Mandy asked, 'How come you're not working?' Rod was normally drumming with his group. It was rare for him to be around on a Monday night.

'Band's split up,' he said. 'I'm joining a new one. Got a couple of weeks break and then I'm off south to East Sussex for the summer.'

'Bet Jenny's pleased.'

He stared at her for a long moment. 'Oh - you know Jen. Supportive of everything I do. Not!' he finished sarcastically. 'She hates me being on the road. If she wanted a stay-at-home she should have married a bloke in a suit with an office job, like Mike.'

'You two had a row? Is that what this is all about?' Mandy took a sip of wine. 'It's finally dawned on you that Jenny doesn't understand you.'

Rod looked down at his drink. 'Well, she doesn't,' he mumbled, 'understand me, I mean. Never has done. But then I guess I've never understood her either.'

Mandy nodded. Once Jenny got her claws into Rod there was no way she was letting go. She took another sip of wine.

He cleared his throat. 'I need to tell you something, Mandy. It's, erm, not easy for me. It might wreck our friendship.' He shrugged. 'But I'm gonna have to take that chance.' He came and sat beside her. 'I've carried it around with me forever. In here.' He patted his chest. 'In my heart - I mean. It won't go away. I can't handle it any longer.'

She gripped the stem of her glass and drew a deep breath, feeling her cheeks heating, and something that felt like icy water trickling down her back. He was so close she could smell his aftershave, woody and masculine. The scent made her stomach flip. She focused on the dimple in his chin.

'Mandy, look at me… please.'

She swallowed hard and looked into his eyes, seeing something in their blue depths that she'd never seen before.

'You haven't a clue, have you?' he said softly.

She shook her head. 'Rod, you're scaring me. What is it?'

'I'm in love with you,' he said.

*

CHAPTER TWO

The glass slipped from Mandy's fingers, the wine spreading in a big red stain on the cream rug.

Rod leapt to his feet, snatching a handful of tissues from the box on the coffee table. Mandy stared at him as he dabbed at the mess, her mouth wide but silent. She heard the front door opening.

'Only me, Mum.'

Her daughter's voice brought Mandy to her senses. 'In here, Nic.'

Nicole's head popped around the door. 'Hi, Mum. Hi, Uncle Rod. You okay? Aunty Jen not with you?' Her eyes went to the rug. 'Oh, oh. Who's been clumsy then?'

'That was me I'm afraid,' Rod mumbled. 'I, err, popped in to see your dad, but he's out. Your mum gave me a glass of red and I missed the coffee table when I put it down.'

'I'll grab a cloth and the Vanish,' Nicole said.

'Why did you tell her it was your fault?' Mandy whispered as Nicole left the room.

'I said the first thing that came into my head. I could hardly tell her the truth.'

'I think you'd better go. Before you say anything else you might…' Mandy trailed off as Nicole came back and bent to spray the stain. 'Leave it, Nic. I'll do it. You get off to bed, love. I'm just going to see Rod out.'

'Okay. Goodnight.' Nicole gave her mum a kiss. 'Night, clumsy,' she said to Rod with a grin.

'Night, sweetheart.' Rod gave his goddaughter a hug.

Mandy followed Nicole out of the room and came back carrying Rod's coat.

'Mandy,' he began and pushed the door closed. 'I meant what I said. I'm sorry, but I *do* love you. I always have done.'

'Stop it, Rod. You love Jenny, you know you do.'

'I care about Jenny, but I don't love her,' he said, taking hold of her upper arms. 'This isn't a wind up. I can't carry on any longer; it's doing my fucking head in. Maybe I should have found a better way to tell you. But I couldn't think of another. You must have seen the way I look at you when we're all out together. I can't take my eyes off you.'

Mandy nodded. She'd seen it alright, but had chosen to ignore for fear of where it might lead. 'I can't deal with this. Jenny's my friend. Why have you said it? How will I look her in the eye now? Just go, please.'

'I'm going nowhere. I need to talk to you properly. Can we meet up one day this week? When's your day off?'

'Wednesday, but…'

'I have to see my new agent on Wednesday. Come with me for the ride and then we can talk. His office is in Shrewsbury. I shouldn't be more than an hour or two. Maybe you could pop in and see your friend Lesley while we're down there.'

'My God! You've got it all planned.'

'Well it makes sense,' he persisted. 'And I didn't plan it. Just seems like a good idea. I know you often go down to Lesley's on a Wednesday.'

'Yeah, but this week I've arranged to have lunch with Jenny.'

‘Shit! Can’t you cancel? Please, Mandy, there’s so much more I want to say to you.’ He stared at her as though willing her to say yes. ‘Shall I pick you up here, at say - ten? Please,’ he said, one more time.

She chewed her lip. ‘Okay, but go now. My head’s in a whirl. Nic’s bound to tell Mike you were here tonight. I’ll stick with the story you told her. That you forgot he was going out.’

‘Okay. I didn’t mean to upset you. Maybe I shouldn’t have dropped this on you, but I’m not sorry that I did. We’ll talk on Wednesday. If you want nothing more to do with me I’ll understand. But please, Mandy, think about what I said. I meant every word.’ He planted a light kiss on her cheek and left.

*

On the drive home Rod gripped the steering wheel, using all his effort to concentrate on the road. He couldn’t believe he’d done it. He hoped to God he hadn’t fucked things up. He thought back to when he first met Mandy in the record store. They were both sixteen. He fancied her then, but she was dating an older guy and seemed quite happy. Then one night she was at The Manor Lounge Club with Jenny. He assumed she’d dumped the boyfriend. He asked her to dance then later asked her out. She told him her boyfriend was on holiday.

A few months later they were at the engagement party of mutual friends. He followed her upstairs and hung around on the landing. When she came out of the bathroom he pushed her back inside. He’d just shared his first joint and was feeling invincible. He pulled her into his arms and kissed her. He expected her to shove him away, but she wound her arms around his neck and kissed him back. She still refused to date him though because of the older guy. She fixed him up with Jenny and only weeks later started seeing Mike and that was it. The following year they were all married. He'd felt trapped ever since. He'd only dated Jenny in the first place because he thought he'd be spending a lot of time in Mandy's company. Then he'd got Jenny in the club and felt obliged to marry her. But he'd never forgotten that first kiss with Mandy, and he knew *she* was unhappy with Mike.

If he had to spend many more years with Jenny he'd slit his wrists. She was an okay wife and a great mum but they had no shared interests. She'd asked him to give up drumming when he married her. It was one sacrifice he wasn't prepared to make. He'd told her; accept him for what he was, or not at all. For the last twenty-four years she'd tried to change him. He'd had enough. He'd recently lost a close mate in a car accident. Mac had been the singer in his first band. His death had made Rod realise that life was too short. It was time to move on. But he wanted to move on with Mandy - if she'd have him.

*

Mandy heard the front door open as Mike came in and began to unload his gear. She turned onto her side, switched off the bedside lamp, curled into a tight ball and closed her eyes. She couldn't get Rod's anxious face out of her mind. She was sure he wasn't having her on with his declarations of love. She'd never seen him so serious. It must have taken some guts to come here and tell her that. She wondered how long he'd been trying to pluck up the courage. She'd always had a special bond with Rod and thought back over the last few years. Their family holidays together. He'd helped her get over her fear of water and taught her to swim. Had held her bikini-clad body in the pool; never once touched her inappropriately. He'd smoothed sun-cream on her back and other areas she couldn't reach; guided her arm in the right position when they'd been ten-pin bowling, his other hand on her hip. All the times they'd laughed and joked together.

She heard Mike clattering around in the bathroom now. The dogs grunted softly as they greeted him from their baskets on the landing. He came into the dark bedroom, banging into the chair by the window.

'Fuck it!' he cursed under his breath, throwing off his clothes.

The bed creaked as he climbed in beside her. He made no effort to see if she was still awake, to say goodnight, or even give her a hug. She could smell his citrus aftershave mingled with beer. She recalled Rod's woody scent and the way it had made her stomach flip. It was a long time since Mike had made her feel like that. She'd tried her best to put a spark back into their marriage, candlelit dinners, sensual underwear, but it was hard work and the feelings of love she'd once felt were no longer there. For her, there was nothing left to ignite. What harm could it do to go to Shrewsbury with Rod on Wednesday? She enjoyed the little thrill that ran through her as she made her decision.

*

On Wednesday morning Rod was outside the house on the dot of ten in his battered black BMW estate. Mandy got in beside him, feeling like a nervous teen on her first date. His smile was welcoming. He leant over and pecked her cheek. She smiled back and felt herself relaxing.

'Does Jenny know I'm going to Shrewsbury with you?' she asked as he pulled onto the busy A6. 'Only when I left her a message to cancel lunch I told her I had to go and see my bank manager.'

'She doesn't even know I'm going to Shrewsbury,' Rod replied. 'I told her I've got a band meeting. She's not speaking because of the summer season. I don't know what she expects of me. I can't pay the mortgage unless I work. I love performing. I'll be doing more singing with this new band. I'm really looking forward to it. I'm too bloody old to change careers.'

'You shouldn't have to,' Mandy said. 'You're very good. You've got a great voice. By the way, I told Mike that I'm going to Lesley's, but not that I'm going with you. I said I was getting the train.'

'We're sneaking about like we're having an affair already,' he said.

'An affair!' Mandy stared at him. 'No way am I having an affair with you, Rod.'

He looked at her, eyebrows raised. 'So how do you propose we get to know one another better?'

'We've been friends for thirty years. I think I know most things about you. Anyway, I thought the idea was to talk some more.'

'Yeah, and we will. What I said the other night – I meant it. I love you. I'd like to spend some time with you. Even just like this. Being alone together now and again would be great. I've got two weeks before I'm off down south and I'll be away for months.'

'And will Jenny be spending any time with you while you're away?' She was surprised to find she felt slightly jealous at the thought.

'I doubt it. I'll nip back now and again to catch up with her and the kids.'

Mandy stared out of the window. They were passing Manchester Airport. 'Be nice to go away somewhere hot together.' The words were out before she could stop them. She felt her cheeks warming.

Rod looked across and grinned. 'Ah – you'd consider going away with me then? You do realise that'd mean we'd have to spend nights together?'

She looked away, feeling flustered. The way Rod was looking at her sent a warm glow right through her. She liked it.

'Cat got your tongue?'

'No, you've made me feel embarrassed.' She slapped his arm.

'Mandy,' he said, his tone more serious now, 'would you like to spend a night with me?' He kept his eyes on the road.

'Maybe.' This was a crazy conversation. Not one she should be having. But for reasons beyond her she wanted it to continue.

'Did you have time for breakfast?' He changed the subject.

She shook her head.

'We'll stop at a Little Chef.'

*

They found a table by the window, ordered Early Starters and pots of coffee. The waitress brought them a laden tray.

'Tuck in.' Rod poured the coffee. 'Never let it be said that I don't know how to treat a lady!'

'Audrey Hepburn got hers in Tiffany's,' Mandy said with a laugh. She buttered a slice of toast. 'Can't believe we're doing this.'

'We're only having breakfast.'

'Yeah, but we're doing it behind Mike and Jenny's backs.' Her mobile rang and she fished in her handbag, hoping it wasn't Mike, or even worse, Jenny. Lesley's number flashed on screen. 'Hi, Les. – Yeah, I'm on my way. Just having breakfast. Won't be too long. Okay, see you soon.'

‘Does Lesley know you’re with me?’

She nodded and dipped a piece of sausage into her egg yolk. ‘I told her I was getting a lift from you. She called to say that if she’s out with the dogs the key will be under the red plant pot.’

‘Anyway,’ Rod said, lowering his voice. ‘Back to spending a night together. What about next Wednesday? Tell Mike you’re staying overnight at Lesley’s. I’ll book a room somewhere away from Pickford. Get you back to work for Thursday lunchtime.’

‘God, I’m not sure,’ Mandy said, a feeling of utter panic dancing in her stomach. ‘What if Mike finds out? He’ll go mental. So will Jenny.’

Rod was quiet for a moment. ‘Think about it. We’ll talk some more on the way home.’

Mandy stared down at her plate. She was so tempted to say yes, but she also felt terrified. She looked up to find Rod’s eyes burning into hers. ‘I’ll see,’ she whispered.

In the queue to pay Rod slipped his arm around her waist; she didn’t pull away. It felt comfortable and she leaned into him.

*

They parked outside Lesley’s black and white timbered cottage. She came strolling up the lane accompanied by two muddy cream Labradors. Lesley, her husband Jack and their sons had moved from Pickford two years ago to seek The Good Life in rural Shropshire.

The dogs were packed off to the utility room for rubbing down later. Lesley led the way into the comfortably furnished conservatory at the back of the house. The room overlooked a large garden that sloped away to a small lake, home to a couple of swans and a dozen or so ducks.

‘The blinds still look good,’ Mandy said. She’d made the cream calico Roman blinds last year. ‘Rod, just come and look at the fabulous view from this window.’ She went over to the patio door, wondering why Lesley had left it open while she was out. That was something you wouldn’t dare do in Pickford. She walked straight into the glass, banged her head with such force that she bounced backwards into the room and landed at Rod’s feet. He was on his knees in seconds, cradling her in his arms. He ordered Lesley to grab a cloth and some ice.

Mandy could see stars, but was also aware of Rod’s anxious face and his sensual scent. She felt doubly dizzy with him holding her so close. He smoothed her hair from her face and dropped light kisses on her lips. ‘It’s okay, it’s okay,’ he whispered.

Lesley returned with a tea towel and a basin of ice cubes. Rod tipped the ice onto the cloth and held it against Mandy’s forehead.

‘Why the hell did you walk into the door?’ Lesley asked, looking totally bemused.

‘I thought it was open!’

‘Err- no, but I can see why you thought that. It’s usually covered in dog-snot, but I cleaned it yesterday. You dope, Mandy! You’ll have a right headache now.’

Rod was still on his knees with his arm around her shoulders. Mandy could see Lesley looking curiously at them.

‘Never had a woman fall at my feet before,’ he muttered, jumping up. ‘I’d better get off to the meeting. Will you be alright?’

‘She’ll be fine,’ Lesley said. ‘I’ll give her something for the pain and bring her into town later. Do you want to meet us in the wine bar on Barker Street for lunch?’

Rod nodded and blew a kiss at Mandy as Lesley saw him out.

Mandy got unsteadily to her feet and sat on one of the sofas, her head throbbing. Lesley came back into the conservatory with a glass of water, two paracetamol and a questioning look in her eyes.

'So, are you going to fill me in with what's happening between you and Rod?'

'There's nothing happening. I took advantage of a lift down here to visit you, that's all. Saves the train fare.'

'Does Mike know you're with him?'

'No.'

'Thought not. Rod's got the hots for you. The look on his face when you smashed into that door said it all.'

Mandy sighed and twisted her hands. 'Don't say a word to anyone. On Monday night he told me, well - he told me he's in love with me.'

'That much is obvious. How do you feel about him?'

Mandy thought for a long moment. 'I really like him. I always have done. He's kind and funny. And I know this might make me sound like a right stupid kid, but he makes me feel all warm and fuzzy inside. I haven't stopped thinking about him since Monday.'

'Will you sleep with him?' Lesley was always direct.

Mandy could feel her cheeks burning yet again. 'I think I want to, but don't know if I dare. What if it gets all out of control once we start?'

Lesley sat down next to her. 'Want my honest opinion?'

Mandy shrugged. 'You're going to give it to me anyway, aren't you?'

‘I shouldn’t be encouraging you, but what the hell. You’re so fed up with Mike. I can’t see you staying with him for much longer. And let’s face it; Jenny’s pissed Rod off for as long as I can remember. You and he will make a great couple. You might regret it forever if you don’t even give it a chance. Go for it, Mandy. What have you got to lose? It might be the best thing you both ever do.’

*

CHAPTER THREE

Mandy stretched out on the bed, racking her brain as to how she could spend a night away with Rod. She heard the bathroom door opening and as Mike wandered in, the perfect excuse occurred to her. 'I'm, erm, staying overnight at Lesley's next Wednesday,' she said, hoping her face wasn't turning pink. 'We're going to her friend's party at The Buttermarket.' Rod had dropped her off at Pickford Station. They'd agreed he'd book a motel room. He'd promised to pop in the shop to see her tomorrow lunchtime.

'Whatever,' Mike said, brushing his hair in front of the dressing table mirror. 'You okay for cover at work?'

'Sarah and Carol will take care of things. I haven't had a day off for weeks, well - apart from today, of course.'

'Okay.' He reached into the wardrobe for a sweatshirt and jeans.

Mandy watched him dress. Why didn't she fancy him? He wasn't bad looking; slim and nearly six-foot tall. Had friendly blue eyes, a neat dark beard, always dressed trendy and smelt clean. But there was nothing there.

'I'm off out in a minute,' he announced. 'I'm meeting Steve from work for a drink. Oh, yeah,' he added, picking up his car keys, 'Jenny called earlier. When you ring her back, ask her and Rod over for a curry on Friday. It'll give me a chance to catch up with him.'

Mandy could feel her cheeks heating and looked away. ‘Do I have to? Why don’t we just relax together?’

‘Don’t be such a misery. They’re our best mates. Right, I’m going. Don’t wait up.’

She watched him stride out of the room and breathed a sigh of relief when she heard the front door slam. Her headache was back with a vengeance, but at least the swelling had gone down. Mike hadn’t even noticed. And there was no way she was phoning Jenny tonight, listening to her wittering on about Rod being away all summer.

Her jacket was draped over the back of the bedroom chair. She reached for it and held it to her nose. She could smell a faint trace of Rod’s aftershave. Again, she felt her stomach flip.

*

‘So what do you reckon?’ Mandy asked Rod the following day.

‘It’s up to you.’ They were in the workroom at the back of the shop. Rod sprawled out on the comfy chair, surrounded by rolls of fabric and a mountain of half finished curtains.

Mandy had given Sarah and Carol an early lunch. Rod dropped the catch and hung the “back in thirty minutes” sign on the door.

The way he was looking at her made her feel tingly inside, right down to her toes. His eyes followed her every move as she fiddled with a roll of curtain tape. ‘I don’t know that I can face Jenny,’ she muttered.

‘Why? We haven’t done anything. Let’s not start acting guilty just yet. Try and be normal in front of Mike and Jenny. Call her later, invite us over and we’ll have a nice night. Get a couple of drinks down you, you’ll be fine.’

'I suppose you're right,' she said, pacing the floor now, her hands shaking. She was so conscious of that woody scent. 'We haven't done anything, but we've talked about it. Doesn't that make us guilty by thought?'

'Mandy?' He got to his feet and reached for her, held her in his arms. He ran his hands through her hair. 'Do you want me? If you don't I'll walk away now. We'll carry on as normal and never mention it again.'

'Of course I want you,' she said, loving the feel of his arms around her. His eyes never left her face. She willed him to kiss her, really kiss her. She stroked his cheek and shivered, closing her eyes as his lips came down on hers. He crushed her to him, kissing her long and hard. They drew apart and he sat back down on the chair, pulling her onto his knee. He gave her no time to catch her breath and kissed her again. She kissed him back, wanting it to go on forever, pressing herself against him, needing more.

He held her face between both hands and whispered. 'That felt so right, and don't tell me it didn't.'

'It did.' Nothing had ever felt so right to her in fact.

'I can't wait for next week,' he said, hugging her.

'Me too. But I'm a bit nervous.'

'Not of me, I hope.'

She chewed her lip. She was nervous of everything. Disappointing him for starters. What if he hated her body on sight? She was slim, but things weren't quite as firm as they used to be. What if she couldn't turn him on? Although sitting on his knee here, she could feel that wouldn't be a problem. If becoming lovers ruined their close friendship, then what? It wasn't something you could take back.

And then there was Mike and Jenny and all their kids; the feelings of so many to consider. There were hundreds of thoughts running through her head, so much so, she felt it might explode.

The sensible wife-and-mother-side knew she should say forget it. But the not-so sensible side didn't want to, and Rod's sincere face, and him telling her he couldn't wait, well - how could she say no?

'It's not you, Rod. It's the thought of Mike and Jenny finding out that's bothering me, and all the upset that would cause.'

'I know. But Lesley will cover for you. I'll tell Jen I've got a last minute gig in Cardiff. She won't question it. I often stand in with a band down there at short notice.'

'Won't she expect you to hand some money over then?'

'Wouldn't get much for one night. Digs and diesel would take a chunk. I'll slip her a few quid. That'll keep her happy.'

Mandy traced the dimple in his chin. 'You've thought of everything.'

He hugged her, set her down and got to his feet. 'I hope so.'

She pulled him close and kissed him again. 'See you tomorrow then.'

*

Mandy stacked the plates on top of the warmer and lit the tea lights. She poured two glasses of Chardonnay and handed one to Jenny. Mike and Rod had nipped out to collect the take-away.

'Come and sit in the lounge.' Mandy led the way and gestured for Jenny to take a seat.

'Oh dear, he *did* make a mess.' Jenny pointed to the faint red stain on the cream rug. 'Dozy sod.'

'Who?' Mandy frowned. She wasn't aware that Rod had told Jenny of his visit on Monday.

'Rod, of course. Your Nicole told our Beth he'd dropped his wine when he called round.' She laughed, her hand fluttering to her chest.

Mandy forced a smile. 'Oh - yeah. Do you know, Jenny, I've had such a hectic week, I'd forgotten all about it.'

'They say pouring white wine on red helps. But you have to do it right away.'

'I believe so,' Mandy said, thinking - when your husband announced he was in love with me - cleaning the rug was the last thing on my mind. 'Bit late for that now though.'

'Never mind, you can take it to the cleaner's and get them to pre-treat the stain. You should ask Rod to pay for it.'

'Please stop worrying about my rug,' Mandy said, a bit sharper than she meant to. 'Sorry,' she added as a frown crossed Jenny's pale face. 'I'm a bit tired, been a busy day. Like your dress, by the way.' The dress was a silky black and white shift that clung to Jenny's curvy hips, but the black drained her colour. She needed something brighter to warm her complexion. Chocolate brown or a warm cream would have looked better. Pointless telling her though; she'd never had a sense of what looked good on her and usually stuck to wearing tailored pants and over-fussy shirts.

'Thanks. Beth made me buy it in Next.' Jenny twiddled a mousy-brown strand of her chin length bob. 'She said it's time I dressed for my age rather than her granny's.' She took a sip of wine. 'Did you know that Rod's going to be away for most of the spring and summer?'

'Is he? Bet you'll miss him.'

'Hmm. I'll have to get someone in to help with the garden.'

Mandy almost choked on her drink. 'That all you'll miss him for?'

'He usually cuts the grass when he's around. I can't handle the mower. It's too heavy for me.'

'But surely you'll miss him for more than grass cutting?'

'Well I won't miss him arguing with me every five minutes.' Jenny stared into her glass. 'It must be so nice to be as happy as you and Mike are.'

Mandy frowned and took another slug of wine. 'I suppose it is.' She tried to keep the sarcasm out of her voice. Couldn't Jenny see how unhappy she was? Mind you, for the last few months she hadn't spent much time with her, Lesley being her preferred confidant these days. Jenny was always in her own little world. She saw what she wanted to see. 'You and Rod are happy enough, aren't you? You always seem – err – close.' Close might be stretching it a bit, but she needed to know from Jenny what the current state of play was with their marriage. It was something she'd never even thought about. Like everyone else, they seemed to plod along okay. It was only after Rod had told her he didn't love Jenny that she realised there was a problem.

'We used to be close,' Jenny said wistfully, a faraway look in her brown eyes. 'But I suppose we're like most couples who've been married a long time.' She lowered her voice, even though there was no one around except for the dogs in the hall. 'When I had Beth things dwindled. After my hysterectomy I kind of shut up shop, if you get my drift.' She smiled at her own joke. 'Rod used to get annoyed with me, but he seems to have accepted it now.'

Jesus, Mandy thought. Poor Rod, Jenny had her hysterectomy ten years ago and Beth was a bit younger than Nicole - almost seventeen. Even she and Mike managed it occasionally; birthdays, anniversaries, any celebration that involved consuming copious amounts of alcohol to get her through it.

'I think Rod strays a bit when he's away,' Jenny confided. 'But as long as he doesn't bring trouble home, I turn a blind eye. Apart from that, I suppose you could say we've got a more or less perfect marriage.'

This time Mandy *did* choke on her drink. Perfect marriage! Arguments, no sex and a straying man! Bloody hell; it was worse than hers and Mike's. She didn't like the thought of Rod straying either. It made him sound like a randy tom; although she couldn't really blame him. She shoved the thought to the back of her mind and topped up their glasses. At this rate she'd be more than drunk before they got around to eating. She heard the front door open and Mike and Rod strolled in, arms full. Rod winked at her from behind Mike's shoulder and the back of Jenny's head. She turned away, smiling.

*

'Tuck in,' Mandy said, taking the lids off everything. 'Be careful because the plates'll be hot.'

'You two got any holiday plans?' Mike asked as they helped themselves to food.

'Not at the moment,' Rod said.

'Ah well, no doubt Jenny will join you for a week or two while you're away. We're thinking of Malta in April or May, aren't we, Mandy?'

Mandy nodded. Mike and Jenny moved away from the table and carried their laden plates into the lounge. She spooned chicken korma onto her plate and tore a piece off a Peshwari Naan. She was conscious of Rod standing very close behind her. Her stomach looped and she gave an involuntary shiver.

'I was rather hoping that *you'd* join me for a week or two,' he whispered.

She turned to face him and pushed the door closed with her foot. 'How?' she whispered back. 'I've got a business to run.'

'Well, if you can take time off to go away with Mike...'

'Pack it in, Rod, please. I knew you two coming here tonight was a bad idea.' Then before she could stop herself she added, 'Jenny thinks you stray when you're away.'

'What?' His face darkened and he put his plate down on the table. 'Why would she say that?'

'She just came out with it. Well - do you?'

He was quiet for a moment and then looked at her. 'I have in the past. But not for ages.'

'You sure?'

'Jesus, Mandy, of course I'm sure. Don't let what she says put you off our plans for Wednesday.'

'Shh,' she whispered. 'It won't.' She kissed him, keeping one eye on the door.

'I'll call you tomorrow,' he said as they broke apart. 'No, sod it. I'll come to the shop again. We'll arrange a time and place for me to pick you up.'

She nodded and left him to pile up his plate. In the lounge Mike was chatting animatedly to Jenny. Mandy sat down beside him.

'Thought you'd got lost,' he said, topping up her glass.

'I was just asking Rod about the new band.'

'You take more interest in him than I do,' Jenny laughed.

Mandy raised an eyebrow and took a slug of wine.

*

The March wind whipped her long hair across her face. Mandy wished she'd put on something warmer than a leather jacket and short skirt. Thank God she'd decided on winter tights and knee-length boots. She wound her red silk scarf a bit tighter around her neck and adjusted her shades. It wasn't a sunny day, they were for disguise. She flicked up the collar of her jacket and stared down Station Approach.

Her legs felt weak as Rod's car turned in. He flashed his lights and pulled over. She picked up her overnight bag and ran round to the passenger door, but not before she'd spotted a familiar figure striding up the road towards them. She jumped into the car. 'Put your foot down, quick,' she said, sinking into the seat.

Rod screeched around the corner and stopped. 'What's wrong?' He looked over his shoulder. 'Why the panic?'

'Nicole's boyfriend's over there.' She gestured with her thumb towards Pizza Hut.

'Well you can come out now,' he said, grinning. 'He's gone inside and I'm sure he didn't clock us. You can take your shades off, too.'

'It's not funny,' she said, wriggling upright. 'Just get me out of bloody Pickford before anyone sees us.' She settled back in her seat and tried to relax. 'So where exactly are we going?' she asked, once they were whizzing up the motorway.

'A Travelodge on the M62. It's not too far and saves us spending half the day driving. We can have the room from one and we don't have to be out until twelve tomorrow.'

'Great. We don't need to rush back either. I told Sarah I wouldn't be in at all until Friday.'

'Good. Sorry it's not anywhere posh. I'm a bit skint and obviously I couldn't book it on my credit card. Miss Marple would be sure to spot it.'

'A Travelodge is fine by me,' Mandy assured him. 'And we'll go halves.' Poor Rod was always skint. Jenny made sure of that. A picture of Jenny's trusting face came into her mind and she blinked to clear the vision. She glanced sideways at Rod, whose eyes were on the road as he flitted from lane to lane. She wondered if he was thinking about Jenny and how she would feel so betrayed if she knew of their plans. She thought about Mike and how angry he would be. But then, Mike hardly ever told her that he loved her these days. He wrote it in cards, well - he wrote, All My Love, but that was pretty standard for Mike - and her, come to that. They didn't go over the top. Not like Jenny, who always spelt Rod's name in little x's on cards and splashed words of love all over the place. If she felt that way, why the heck was she physically unable to show him that she loved him? But then again, if she did, Rod might not have asked her to spend a night with him. Mandy pushed all her scrambled thoughts to the back of her mind and concentrated on the day ahead, before she silently talked herself out of it. The thought of being loved and kissed by Rod was overwhelming and made her feel warm and fuzzy inside. Those sorts of feelings had been sadly lacking in her life for far too long. She stole another look at Rod's profile. He looked happy. His blue eyes were shining and his lips looked decidedly kissable. It wouldn't take much to make her fall deeply in love with him. She was more than halfway there already.

'Want some music on?' His voice broke her thoughts. 'I got a new CD from my friend in the States. It's a country rock band called Restless Hearts. They sound a bit like The Eagles. In fact, they took their name from the lyrics of New Kid in Town.' He slid the CD into the player and sang along to a couple of the songs.

Mandy loved his voice. She'd always enjoyed watching him performing with his various groups over the years. She knew Mike was envious of Rod's career. Although he enjoyed playing with his band, he would never take the chance and sacrifices to go pro because of the erratic financial side of things.

'Listen to the next song,' Rod said. 'It's got great lyrics.' He sang along again, glancing at her from time to time.

'Whatcha think?' he asked when the tale of unrequited love was over. 'Magic or what?'

'It's very you,' she said. 'What's it called?'

'Fast Movin' Train.'

He was quiet for a moment.

'Shall we adopt it as ours?'

'Ours?' Mandy had never had a song with Mike, although she'd always thought the words to Cass Elliott's, It's Getting Better were appropriate, even though it never really did. 'Yeah, let's.' She couldn't believe he'd made such a romantic gesture already. He kissed her hand and the warm, fuzzy feeling spread right through her.

*

It was only just gone twelve when Rod pulled off the motorway into Hartshead Services.

'Hartshead Moor,' Mandy said, liking the name.

'Yeah, I thought it appropriate,' Rod said. 'Seeing as my heart's ruling my bloody head at the moment. Soon as I saw it on the list I thought, that's the one.'

Mandy pulled his face to hers and kissed him, shivering as he kissed her back. She smiled as they drew apart. Two romantic gestures already and they had over twenty-four hours to go.

'We're a bit early for booking in,' Rod said. 'Shall we grab a coffee?' He took her hand and led the way.

He went to order and Mandy found a table. She stared at his back with longing. She couldn't wait to get him alone. He turned, as though sensing her watching him.

'Love you,' he mouthed.

'Love you, too,' she mouthed back, surprising herself. His face lit up and she blew him a kiss.

*

Rod looked around the room as Mandy went to pull the curtains. It was basic but clean and tidy and the big bed looked very inviting. He couldn't wait to get her into it. He smiled as she kicked off her boots and hung her scarf and jacket over a chair. A sudden thought occurred to him and the smile left his face.

'Back in a minute.' He dashed from the room, cursing himself for being forgetful. He thought he'd covered everything. He ran into the services shop and glanced around. Where would they be? There - on the shelf by the till, thank God. How many, three, eight, twelve? He grabbed an eight pack, paid the girl and dashed back to the room. Would Mandy think he was being over-presumptuous, buying eight? But three wouldn't be enough, he hoped.

He walked back into the room and she stared at him, a questioning expression in her eyes. 'Guess what I forgot?' He fished the condoms from his jacket pocket.

'Oh my God, I never even thought!' she exclaimed.

'Nor did I. Good job they had some in the shop. Is the room okay?'

'It's fine,' she said, looking away.

He tossed his jacket on top of hers. 'Come here,' he said, and she moved into his arms. Her cheeks were flushed and he could feel her shaking. He tilted her chin. 'Nervous?'

She nodded. 'Very.'

'Me too.' Voices in his head were screaming that he shouldn't be here, but there was no way he was backing out now. He kissed her and felt her relaxing against him.

He pulled her sweater over her head and she did the same with his T-shirt. He ran his hand down her back, gripped her buttocks and pulled her close. She was a couple of inches shorter than his five-foot-seven and he loved the way she melted into him, the perfect way they fitted together.

She rubbed her face against his hairy chest, breathing deeply.

He lowered her onto the bed and they slowly undressed each other, kissing and caressing all the time. He could feel the blood rushing to his groin and groaned, desperate for her to touch him.

Mandy ran her hands over his arms and upper chest. 'Lovely body,' she whispered, moving as close to him as she could.

'You're beautiful,' he said and leant up on one elbow, looking into her eyes. 'I love you, Mandy. I've waited forever for this.' He traced from below her chin with his fingertips and squeezed her breasts, loving the way her nipples stiffened as he ran his tongue over them. She groaned, reached for him and gently caressed his erection. He held his breath. Her hands were soft and warm. It was ages since a woman had touched him and it felt so good. She moaned softly as his fingers slipped inside her and explored. He moved slowly down her body, raining kisses, searching her, and then moved back up as she arched to meet him. He pushed inside her, thrusting with an energy he'd forgotten he possessed. They were on the bed, the floor, the chair, then back on the bed again. Time passed slowly as he made love to her in every position possible, and some Mandy told him she didn't even know existed. He looked up at her face, her eyes closed, lips parted as she rode him. He tipped her onto her back and as her breathing deepened, slid his hands underneath her, thrusting deeply. Her orgasm was explosive, noisy and went on forever. He cried her name over and over as he came.

'Fucking hell, woman!' He flopped onto his back. 'You've blown me away.'

He saw tears tumbling down her cheeks and held her close.

'What's wrong?' He wiped her face with his fingers.

'Was it ever like that with Jenny?' she whispered.

He stroked her hair from her face and dropped a kiss on her lips. 'It's never been like that with anyone. Not ever. What about you?'

'The same. It was wonderful, the most amazing I've ever had.'

Rod looked at his watch and smiled. 'It was a bloody marathon! We were at it nearly three hours!'

'My God, I doubt my sum total over the last ten years would amount to that!' She stroked his cheek and kissed his dimple. 'We've got all night to look forward to. I love you, Rod. I really do. You've made me feel - oh - I don't know, special, like a woman again.'

'You *are* a woman, a perfect woman. I love you, babe, more than you'll ever know.'

They lay curled together for a while talking quietly.

'I wish we could stay here forever,' Mandy said wistfully.

'So do I,' Rod murmured. 'I could do with a ciggie.' He sat up, reached for his jeans, rooted in the pocket and lit up.

'I'll make some tea,' Mandy said and slid out of bed. She handed him an ashtray and reached for his T-shirt.

'Don't put it on.' He stared at her with narrowed eyes as he blew a cloud of smoke into the air.

'Why not?'

'Because I want to look at your body.' Her face was glowing, lips swollen and her pupils, huge in her sparkling eyes. She looked like she might burst with happiness. He felt the same. It was the most wonderful feeling in the world and one he'd never experienced before. She picked up the kettle and took it into the bathroom. He couldn't take his eyes off her while she made tea.

Rod finished his cigarette and took the cup and saucer Mandy handed him. 'Well, this is very civilized,' he said as they perched on the edge of the bed, sipping tea. 'I mean - after all that...' He looked pointedly at the bedding and their clothes in a heap on the floor.

Mandy looked at him and blushed. 'I never knew I had it in me to be such a whore!' She took his cup and moved back into his arms. 'Now see what you've started!'

*

'You okay?' Rod asked as they pulled off the motorway and headed towards Pickford. They'd left the Travelodge at twelve, driven around for a while, stopped at a pub for lunch and then steamed up the car windows in a disused farm gateway until four.

'I don't want to go home,' Mandy said, stroking his thigh.

'Neither do I. But we've no choice, I'm afraid. I'll come and have lunch with you tomorrow and Saturday, if you like.'

She nodded. 'I *would* like.'

'Will you think seriously about joining me occasionally while I'm away?'

'I don't need to think. I'll do it. One way or another, I'll do it.'

Rod breathed a sigh. If only she could be with him all summer.

'I'll get sorted with digs and stuff and then we'll arrange something. We're playing Brighton, Hastings and Hove a lot, so that should be nice. We'll have all day and night together and you can come to the gigs.'

He pulled up at the station and drew her into his arms, kissing her deeply. 'Thanks for the most wonderful time of my life,' he whispered into her hair.

'It was my pleasure, and thank *you.* It's going to be so hard to act normal when I get home. I'm dreading it. Do you think Mike will be able to tell?'

'No. Just keep cool. We're not in a position to do anything else at the moment. You've spoken to Lesley, so you know he's not called you there for any reason and he hasn't rung your mobile. He couldn't give a flying fuck. If it wasn't for your business, we could have stayed another night.' He kissed her again. 'Love you, babe.'

'Love you too, Rod,' she said, reaching for her case. 'See you tomorrow.'

He watched her walk away towards the taxi rank. She turned, blowing him a kiss before climbing into a black cab. He pulled back onto the A6. He wanted to be with Mandy more than he'd ever wanted anything. But he knew that to achieve it would cause problems of monumental proportions.

*

CHAPTER FOUR

Mandy dropped the phone onto the cradle and turned to Rod. 'That was Mike. Jenny called. Suggested we all go to the cinema tonight while you're still around. Maybe have a pizza first.'

Rod raised a surprised eyebrow. 'Do we have a choice? What film does she want to see?'

'Backbeat. The one about The Beatles in Hamburg.'

'Ah, yes. She was going on about that last night. Wouldn't mind seeing it myself, but I'd rather just go with you.'

'Me too.' She wound her arms around his neck and kissed him. 'But we can't.' She brushed his face with her fingers. 'You're all sugary!'

'It's that donut.' Rod sat down on the chair, pulling her with him. 'Did you drop the catch on the door?' It was Saturday lunchtime and they were alone in the workroom at the back of the shop.

'Yeah! Why? What do you have in mind?'

'What do you think?' He said, sliding his hands under her sweater and cupping her breasts.

She caught her breath. It was impossible to fight the wonderful feelings he was giving her, and she didn't want to anyway. 'Half an hour. Then I really do have to reopen.'

*

Mandy reached for a slice of garlic bread. Rod was seated opposite her in Pizza Hut. He wrapped his feet around her feet, giving them a squeeze. She raised her eyebrows to warn him that Mike and Jenny were on their way back from the salad bar.

'I enjoyed lunch today,' he whispered, with the emphasis on lunch.

'So did I,' she whispered back. She felt her cheeks heating at the memory. They'd found a new use for the cutting table. Mike sat down beside her.

'I'm really looking forward to the film,' he said. 'Good idea of Jenny's.'

Jenny took the seat next to Rod. 'Well it's the last chance we'll get to be together for a while,' she said. 'And anything to do with the Beatles is usually good.'

'I'll never forget the day Lennon was murdered,' Mike said, tucking into his pizza. 'You were in bits, weren't you, Mand? Stuck out in Calgary and no one to share your grief with.'

Mandy nodded. 'It was awful. I spoke to Jenny the following day though, didn't I, Jen?'

'You did,' Jenny replied. 'I couldn't even tell it was you at first, you were crying that much.'

'It was a bad time all round really,' Mandy said. 'I hated Calgary. And being alone that day just made matters worse.'

'Let's not spoil the night by dwelling on the Calgary thing,' Mike said.

Mandy reached for another slice of garlic bread at the same time as Rod, and their fingers touched. She felt a lightning jolt shoot through her. Rod's look told her he'd felt it too. It was probably as well he was going away in a couple of days, she thought, before Jenny organized anything else. All she wanted to do right now was jump on Rod and make love to him again. Instead, she indulged in chit-chat with Jenny about the kids until Mike insisted they leave for the cinema.

*

Backbeat left Mandy with a heavy feeling in her heart. She didn't know if it was for herself, Stu Sutcliffe and Astrid Kirchherr - for their tragic relationship - or John Lennon. Rod had made it his business to sit next to her with Jenny to his left and Mike next to Jenny. Rod had let his knee rest against hers and when he'd reached for her hand the others didn't notice and they laced fingers down by his leg all through the film. He kept glancing at her and squeezing her hand. She could feel tears welling as they parted company on the car park. She gave Jenny a hug and a peck on the cheek and Jenny promised to call her mid-week to arrange lunch one day. Rod kissed her goodnight on both cheeks, whispering that he'd call her on Monday.

'You okay, Mand?' Mike asked, linking her arm as they walked to the car. 'You've hardly spoken all night'

'Yeah, of course. The film made me feel sad, that's all. I just wonder how on earth Astrid and John found the strength to pick up the pieces after Stuart's death.'

Mike nodded. 'It was very gut-wrenching. Fancy last orders at the Dog?'

'Not really. I'm tired. You go, but drop me at the house first.'

*

Mandy threw off her clothes and lay on the bed, wrapping her arms around herself. Tears flowed freely now and she sobbed into the pillow. She didn't really know why she was crying. Maybe sadness for a life she might have had with Rod, but then she wouldn't have had her beautiful daughters, and she'd never swap them for anything. She and Rod might have had kids – a son – she'd have loved a son. Rod had two. She was really going to miss him next week and would be living for his phone calls and making plans to visit him. Since their night away she'd felt more distanced from Mike than ever. It made her realise how wide the gulf between them really was. She'd felt so comfortable and relaxed with Rod. The way he looked at her with adoring eyes took her breath away. She could be herself with him. None of that walking-on-eggshells thing she always did around Mike.

Rod made her feel alive – eighteen again. How she wished they could go back to that time. She didn't dare let herself think about a future together. Probably an affair was all they'd ever have. But for how long, before Mike or Jenny guessed? What the hell would happen then? She couldn't believe that it was less than two weeks since Rod had dropped his bombshell, nor how quickly and deeply she'd fallen in love with him.

*

Rod took a long drag on his cigarette and looked up at the stars. Shivering, he pulled his leather jacket around him. He was sitting in his favourite thinking place, at the bottom of the garden, on an old stone bench that had been in his parents' backyard since his childhood. Mum had passed away eleven years ago, only fifty-five – massive heart attack. Dad had shacked up with an old friend and moved into her flat. Rod had brought the bench here when the family home was sold. He recalled Mum, sitting on it, with him on her knee, reading stories and singing songs that he'd join in with, making up his own lyrics to the tunes. He'd always loved to sing and his parents had encouraged him. He was an only child of only children, but had never felt lonely without siblings or cousins. Mum and Dad had always been there for him. Mum had taught him to play the piano. When he decided he'd like to play the drums, they'd bought him his first kit, a silver sparkle Rogers set, on HP from The Music Exchange. It had been his pride and joy and seen him through several bands in the sixties.

He really missed his mum and still felt guilty at disappointing her when he'd knocked Jenny up. But she'd been an all forgiving and doting grandma when James arrived and in her element when Ben and finally Beth put in appearances. He wondered what she would make of his affair with Mandy and saluted the brightest star. 'Sorry, Mum,' he whispered, knowing she wouldn't approve. He swallowed the lump in his throat now; thinking of the Rogers kit, stuffed at the back of the garage under God knows what. He should dig it out, clean it, re-skin the drums and sell it. There was a market for vintage kits. Maybe he would one day, when he was really skint.

Jenny had gone to bed as soon as they arrived home. He wished he could have gone home with Mandy. He wondered if he dare call her. Knowing Mike, he'd have suggested last orders. Knowing Mandy - she'd probably said no. If he called her mobile it wouldn't disturb the rest of the house, she usually stuffed it in her handbag.

His fingers hovered hesitantly over the keypad. 'Fuck it!' He dialled. It rang for a few seconds and then she answered, sounding like she had a cold.

'Hello.'

'You alone?'

'Yeah. Mike went to the pub. I can't stop crying, Rod and I don't know why.'

Rod felt like crying himself. 'I can't get you out of my head. Seeing that film took me right back to our teens and thinking about all that we'd missed.'

'I know, and that's my fault,' she sobbed.

'Mine too. I should have made a move after you dumped Chris and before Mike asked you out.'

'Why didn't you?'

He was silent for a few seconds. 'Because I couldn't stand you rejecting me again.'

'Oh, Rod. That makes me feel even worse. What on earth are we going to do?'

'We'll talk things through this summer and make some plans. I want to spend the rest of my life with you. But we're in for a rough ride. Do you think you can cope?'

'I don't know. The girls will hate me if I leave their dad. They'll probably never speak to me again.'

'Well I don't think I'll win any father-of-the-year awards with my lot. It won't be easy.'

'The dogs are grunting.' Mandy's voice dropped to a barely audible whisper. 'Mike's coming in. I'll talk to you on Monday. I love you so much.'

'And I love you, more than you know. Goodnight, babe.' He ended the call and sighed. Fucking hell, sorting it all out was gonna be a nightmare. Jenny would be devastated and Mike would probably want to kill him. The kids would side with Jenny; he'd no doubts about that. He'd got fuck-all security to offer Mandy. But there had to be a way. Now that he'd got her, he wasn't about to let her go. The creak of the garden gate disturbed his thoughts. Ben strolled towards him. His youngest son reminded Rod of himself at the same age; cocky, with an assured swagger. They were the same height and build, same blue eyes and brown hair.

'Hiya, mate.' Rod offered him a cigarette.

'Ta, Dad.' Ben sat down and lit up, blowing a cloud of smoke into the air. 'What you doing out here. Had another barney with Mum?'

Rod shook his head. 'Having a word with your Gran,' he said, gesturing towards the sky. 'We've been out with Mike and Mandy. Mum was tired. She's gone to bed. I'm just sitting here thinking. While I'm away this summer, make sure you look after Mum. Help her with the garden and stuff.'

'You'll be home occasionally, won't you?'

Rod shrugged. 'Now and again. When I get the chance. Be working most of the time though. Where've you been tonight?'

'Boar's Head, watching a band. Then back to Tanya's mum's place.'

'Is it serious, you and Tanya?' Rod took a long drag on his cigarette and realised that this was probably the longest conversation he'd had with Ben for ages.

Ben shook his head. 'We're good mates. I like her, but she's got a kid, hasn't she? I don't really want to take on a kid.'

'Don't blame you, son. Especially when it's not yours. What about the baby's father? Is he still inside?' Tanya's ex was a local drug dealer who'd beaten her and the child regularly and was serving time for ABH and possession.

Ben nodded. 'He's got another year. But his mates watch Tanya all the time. Freaks me out when I'm with her.'

'Freaks me out too,' Rod admitted. 'I dread to think what he might do to you if he gets his hands on you when he's released. Find yourself a nice girl without baggage. Someone you can bring home to Mum.'

'Do me a favour,' Ben smirked. 'Bet you never did.'

'I didn't get the chance. I was married and a father twice over at your age. Not that I'm saying your mum wasn't a nice girl,' he added.

Ben laughed and almost fell off the bench. Rod could tell from his voice and his glassy expression that he was stoned. More than stoned. He worried about Ben. He'd dropped out of college, had a succession of dead end jobs and was currently unemployed. 'Get down to the job centre next week and sort yourself out. I can't afford to keep giving you handouts.'

'I'll sort it,' Ben said. 'And don't you worry about Mum. We'll all pull our weight.'

Rod got to his feet and patted Ben on the shoulder. 'See you tomorrow. I'm off to East Sussex on Monday.'

'Lucky you,' Ben said. 'Wish I had your life.'

'Nothing to stop you, son. Join a band. You've got a guitar, talent and no ties. Get your act together before it's too late.'

Rod said goodnight and made his way indoors. He stood in front of the bathroom mirror, staring at his face, pale from tiredness with shadows under his eyes. He ran his hands through his hair and wished they had a spare room he could sleep in so he could dream about Mandy and lunchtime. He took a deep breath and went into the bedroom, hoping he wouldn't call out her name in his sleep. Jenny was curled on her side, still awake. He undressed, slid in beside her and she turned towards him.

'I've been waiting for you.' She reached for him. 'I'll miss you.'

'Yeah, I'll miss you, too.' He turned on his side with his back to her. First time she'd made a move in God knows how long and he really couldn't be arsed.

'Rod,' she slipped her arm around his waist. 'What's wrong?

'I'm tired,' he snapped. 'Just go to sleep, Jenny.

*

CHAPTER FIVE

APRIL 1994

'Who's the hunk?' Mandy asked, looking out through the front window of her friend Dee's terraced cottage. A tall young man with a shaved head and a tight black T-shirt that showed off well-developed muscles was re-building the low stone wall that bordered the small front garden.

'It's David, from next-door-but-two,' Dee replied. 'Saw me struggling and offered to help. He had some rocks left over from building his own wall.'

'That's kind of him. Useful having a handy neighbour and he's got a gorgeous bod.'

'He has,' Dee agreed.

'Lucky you.'

'He's only helping me out. And he's twelve years younger than me, so don't go reading anything into it. Let's get stuck into the fish and chips and you can tell me what's on your mind. You sounded a bit desperate on the phone.'

Mandy followed Dee into the kitchen with its stripped-pine units and low-beamed ceiling. In the dining area the patio door led out to a small white-painted courtyard with colourful spring flowers in blue tubs and wicker hanging baskets. 'The yard looks very Greek. I love this cottage, Dee. You're so lucky to be divorced and have your own space.'

'Not so sure about the divorced bit,' Dee grimaced, reaching plates off the dresser. 'It was hard at first and I've had to work my arse off to hang on to the place. But since the kids left home it's been easier, just me and the cats to worry about. Shall I offer David a chip butty?'

Mandy nodded. 'Yeah, and a cuppa.' Dee worked long hours in Manchester as a PA and often came home fit to drop. Mandy opened the parcels of food while Dee buttered bread and brewed mugs of tea.

'I'll ask him in,' Dee said. She shook a pile of chips onto a slice of bread and slapped another slice on top. She left the kitchen and came back seconds later with David on her heels. 'This is David, and this is my friend, Mandy.'

'Nice to meet you, Mandy.'

'Likewise.' Mandy stretched out her hand.

'Sorry,' David said, rubbing his hands on his shorts. 'I'm a bit mucky.'

'You can wash your hands at the sink,' Dee told him. 'Use the towel on the side there.'

Mandy stared at David as he stood with his back to them, liking what she saw. She raised an eyebrow at Dee who blushed slightly and twiddled with a blond curl. David dried his hands, turned and smiled.

'It's good of you to help Dee with her wall,' Mandy said. 'She's been trying to fix it for ages.'

'I know.' David sat down and picked up the chip butty Dee pushed towards him. 'I'd have offered my services sooner, but every time I tried to catch her eye she ignored me.'

'I didn't,' Dee protested. 'I'm blind as a bat without my lenses. I'd no idea you were trying to attract my attention.'

David smiled, his brown eyes twinkling. He wolfed his food, washed it down with a long swig of tea and stood up. 'I'll go and get finished. Your mate's a hard taskmaster,' he said to Mandy.

'And you're a cheeky bugger,' Dee said with a laugh. 'I'll give you a hand later when Mandy's gone.'

'He likes you,' Mandy said, when David had left.

'Hmm. Maybe. Anyway, spill the beans now you've finished your meal. What've you been up to? You're looking all secretive. I spoke to Lesley the other night, so I know you were down there a couple of weeks ago.'

'Ah, thought she might have called you. I suppose she told you I went there with Rod Davies?'

'She did. So - what's going on? Lesley said you'd get round to telling me when you were ready.'

Mandy knew she could trust Dee with her life. They'd met after Calgary when her middle daughter Louise befriended Dee's daughter Sally at school. She told Dee the events of the last two weeks. 'I'm worried that Mike may get a bit suspicious if I say I'm staying at Lesley's again,' she continued. 'Can I tell him that you and I are having a few days in Wales or somewhere instead? And is it okay to leave my car outside your place and grab a lift into Manchester with you Tuesday morning? I'm going by coach to Victoria and the train from there to Brighton. Rod said it's the most direct and cheapest route. He's meeting me at Brighton station.'

'Of course you can have a lift,' Dee said, patting Mandy's hand. 'I'll cover for you with Mike, don't worry. Stay here on Monday night, so you don't have to get up really early. It'll save you getting into a sweat about Mike asking awkward questions.'

'Thanks,' Mandy said, breathing a sigh of relief. 'He'll have a go at me for taking more time off work. But I haven't had a holiday for over a year, so a few days here and there won't hurt. Sarah will take care of things and tell Carol what she thinks she needs to know.'

‘That’s where you need to be careful,’ Dee warned. ‘You can trust Sarah, but Carol’s a bit straight-laced, so the less she knows, the less chance there is of her landing you in it. Just be careful, Mand, that’s all I’m saying. Rod’s a great guy. I’m sure you’ll have a brill time with him, but be really certain it’s what you want, because divorce is shit.’

Mandy nodded. ‘It freaks me out to even think about it. But I want to spend time with Rod, so it’s a chance I have to take.’ She stood up and gave Dee a hug. ‘I’ll go now and leave you to help David before it gets too dark to see. See you again, David,’ she said as he straightened up when they walked outside. ‘You’re doing a smashing job.’

‘Thanks. Knew as soon as I offered Dee my rocks she’d jump at the chance,’ he said with a smirk.

Dee blushed and smacked him on the arm. Mandy got into her car, thinking they looked good together. Dee had been alone for far too long. She didn’t look forty-four and David didn’t look twelve years younger. They sort of evened each other out. Fingers crossed something came of it. She pulled into a layby down the road. With a bit of luck she might just catch Rod before the band went on stage. She rooted for her phone and spotted two missed calls from him. Damn. She hadn’t even heard it ring out. The signal was hopeless in this area. She dialled his number, praying he’d answer, and he did.

‘Hi, you. Sorry I missed your calls,’ she began. ‘Everything’s sorted for next week. Dee’s going to help me.’

‘Oh, fantastic. Can’t wait. I’m really missing you. I’ve got a great room, right at the top of the house. It’s dead private. There’s even a sea view if you stand on your toes.’

'Rod, as long as we're together, I don't care if we have to sleep in the car. If Mike's out when I get home, I'll call you in between your spots. By the way, I've got to have lunch with Jenny tomorrow. I don't want to, but I can't see a way out. She's bringing Ben as well 'cos it's his birthday. I can hardly say no to my godson.'

'Bit difficult. She'll probably have a moan about me being away, so just agree with her. Keeps her happy. I'll have to go now. We're on soon and I need to get changed. I love you.'

'I love you too, soo-oo much. Take care.'

*

Mandy could feel her eyes glazing as Jenny waxed lyrical about the new job she was due to start, how lucky she was that it was a local school and she could walk there instead of driving. They were eating in Brambles, at a table by the side window, overlooking the canal locks.

'It's great the school's only round the corner,' Mandy agreed. 'At least you won't be stuck in heavy traffic every morning.'

'Shame it's only temporary,' Jenny went on. 'But the secretary might decide not to come back after her maternity leave. It's term time only, which means I can go and spend time with Rod in the school holidays. Beth said she'll come with me. He's staying in Brighton. It'll be lovely if the weather's nice. We can't afford a proper holiday this year, but I've been saving to take Rod on a surprise weekend to Paris in August for our silver wedding.'

Mandy felt her stomach tighten. Jenny went on, 'He says his accommodation isn't really suitable to put us up. He's flat sharing with the lads in the band, and they've only two bedrooms between five.'

Mandy nodded. What Rod had told Jenny wasn't true. The band was staying in a rented house and they had a bedroom each.

'Still, he could always treat us to a few nights in a cheap hotel,' Jenny continued.

Mandy toyed with her pasta, her appetite gone. It was her and Mike's silver wedding anniversary in May and she hadn't really given it a thought. They'd talked about the trip to Malta to coincide, but she'd done nothing about it. She couldn't face going away with Mike, and the thought of Rod and Jenny having a romantic weekend in Paris made her feel physically sick. She looked at Ben and changed the subject. 'Did you get anything nice for your birthday, Ben?'

Her godson nodded, his blue eyes twinkling just like his dad's when he smiled.

'Yeah, a new phone and a Walkman off mum and dad. Granddad taxed my car and James and Beth gave me vouchers.'

'That's great.' Mandy handed him an envelope. His face lit up as he ripped it open.

'Thanks, Aunt Mandy,' he said, reading the card and then pocketing the thirty pounds she'd slipped inside.

'You're welcome,' Mandy said as he pecked her on the cheek.

'Fancy going out next Tuesday night?' Jenny asked, running her finger around the top of her wine-glass, making a noise that set Mandy's teeth on edge. 'Frankie Valli and The Four Seasons are playing the Apollo. There's still tickets available.'

Mandy looked away before replying. Jenny looked so earnest and here she was, living a lie. 'Err, I'd love to, but I'm going away for a few days with Dee next week.'

'Oh, really? Anywhere nice?'

'Snowdonia.' The lie came out easily. 'We're renting a little cottage.'

'Sounds lovely. Don't suppose you've got room for one more?' Jenny looked hopeful.

'Sorry, no,' Mandy replied quickly. 'Dee's cousins are already there. They can just about squeeze us in. Another time, eh?'

'That would be nice.' Jenny took a sip of wine.

Mandy glanced at her watch. 'I should be getting back to work. I've loads to do so I can take the time off.' She signalled to the waiter and settled the bill. 'You two finish the wine. Enjoy the rest of your birthday, Ben. See you soon.' She dropped a kiss on Jenny's cheek, gave Ben a hug and left.

Outside she took a deep breath and walked towards the canal towpath. Might as well take the long walk back across the park and clear her head. It was hard lying to Jenny. She felt really guilty. Like Rod had said, it wasn't going to be easy.

*

Mandy stared out of the window as the train sped through unfamiliar countryside, stopping at places she'd never heard of; Three Bridges, Hayward's Heath, Wivelsfield and Hassocks. The coach journey to London had taken ages, stopping several times along the way. She'd had the back seat all to herself and had been able to spread out, spotting signs for places whose names she recognised, Golder's Green, Swiss Cottage and St John's Wood. When they drove past the Abbey Road studios her heart had almost stopped as they trundled over that zebra crossing. She'd looked back wistfully, picturing The Beatles standing on it, and wished she had her camera with her. She'd almost packed it but thought better of it. She'd never be able to explain away photos of her and Rod in Brighton, should anyone get their hands on them.

She'd managed to find Victoria station easily enough; it was almost opposite the coach station. The announcement of "Next stop, Brighton" set the butterflies in her stomach fluttering. Please let Rod be there. She'd spoken to him at Victoria, but the phone signal since had been intermittent. They had three whole nights together. She wasn't going back until Friday. Rod had asked her to stay for the weekend, but she couldn't risk it. There was every chance that Jenny may bump into Dee in town on Saturday, or Mike might see her in the pub. It wasn't fair to ask Dee to hide away all weekend just to save her neck. Besides, there was no one to cover the shop. Sarah was going to a wedding and Carol's husband wouldn't let her work Saturdays. Her hands shook as she gathered her bags together.

Through the train window she spotted Rod way down the platform, looking anxious. He had on denim jeans and a plain black T-shirt. His hair was standing on end as though he'd been running his fingers through. He was scanning the passengers as they alighted. He hadn't caught sight of her, giving her the chance to look at him. She felt her heart thudding as he turned and spotted her. His face lit up and then he was hurtling towards her. She dropped her baggage. He flung his arms around her, drawing her close. He kissed her and sighed into her hair. She felt her eyes filling and as they drew apart she saw that his were moist too.

'Thank God,' he whispered, picking up her case and bags. 'Come on, let's grab a taxi.'

'Where's your car?' Mandy asked as they clambered into a black cab.

'Back at the house.' He slipped his arm around her waist. 'It's so good to see you. I was dreading you backing out at the last minute.'

'As if.' Mandy kissed him. 'Nothing was gonna stop me doing this.'

*

'It's really nice,' she said, wandering around the attic bedroom, which was comfortably furnished with a double bed, matching pine wardrobe, chest of drawers and coffee making facilities. 'Great that you've got your own shower room, too.'

'I'm the only one, who doesn't share a bathroom,' he said. 'Although that extra flight of stairs is a killer. But look.' He pulled her over to the open window. 'Stand on this chair and you can see the sea.'

Mandy climbed up and stuck her head outside, looking down across the sloping roof at the sea glistening in the distance. She could hear seagulls making a racket, could smell the sea, and felt a rush of excitement as she spotted the bulk of The Palace Pier and the flickering lights of the fairground rides. She loved the seaside, it made her feel young again, a teenager at heart. They could ride the waltzer, the big wheel and eat candy floss. She took Rod's hand and looked into his eyes as he helped her down. She could see the hunger in them, feel the electricity in his touch and shivered as she snuggled into his arms. 'Can we walk on the beach later?'

'Much later,' he whispered, stroking her cheek. 'I'm desperate for you.' He kissed her lips, her cheeks and the hollow of her neck, undoing the buttons on her top and pushing it back over her shoulders. She pulled his T shirt over his head and he unhooked her bra and let it fall to the floor. She could feel his erection pressing against her and undid his jeans and slid her hand inside, caressing him. He moaned and bent to take a nipple in his mouth. Mandy held his head, running her hands through his hair. He lowered her onto the bed and pulled off the rest of her clothes with a sense of urgency. She finished stripping him and he moved down her body, dropping little kisses across her stomach and the inside of her thighs.

She could feel every nerve in her body on fire, smell his sensual scent mingling with her own and groaned as his tongue and fingers searched. She felt like she was floating and close to orgasm but fought it, wanting to savour the sensations for longer. She reached for Rod and pulled him up beside her, kissing him deeply and loving her own scent on his face. She bent to take him in her mouth, running her tongue slowly up and down his erection, hearing him groan softly and whisper her name. She stole a look at him; he was leaning backwards on his elbows, watching her, a look of pure bliss in his eyes.

Her heart was filled with love; she was responsible for giving him that look, for pleasing him and having him need her. She wanted to love him forever and couldn't imagine a time when she wouldn't want him. She needed to ride him and climbed on top. He reached for her breasts and held them, running his thumbs over her nipples while she ground against him, her hair flopping down over her eyes. Rod flipped her onto her back and thrust into her, kissing her, rolling his tongue against hers, telling her he loved her and would never leave her. She couldn't hold back any longer and cried his name, grabbing his buttocks, pulling him closer as she came. Almost simultaneously Rod let out a yell and collapsed on top, breathing deeply in her ear.

Outside the sound of the gulls returned, the scent of the sea was almost as heady as the wonderful scent of her and Rod. She'd never felt such love. He was the one she'd been waiting for all her life. If only she'd known it sooner. But they were here now - soul mates - forever. She snuggled into him with a feeling of utter completeness.

*

Mandy stirred and opened her eyes. She felt disorientated for a moment. An arm rested across her middle and she turned to see Rod's blue eyes looking into hers. She smiled and kissed the tip of his nose.

'Thought you were going to sleep until morning,' he teased. 'Did I wear you out?'

'Just a bit. You - and the journey. What time is it? I'm starving.'

'Almost ten-thirty. Let's take a shower and get something to eat.'

'Will there be anywhere still serving food?' she asked, climbing out of bed and stretching her arms above her head. She rummaged in her handbag for a scrunchy and fastened up her hair.

'Loads of places,' Rod replied, jumping up and leading her into the bathroom. He turned on the shower, pulling her in with him. 'Brighton doesn't shut down like Pickford. We can eat on the beach and then take that walk. There's a great diner on The Esplanade. They have live music as well.'

'Sounds good,' she said, laughing as he lathered her with shower gel.

*

CHAPTER SIX

Rod balanced a bottle of lager on the pebbles and reached into his pocket for his ringing phone.

'Jenny,' he muttered, staring at the screen. He rejected the call, switched off the phone and put it away.

'You should have answered. Might be urgent,' Mandy said. 'Why would she call you at this time if it wasn't?'

'Whatever it is can wait,' he said. 'Everything was alright when I spoke to her earlier.'

Mandy nodded and took a sip of her drink. They'd dined at The Source, watched a Van Morrison tribute singer and then strolled down the beach to sit by the sea.

'It won't be important, just her wittering on.' He knocked back the last of his drink.

'Okay, if you're sure.' She cuddled up to him, shivering. 'I'm cold now. And I could use the loo. It's the lager and those lapping waves!'

'Come on then.' He pulled her to her feet. 'Let's head back.' He slipped his arms around her waist and kissed her. They crunched up the beach hand in hand, stopped to return the empty bottles at The Source, and Mandy nipped inside to use the toilet. They ran up the steps to the Promenade where people were milling around in small crowds, talking and laughing.

'I can't believe how lively everywhere is so late at night,' Mandy said.

‘Places stay open ‘til the early hours,’ Rod told her. ‘The rest of the band will still be out. You’ll meet them tomorrow.’

‘Are they all single?’

‘Couple of them are married with kids, the others are divorced. They all pretty much live the bachelor life down here.’

‘What about their wives?’ Mandy frowned. ‘Don’t they object to being cheated on?’

He shrugged. ‘They probably don’t have a clue.’

‘Bit like Jenny then.’

Rod stopped walking and swung her round to face him. ‘This is different - for us - I mean. I want to be with you and only you. The lads are out for what they can get. I’m not. I thought you felt the same.’

Mandy nodded. ‘I do, you know I do. I just feel a bit guilty, that’s all. I still think you should have taken that call.’

‘I’ll check my phone for a message when we get back. She thinks I’m working tonight anyway, so God knows why she called me. She must realise I’m unlikely to hear the bloody thing.’

‘All the more reason to think it might have been urgent then.’

‘Okay!’ he held his hands up. ‘You win.’

*

Back at the house Mandy hurried upstairs ahead of Rod, grabbed the kettle and went into the bathroom to fill it. When she came out he was frowning, phone to his ear, free hand running through his hair.

‘What is it?’ she asked as he chewed his lip.

‘She left a voice-message. I’m gonna have to call her back. She sounds upset, but doesn’t say why, other than that she needs to talk to me urgently.’

‘Go downstairs and call her privately.’

Rod agreed and left the room. Mandy flopped onto the bed and sighed. She hoped Jenny hadn't discovered she was down here with Rod. What if she'd spoken to Mike and the pair had put two and two together? But no, that was impossible. For all his indifference, Mike would have called her by now, ranting and raving and ordering her to get back home. He'd responded to her earlier text, informing him that she and Dee had arrived in Wales. He'd sent a text back, saying, "stay safe" and added a couple of xx's. Her imagination was running away with itself as usual. Jenny couldn't have found out. No one knew except for Sarah, Dee and Lesley and there was no way they would say anything.

Rod came back in, shaking his head.

'What is it?' she asked as he joined her on the bed, taking her hand. 'Is everyone okay? No accidents or anything?'

'No accidents. Jenny took three hundred quid out of the bank today to pay the balance for a weekend in Paris.' He stopped and looked at her.

'And,' she prompted, feeling very sick. 'Your silver wedding trip. Jenny hasn't wasted much time organizing that.'

'She put the money on the dining table in an envelope,' he continued. 'It's gone missing.'

'Maybe she put it somewhere else and got confused. I do things like that all the time.'

'She's had the house upside down, accused all the kids in turn of taking it and caused a big row with Beth and James.'

'Oh God!' Mandy exclaimed. 'Your kids wouldn't steal money from their own mother.'

Rod raised a weary eyebrow. 'She said Ben stormed out with his girl and the other two stayed behind to help her look. But they couldn't find it. James and Beth think Ben took it because he left the scene of the crime. Jenny says they're ganging up and saying Tanya probably egged him on. For fuck's sake, Ben might be a bit of a lad, but he wouldn't steal. And what she thinks I can do about it, stuck down here, God only knows.'

'It'll probably turn up tomorrow,' Mandy said, squeezing his hand. She drew a deep breath and tried to keep her voice from wobbling. 'But if it doesn't, how will she pay for the trip?'

'No idea. I don't wanna go to Paris with her anyway. She's planned it behind my back. It was supposed to be a surprise, but she never thought to ask if I'm working that weekend or anything. That's one of Jenny's problems, she never bloody thinks. I had a go at her, told her I don't want to go. Now I feel bad for upsetting her even more.' He rummaged in his pocket for his cigarettes and lit up, taking a long drag. 'It's not until August. I was kind of hoping you and me would have made a decision about what we're going to do by then. Maybe we'll have moved in together.'

Mandy stared at him. While relieved that Rod didn't want to go away with Jenny, she felt a bit sorry for her. But she also felt panic sweep over her at the idea of her and Rod moving in together. August was only four months away and she hadn't thought they'd do anything for ages except see each other as often as they could and make a few tentative plans. Four months to sort everything. It would be impossible. When she was lying in Rod's arms, there was no other place she'd rather be. Making love with him was out of this world. She knew that she wanted to spend the rest of her life loving him, but to think beyond the next few days was more than terrifying.

'Don't cry, Mandy,' he said, running a finger down her cheek where she could feel a lone tear trickling.

'We won't let my problems spoil our time together. I'm sure Jenny'll find the money tomorrow and make it up with the kids. I'll apologise when I speak to her again. But I'm not going to Paris.'

*

Mandy glanced around the smoky club, taking in the subdued lighting, the corner stage, where Rod's new five-piece band Timeless had done an earlier sound check, and the crowd of young people queuing at the bar. Rod was getting the drinks in with Jed the bass player. He turned and winked at her. She smiled and blew him a kiss. The young woman sitting opposite her, who Rod had introduced as Penny, Jed's girlfriend, offered her a cigarette.

'I don't smoke, thanks,' Mandy said. Penny shrugged, lit one for herself and took a drag.

'How long are you down here for?' Penny asked, flicking back her shoulder-length blonde hair.

'Until Friday,' Mandy replied. She felt a bit under dressed in her white jeans and black halter-neck top, next to Penny's figure-hugging, purple Lycra dress, her nails painted the exact same colour. Rod had told her the club had an informal dress-code so she didn't need to wear anything too fancy. He'd reassured her that she looked good enough to eat before they left the house. She'd spent ages getting ready while he lay on the bed watching her. Then he'd messed her hair up and kissed off her lip gloss when he'd pulled her down beside him, telling her he preferred her naked and wouldn't be able to keep his hands off her tonight.

Penny, who'd tottered into the club on killer heels that would have had Mandy towering way above Rod, but just brought Penny up to Jed's shoulder, asked, 'Have you known Rod long?' as Rod and Jed returned.

Rod smiled and told her, 'I've known Mandy almost thirty years.'

Penny raised a surprised eyebrow. 'Thought you were in a new relationship, the way you are with each other.'

Mandy picked up her glass of red wine and took a sip. She could tell by the glint in Rod's eye that he was about to spin Penny a yarn. He'd told her earlier that Jed's woman was much younger than they were and blonde enough to hang onto every word. Much younger was an understatement, Mandy thought. Penny looked a similar age to her eldest daughter, while Jed was the same age as Rod.

'Silver wedding this year,' Rod said, offering cigarettes round.

'Really?' Penny's eyes were wide. 'Wow, how many years is that?'

'Twenty-five,' Rod replied. 'And I love her more than ever.'

Mandy played along with him. 'It only feels like a few weeks,' she said. 'I can't believe how the time has flown.'

'Aw, well I think it's lovely, the way you're so into one another,' Penny said, batting her lashes at Jed. 'Don't you, Jed?'

Jed nodded and winked at Mandy. She wondered how much Rod had told the other band members about their relationship. Whether they thought she was his wife - or what? He hadn't mentioned it and she never thought to ask. She'd met the other members of Timeless earlier and they were a friendly bunch. She could see why Rod preferred to spend his time down here rather than stay home with Jenny and do local gigs. Penny was still questioning Rod, asking how often they got together with him working away. Mandy turned her attention back to the conversation.

'She joins me as often as she can, work and kids permitting,' Rod was saying.

'How many kids do you have?' Penny had such an earnest look on her face. 'And how old are they?'

Mandy knew exactly what Rod was going to say before the words were out of his mouth. What surprised her was how he remembered not only how old his own kids were but hers as well. Mike was hard pushed at times to even remember their daughters' birthdays.

'We've four daughters and two sons,' he said. 'There's two at twenty-four, two at twenty-two, and two at seventeen.'

'Three sets of twins, how lovely,' Penny gushed. 'I'd love twins, wouldn't you, Jed?'

Jed grunted into his beer and Mandy choked on her drink. She aimed a kick at Rod's shin. 'No, Penny, not twins, there's eleven months between each pair.'

'God, you must have been worn out, all those babies to look after.'

'Erm, just a bit,' Mandy said, raising an eyebrow at Rod, who was smirking.

'Pack it in,' she mouthed.

'Would you like another?'

'Another glass of red, please,' Mandy said, trying to change the subject.

'I meant more children,' Penny said with a laugh.

'No thanks,' Rod said. 'We've done our bit. We're counting the days to being just a couple. A kid-free zone. Bliss.' He clinked his glass against Mandy's. 'Isn't that right, Mand?'

Mandy nodded. He'd be lucky. She was pretty sure that Nicole would want to live with her and Rod eventually, maybe even Louise and possibly Ben, who was closer to Rod than he was to Jenny. Once they'd all got over the shock and got used to the idea that is.

'Your kids are fortunate to have such close parents,' Penny went on. 'Mine split up when I was sixteen. Right in the middle of my GCSE's. No wonder I failed them all. My little brother was only ten at the time. I've never forgiven Mum for walking out on us.'

Mandy stood up and grabbed her handbag. 'Back in a minute,' she said and made a dash to the ladies. She locked herself in a cubicle and leant against the door, breathing deeply. Alright, their kids were older than Penny and her little brother, but Nicole and Beth would be doing A levels next year. They were currently studying hard with course work. They couldn't be contributory factors to their respective daughters failing exams and not getting into Uni. Nicole and Beth would never forgive them for destroying their dreams and she'd never be able to forgive herself. It was all very well her and Rod having wild ideas of spending the rest of their lives together, but what about the lives they'd be ruining.

They'd had a wonderful day, staying in bed until lunchtime and then an all-day breakfast in a little café on The Lanes. Jenny had called Rod first thing to say she'd found the envelope of missing money. It seemed that Beth had scooped it up when she'd shoved the laundry, piled up on the dining room table, into the basket. No one had thought to check there and they'd all apologised to Ben. Rod had been pleased but told Jenny to cancel the Paris trip. There'd been a few cross words between them and he'd disappeared into the bathroom. She could hear his voice raising and then he'd stormed out and apologised to Mandy before throwing his phone under the bed.

They'd strolled up the promenade to the Marina and wandered around, looking at the yachts and wishing they were rich enough to own one and sail off to far-away places, just the two of them. Nice dreams, and it was easy to pretend they would all come true, well maybe not the yacht, but faced with reality, she felt more frightened than she'd ever felt in her life. She couldn't envisage staying with Mike forever, but just now, in her head, she couldn't see how there would be a choice. She and Rod would just have to continue having an affair, certainly for the foreseeable future.

*

The other three band members and a couple of young women had joined the table when Mandy got back. She sat down next to Rod and he took her hand. He had a worried look in his eyes. She smiled and squeezed his hand, to reassure him that she was okay.

'Come on,' he said, pulling her to her feet.

'Where are we going?'

'A little walk down the street. We've half an hour before we go onstage.'

Mandy linked her arm though his as they strolled down to the promenade.

'Why did you rush off? Did Penny's comments freak you out?'

'Yes,' she said, feeling her eyes filling. 'It's just a nightmare. Everybody's gonna be so hurt.'

Rod stopped and pulled her into his arms. 'Don't get upset. Let's just enjoy tonight. I did say it wouldn't be easy. But you said it's what you want.'

Mandy swallowed hard and wiped her eyes on the tissue he fished out of his pocket. 'It is, but I don't know how we can make it happen. They'll all end up hating us like Penny hates her mum.'

‘They won’t. Well they may do at first, but time heals and we’ve got each other for support. And we will get through it, Mandy, I promise you.’ He kissed her and gave her a squeeze. ‘I was keeping this a secret, but I’ve got a surprise for you.’

‘You’ve always got a surprise for me.’ She smiled through her tears.

He laughed and kissed her again. ‘That’s better. But it’s not what you think. Well not until later anyway! I’ve two solo spots tonight. I’m doing an Eagles spot in the first half and then I’m trading places with Jim on keyboards in the second half and doing a mixed spot towards the end.’

‘Oh, that’s great, I’m really looking forward to hearing you sing again,’ she said as they turned back towards the Majestic Club.

*

Mandy smiled as Rod looked directly at her from his center-stage position at the keyboard. The band was doing their final spot and he was singing solo.

‘The next song might not be familiar to most of you,’ he began, ‘but it means a lot to me and my lovely lady over there. Tonight’s the first time I’ve performed it, so please be gentle with me.’

Mandy clapped her hand to her mouth as she recognised the opening bars of *Fast Movin’ Train.* She could feel herself filling up as Rod sang their song, never taking his eyes off her until he took a bow at the end to much cheering and clapping. Mandy couldn’t believe that he’d taken the time and trouble to learn that song. And he’d done it all for her. What a wonderful, loving gesture. No matter what the future brought, she knew she’d treasure those few precious minutes for the rest of her life.

*

Friday morning Rod ordered a taxi to take them to the station. Mandy didn't want to leave him and they clung together on the platform, both fighting back tears.

'I'll be home next Sunday,' he told her. 'I've got a couple of days off, so I'll drive back and try and spend as much time as I can with you. Don't make any plans.'

'Okay,' she said, then, 'Shit, it's Jenny's birthday next Sunday!'

'I know. That's why I'm coming home. She knows I'm off then. I can hardly stay down here when it's her birthday. No doubt she'll want to do something that includes you and Mike. So be prepared for the phone call.'

She nodded. 'I suppose she will. I guess I'll have to get used to feeling guilty.'

'Won't be for long,' he said. 'We'll sort things out this summer. I've got all the earache of the cancelled Paris trip to contend with next week.'

'I don't envy you.' She held him close and kissed him as a request for passengers to Victoria came over the tannoy.

'Call me as soon as you get a signal,' he said, helping her on the train with her baggage. 'Just keep calling me. I love you. Take care, baby.'

'I love you, too,' she sobbed against his shoulder. 'You'd better get off before they blow the whistle.'

He kissed her one last time and leapt off. She sat down and pressed her face to the window as the train pulled out of the station. She waved and blew kisses until she could no longer see him. She sat back on her seat with the bleakest and emptiest feeling in her heart that she'd ever experienced. There had to be a way to work things out to suit everyone, because she couldn't be without Rod in her life.

*

Dee was waiting for Mandy in the bus station café in Manchester.

'You look like you've had a great time,' Dee greeted her. 'You look so different, glowing and contented.'

'I am,' Mandy said, hugging Dee. 'Thanks for meeting me.'

'I promised I would,' Dee said. 'Do you fancy a Chinese, seeing as we're in town. You can tell me all about your trip. Let's put your bags in the car.'

As they walked up the car park ramp Dee said, 'There's something I need to tell you, but I don't want to you to worry about it and let it spoil what you've just had.'

'What?'

'Now don't freak out, but Mike drove past my place twice last night.'

'What? Why?'

'I don't know why. I guess he was checking up on you.'

'But why would he do that? Shit! Your car, he'll have seen your car! I told him we were going in yours.'

'Ah, well David borrowed my car last night. He was out in it when Mike drove past. I spotted him from upstairs and hid behind the curtain. He slowed down and looked at the house, drove to the bottom of the road and then back up again. Fortunately the windows were all closed and there were no lights on. Your car was there of course, but mine wasn't. So that was lucky.'

Mandy shook her head. 'I'll have to play things by ear now. I can't ask him what he was doing, can I?'

Dee patted her arm. 'Just be wary. Maybe he suspects you're having an affair. But hopefully he won't have a clue it's with Rod.'

*

CHAPTER SEVEN

Mandy let herself into the house and dumped her case on the floor. The dogs ran to greet her, snuffling against her legs, stumpy tails barely wagging. They had a worried air, as though someone had yelled at them for making a mess. 'Hello, babies.' She bent to fuss them. 'Did you miss your mummy? What have you been up to?' She could hear raised voices, doors slamming and then Mike was running down the stairs, shaking his head.

He gave her a quick hug and a peck on the cheek. 'Hi. Did you have a nice time?'

'Great, thanks.' She could feel her face warming. Was he giving her a strange look? 'What's wrong with the dogs, and why were you shouting? Where's Nic and Louise?'

'Upstairs, sulking,' he said. 'And there's nothing wrong with the dogs that a good walk won't put right. I've asked that lazy pair to take them out. I'll take your case up. You'd better go and see the girls. They've got "I Hate Dad" heads on tonight.'

Mandy followed him up the stairs, the dogs close on her heels, bumping the backs of her knees as though they didn't want her out of their sight. Mike went into their bedroom and banged the door shut. She shook her head and knocked on Nicole's door.

'Come in,' a tearful voice called.

'Hi, you two,' Mandy said, walking into the room, where her girls, the image of each other with their long dark hair and blue eyes, were sitting side by side on the bed. Nicole was crying and Louise's mouth was down-turned, mutiny in her eyes. 'What's going on?'

'It's him,' Louise began, jerking her thumb at the door. 'He's done nothing but rant at us since you went away. Walk the dogs, turn it down, and unload the dishwasher! He just gave Nic earache for putting her jeans in the drier. Said it's a waste of money. He moaned about us leaving lights on and he's got a right cob on about the phone bill!'

In spite of the tension, Mandy smiled. 'Ah, sounds like he's on his annual economy drive. And he's right, Nic you should put a full load in the drier, not just one pair of jeans. And I'm always telling you to turn the lights off when you go out, too. Don't know why he's going on about the phone bill though. You use your mobiles most of the time. I'll go and speak to him. Have you eaten?'

'Yeah, ages ago,' Louise said. 'He made us sausage and mash, but the mash was lumpy. Nic made Crème Brulee for dessert.'

'Right.' It would never dawn on Louise to make tea for her dad, not unless he suggested it anyway. She took it for granted they'd all get fed. How the hell would they manage without her? But then again, Louise was working and at twenty-two, old enough to look after herself. It was Nicole she was most worried about leaving behind. She swallowed hard. 'Take the dogs to the field. Give them a good run. I bet they've not had a walk since Monday.'

Nicole jumped up and gave her a hug. 'I saved you some dessert, 'cos I know it's your favourite. I've really missed you, Mum. Glad you're back. Did you and Dee have a good time?'

'Yes, thanks, it was a lovely break. Nice and peaceful, just what I needed.' A bit of peace now wouldn't go amiss, she thought as the dogs followed the girls down the stairs. All she wanted to do was take a bath, have an early-ish night and dream about Rod. She went into the bedroom, where Mike had the contents of his briefcase strewn on the bed, bills and bank statements piled to one side.

'I'm switching the direct debits to another account,' he said, without looking up.

'Why? What's wrong with the account they're in now?'

'It's more manageable to keep the household outgoings separate. Then I know where we're up to. All part of good project control.'

'For God's sake, Mike, we're your family, not one of your flipping contracts.' She rolled her eyes. She hated it when his job of Project Control Manager crept into their everyday lives. 'Oh - do whatever! I can't be bothered arguing right now. I'm tired. And why have you given the girls a hard time over the phone bill? They hardly use the landline.'

He snatched up a bill and shook it at her. 'It's no wonder British Telecom can afford plush new offices in Manchester. It's me that bloody well pays for it! I've organized itemized bills so the girls can pay their share. This one came yesterday. The most expensive calls are to a mobile number and I certainly didn't make them.'

A wave of heat surged through Mandy. She took the bill from Mike with her heart thumping. He'd highlighted one number over and over. Rod's number. She'd no idea Mike had arranged an itemized bill. He obviously didn't recognise the number. He hated mobiles and hardly ever used his own, claiming to be all fingers and thumbs with being left-handed. As far as she knew he only had the house and her own number stored in his phone. She'd stupidly used the landline because her credit was running low, and she desperately wanted to speak to Rod. But the calls had been lengthy and totalled over twenty pounds. No wonder Mike was going mad.

‘Hmm,’ she muttered. ‘I don’t recognise the number. Must be one of their mates. But if it makes you feel any better, I’ll give you the money.’ What if he had recognised it and was testing her. Maybe that was the reason he’d driven past Dee’s last night.

‘There’s no need for that. I’ll just bloody pay it as usual. But from now on, I want no calls to mobiles from the house phone. I’ve already told the girls. If they want to use the phone to make expensive calls they’re gonna have to pay for them. I’m sorry if they got upset, but just wait until they leave home, they’ll have to learn to manage then. They’ll know what it’s like to struggle, like we had to.’

‘Oh come on, Mike, we haven’t struggled for years. You’re going a bit OTT.’ She drew a deep breath. Her palms felt sweaty and her heart was still racing. Keeping her voice light, she asked, ‘Err, something bothering you? Something other than the bills, I mean?’

He gathered up all the papers and stuffed them back in his briefcase. ‘Why do you ask?’

She shrugged. ‘You just seem on edge, that’s all.’

‘I’m fine. A bit tired. Those two have gone out of their way to wind me up this week. I need a drink and some space.’ He grabbed his jacket from the bed. ‘While I remember, I’ve invited Mum to Sunday lunch. It’s Dad’s anniversary and she gets a bit maudlin if she’s left on her own. I’ll take her to the cemetery first. Right, I’m popping out for a pint. See you later.’ He pulled her to him, planted a kiss on the top of her head and left the room.

Mandy stared after him. Why had he given her a hug? She sat down on the bed and sighed. He couldn't even be bothered staying in on her first night home. Not that she minded. It would give her the chance to call Rod.

She unpacked her case, ran a bath and lay back in the bubbles, reflecting on the last few days. She'd shared a joint with Rod after last night's gig, the first she'd had for years. She'd coughed her guts up at first, but the cannabis made her feel free; no inhibitions. Not that she had any with Rod anyway, but she felt she could do anything she wanted to if she tried and it had added further passion to their lovemaking, something she didn't think possible. She smiled as she recalled Rod's teasing that he could have a rest when she went home as he was in a permanent state of erection when he was with her. He made her laugh a lot. She felt she was re-discovering the person she used to be, before marriage and responsibilities took over.

They'd had another lovely day again, yesterday, feeding one another strawberries for breakfast, and making love until lunchtime. They spent the afternoon on the beach, planning a future.

'I think we should wait until the girls finish their A levels before we say anything,' she'd suggested.

'I don't want to wait another year,' Rod had said. 'There'll never be a right time so if we do it at the beginning of the college holidays they'll have all summer to get their heads around things. They'll be fine eventually, honest.'

'That's you just hoping for the best,' Mandy said. 'It's going to be a lot worse than you think it will be. I'm dreading it. Mike will want to kill me - and probably you.'

‘If Jenny doesn’t get to me first,’ he said with a wry smile. ‘We need a place to live; a bolt hole to head to as soon as the shit hits the fan.’

Mandy nodded. ‘I’ll have a look round. See what we can afford.’

‘I’ll give you some money to save and send some each week. I don’t have much to spare, but I’ll do my best.’

‘I’ll put some to it. We’ll need about a grand to get us in somewhere. When Sarah moved in with her boyfriend they paid two months up front and a charge for signing the lease.’

They’d talked themselves into a sense of security that all would be well and the feeling had stayed with her until she’d seen that bloody phone bill.

She reached for her mobile and pressed redial. Rod answered right away. After exchanging "I love you’s" and "I miss you’s" she told him about Mike driving past Dee’s and the itemized bill.

‘Shit! Just be careful, Mand, we don’t want it blowing up in our faces until we’re sorted.’

‘I know. Don’t worry; I doubt he recognised your number, unless he’s not letting on. Reject the call if he tries to ring you. Dee’s car wasn’t outside her house, so there’s nothing he can deduce from that. I just wish I knew why he drove past. I can’t ask him, obviously.’ She lowered her voice. ‘The girls are back with the dogs. Talk to you tomorrow. Thanks for the best time of my life. I love you.’

‘I love you too and thank you for the best time of mine. Can’t wait for more.’

She climbed out of the bath and was towelling herself dry when the house phone rang out. She heard Nicole answering and then, ‘Mum, Aunty Jen’s on the phone. Where are you?’

'In the bathroom. Tell her I'll call her back.' The last thing she felt like doing was talking to Jenny tonight. But if she didn't get back to her, she would only call again and Mike might be home and then it would be more difficult to keep cool. She knew she couldn't avoid Jenny, but after the wonderful time she and Rod had enjoyed, lying to her about the Snowdon trip was going to be really hard. Fortunately Dee had made her a list of places they'd "visited" and pubs they'd "been" in. She'd have to bluff it the best she could.

*

With the dogs stretched out either side of her on the bed, as close as they could get; their heads resting on her shoulders, Mandy lay back on the pillows and called Jenny. It took a while for anyone to answer and she was about to hang up when Beth picked up. 'Is your mum there, Beth? I'm returning her call.'

'Err, yes, just a minute.' The line went muffled, as though Beth had her hand over the receiver. 'Aunt Mandy, can she call you tomorrow? She's a bit upset. She's had words with Dad and she's hoping he'll call back. She wants to keep the line free.'

'Okay, no problem. But tell her I'll call her when I get a minute. I've got a very busy day tomorrow.' She said goodbye, hung up and breathed a sigh of relief. She checked the time. Rod would be in-between spots. She cocked an ear, the girls were playing music. She grabbed her mobile again. He answered right away.

'Oh, babe, I was hoping you might call back. I hate that I can't ring you.'

'Can't talk for long in case the girls hear me,' she whispered. 'Jenny rang. I tried to return the call, but she wouldn't talk 'cos she's hoping you'll ring back, Beth said you'd had words.'

'Yeah, we did. All I said was what part of "I'm not going to Paris" don't you understand, and she starts yelling at me. I haven't got the patience to deal with it right now. I'm getting changed and having a quick fag. We're back on in ten. Wish you were here. Penny said earlier what a lovely lady you are and I could have cried. Don't even think I can wait until August.'

'Oh, Rod.' A sob caught in her throat and a tear trickled down her cheek. 'It won't be long. We need money behind us and a plan of action in place first. As soon as we tell them, I'll have to leave home.'

'I know, but while I'm down here you could be with me. We wouldn't have to worry about getting somewhere to live.'

'But when your summer with the band ends, we would. You'll have to find more work and I've got the business to run. We'll need every penny I can earn. You'll be home in September; it's not too long to wait. I'll spend time with you as soon as I can get away again. Just hang in. I love you. I'd better go now before someone hears me. Talk tomorrow.'

'Love you, too. I've got to sing Fast Movin' Train and you're not here.'

'Can't you substitute it?'

'Wish I could, but the lads like it; it's part of the set now.' He was quiet for a few seconds. 'Night, babe. Talk to you tomorrow.'

'Night, darling.' She hung up, tears streaming now. She heard the front door opening. Mike was back. She pushed the dogs off the bed and shoved the towels they'd been lying on underneath it. She took Max and Poppy onto the landing and ordered them into their baskets. They looked disappointed, their big brown eyes sad. 'Sorry,' she whispered. 'He doesn't like you on the bed.' She'd love to take the dogs with her when she left Mike. But most rental properties had a no pet's policy and she wouldn't be able to afford kennels when she went to stay with Rod. Maybe when things settled down she and Mike could have shared custody of them, like people did with kids.

*

'Get Nana another whisky,' Mandy said to Nicole.

Mike's tubby little silver-haired mother was eating a chocolate brownie in the lounge, her feet up on a brown velvet pouffe, that only came out when she visited, along with the hideous green vase she'd given Mandy last Christmas. Mandy had stuffed it with an equally hideous supermarket bouquet that she'd chuck in the bin later.

'Do you want ice and ginger ale, Nan?' Nicole shouted above the noise of the cooker-hood fan.

'Just the ginger, love,' Nana called back. 'These cakes are lovely. Can I have another?'

Nicole sloshed the whisky into a tall glass and topped it up with dry ginger while Louise took the plate of chocolate brownies through. Nicole followed and handed Nana the drink. Nana helped herself to a brownie and took a large bite.

'Beautiful,' she said. 'You're a good little cook, our Nic.'

'Thanks, Nan. Just going back in the kitchen to help Mum. Will you be okay on your own for a while?'

'Yes, love, I'll be fine. Just put me the Eastenders omnibus on before you go.'

The girls came back as Mandy was lifting the chicken out of the oven to baste. Nicole was shaking her head at Louise in a meaningful way.

'It was the wrong plate, Muppet!' Nicole muttered under her breath. 'Those bigger ones are for us, for later - you know.'

‘Oh shit!’ Louise exclaimed, her eyes wide. ‘Well there’s nothing I can do now. She was stuffing it in her gob like she’s not been fed for weeks.’

‘What are you two on about?’ Mandy said, wiping her sweaty brow with the tea towel. ‘Nana can have whichever size cake she wants. Don’t be so mean.’ She saw a look pass between the pair. ‘What?’

‘Oh, nothing,’ Nicole said airily.

Mandy frowned as Nicole turned her back, her shoulders shaking while Louise, trying hard not to giggle, began busying herself at the sink, rinsing coffee mugs.

‘Right,’ Mandy said, as they both choked on laughter, ‘what have you done? You’d better tell me quick before your dad gets back from the pub.’ Mike always managed to nip for the proverbial quick pint whenever he invited his mother for lunch.

Nicole was almost hysterical. ‘Nana’s eating a hash brownie,’ she confessed, ‘a very big hash brownie! Sorry, Mum, they were for us to take to a party tonight.’

‘Hash brownie,’ Mandy echoed. ‘What - you mean…? Oh, for God’s sake, Nic, she’ll be stoned, not to mention pissed with the amount of bloody whisky you put in that tumbler! Your dad will go nuts. You know he doesn’t approve of drugs.’

‘I know,’ Nicole said. ‘That’s why it’s gone in the cakes rather than we smoke it in the house.’

Mandy shook her head and dashed into the lounge. Her mother-in-law looked decidedly flushed, but that might be the whisky, or the gas fire, and she did have slightly high blood pressure. ‘You okay, Mum?’

Mum dragged her eyes away from Eastenders and smiled at Mandy, who took the empty glass from her. Christ, but she could certainly knock it back for an eighty-five-year-old. Like mother, like son, she thought.

'I'm fine, love. I feel very relaxed. I might shut my eyes for five minutes. Just wake me when dinner's ready. I'll only get under your feet if I try and help you in the kitchen.'

Mandy left the room and closed the door behind her. She leant against it and sighed. Nicole and Louise came into the hall, looking worried.

'Is she okay?' Nicole asked.

'She's fine, so far. No thanks to you two. She's gonna have a little nap until dinner's ready. Who gave you the cannabis?'

'Ben Davis,' Louise said. 'He always has a bit to spare.'

Mandy nodded. Why didn't that surprise her? Just like his father. She felt a rush of heat as she thought about his father, and their last night together. She excused herself, ran upstairs to the bathroom and locked the door. She sat down on the side of the bath and took a deep breath. She was dying to talk to Rod. She hadn't had a minute on her own today, but Mike would be taking his mum home later and the girls would be out. Rod had called her every hour yesterday and she'd stayed behind at the shop until eight, finishing an order for fitting next week. She'd even been able to speak to him on her way home, before he went on stage.

She'd plucked up the nerve to call Jenny late afternoon, after putting it off nearly all day. The conversation had been a bit strained. Jenny was still tearful and smarting from Rod's refusal to go to Paris.

'He's being so horrible. I don't know what I've done to upset him. It's such a special anniversary. I can't understand why he doesn't want to go. Do you think I should book a surprise weekend in London instead?'

‘Erm, I think you should leave it, Jenny. If he’s anything like me, he won’t like surprises. I’d rather be involved in the plans. Try and speak to him without falling out.’

‘He’s home next week for my birthday. I’m going to work on him then.’

Mandy almost said she knew he was coming home but stopped herself just in time.

‘So will you and Mike come for a meal on Sunday? You can persuade him that Paris is a good idea. He’ll listen to you.’

‘Can I get back to you on that?’ Mandy searched for an excuse. ‘Mike may have a gig.’ She answered Jenny’s questions about Snowdon and then thankfully the shop bell rang and she’d said goodbye.

She splashed her face with cold water, patted it dry and went back downstairs. The girls were in the kitchen, sharing a hash brownie. ‘Don’t you think you should wait until later to eat that?’

‘It’s only one between us,’ Nicole said. ‘It’ll chill us for when dad comes home. He’ll go loopy if Nan’s out of her skull.’

‘I’ll tell him she’s had too much whisky,’ Mandy said. ‘Hopefully she’ll be okay. Go and set the table. Put the new wine glasses out. They’re a bit smaller than the old ones and the less alcohol your Nan drinks between now and going home, the better.’

*

‘More veg, Mum?’ Mandy kept a close eye on her mother-in-law, making sure she ate plenty to soak up the whisky. Her eyes were a bit glazed, but other than that she appeared to be okay.

‘No thanks, Mandy. I’m quite full. I’ll leave room for the pudding. I’ll have another drop of wine though.’

Mike re-filled her glass. 'Mandy?' He gestured with the bottle. Mandy shook her head and he re-filled his own. 'Better make this my last. Don't want to be over the limit for driving you home, Mum.'

'You have another if you want, love,' his mother said. 'I can always get a taxi.'

'I think Mike should take you, Mum. He can see you safely inside then.'

'You're a thoughtful girl,' Mum said. 'Have you decided what you're doing for your silver wedding yet?'

'Err, no.' Mandy sighed inwardly. 'We don't want a party or any fuss. Do we, Mike?'

'Apparently not,' Mike said, sitting back in his chair. 'We've made no plans.'

'I think you should go to Malta, Mum, like you said you might do,' Louise chipped in.

'I'm too busy at work to take a full week off,' Mandy said. 'I'm sure your dad is, too.'

'I can manage a week,' Mike said. 'Certainly a long weekend. I'll get some brochures next week.'

Mandy chewed her lip. Mike was looking at her closely, too closely. 'We'll see.'

'Well, whatever you decide, I'd like to treat you,' Mum said. 'A gift from me. You work too hard, Mandy. You both need a break. The girls are old enough to leave on their own for a few days, or I could always move in and look after them.'

'It's okay, Nan, we can manage,' Nicole said. 'You should go for it, Mum. A romantic week away will do you both good. Just book it, Dad, surprise her.'

'I don't like surprises,' Mandy said and jumped to her feet. She felt Mike staring at her again and began to gather the dishes together. 'Louise, take these through to the kitchen and I'll serve up the apple crumble. Would you like cream or ice-cream, Mum?'

'Ice-cream, please, love. I meant what I said.' She patted Mandy's hand. 'Whatever you decide, it'll be my treat.'

Mandy hurried out of the room and went down to the cellar. The utility room was cool and she leant against the sink and took a deep breath. No way was she going away with Mike. What a farce. Maybe Rod was right and they should do it sooner. She didn't think she could keep up the act for another four months. Then again, there were Nicole's exams. They needed to be over and done with and all the other stuff put into place. Bloody hell, what with Jenny mithering about Paris and Mike and bloody Malta, her head was in a whirl. Living a double life was not easy. She took another deep breath, got the ice-cream out of the freezer, fixed on a happy-family smile and dragged her feet back up the cellar steps.

*

CHAPTER EIGHT

Mandy looked up from her magazine as Mike came into the lounge and dropped a handful of glossy books onto the coffee table next to her glass of red wine.

'Holiday brochures,' he announced. 'Have a look, pick somewhere you fancy and I'll book it tomorrow.'

'But I told you I'm too busy to take a week off.'

'Okay, we'll have a long weekend then.' He turned to stare at her. 'Anybody would think you don't want to go on holiday with me, let alone celebrate our anniversary.'

She could feel her face warming and searched for an answer. 'Actually, Mike, I could say the same about you. Until your mum mentioned it on Sunday, you've steered clear of the subject for weeks. I thought you'd conveniently forgotten because you don't want to spend time with me!' She watched as his mouth fell open.

He came to sit beside her and took her hand. 'That's not true,' he began, twisting her wedding ring around her finger. He was quiet for a moment as though considering his reply. 'You know what, Mandy? You never seem to want to be in the same room as me. I sense your irritation with me all the time. That's why I make myself scarce. I can't stand the tension. It's easier to go to the pub and come back when you're asleep.'

She gasped at his directness, but let her hand remain in his. It seemed a bit churlish to snatch it away, even though she wanted to. 'I'm sorry,' she said, looking down at the magazine on her lap. 'But what more can you expect when you're always so indifferent towards me. You never make me feel special. When was the last time you gave me a compliment? Or bought me flowers or perfume, or anything, other than at Christmas or my birthday? You can't remember can you?' she said.

He shook his head. She snatched her hand away now. His was clammy and it made her feel sick. 'You can't remember, because it's years ago! Face it, Mike, your bloody job means more to you than I do.'

His face paled as he stared at her. She was very tempted now to ask him why he'd driven past Dee's place. Then before she could stop herself she began, 'While I was away, erm, Sally called and told Dee she saw you drive past the house twice.' Dee's daughter often stayed with her mum. Why hadn't she thought of that before and confronted him at the beginning of the week, instead of worrying. 'Why did you do that, Mike? Sally nearly called here to ask if something was wrong. She thought, err, that maybe you wanted a contact number for where we were staying. But Dee told her I had my mobile with me and that if you wanted me you would call me on that.' She stopped, her mouth dry and her stomach wobbly. She could hardly believe she'd asked him and dreaded his answer. His silence was worrying. 'Well - come on,' she said, before she lost her nerve completely. 'Why did you do it?'

'I'm not sure,' he muttered, eventually. 'Well - yes, I am. I didn't really believe that you'd gone away with Dee. I suppose I was checking up on you.'

'What? Why would you think that?' She felt a bit braver now, but really guilty at the same time.

He shrugged. 'You never go away without me, apart from the occasional overnight stay at Lesley's, and you've been even more distant than usual lately. To be honest, Mandy, I thought you were up to something.'

'What sort of something?'

‘I err, thought you might be seeing someone,’ he said, looking her directly in the eye.

She looked away for a second then met his gaze. ‘What? And when do you suppose I find the time for that? I’ve a business to run, the girls, dogs and this place to look after, with hardly any input from you. When I take a flipping break because I’m worn out, you think I’m having an affair. Well that’s rich.’ She felt angry now, but with herself more than anything. He looked really upset. How the heck was she going to get another few days away with Rod now if Mike was starting to check up on her? But she had to. She ached for him. It was gnawing at her and it wasn’t a feeling she was used to. She couldn’t wait to see him at the weekend. She’d arranged to fit a Roman blind on Sunday morning, but it wouldn’t take her long and then she planned to go to the shop and wait for Rod who would join her as soon as he hit Pickford. The thought of making love with him again made her stomach flip. She picked up her glass and finished her wine.

Sunday night was going to be awkward. Jenny had spoken to Mike on Tuesday while Mandy was out with the dogs and he’d agreed that they’d join her and Rod for a meal to celebrate Jenny’s birthday. When she got back he’d asked her why she’d told Jenny he had a gig and she replied that she was sure she’d seen it written on the calendar. She was getting good at lying, but the stress was taking its toll. She’d lost five pounds in weight since the affair started. She jumped, aware that Mike was speaking to her. ‘Sorry?’

‘You were miles away,’ he said. ‘I apologised for doubting you. I’m really sorry.’ He picked up her empty glass. ‘Another?’

‘Oh, no thanks.’ She smiled warily. ‘Apology accepted.’ She felt awful. It should be her apologizing.

She needed to get out of the room and away from him. She jumped to her feet. 'I'll see to the dogs.'

He grabbed her hand and pulled her back down beside him. He moved in closer, slipping his arm around her shoulders. 'Forget the dogs. We need to sort out our problems. Twenty-five years is a long time to be married.'

'Yeah,' she agreed, pulling away. 'It is. Especially when you didn't really want to marry me in the first place.'

'Oh, Mandy!' He looked into her eyes. 'That's not true, you know it isn't.'

'You only married me because Becky was on the way.'

'I asked you to marry me long before you were pregnant. I married you because I loved you, you stupid girl. I still do.'

She stared at him. 'Do you? Why do you never tell me then?' When she thought of how many times Rod had told her he loved her, and in so short a space of time, there was no contest. 'And you never show me. We live this bland existence, just muddling through. It's soulless and boring. I feel like I've been living with a stranger for years, Mike and it's getting me down.'

'I had no idea you felt that way. You never say anything. I can't put things right if I don't know what's wrong.' He pulled her closer again and kissed her lightly on the lips. 'The girls are out. Come to bed with me. Let me show you how much I still love you.'

She flinched at his kiss, her stomach tightening, and not with passion. She pulled away again. 'Erm, not tonight, Mike. I've err, got my period.' It wasn't a lie and she wasn't fobbing him off, she did have her period, thank goodness. She and Rod had taken a few too many chances last week. She saw the disappointment in Mike's eyes but didn't feel too guilty. He'd often turned her down in the past, saying he was tired. His declarations of love were a bit too late. She felt numb as she got to her feet. 'The dogs need feeding. Would you like something to eat?'

He shook his head. 'I'll get something later. Look, I'm sorry; I should have known you wouldn't cheat on me.' He hesitated. 'I mean - you wouldn't - would you, Mand?'

She sighed. 'Like I said, Mike, I'm too busy, I wouldn't have the time.' She realised as soon as the words were out that it was the wrong answer. 'Err, sorry, that didn't come out right. No, I wouldn't cheat on you.' She left the lounge and ran upstairs to the bedroom, shutting the door. She sank to the floor beside the bed and sobbed into her hands. What a mess. She was terrified of what was to come and desperate to talk to Rod. She felt so empty inside when they weren't together. There were times when she hated herself for not dating him years ago. If only... Her thoughts were disturbed as Mike called 'I'm going out.' She heard the front door slam shut and got to her feet. Rod would be on stage right now. She pulled her phone from her pocket and sent a text, asking him to call her as soon as he could. She just needed to hear his voice, but she wasn't going to tell him what Mike had said. She didn't want him worrying while he was stuck down there on his own. It could wait until the weekend.

*

'Hiya, babe, I know this a big ask, but I need some help.'

Mandy smiled into the receiver. 'Hi, Rod. Go on, what is it?' It was Saturday lunchtime and she'd just put the "back in thirty minutes" sign on the shop door and settled down on a bean bag with a Tuna Mayo baguette, courtesy of her friend Sue, who was making coffee for them in the tiny kitchen.

'I need a present for Jenny's birthday. Any ideas? Beth normally chooses stuff for me, but I can't get hold of her.'

'Perfume,' Mandy suggested. 'She told me yesterday when she called that she's almost out. She's hoping to get some for her birthday.'

'Oh, brill. What sort?

'Don't you know?' Mandy smiled, glad that he didn't.

'Not a clue. I never get that close to take much notice. Now you - well - I know exactly what you smell like!'

'Do you?' she said, feeling her cheeks going warm and picturing his face and cheeky grin. 'You're just being rude now. Tell you what; I'll nip to the perfume shop in the precinct. I know what she uses. They'll gift wrap it too. You can collect it from here tomorrow.'

'Fantastic. You're a doll. Make sure it doesn't have a local shop label stuck to it before they wrap it. What you doing right now?'

'I'm about to have lunch with Sue. She's just brought the coffees through.'

'So you can't talk dirty to me?'

'Not at the moment,' she said, laughing. 'You'll have to wait.'

'Later then? Promise? I'll let you go. Say hi to Sue for me. Love you.'

'Love you too.' She hung up.

Sue handed her a mug and sat down on the chair. 'I take it that was Rod? Mike never makes you smile like that.'

'It was. He says hi. I've got to get perfume for Jenny's birthday. He hasn't a clue what she wears.'

'Well that sounds about right. My ex always got it wrong.'

'I have to give Mike his due there, he buys perfume for my birthday and always gets it right.'

'Probably asks the girls to choose it,' Sue said, taking a sip of coffee. 'Or maybe he has another woman to do his pressie shopping, like you're doing for Rod.'

'Huh, I should be so lucky. Mike and another woman. Now that would be an answer to one of our problems. We'd just have to fix Jenny up with someone, and we can walk away without feeling too guilty.'

'Jenny won't let Rod go without a fight. And I don't think Mike will give you up that easily either,' Sue said. 'Have you and Rod really thought this through, seriously. I mean, great sex is one thing, making plans is fine, but putting them into action, well, I don't envy you.'

'Well you did it. You've got your own place now. And you can see Pete whenever you like.'

'Yeah,' Sue sighed. 'Whenever he can escape from his wife, that is. Which is getting less and less as the weeks go by.'

'I thought he was leaving her and moving in with you. Wasn't that the plan?'

'It was. But he keeps making excuses as to why he can't come yet. His daughter's too young, his wife won't be able to cope financially on her own. Then there are our jobs. Doesn't bode well, two teachers in a catholic school having an affair. And keeping it a secret is a nightmare. Last week, when we came out of school late, some little shit had spray painted the wall in foot high letters - Mr Jackson is shagging Mrs Travis in the Art Room cupboard! I tell you, nightmare.' Sue shook her head. 'But at least I'm free now. I'll give him another six months, and if he's made no effort, then he gets his marching orders and I'll move on. What I'm trying to say is, it won't be easy, Mandy.'

Mandy nodded. 'I know.' She also knew that Sue was putting on a brave face. She idolized Pete and had given up so much to make a home for them. The least he could do was make a few sacrifices for her.

'Will you take a look at something while I'm here?' Sue put down her cup, hoisted up her sweater and pointed to her left breast. 'See if you can feel anything.'

Mandy ran her fingers lightly over the soft white skin and gently kneaded the flesh. She swallowed hard and looked at Sue. 'You've got a lump. A big one. You need to get it checked out. How long have you had it?'

'I found it a couple of weeks ago. Pete's been nagging me to get it seen to, but I'm scared, Mandy.' Her blue eyes filled with tears and Mandy put her arms around her and gave her a hug.

'It might just be a cyst. Mum had a lump a few years ago and it turned out to be nothing to worry about. But you have to go to the doctor. Promise me you will?'

Sue nodded. 'I'll call them on Monday.'

They finished their lunch in companionable silence. Mandy took the empty mugs into the kitchen. 'You will call the doctor, won't you?' she said when she came back.

'I promise,' Sue replied. 'Now go and get Jenny's perfume and I'll look after the shop for five minutes.'

*

Mandy felt close to tears as she headed for the perfume shop. She'd heard people say that stress can be a contributory factor to certain cancers, and Lord only knew how much stress poor Sue had been through in the last year or two. She wished she could tell Pete to get a move on and sort himself out. Once she and Rod had plucked up the courage to tell Mike and Jenny, then that would be it, they'd move in together.

She'd done some checking out of rental properties and the ones they could afford were few and far between. Rod had told her he'd still have to make a substantial contribution to his house and family. Jenny didn't earn that much and there was no other money going into the household. He said Ben would need to get a job to pay his way and eventually he'd hope that Jenny would agree to sell their place, but he'd told her not to hold her breath on that score. She'd told him Jenny shouldn't have to lose her home and she would ask Mike to buy her out of theirs, but she just knew that he'd make it as hard as possible for them.

They were going to be so poor. Her shop rent and business rates were high. It was a pity the flat above the shop was already taken, or she might be able to persuade the landlords to do her a deal on both properties. Even if Mike did buy her out and she used the money as a deposit on a small place, she probably wouldn't be able to get a mortgage on what she was left with after all the other outgoings were deducted. She couldn't even make cutbacks on staff; she needed the help of both Sarah and Carol.

In the perfume shop she chose Jenny's favourite Rive Gauche. There was a special offer pack with a free gold-plated butterfly brooch. Right up Jenny's street, she thought as the assistant gift wrapped and attached a small pink bow. She said goodbye and wondered if Rod had thought to get a card. She'd bet her life he hadn't, so popped in to Clintons and picked a nice glossy card with a spray of pink flowers and a simple birthday message. Did he normally get one with wife on? She racked her brains, trying to remember from past birthdays when she'd looked at Jenny's cards. She couldn't recall anything wifely or over-sentimental. Oh well, she'd done her best, over and above the call of duty.

*

'You look lovely, Jen,' Mandy said as a smiling Jenny took her and Mike through to the lounge. 'New outfit?' She noticed the little gold butterfly brooch pinned on Jenny's top and liked the way her light brown hair swung neat and shiny around her carefully made-up face. Mandy didn't think she'd seen Jenny look as radiant for years. She felt a twinge of jealousy. Surely Rod hadn't put that happy smile on her face?

'Thank you.' Jenny said, looking down at her rainbow coloured voile skirt and matching loose top. 'Reminds me of our hippy days. Do you remember them, Mandy? We used to wear floaty dresses and skirts and lots of bangles. Just before we started dating Rod and Mike.'

'Of course I remember.1967, The Summer of Love,' Mandy said wistfully. The summer of Sergeant Pepper, free love and flower power. And the summer Rod had asked her out - twice. Why oh why hadn't she said yes?

'Take a seat and I'll get you a drink,' Jenny said. 'Red or white?'

'Red for me, please,' Mandy said.

'A beer for me, please,' Mike said. Jenny left the room and Mandy wondered where Rod was. She could hear floorboards creaking above, which was the bedroom he shared with Jenny, so presumed he must be getting ready. She'd bet he was tired. He'd left Brighton before seven, after working until two am. When he'd arrived at the shop he looked pale and a bit disheveled and apologised for not having a shave. She didn't mind, she was just so glad to see him. She told him about Mike's accusations, but that she felt she'd convinced him he was wrong. Rod shrugged and said they'd need to be careful in front of Mike and Jenny. They'd thrown cushions on the floor in the workroom and made long, slow love, so that by the time he was leaving, he told her he was more than knackered and needed a sleep before tonight. He'd approved of the card she'd chosen and wrote it out there and then. Mandy could see it in pride of place on the fireplace right now. The lounge door opened and her heart leapt as Rod strolled in, looking good in black jeans and a purple T shirt, his hair freshly washed and spiky. She caught a whiff of woody aftershave and felt her stomach flip. He looked directly at her and smiled. She relaxed and smiled back.

'Hi, mate, good to see you,' Mike greeted him. 'You're looking well. Obviously suiting you, working down south. How's it going?'

'Err, yeah, it's great to see you two as well,' Rod replied. 'It's going good down there. Some weeks are better than others.'

Mandy could feel her face heating and got to her feet. Did he mean her week or the gigs? 'I'll see if Jenny needs any help,' she said. 'Leave you two to talk bands.' She had to squeeze past Rod who was standing in-between the sofa and chair so that her hip brushed his. It was the lightest touch, but it set her nerve endings tingling. She hurried out of the room without looking back. She was dreading tonight. He'd told her earlier that he was, too. Mike had done his usual head-in-the-sand thing and hadn't mentioned their argument from the other night. It suited her. Back to normal, but he'd brought her flowers on Friday, so something must have stayed in his mind. Guilt for accusing her, no doubt. She wished he hadn't bothered, because it made her feel guiltier than ever.

Jenny was pouring wine into two goblets, her face flushed. She wafted herself with a tea-towel and smiled at Mandy.

'Been checking the Lasagne?' Mandy asked, sitting down on a bar stool.

'How did you know I'd made that?'

'The garlic scent gives it away,' Mandy said, with a grin. 'Plus, you always make it when we come round.'

'Oh, am I really that predictable?' Jenny looked worried.

'Of course not. We love your Lasagne. You know you make it better than me. Mike thinks it's wonderful.' She smiled as Jenny's face relaxed. 'So, is it good to have Rod home?' She tried to keep her voice light.

'Yes, of course. Although saying that, I haven't even had five minutes with him yet. He was late getting back. He said there were road works on the motorway. He went straight to bed because he was exhausted and he's just spent an hour in the bath. I thought he'd fallen asleep again. He's going back on Tuesday. We've only got tonight and tomorrow. He gave me my present and card as soon as he came in though.'

'Oh, nice. What did he get you?' She felt relief. Rod hadn't put the smile on Jenny's face. But this was hard. She looked really happy.

'My favourite perfume. This little butterfly brooch came with it. Wasn't it thoughtful of him to choose it? He knows I love butterflies. It was beautifully wrapped too. The shop'll have done that I expect. He's not very good at wrapping. I usually just get the gift in a bag with a receipt stuffed inside in case I don't like it! I'll take the boys a beer and then I'll come back and carry on in here. Do you want to go back in with them or stay here and chat to me for a few minutes?'

Mandy took a deep breath before replying. Sit in there with hubby and lover, or stay here with lover's wife, what a choice. 'I'll stay here and help you. I'll feel like a spare part in there while they talk music and stuff.' She took a sip of wine as Jenny left the room.

When she came back Jenny was flushed and giggling. 'Your Mike's a one for the compliments, isn't he?'

'He has his moments,' Mandy said dryly. 'Why, what did he say?'

'Told me I look a million dollars in this new outfit.'

'Did he now? And did Rod say anything?' Mandy felt annoyed. Mike hadn't bothered complimenting her before they left home, even though she too had on a new outfit.

'Did he heck! He hardly noticed me. He was slugging his beer down as though he'd had none for a year.' She shook her head. 'The table's all set. I'll light the candles and take the food through. Will you carry the salad bowl for me and bring that bottle of wine?'

'Right, I'll give them a shout,' Jenny said, when she and Mandy had transported the food to the dining table. She slipped a CD into the player and left the room. Rod and Mike followed her back in. 'Sit anywhere,' she said waving her hands vaguely.

'What's this bloody music you're playing?' Rod said.

'Beautiful South,' Jenny replied, frowning. 'I like them.'

'Well I bet our guests don't.' He stopped the player, put in another disc and turned up the volume. The Travelling Wilburys, Handle Me With Care, blasted out. 'That's better,' he said. 'You've got no musical taste, Jen. You can't inflict the Beautiful South on our visitors.'

'Okay,' Jenny snapped. 'Don't go on.'

Mandy sat down and Mike sat beside her. Jenny took the seat opposite Mike and Rod sat opposite Mandy. She felt his feet rubbing her shins immediately and realised he had no shoes on. She stared at him, willing him to stop, but not really wanting him to. He smiled and she could see his eyes were slightly glazed. He'd been smoking dope. Shit. That didn't bode well. He'd be feeling frisky.

'Help yourselves,' Jenny said. 'You can have an extra big portion, Mike. I know how much you love my Lasagne.'

Mike smiled and dug in. 'Thanks, Jen. I have to say, you'd make someone a great wife!' He laughed at his own joke. Jenny giggled and tapped his hand.

'You two got the hots for each other,' Rod said, laughing. 'No, ah well, pity. You could have taken her off my hands, Mike.'

'Rod, that's not very nice,' Jenny said, frowning. 'Get something to eat. You're drinking on an empty stomach and you know how argumentative that makes you.'

'It was a joke, Jen, just a bloody joke,' Rod said, raising an eyebrow in Mandy's direction.

Mandy looked away and helped herself to food. Rod topped up her glass and offered the bottle round.

'So, let's drink a toast to Jenny,' Mike said. 'Happy birthday, sweetheart. And thanks for this lovely meal. You've excelled yourself as always.'

Jenny blushed and Mandy saw her look across at Rod who was concentrating on his plate. He was ignoring Jenny. Whether it was deliberate or not, Mandy couldn't tell. After a while she excused herself and went upstairs to use the bathroom. The window was open but the room was still damp from Rod's bath and she could smell cannabis in the air. He'd obviously had his sneaky joint in here. She could also smell his aftershave. The combination was heady and made her think about Brighton. Tonight was not a good idea. She had a heavy feeling in her heart and hoped it wouldn't end in tears. Jenny was trying so hard to please and Rod simply wasn't interested. If the subject of Paris came up, then God help them. She used the loo and made her way back to the dining room.

The lack of conversation was overwhelming as they finished their meal. Jenny began collecting the dirty dishes and Mandy, glad of something to do, jumped up to help. She could sense Rod's eyes burning into her back. Mike seemed oblivious, but was it all an act, and was he observing more than he was letting on? He seemed relaxed, maybe he was okay. She was glad she'd offered to drive, so no more wine. One of them needed their wits tonight, although another drink would have helped calm her nerves.

In the kitchen Mandy loaded the dishwasher while Jenny took a glass bowl of strawberries from the fridge and tipped a tub of cream into a china jug. 'Carry the strawberries and cream for me, Mand. I forgot to get the best dishes out of the lounge cupboard.'

Mandy took the dessert into the dining room and put it on the table. Rod's eyes lit up and he grabbed her hand. She tried to pull away, but he held on tightly. 'Relax,' he said, 'Mikes gone for a pee. Umm, strawberries. You know what that reminds me of!'

'Yes, I do. But stop it; Jenny'll be back in a minute.'

'She's rattling pots. We'll hear her when she stops. I love you.'

‘I love you, too,’ she whispered. ‘God, this wasn’t a good idea. It’s really hard.’

‘So am I, looking at you in that short skirt!’

‘Rod! Behave.’ In spite of her fear she almost choked, trying not to laugh. She sat down as Jenny came back in the room, her hands full of glass dishes.

‘Here we are,’ Jenny said. ‘They were right under everything else. Oh and here’s Mike back too.’

‘Oh goody,’ Rod mouthed at Mandy, who kicked his feet.

‘Help yourselves to the strawberries,’ Jenny said. ‘They’ve been soaked in Amaretto, so they should be really nice.’

Mandy spooned some strawberries into a dish and refused the cream.

Rod was looking in her direction. He reached a strawberry out of the bowl and popped it into his mouth, rolling it around his tongue. He licked his lips suggestively and grinned at Mandy. He’d really got it on him tonight. If they’d been on their own she knew they’d have had a fantastic time and she knew he knew it, too. Jenny and Mike were tucking in to their dessert, seemingly oblivious to the flirting. Mandy decided she’d plead a headache as soon as they’d finished eating. She had to be up early anyway. Rod had told her he’d see her at the shop for an hour tomorrow morning before she opened.

Rod helped himself to more strawberries and poured some cream over them. He took a mouthful and gagged. ‘What the fuck’s in that jug?’

‘Cream,’ Jenny replied. ‘Why, what’s wrong? Mike’s not complaining and mine’s fine.’

‘Well it doesn’t taste like cream to me. It’s thin, like bloody milk.’

'Ah, that's because it's Elmlea. It's better for your heart, it's low fat,' Jenny told him, smiling.

Rod got up and took his dish into the kitchen. Mandy could hear him scraping the contents into the bin. He came back, sat down again, and opened another bottle of wine. He gestured the bottle around the table. Mike and Jenny pushed their glasses across. 'I don't like that false cream stuff,' he said, topping them up. 'Mandy, do you want another?' She shook her head and he carried on, looking at her. 'I prefer something fuller bodied with my strawberries!'

Mandy pushed her dish away and stood up. 'I've got a really bad headache starting. I'll go and sit in the lounge for a few minutes, if you don't mind.'

'You look a bit flushed,' Jenny said. 'Go and put your feet up.'

'I'll give you a hand to clear the pots, Jen,' Mike offered.

'Thanks, Mike.'

'Can I get you some paracetamol?' Rod said to Mandy, jumping to his feet.

'Please, and a glass of water would be nice,' she replied and left the room.

He was with her in seconds. 'Here you go.' He sat down beside her and handed her the glass and two tablets.

She could hear pots clattering and the dishwasher being stacked and the low murmur of Mike and Jenny's voices down the hall. 'I haven't got a headache,' she whispered. 'It's an excuse to get away early. Jenny's desperate to spend some time with you alone. Much as I hate the thought, it is her birthday, you are her husband and she hasn't seen you for weeks. All you've done tonight is be horrible to her. I want to get out of here before she brings up the Paris subject and you hit the roof. Just try and be nice for a short while. She's got herself all dressed up for you and she looks lovely.'

'I know.' He stared at her. 'But I don't want to be here. The thought of sharing a bed with her, even for a couple of nights, does my head in. I had to have a small joint earlier to get me through tonight.'

'I can tell. But just try and be nice, it won't hurt you.'

'I'm not shagging her!' He had a mutinous expression and it made her smile.

'I didn't ask you to. I hoped you wouldn't want to anyway. Just be nice, that's all. Tell her you're tired, too full, whatever. But don't be horrible. It doesn't suit you. Just sit and talk with her for a while.'

'I'll do my best. Go up to the loo. I want to kiss you before you leave. I'll make an excuse to get something from upstairs to show Mike.'

*

Mandy sat down on the side of the bath and took a deep breath. She could hear music so that would deaden any sound from up here. There was a tap on the door and Rod slid in.

'They're in the lounge with a tray of coffee and brandies,' he told her. 'I've put another CD on. Told them you've come up to get a damp flannel for your head. They're both a bit pissed, so we'll be okay for a few minutes.' He pulled her into his arms and ran his fingers through her hair. 'God, I want you again.' He pushed her up against the wall and ground against her, kissing her hard. He smoothed his hands down over her hips and inched her skirt up.

She stopped him 'Rod, we can't. Not with them downstairs. This is madness. You said earlier we have to be more careful.' He groaned as she pulled away. 'I'll see you tomorrow morning,' she said. 'I'll go downstairs now. You stay here and try and get rid of err, that!' She looked pointedly at his groin and shook her head. 'God, what are you like?'

'It's your fault. You turn me on so easily.' He kissed her one last time. 'I'll see you in a few minutes.'

'How are you feeling now?' Jenny asked as Mandy went back into the lounge.

'Not bad. But I think we should get going in a few minutes, Mike, when you've finished your coffee.'

'Okay. Where's Rod?'

'I heard him rummaging around in the bedroom while I was upstairs. Ah here he is now,' she finished as Rod came back in the room.

'Can't find the Mojo magazine with that Eagles article I was telling you about, Mike,' he said. 'Anyway, they're recording a new album, Hell Freezes Over. And they're planning a tour. Remind me to look again the next time you come over.'

Mike nodded. 'Fantastic. It must be fourteen years since the last album. I remember Don Henley saying he'd only work with the band again when hell freezes over! Looks like it has. We'll have to get tickets for the tour.'

'For sure,' Rod agreed. 'It's something to look forward to.'

Mandy smiled. 'It is. Shall we be off then, Mike? I'm really tired.'

'Actually,' Mike began, 'while you two were out of the way, Jenny's had a great idea. She was telling me you're not keen on going to Paris, Rod, with working away all summer. And Mandy doesn't want to go away either just at the moment, because the shop's too busy. Well what about this? Why don't we all go away together when Rod's finished his stint and Mandy's summer rush is over. We could hire a villa or something, somewhere really nice.’

*

CHAPTER NINE

MAY 1994

Mandy rooted in her handbag for the stamp she was sure was in the little pocket where she kept her lippy and loose change for the car park. The stamp wasn't there and she remembered now she'd used it the other day to send payment for an invoice. 'Damn!' She really needed to post the card tonight or it wouldn't get there for Lesley's birthday on Friday. Mike always had spare stamps in his briefcase, but he was out rehearsing. The briefcase was on the floor by the wardrobe, but was no doubt locked. She tried the catches, they sprang open and she delved into the compartment in the lid, marvelling at how neat and tidy everything was. Not like her case, all higgledy-piggledy. She found a book of first class stamps, tore one out, and put the rest back exactly as she'd found them. She was about to close the case when she spotted a small black diary. She stared at it. She had no idea that Mike kept a diary, apart from the big office one he occasionally brought home.

She knew she shouldn't read it. She'd go nuts if anyone read hers. But then again, she always got one with a lock. Perhaps as well these days, because she recorded details of her relationship with Rod. But that diary was kept at the shop. Locked or not, no way would she dare to bring it home. She picked up the diary and flicked through it. She spotted her name on one page and read the entry. The fine hairs on the back of her neck prickled. The date was the week they'd had the argument, when Mike suspected her of having an affair.

Mandy's doing my head in. She hardly speaks unless I speak first. She looks different, happier almost. She laughs and jokes with the girls, but acts miserable around me. I can't accuse her of anything without proof, but I'm sure she wasn't away with Dee.

The entry before it was after his mother came for Sunday lunch.

Mum offered to pay for a silver wedding trip. Mandy doesn't want to do anything. I'm sure she's seeing someone.

She turned a page and found an entry written on the day after Mike had asked her if she was seeing someone.

Blew it last night. Asked Mandy if she'd got someone else and she denied it. We had a row. I apologised to keep the peace, but I don't believe her. Wish I'd kept my mouth shut until I've got some proof. She's different and there must be a reason. I'm keeping an eye on her.

Butterflies doing wheelies in her stomach, Mandy quickly turned the pages to the present month. There weren't many more entries, just a few random ramblings about how he kept looking for clues but had found nothing so far. Well he wouldn't, because nothing was happening other than her and Rod's frequent calls. She couldn't get away at the moment and Rod was too busy to travel north. He'd got a weekend off mid-July and the odd day in between, but not enough time to drive back and forth to Pickford.

She'd booked to go to a fabric and home interiors show at the NEC next Wednesday. Rod was driving up to Birmingham to spend the night with her. She couldn't wait. She missed him so much. She just hoped that Mike wouldn't suddenly decide he wanted to go with her. He'd mentioned he might, saying that it was time he took a bit more interest in her business. Huh, more like checking up on her. She'd told him he'd be bored. It was only work, not pleasure. She wouldn't want to go to work with him, so why would he want to come with her when he'd never been bothered before. He suggested she take Nicole for company. But Nicole had exams. Fingers crossed he wouldn't mither again.

She put the diary away, shut the briefcase and stuck the stamp on the envelope. A walk around the block to the postbox might clear her head. She called the dogs and clipped on their leads. Max and Poppy leapt up and down like mad things, eager to be off.

Jenny had been over at the weekend. She and Mike had pored over holiday brochures. They'd chosen a villa in Malta for September to coincide with Rod being home. They'd booked it for the week before Jenny went back to work for the new school term. Mandy had gone along with their enthusiasm, nodding and agreeing that the pool looked lovely. How relaxing the break would be for them all. But she couldn't really care less. By September she and Rod would be living happily together and in the meantime she'd got next Wednesday to look forward to.

*

'You okay?' Mandy said as Rod stretched out on the bed in the Holiday Inn. 'You're a bit quiet.'

'I'm fine.' He held out his hand for her to come and join him. She lay down beside him and snuggled close. They'd met up on the NEC car park, had a bite to eat and then checked into the hotel.

'You're not fine,' she said. He wasn't his usually bubbly self and he looked pale. 'Tell me what's wrong.'

He sighed. 'I don't feel too good. Got pains in my chest. Think the coffee and donut I threw down my neck at the services are lying heavy. Maybe I shouldn't have had that meal just now either.'

'Might be indigestion. I've got some Tums in my bag.' She jumped up and brought him the Tums and a glass of water.

He chewed a couple and washed them down. Mandy took the glass back into the bathroom. When she came out he was sitting hunched over, groaning. She sat beside him and gently rubbed his back. 'Shall I get you some ginger ale?'

'Will it help?'

'Might do. I used to drink it when I was pregnant and had heartburn. You need to do a big burp.'

'Okay.'

She could see tiny beads of sweat above his top lip and his hair was damp, as though he'd just showered. 'Won't be a minute.' She hurried from the room. At the bar she got three bottles of Canada Dry and a miniature brandy for herself. Back in the room, Rod was slouched against the headboard. She poured a glass of ginger ale and added a drop of warm water. 'Try this and sip it slowly.'

He did as he was told. 'Have you got pain anywhere else?'

'Across my shoulders. I wonder if I trapped a nerve or something when I packed my gear away.'

'You might have. Do you have pain in your arms?' She remembered that Rod's mum had died suddenly following a heart attack. She'd read somewhere that apart from pain in the chest, pain down the left arm was also a symptom.

He shook his head and finished his drink.

'I've got some paracetamol in my bag. It might ease the pain in your shoulders.'

He smiled. 'Mandy, I'm really sorry. I didn't come here to be ill. All the way up the bloody motorway I've thought about nothing else but your body and making love to you.'

She took the empty glass and kissed him lightly. 'All that matters is we're together for a night. Our relationship's about more than sex. Well, it is for me, anyway.'

'It is for me too. But I was so looking forward to being with you again.'

'And you are. You might feel better later. Sit upright properly now and see if you can get some wind up while I fix my brandy.'

Rod shuffled upright. He let out a loud belch and sighed. 'Ooh, sorry about that. Christ I feel better already.'

She got him the paracetamol and another glass of water. 'You might as well as take these, in case you've also trapped a nerve. They won't do you any harm.'

'That handbag of yours is a one-woman chemist's shop.'

'I'm always prepared,' she said, laughing. 'Talking of which - did you get the condoms?'

'No,' he said, looking sheepish. 'Sorry, didn't have time.'

'Oh, Rod, you've known for ages we were meeting here. You've had plenty of time. I'll try and get some from the ladies. If not you'll have to go to the gents.' She left the room again, shaking her head. Bloody hell, she could have got some herself before she left Pickford. But Rod had said he'd do it. Neither of them liked using condoms, but she was terrified of taking too many chances. They'd been lucky so far.

Two young women were touching up their makeup in the ladies. She popped into a cubicle until she heard them leave, wondering why the hell she was hiding. Not like she was under-age or anything. She spotted two machines placed discreetly in the alcove behind the door; one with tampons, the other, condoms in two choices, flavoured or sensitive. Wouldn't you know it, sensitive was off the menu, chocolate being the only choice. She bought them anyway.

Rod was in the bathroom when she got back. 'You feeling okay now?' she called.

'Yes thanks. Just having a quick shower to wake me up,' he called back.

She went into the bathroom and stripped off. 'Mind if I join you?'

He held the shower curtain to one side and took her hand. 'Be my guest. Any luck?'

'Yes and no,' she said with a grimace.

'What?'

'Chocolate flavour. It was the only choice.'

'Fucking hell, Mand.'

'It's better than nothing.'

'I've been thinking,' he began, lathering her with shower gel.

'About what?'

'I'm gonna get the snip.'

'You'll have a job tonight.'

He smiled and flicked bubbles at her. 'I'll get it done privately, down in Brighton. Jenny needn't know anything about it then.'

'We can't afford it. We need money for a place to live. Why don't you wait until we move in together and get it done on the NHS?'

He tweaked her nipples with soapy fingers. 'The way we are with each other, I need to get it done sooner rather than later. I'll find the money somehow.'

She was touched that he'd even think about doing that for her. He'd flatly refused to have a vasectomy when Jenny asked him, even though Mike had told him it was okay once you got over the first few weeks. There was little she could do about contraception herself. The pill didn't suit. She'd tried a coil and got pregnant with Nicole almost right away, prompting Mike to have his vasectomy.

Rod turned off the shower and wrapped towels around them both. 'I'll sell my old drum kit. I'll take it into Johnny Roadhouse; see what they'll offer.'

'Don't get ahead of yourself. See how much a vasectomy costs first. If you sell your drum kit Jenny will be after you to put the money towards Malta.'

'Not a chance.' He held her close and kissed her.

She ran a finger down his cheek. He was a better colour now. 'Are you sure you're feeling alright?'

'Yeah, a bit tired. Had a really late night. We did two gigs. An early doors session and an after midnight spot at another club. I've only had a couple of hour's kip in the last two days.'

'No wonder you don't feel well. I bet you've not eaten properly either. You can't live on junk food and fags and expect to feel on top of the world. You're not a teenager, Rod. You have to start looking after yourself properly.'

'Yes, mother!' He dried her back with his towel. 'You can take care of me soon.' He lifted her and carried her into the bedroom, dropping her onto the bed so that she bounced and started laughing.

'You'll give yourself a hernia, ' she said and pulled him down beside her.

'I'll take my chances.' He kissed her, running his fingers through her hair. 'I've missed you so much. I think about you all the time. I can't wait for us to be together.'

'Not long now,' she whispered. She still hadn't told him about Mike's diary entries. He had enough going on in his head without her adding to his worries. She pushed everything to the back of her mind and lost herself in their lovemaking. When Rod reached for the condoms and tore the top off a packet with his teeth, she almost gagged at the vile smell of rubber and chocolate.

'Fuck it,' he muttered, flinging it to the floor. 'I'm not using that. I'll be careful.'

Mandy nodded, too far gone to care and willing to agree to anything.

*

'I don't want to go back.' Rod hugged Mandy close. 'It's gonna be ages until I see you again.' They were sitting in his car on the hotel car park, saying a last goodbye.

'I wish I could come down to Brighton, but I need a good excuse to take more time off work and seeing as I've refused to go away with Mike, it just wouldn't wash.'

'I know. If I get any spare time at all, I'll come up. You know that, don't you?'

'It's such a long way though, just for a day. As long as I can talk to you frequently then I can cope. I'd better go, and you need to get back for work tonight.'

'I love you.' He kissed her one last time.

'Love you, too,' she said, fighting back tears.

He watched as she got into her car, and then followed her off the car park. He hated this, saying goodbye, when she could be with him all summer if only things were different. He hadn't called home in over twenty-four hours and had switched off his phone as soon as he got to Birmingham. He supposed he should check in before he got on the motorway. He'd need his phone on again anyway in case Mandy called him. He pulled over and switched on. 'What the fuck?' he muttered as it beeped continuously. Six missed calls from Jenny, two from Beth and a barrage of text messages, all asking him to get in touch urgently.

'Jen,' he said when she answered, sounding tearful. 'What's wrong?'

'Where the hell have you been?' she demanded and he held the phone away from his ear. *'Why'd you turn your bloody phone off?'*

'I've been busy working and stuff. I left my phone in the dressing room at a club. Only just got it back.'

'Well you could have used someone else's phone to call me.'

'Yeah, and I would have done if I'd known you were trying to get hold of me. So what's the panic?'

'It's Ben. I found used needles when I was cleaning his room last night.' Her voice wobbled as she spoke.

'Shit!' Rod's stomach tightened. 'Did you say anything to him?'

'No. He's not here. He's away with Tanya and her mum. His room was a shit tip, dirty clothes and pots all over the place. If it hadn't been such a mess I wouldn't have gone under the bed. That's where the needles were, and used condoms, too. It's not on, Rod. I shouldn't have to clean those up. It's that girl. She's made him like this, her and her filthy ways. I don't know what to do.'

Rod sighed, thinking of the condom he'd chucked on the floor last night. Like father, like son. He didn't know what to do either. And stuck down in Brighton he was no use to Mandy, Jenny or Ben. But he needed the work. If he could just get through this summer, he had a few ideas up his sleeve that wouldn't take him away again, apart from odd nights. 'Has he got his phone with him?'

'Yes, but he only answers when it suits. Then he bites my head off. Just like you!'

'Alright, don't have a fucking go at me. I'll call him. Has it occurred to you that the needles might be Tanya's?' He knew Ben smoked weed and took Ecstasy occasionally. Ben had admitted it when he'd confronted him a couple of years ago. Rod had made him promise never to touch the hard stuff. He'd seen too many mates in his teens and twenties bite the dust from drugs. He never smoked dope in front of his kids or Jenny. He wouldn't dream of it. Yet he'd shared a joint with Mandy without a second thought and it had been the most natural thing in the world to do. But then, everything was natural with Mandy. She didn't nag him and he could just be himself. He was aware that Jenny was speaking again. He interrupted her. 'Leave it with me. I'll speak to him before you start accusing him of anything. Have you told Beth and James?' He supposed she must have done or Beth wouldn't have left him texts.

'Yes, they're angry with him, too. James would have had a go if he'd been here. But he's away with work at the moment.'

'Well just remember what happened the other week when you all accused him of stealing money,' Rod reminded her. 'I'll call you later when I've spoken to him.' He said goodbye and ended the call. He sat for a few minutes, wondering what to do. Pointless calling Ben now, he'd be unlikely to be up. He dug his fist in his chest and took a deep breath. Bloody indigestion was starting again. He shouldn't have had the fried breakfast. But it was part of the room deal and it seemed daft to miss out when Mandy had paid for it. He was suffering now. He reached in his jacket pocket for the Tums she'd given him, popped a couple in his mouth and headed for the motorway.

*

'Ben, it's Dad. Call me as soon as you get this message.' Rod sat back in his chair and looked out of the window. He'd stopped for a pee, coffee and fag at Pease Pottage Services. Not far to go now. He felt the urge to hear Mandy's voice and called her. She sounded sad. Told him she was missing him already and was wracking her brains as to how she could get away to join him in Brighton. He said he'd have a think too. He told her about Jenny's find, but that Jenny probably wouldn't say anything to her. 'She can't handle anyone thinking badly of our kids, not even close friends. She feels a failure with Ben at times.'

'Ben's lovely, Rod. He's just like you! Don't worry. They might not even be his needles. Most likely that Tanya's.'

'Hmm, possibly. I've had pains in my chest again. Been chewing your Tums all the way down here.'

'I think it's stress. Promise me you'll go and see a doctor if it continues.'

'I will. I'll talk to you later. Call me as soon as you can. I love you.'

'And I love you, too. Drive carefully.'

*

Mandy was folding curtains, the last of Friday's workload, when Sue strolled into the shop. One look at her friend's pale face told her the news wasn't good. 'How did it go?' she asked, putting the curtains on the cutting table and clearing the chair of fabrics and cushions. Following an initial visit to the doctor's Sue had had a biopsy and been back to hospital today for the results.

'Not great.' Sue's eyes filled with tears and Mandy gave her a hug.

'Sit down; I'll put the kettle on.' She made coffee while Sue took off her coat and produced a paper bag containing two strawberry tarts.

'It's cancer,' Sue said as Mandy handed her a mug. 'I've two choices. Lose my breast or have a lumpectomy. Either way I'll need chemotherapy.'

'God, I'm so sorry. What have you decided?'

Sue shrugged. 'Nothing yet. Pete's coming over tonight. I'll see what he thinks.'

'You have to do what's best for you,' Mandy said.

'Yeah, but I'm going to look a right mess with only one breast.'

'Dee's friend had a mastectomy last year and a reconstruction. You'd never know. She's doing really well.'

'Oh, I just don't know, Mand. I feel numb inside. Pete will hate it if I lose a breast. He as much as said so last week.'

Mandy felt anger rising. Pete was such a selfish bastard. 'He'd hate it even more if he lost you.' She handed Sue a box of tissues and sat down on the bean bag. 'Like I said, you have to do what's best for you. I'll help you all I can.'

'I'll lose my hair,' Sue wailed. 'It's taken me ages to get it to this length, too.'

Mandy felt helpless. Nothing she could say would ease Sue's fear and bewilderment. Her friend was proud of her shoulder-length blonde hair. It framed her elfin face and set off her sparkling blue eyes and wide smile. Mandy absentmindedly put her hand up to touch her own hair. How would she feel if she lost it? And would

Rod want her with only one breast? But surely love was about more than just appearance? She hoped he'd still love her, regardless.

'Your hair will grow back, Sue. Like I said, I'll be there for you every step of the way. Take you to hospital for your treatment and bring you home and look after you.'

They clung together for a few minutes then Sue pulled away. 'Let's talk about something else. How's Rod? Did he meet you in Birmingham?'

Mandy nodded. She told Sue about the trip and also about the discovery of Mike's diary.

'He'll watch you like a hawk now. Just like my ex did with me. Always look over your shoulder when you're out with Rod. Mike may have a detective following you.'

'Don't think he'd go that far,' Mandy said. 'Besides, I never go out around here with Rod. When I'm out alone Mike can easily check up on me and make himself look an idiot. In fact, I wish he bloody well would.'

'When are you seeing Rod again?'

'It'll probably be July now. I can't think of any good excuses to get away again.'

Sue was quiet for a moment and then smiled. 'I can. Tell Mike about my cancer. Then tell him you and I are having a long weekend at my friend's in Berkshire before I have my operation. He won't begrudge us that, surely? We'll go next weekend, well you will. Get the train on Friday morning and Rod can meet you in London.'

Mandy felt her jaw drop. 'Honestly? I'll have to see if Sarah can look after the shop. But dare I? What if Mike checks up on me? He might try and call you or something.'

'Mand, stop flapping. Let me worry about that. Just do it. Please. Life's too short. Grab the chance while you can. Make Rod a happy bunny!'

'He'll be thrilled,' Mandy said, filling up again. 'Thank you so much. I'll do anything for you. You know that, don't you?'

'I do,' Sue said, smiling. 'And you will, believe me. You'll want to run a mile at the sight of me in the next few months, sickly, bald and moaning.'

'Never.'

*

Rod lay on his bed, staring at the ceiling. He felt really down and wished Mandy was there beside him. He jumped as his phone rang out. Mandy, calling to say goodnight? He felt almost disappointed to see Ben's number, then felt a rush of guilt and tried to get his head into strict-father mode. 'Ben, how you doing, son?'

'Alright, thanks, Dad. What's up? You sounded anxious in your message.'

Rod came straight to the point. 'Your mother found used needles under your bed. She's in a right state, worrying. You promised me you wouldn't touch the hard stuff.' There was silence for a few seconds. Rod could almost hear Ben's brain ticking over while he searched for an excuse.

'Ah, sorry, Dad. They're not mine. A mate of Tanya's left them. Meant to chuck 'em away. I forgot. Really sorry to freak Mum out.'

Rod drew a deep breath. 'Don't believe you, Ben. Tell me the truth. Where the fuck are you getting money from to buy heroin, or weed for that matter?'

Ben was silent again before replying. 'I tried it once. Didn't like it. And I get my weed off Tanya's mates for free.'

'Do you think I was born yesterday?' Rod yelled. 'Drugs cost; you're skint. I'm telling you now, don't you dare take drugs, that girl, or her mates to the house again. I don't want them anywhere near Beth or your mother. In fact, I want you to come down here and stay with me. Bring your guitar. I'll try and get you some work. Ask Mum to sub you the train fare. I'll see her straight.'

'Can you really get me some work?'

'I'll try,' Rod replied, glad to hear enthusiasm in Ben's voice. Anything to get him away from that skanky girl and her druggy mates.

'Tanya'll be really chuffed. She's always going on about us getting away from Pickford before her ex gets out.'

Rod drew another deep breath. 'The invite's for you only. I don't want Tanya here. And anyway, she's got her kid to think about. There's no room for them as well. You'll be sleeping on the floor as it is. I want to try and get you sorted, earning some money. You can't afford to support her. She's not your responsibility. And it's not that long ago you told me she was just a mate and you weren't serious about her.'

'Things have changed. If she can't come then forget it. I'm leaving home anyway. I'm pissed off with Mum's nagging. Me and Tan are trying to get a place of our own.'

Rod swallowed hard. That was not what he wanted to hear. 'Where will you go?' The thoughts of Ben living away from the family worried him. Jenny could keep an eye on him while he was under the same roof. Out of sight - well - he dreaded to think. But what if Ben was telling the truth and he really wasn't doing hard drugs? Maybe standing on his own two feet would be good for him. He'd have to find a job to pay rent. If he took on Tanya and her child, they'd struggle to afford drugs. Ben might grow up a bit, like he'd had to at that age with two kids and Jenny to support. 'Okay, son. If that's what you want. Good luck to you. Just two things. Keep me up to date with where you're living. And check in with your mum occasionally. I know she nags but she's worried about you. I'll catch up with you when I'm next home.'

'Okay, Dad. Maybe one day we'll visit you down there.'

*

Mandy could feel the smile splitting her face as Rod sang *Fast Movin' Train*, his eyes on hers. She couldn't believe she was here. The same club - The Majestic - and Penny sitting opposite her again. She was determined to make the most of this weekend. It would probably be the last with any piece of mind before they dropped their bombshell. Rod would be home in July, but he had his dad's seventieth birthday to celebrate and bridges to build with Ben, who, much to Jenny's disgust, had moved into a houseboat on the canal this week with his girlfriend and her child. Mandy was aware of Penny tapping her arm and pointing to her empty glass.

'Refill?'

'It's my turn to get a round, Penny.' She got to her feet. 'I'll get a couple of pints in for Rod and Jed, too.'

She made her way to the bar, glancing at Rod, who was finishing the second spot with *Hotel California*. He looked tired tonight. Had dark shadows beneath his eyes and his face was pale. He'd rushed up to London to pick her up, wanted to make love as soon as they got to Brighton, and then the mad dash to get ready and set up the gear for tonight. No wonder he was tired. He needed looking after. She couldn't wait for the gig to end, to be back in his room with him.

By the time Mandy got served, the group was making its way off stage. She carried the tray back to the table and sat down. Jed came rushing over, his expression anxious, and grabbed her by the arm. 'It's Rod, you'd better come quick.' He bundled her into the dressing room where Rod was slumped on a chair, looking waxen. The rest of the band were in various stages of undress, but didn't seem bothered by her presence. They were more concerned about Rod, worry showing on their faces. She knelt beside him and took his hand, her stomach lurching. 'Have you got chest pains again?'

He turned terrified eyes to her, nodded and pointed to his left arm. 'And here,' he whispered.

'Call an ambulance,' she ordered Jed. 'Tell them to hurry.'

*

CHAPTER TEN

Mandy had never felt so frightened. She couldn't stop shaking. Jed slipped a comforting arm around her shoulders as they sat in the relatives' area of Brighton General. The short ambulance ride had been traumatic. The paramedics had allowed her to accompany Rod. They'd worked on him, making him comfortable, giving him a shot of something to relax him, and oxygen via a face mask. His waxy colour, laboured breathing and blue-tinged lips scared her more than anything she'd ever been scared of in her life. Jed had followed in a taxi. Rod had been rushed away on a trolley to God knew where. She and Jed sat in silence for what felt like hours.

'Is there anyone you need to call?' Jed asked eventually.

'Oh, I don't know,' she muttered. She couldn't call Jenny, or any of Rod's kids. They had a right to be here, more than she did, but she couldn't call them. That would be up to the hospital and Rod.

'What about your kids?'

'Err, not just yet. I don't want to worry them.' Did Jed still think she was Rod's wife? He must do, bloody hell. Panic washed over her. Please be okay, Rod, she chanted silently in her head. Don't leave me to deal with all this on my own. I can't live without you. Tears poured silently down her cheeks and great shuddering sobs racked her body. This really couldn't be happening, it was a dream. She'd wake up any minute, wrapped in his arms. A door at the end of the corridor swung open and a nurse walked towards them.

'Mrs Davies?'

Mandy nodded and got slowly to her feet, her legs wobbly.

'Come through, please. Your husband wants to see you.'

'Go ahead,' Jed said. 'I'll wait here.'

Mandy followed the nurse into a small room where a pale-faced Rod lay on a bed, monitor wires attached to his bare chest. She almost collapsed with relief when she saw him smile behind the oxygen mask and hold out his hand. The nurse left them alone and Mandy clasped his hand and burst into tears again.

He pulled the mask down and said,' I'm okay. Don't think it's anything too serious. It looks more frightening than it is. They've done an ECG and I'm waiting for a doctor to come and explain what happened.' He rubbed his free hand over his hairy chest. 'They've shaved some hairs off me to stick these things on.'

'Rod, I thought I was losing you,' she sobbed. 'I was so scared.'

'You don't get rid of me that easily. At least I'm in safe hands. Is Jed still with you?'

'He's waiting outside.'

'You go back to the house with him. They want to keep me in overnight, but I'm sure I'll be out tomorrow. I'm so sorry, sweetheart. After all that planning to get here as well. I'll make it up to you, I promise.'

Mandy nodded. 'I'm just glad I'm here. I'm staying in Brighton until I know you're okay. I don't care how long it takes. I'll get round it somehow. Are you going to let Jenny and the kids know?'

'No. I should, but she'll want to come down and I can't deal with her right now. I just want to spend time with you, not have her fussing all over the place.'

'Okay, if you're sure.' She looked up as the door opened and a young man, carrying a file, walked in. 'Do you want me to stay while the doctor's here?'

'Please.' Rod squeezed her hand tightly.

'Mr Davies.' The doctor smiled at Rod and nodded in Mandy's direction. 'How are you feeling now?'

'Better than I did, thanks,' Rod replied. 'So, how am I doing? Was it a heart attack?'

'Not this time. But you have an irregular heart rhythm. I want you to stay on the monitor overnight and we'll run more tests tomorrow.'

'What sort of tests?'

'We'll do an angiogram. It will tell us if you have any blocked arteries, and we'll do a stress test. How frequently do you get the chest pains?'

'They can come on at any time,' Rod replied. 'Mainly when I'm rushing around and not eating regularly. I thought it was indigestion.'

'The symptoms of heart problems are very similar,' the doctor said. 'I see from your notes that you've a family history of heart disease and that you're also a smoker.'

Rod nodded. 'My mother died from a heart attack. And yes, I smoke about twenty a day. Suppose I'll have to cut down now?'

'I'd advise you to give up completely. We'll be able to help you with that. I'll leave you to get some rest now and will see you in the morning.'

Mandy smoothed Rod's hair off his face and bent to kiss him as the doctor left the room. 'I'd better go, too. Jed looked fit to drop out there.'

'I'll see you tomorrow,' Rod said. 'I'll call you as soon as I know what's happening. They won't let me use my mobile in here because of the monitor, but as soon as I can ring you I will. Try not to worry. I'll be fine. Jed'll look after you.'

Mandy nodded. 'I love you. See you soon.'

'Love you, too. Goodnight, baby. Sorry I scared you.'

'Won't Jenny worry that you haven't called her tonight?'

'I spoke to her this morning. I'll tell her I left my phone in the dressing room again. I really can't be arsed mithering about it now. And don't you go worrying about her either. I'll sort it tomorrow. Give us a hug now, before they throw you out.'

*

Rod lay awake, staring at the wall-clock. It was 4 am. Every time he managed to doze, a nurse popped in to do his "obs". His blood pressure was back to normal and he had no temperature. Last time she was in he'd had a sharp chest pain and she'd sprayed something minty under his tongue. The relief had been instant. He could do with a spray like that to take home. If whatever was wrong with him was that easy to control he could cope with it. He was desperate to speak to Mandy. He pictured her lying alone in his bed, her hair fanned across the pillows. He felt like crying. The one weekend they'd managed to get together for a while and this had to happen. His phone was on the bedside table. They'd said not to use it, but surely a text wouldn't do any harm. He could switch it off again right away. 'Sod it,' he muttered. He hid the phone under the covers, tapped in *I love you xxx* and sent it. No alarms went off. It didn't appear to have messed with the equipment. The phone was silent for a couple of minutes and then beeped against his thigh. He smiled as he read, *I love you too. Do as you're told and turn that bloody phone off. xxx*

*

Mandy smiled as she sent the text through to Rod. Like her, he must be lying awake, thinking of what they could have been doing right now. But she was glad he was being taken care of. What if he'd collapsed here? She would have panicked. They might not have got to the hospital on time. Then what? Imagine having to call Jenny with that sort of news. It didn't bear thinking about. Her phone beeped again. *Turning off now. Goodnight, sexy angel. See you tomorrow. xxx* She sent a goodnight back and turned onto her side, willing sleep to come.

*

'So, can you put me right?' Rod asked the heart specialist. He'd just been given the diagnosis - stable angina and a blocked artery.

'You'll be able to control the angina with a spray,' the specialist said. 'We'd like to do a procedure called Angioplasty. We put a stent into the artery, which opens up to let the blood flow through properly.' He went on to explain the procedure and how it would be done by insertion through the groin.

Rod could feel his eyes watering at the prospect and forced himself to pay attention as the specialist continued, 'I'm also prescribing Beta-blockers, which will slow your heart rate a little, and a daily aspirin to thin your blood. Makes it easier to flow through the blocked artery. I'd advise you to have a few days off work and get some rest.'

Rod wished Mandy was with him. He couldn't take it all in and would be sure to forget as soon as he walked out of the room. It was three pm now and the tests had taken nearly all day. He'd been weighed, measured, had blood taken. He'd been on a treadmill and had dye inserted into his bloodstream, so they could see what was going on in his heart. All he wanted to do was get back to the house and Mandy. He wouldn't be able to work for a while, so Jed would need to get a stand in drummer. Rod had called Mandy and Jed earlier from the portable payphone a nurse had brought to his bedside. Jed told him not to worry, he knew a guy who'd help out. He'd told Rod to let him know when he was ready for discharge and he'd come and pick him up.

'Can I go home now?' Rod asked.

'Yes. Nurse will get your prescription and we'll arrange a date for the Angioplasty. You can of course have it done at a hospital nearer your home.' He gave Rod a handful of pamphlets about heart disease and how to keep himself fit. 'These will give you all the information you need.'

'Thanks. I'll talk to my erm - wife. See what she thinks. Then I'll let you know.' Rod got to his feet, thanked the specialist and followed the nurse back to his room.

'Wait here for me, Mr Davies,' she said. 'I won't be long.'

'Okay. I'll ring my friend. Tell him I'll be ready to go home soon,' he said as she closed the door behind her.

He needed clothes. He'd been admitted in sweaty stage gear and was currently wearing scratchy paper knickers and a hospital gown in an unflattering shade of green. He was dying to get home, jump in the shower and have a shave. Luckily they'd provided him with a disposable toothbrush and tiny tube of toothpaste, so he wasn't totally manky. He could use his mobile now. Mandy would sort him something to wear. He sat down on the bed and called her.

*

‘Have you spoken to Jenny?’ Mandy asked as she lay on the bed, Rod stretched out beside her. Jed had taken her to the hospital to collect him and they were relaxing after Rod had freshened up.

‘I’ve been wracking my brains to think of a way to tell her without her panicking and getting James to drive them down here,’ he replied. ‘I’ve had texts and messages from her. I suppose I should call soon.’

‘You should. It’s been well over a day since you last spoke to her and you know how she flaps if you don’t call.’

‘I just want a peaceful and stress-free weekend with you, well what’s left of it anyway,’ he said. ‘I’ll say I left the phone in the club again. I’m not telling her about the ticker problem just yet. I’ll drive home Tuesday afternoon with you and drop you at Sue’s. I’ll have to call the hospital on Monday to see if I need a letter or something to give to my GP. I’ll tell Jen when I get back and I’ll arrange to have the op done locally. Don’t fancy being stuck down here on my own with no you to visit me. Do you think you can wangle another night down here?’

‘Yeah. I’m not leaving you now. I’ll call Sue and warn her. Mike can have a text to say I’ll see him Tuesday night. I’m not even going to give him a reason. He hasn’t bothered contacting me since I let him know I’d arrived safely.’ She got up and reached for her handbag. ‘Right, I’ll nip to Waitrose and get something for tea while you call Jenny.’

‘Don’t be long,’ he said with a grin. ‘I need nursing back to health. Those pamphlets from the hospital say regular sex is good for heart patients. The more the merrier, it says. And I never once got the pain while we were making love.’

She laughed. He had a twinkle in his eye again. It was good to see. 'Actually, it says twice a week. Alright, a minimum of twice,' she added as he opened his mouth to protest. 'But you're not wearing yourself out tonight to prove it should say twice daily. Don't forget to take a Beta Blocker; and no sneaky fags while I'm out.' She left the room, ducking the pillow he chucked at her.

*

Rod crossed his fingers as he waited for Jenny to take his call. He hoped she wasn't home, but she was. Her response was curt as he apologised for not getting in touch and said he'd left his phone at the club. 'I've, err, got a few days off mid week, so I'll come home,' he added.

'Days off! Why? I thought you weren't off again until July. I hope you're getting paid while you're not working. We can't afford for you not to get paid.'

He rolled his eyes. Bloody money; it was all she ever thought about. She'd be better off if he'd corked it on Friday night. At least the mortgage would be paid off and she'd be able to do what the hell she liked with the house. 'Well of course I won't be getting paid,' he snapped. 'I only get paid when I work. You know that. You've always known that. I'm self employed, remember!'

'I thought the job was for the whole summer, with just odd days and one weekend a month off? You're going to have to look for something else. I can't pay the bills on what I bring in. You can't swan around all summer. You're not on bloody holiday you know.'

He let her rabbit on a while longer, then, 'That's enough, Jen. For fuck's sake, get off my back. Anyone would think you don't want me home.' He could feel himself getting anxious. He took a deep breath and tried to keep calm. Avoid stressful situations, they told him. Huh. No chance with her. The pain was starting again. He grabbed the angina spray from the bedside table. A quick shot under his tongue and another deep breath. 'I wasn't going to tell you this, because I didn't want you worrying,' he continued. 'I collapsed this weekend. I've been in hospital. That's why I didn't call you. They said I need a rest.' He left out the heart details. There was silence for a moment and he braced himself. The pain was receding now.

'Why didn't you let me know? You could have asked someone to call me. I should be with you.'

Shit! That was the last thing he wanted. 'I'm fine, honestly. The lads are looking after me. I'm taking a couple of days out to relax and then I'll drive home. I'll leave here Tuesday lunchtime.'

'Are you safe to drive all that way? What did the hospital say? I'll get James to drive me down tomorrow. We can bring you home right away. Are you okay to travel?' Jenny's concerns tumbled over one another and he wished he'd kept his mouth shut now.

'Stop fussing, Jen. It does my head in. I don't need James to come for me. I'll call you tomorrow.' He could hear Mandy talking to Jed on the stairs. He needed to end the call but Jenny wittered on.

'Only me,' Mandy said as she came into the room.

Rod put a finger to his lips and rolled his eyes.

'Who's that,' Jenny asked. *'I can hear a woman's voice. Rod, what's going on? If you're lying to me and you've got another woman down there, I'll...'*

'It's Jed's girl,' Rod butted in. 'She's brought me a sandwich. See, I told you they're all looking after me. Now stop worrying and I'll speak to you soon. Got to go now. Bye.' He ended the call and turned the phone off. 'Fucking hell!'

'Sorry,' Mandy said.

'Oh, don't worry. She was flapping, as usual. I had to tell her I'm not too good. She was giving me earache about not earning. Thinks I'm swanning around!' He shook his head. 'Get me a glass of water, love. I need to take my pill. I had to use that spray. She's got me all worked up. What did you get for tea?'

'Chicken breasts and salad,' Mandy replied, nipping into the bathroom for a glass. 'Nice and healthy.' She took a bottle of water from the shopping bag and filled the glass. 'Got you this for taking your pills. That tap water in the bathroom is a bit grim. It's alright for boiling in the kettle, but not for drinking. I'll go and stick the chicken in the oven in a minute. And for a treat…' She held up a punnet of strawberries and laughed as his face lit up. 'But no cream. Not good for you.'

'Who needs cream when I've got you?' He was quiet for a moment. 'Mandy, I'm dreading the next few weeks. If I have that op I'm not going to be in any fit state to tell Jen I'm leaving her, am I?'

She shook her head. 'Not for a while. Let's wait until you're fully recovered. We'll have more money behind us if we leave it until later in the year. You'll have to put off having a vasectomy, too. You may as well wait now until we move in together. Get it done free then.'

He nodded. 'The only thing is, if we wait, we'll have to go to bloody Malta with them and play happy couples. I don't think I could stand that. Seeing Mike all over you, I mean.'

Mandy sighed. 'It's a long time since Mike was all over me. But knowing him he'll feel he has to make an effort in front of you two. I don't want to go either. It'll take a few weeks for the hospital to organise your op.

They didn't say it was an emergency just that you'll feel better if you have it done. With a bit of luck you might not be well enough to fly and the trip can be cancelled. Work on that excuse next week when you're at home.'

'I will. Keep your fingers crossed then. Call Sue and Sarah now. Tell them you'll be staying longer. Turn your phone off when you've finished. I don't want us to be disturbed or have anything else to worry about tonight. The lads will be working. We've got the place to ourselves. Just you, me, peace and quiet.'

*

'Is Sue definitely going to be in?' Rod asked as he pulled off the motorway and headed towards Pickford.

Mandy nodded. 'I spoke to her this morning and she said she will be. She'll take me home later. I said I'd ring when we're close by and she'll have the kettle on.'

'Nice one.' Rod put his foot down. His thoughts returned to this morning's conversation with Jenny. She'd booked an appointment at their GP's for tomorrow morning, she'd told him, and insisted that she would be going too. Not much he could do about that. He'd have to be patient and put up with her fussing for a few days. He was feeling fine now and planned to be out of the house as much as he could while she was in it. He thought that he might take his old drum kit to Johnny Roadhouse and see what they could offer him. If he was going to get a free vasectomy then he might put the money towards a keyboard, a Yamaha like he'd played in his solo spots with Timeless, and wondered if he had the guts to go completely solo. He could make more money, no one to split the wages with. Then he could look after Mandy properly without her having to work all the hours she did at the shop. The more he toyed with the idea the more he liked it. He hadn't mentioned it to Mandy yet, he wanted to surprise her. Drumming was hard work and if there was a chance he might be plagued with heart problems in the future it would be a good idea to start thinking about making life a bit easier. He might still be able to do the odd drumming gig, but not wear himself out, playing every night.

He was aware of Mandy stroking his arm and speaking to him. They were nearly at Sue's place. He hated the thought of saying goodbye again and her going home to sleep in the same bed as Mike. If only he could turn the car around and take her away forever. Her phone bleeped with a message.

'It's Dee,' she said. 'She's sorry to hear you've been ill, hopes you're feeling better and wants me to go for tea tomorrow. She's got a proposition for me. A nice one, she says. Hmm, wonder what that can be?'

'Well let's hope it's something good, eh.'

*

CHAPTER ELEVEN

Rod stared at Jenny who was sitting on the opposite sofa, twisting her hands in an agitated fashion. He'd told her about his heart condition and by the shocked expression on her pale face he guessed she'd be dusting off the policies later.

'It's not too serious,' he reassured. 'I've had a warning. More than my poor old mum got. Hopefully I won't have a heart attack now. Or at least if I do it'll be mild.'

Jenny shook her head, tears streaming down her face. 'I can't believe you didn't tell me. You were all alone down there. James and I would have come for you. You shouldn't have driven.'

'I'm fine.' Seeing how upset she was he felt guilty for not telling her. He went to sit beside her. 'Don't make a fuss, Jen. We'll see the doc tomorrow, sort out the surgery and that'll be it.' He tried to keep the snappy edge from his voice. It wasn't her fault that he didn't want to be here. She was worried and rightly so. 'Err, one thing though. I doubt I'll be able to fly in September. Might take a while to sort out a date for the op. You know what the NHS is like.'

Her face brightened. 'I'm in a private health care scheme through work. You're covered too. We can use it for conditions that aren't pre-existing. I'll call them tomorrow after we've been to the doctors. You might get it done right away and be fine by September.' She dried her tears and smiled. 'The holiday will do you the world of good. Be such a shame if we have to cancel. And Mike and Mandy are so looking forward to it.'

‘They are? How do you know?’

‘I spoke to Mike after you told me you’d collapsed. I was upset and worried and wanted a chat with Mandy, but he said she was away with Sue for a few days. It was Mike who said they were both looking forward to going. By the way, Mike said Sue’s got breast cancer. That’s why she and Mandy have had a little break before she starts her treatment.’ She shook her head. ‘Poor Sue, she hasn’t had much luck lately. What with this, and that married man who’s always messing her around. She should know he’s only out for what he can get. He’ll never leave his wife.’

Rod could feel his cheeks warming and jumped up. He rooted in the sideboard cupboard. ‘Drink?’ He gestured a bottle in Jenny’s direction and poured himself a large whisky.

‘No thanks. Should you be drinking while you’re taking medication?’

‘In moderation.’ He knocked it back, sat down again and changed the subject. ‘How’s Ben, and where are Beth and James?’

‘Beth’s at the cinema with Nicole. James is at his flat. He said he’ll catch up with you tomorrow. Ben, I presume, is at home with Tanya.’ She wrinkled her nose ‘If you can call it a home! He brought some clothes to wash the other day. They stank of wood-smoke and damp.’

‘How is he in himself? Did he seem okay? Was there anything different about him? His eyes, his behaviour?’

‘He looked the same to me. He’s full of a cold. He had a hot bath while he waited for his washing. I gave him soup, Lemsips and ten pounds towards some food.’

Rod nodded. ‘Was he chatty or withdrawn?’

'His usual moody self. He didn't say much. Took a couple of bags of his things away, CD's and tapes. Me and Beth cleared his room last week. James took some stuff to the tip. The rest is in the garage. We painted the walls, shampooed the carpet and bought new bedding. It's all nice and fresh now. I've got a guest room at last.'

'Handy,' Rod said. 'Not that we have many guests. Actually, I, err, could do with using the room. My medication makes me restless and sweaty.' It didn't affect him, but was a perfect excuse not to sleep in the marital bed. 'Better for both of us,' he added as Jenny pulled a face. 'I won't disturb you then. I've got used to sleeping alone. I'm all over the bed, tossing and turning.'

Jenny sighed. 'Whatever you think's best. I'm off to bed now. I need an early night. You should get one too.'

'I'll stay up and wait for Beth. See you tomorrow.' He pecked her on the cheek and swung his legs up on the sofa as she left the room. He breathed a relieved sigh and picked up the mail she'd given him earlier. It was going to take a lot of effort over the next few days not to get stressed. He wondered what sort of reception Mandy had got from Mike when she arrived home. He was dying to call her, but didn't dare.

He tore open an envelope and pulled out a mobile phone bill. Fucking hell! Two hundred and sixteen quid. And Mandy's number featured prominently. How the hell was he going to find the money? What if Jenny had opened it? If he hadn't come home early she might have done. When he wasn't around she usually saw to the bills. She'd have recognised the number right away. Why hadn't it dawned on him after Mandy had told him about Mike and the itemized landline bill? His next bill would be even bigger; he'd called her non-stop this month. He'd have to ask Vodafone to send it to his Brighton address and buy one of those pay-as-you-go phones to call her. He shoved the bill back in the envelope and stuffed it into his jeans pocket. He'd take it to Mandy's shop and leave it there until he could raise the cash. The old drum-kit would have to be sold now. That would really stuff up his keyboard and solo act plans.

*

Rod gritted his teeth and jiggled his knee up and down as he watched Jenny alternate between picking at a thread on the knee of her black trousers and rooting in her handbag for a tissue. They'd been waiting bloody ages, bit pointless booking an appointment when you never went in on time. He felt tetchy, could murder a fag and knowing he daren't have one made it worse. He'd bitten Jenny's head off earlier and felt bad about that, but she'd gone on and on about bleeding Malta and how she was sure he'd be fine by then if he got the op done privately. He clenched his fists as she picked up a copy of House Beautiful and wittered that now she'd done Ben's room she was going to do theirs next. She flicked to a page with a hideous, frilly pink and white bedroom.

'Oh, Rod, I love this,' she gushed as the receptionist called his name. He silently thanked God and jumped to his feet. He'd rather stay in Ben's room forever than lie with her in a candy floss nightmare.

The receptionist handed him a file. 'Doctor Thomas.'

'Thank you.' He strode ahead of Jenny who hurried to catch up with him.

Doctor Thomas looked up and smiled. She'd been his GP for donkeys' years and Rod was surprised that she hadn't retired yet. He smiled back as she fiddled with a greying curl that had escaped her untidy French pleat. She pushed her glasses up her slim nose and gestured towards a couple of chairs.

'I haven't seen you for a long time, Mr Davis.'

'Err, no, not been ill for years,' Rod said and passed her the file. He gave her a brief resume of his heart condition and handed her the letter from the Brighton hospital.

She read it and nodded from time to time. 'Okay, from this I understand you'd prefer to have the procedure done locally?'

'Please.'

'I'll refer you to a specialist. The hospital will contact you in the next few days for a consultation. As you're a referral from Brighton General you won't have to wait too long.'

'We'd like to use my private healthcare scheme,' Jenny chipped in. 'Will that be okay?'

'Yes, of course. I'll get a letter sent out to you as soon as possible and you'll need to contact your health care provider. They'll send a list of hospitals within their scheme. There's an excellent coronary care unit at Manchester Royal.'

'Will he be alright to fly to Malta in September?' Jenny asked.

Rod took a deep breath and dug his nails into his palms. 'Jen, leave it for now, please.' He turned his attention back to the doctor. 'How long will I be in hospital? Am I okay to go back to work for now?'

'You'll be in about forty-eight hours and will need several days rest at home. What sort of work do you do?'

'I'm a drummer. I work erratic hours, but can get plenty of rest in between.'

‘I don’t see why you can’t work up until the operation. I see you’re trying to give up smoking. How’s it going?’

‘Not bad. I really crave a cigarette at times, but I’m coping. I’ve got Nicorette gum and I’m sucking Polo Mints for England.’

‘See how you go on. If you feel you need extra help I’ll prescribe something, but you seem to be doing well on your own. Apart from resting when you feel you need to, make sure you get some exercise too. A brisk walk each day, or cardiovascular exercises, will help. Ask the receptionist for a leaflet.’

‘What are cardiovascular exercises?’ Jenny asked.

‘They get your heart rate going,’ Rod said, thinking about the heart racing exercise he was hoping to get with Mandy later. He’d spoken to her briefly while Jenny was in the shower and they’d arranged to meet at lunchtime. Hopefully Jenny would be going to work. ‘I need a repeat of the prescription the hospital enclosed,’ he reminded the doctor.

‘Of course. Will work entail you going back to Brighton?’

‘Err, yes. I travel back on Friday.’

‘In that case I’ll prescribe two months supply. It’s important that you don’t run out of the Beta blockers.’

‘Thanks.’ He took the prescription, said goodbye and left the surgery, Jenny on his heels.

As soon as they were outside she started. ‘Why did you stop me asking about flying? We need to know if you’ll be okay. We can put the holiday back a week or two if you won’t be well enough.’

‘I think the heart specialist is the one we should be asking, not the GP,’ he said. ‘And I will ask when I see him. Now stop going on about it. You’re doing my head in. Right, I’ll pop to the chemist and I’ll walk home.

Start as I mean to go on. Are you working this afternoon?'

She nodded. 'I'll go home for an hour. They said I could take the full morning off. Might as well make the most of it. There's a staff meeting after school so I'll be a bit late tonight.'

'Okay. I might visit Ben later,' he said. He walked her to the car, pecked her on the cheek and said goodbye. He waved as she drove away and out of habit reached in his pocket for a cigarette. 'Fuck!' He rooted for a Polo instead, made his way to Boots and handed the prescription over. The girl told him it would be thirty minutes. He strolled to the coffee shop, stopping to buy a newspaper on the way, and ordered a cappuccino, forgoing his favoured double espresso. A table by the window, overlooking the precinct, beckoned. He felt quite proud of himself. Less caffeine, no fags, joints and hardly any alcohol. Good job he had time with Mandy to look forward to. He couldn't wait to see her. She'd sounded a bit down earlier. Probably had a row with Mike. He wished it were possible to tell Mike he was taking her back to Brighton with him for good. He hoped he'd be able to cheer her up.

*

Mandy stared at the list in the order book for June and sighed. May was fully booked up now and it looked certain they'd be as busy next month. Loads of new clients all wanting quotes. Not that it was a bad thing, it would keep her mind occupied when Rod went back to Brighton, but she felt so tired and not in the least bit ready to get stuck in. She'd hardly slept a wink last night, worrying about Rod, and Sue, who was going into hospital tomorrow for her mastectomy. The last few days had left her feeling drained, like she was coming down with flu or something. She was looking forward to having tea at Dee's tonight and enjoying a meal that she hadn't cooked herself. She wondered again about Dee's proposition and what it could possibly be. Hopefully something that would lighten her mood a bit. She wondered how Rod had got on at the doctors. He'd be arriving very soon, if he'd managed to get rid of Jenny. She'd send Sarah and Carol on an extended lunch so she and Rod could have a bit of extra time together. She went into the workroom, where Carol, hemming a curtain, and Sarah, sewing rings onto a Roman blind, were humming along to radio two, playing quietly in the background.

'You can take an hour and a half lunch today,' Mandy announced. 'I owe you both big time for all the help you've given me.'

'Oh great,' Sarah said. 'I'll pop home and let the dog out.'

'Well don't rush back. I'm going to close up for a while and arrange some appointments for measuring up.'

Carol glanced up from her work. 'You'll be losing trade if you do that. Would you like me to stay behind and help you? I can get us a sandwich in.'

'No, I can manage thanks. You take a break. You deserve it. I'll see you back here about two.'

*

'You okay? You're very quiet today.' Rod adjusted his position on the old armchair and stroked Mandy's bare thigh as she curled up on his knee.

'I'm fine. Just tired, so much work to do. I wish I could walk away from it all and go back to Brighton with you on Friday. I hate the thought of you being alone. What if you have another funny turn?'

'I'll be fine, love. The medication's working great. I haven't had a bad chest pain for a few days now, just the odd twinge. Can you manage an hour tomorrow lunchtime? I know you're busy, but it's the last chance we'll get to meet up for a while. And I'm gonna have to be really careful with my phone calls from now on.' He reached on the floor for his jeans and rooted in the pocket. He frowned and looked in the other side. 'Shit!'

'What?' Mandy sat upright. 'What are you looking for?'

'The phone bill. I put it in my pocket to leave here until I can raise the money to pay. It's huge and your number's prominent. I don't want Jenny to see it. Christ, it's fallen out.

Mandy jumped up and lifted their discarded clothing onto the table. Rod looked through it but the bill wasn't there.

'Oh God, what if you dropped it in the car or somewhere in the house? Was Jenny going straight to work?'

'No, she was going back home for an hour. Bloody hell, if she finds it we're fucked!' Rod ran his hands through his hair.

'Get dressed. Go home and look for it,' Mandy said, her eyes filling. 'Oh God, we really don't need this. We've no money, nowhere to live and much as I love you I haven't got the energy to deal with all the shit at the moment.'

'Don't cry.' Rod pulled her into his arms. 'I'll sort it.'

'How? Jenny might be on her way here right now.'

He switched on his phone. No missed calls, no angry text messages. Mandy's shop phone had rung out twice while they were making love but he'd told her to leave it. What if it had been Jenny? His hands shook as he pulled on his clothes. Mandy's face looked even paler than earlier. She turned her back to him and dressed in silence.

'Mand?' He touched her arm. She turned and leant against him, sobbing. 'If the worst comes to the worst we'll clear off down to Brighton right away. I won't leave you alone to face the music, I promise,' he whispered. 'I'll call you as soon as I find it.' He kissed her and left. Shit, it never rained and all that crap. Now he really could murder a fag.

He flagged down a taxi on the main road. So much for walking, but the sooner he got back the better. Dare he call Jenny or should he just chance going home and hope she'd gone to work. He'd made the bed and closed the door before they left the house, so there'd be no need for her to go into Ben's old room. But Jenny was nosy and she may have had a snoop around, although there was no reason for her to do that and nothing incriminating in his suitcase that would point to his affair. Surely she'd have called him by now if she'd found the bill. He could feel a chest pain starting as the taxi dropped him outside the house. He used his angina spray. Jenny's car was on the drive, but then it would be, she walked to the school around the corner. The lounge window was open, someone was home.

He let himself in at the back door, the pain receding now. Beth, and Mandy's daughter, Nicole were sitting at the breakfast bar eating beans on toast. 'Hi, girls. No college today?'

'Free afternoon, Dad.' Beth jumped up and gave him a hug. 'You okay? You look a bit mithered. How did it go at the doc's?'

'It went well, thanks. The op's being arranged on your mum's medical insurance. I'm just popping upstairs.' He dashed from the room and hurried upstairs, two at a time. He searched Ben's room and found nothing. He remembered he'd nipped into the garage before leaving for the doctor's, to check on his old drum kit and to make sure that Jenny hadn't boxed it in any further with the stuff she'd stored from Ben's room. He rushed outside and into the garage and breathed a huge sigh of relief when he saw the envelope lying on the floor. He dropped to his knees, feeling overcome. He quickly dialled Mandy's shop.

'Hello,' Mandy answered. She sounded anxious and didn't even say the shop name.

'It's me. Relax, I found it in the garage. Sorry, babe. I hated dashing away after such a lovely time.'

'Oh, Rod.' He heard a sob catch in her throat. *'Thank God for that. And don't worry about dashing away. I'd rather have peace of mind.'*

'I'll pop down after your staff go,' he said. 'Before you go to Dee's. Need to kiss you, give you a hug; make up for leaving you upset. I love you, babe.'

'Love you, too,' she said. *'What are you doing now?'*

'I'm going to visit Ben. See what's what with this boat he's living on. Your youngest is here with mine. They're eating beans in the kitchen. Got a free afternoon apparently. I'll feel like a spare part if I hang around.'

'Hmm, true. You're better out of the way. See you later then.'

*

Rod popped his head around the kitchen door. 'I'm off to see Ben.'

Beth looked up and smiled. 'Hope you have more luck with him than we did. See if you can get him to come back home, without Tanya. I really miss him. I'll need someone with me when you go away in September. I don't fancy being here all alone.'

‘You can come and stay with me and Louise,’ Nicole said. ‘We’ll have a great time, the three of us together.’

‘There, you see. Sorted,’ Rod said. ‘See you later, girls.’ He made for the car and then thought better of it. ‘Walk,’ he muttered. Make up for taking the taxi earlier. The day was dry and quite warm. He took his jacket off, slung it across his shoulder and cut across Memorial Park and onto the towpath towards the canal basin and marina.

Which bloody boat was it? There were at least twenty moored. Some deserted, locked up, maybe weekend homes. An old sandy haired mongrel came towards him, wagging its tail, followed by an elderly woman who was bent almost double. Rod stroked the dog’s ears and it fawned around him, rubbing against his legs. The woman called the dog to heel and stopped to talk to Rod.

‘Hope he’s not got hairs on your trousers, love. He’s forever moulting.’

‘Don’t worry about it,’ Rod said, smiling. ‘He’s a nice old dog. Reminds me of the one we used to have at home when I was a little lad. Erm, do you live on one of the boats?’

‘I do, love. Not looking to buy, are you? Every winter I think I’ll sell mine and get myself a nice warm flat. But then it gets to spring and early summer and I know I could never settle on dry land. Still, doesn’t stop me dreaming.’

‘I’m not looking to buy,’ Rod said. ‘My son and his girl moved into a houseboat recently on this stretch, but I don’t know which one it is.’

‘There’s a young couple, with a little one, three down from me.’ The woman pointed to a boat with washing blowing on the deck. ‘They’re the only new ones. The owner's gone abroad and he's renting out long term.'

'Thank you,' Rod said. 'That'll probably be them. You take care now.' He went on his way and stood facing the boat. There was a wooden ramp leading up to the deck and kids' toys lying around. The boat looked quite decent, painted green and burgundy; the name, Lady Francis, and a garland of colourful flowers, stencilled on the side. The brass rails around the deck were shiny. Tubs of bright geraniums and greenery dotted about made the place look cared for. Not what he'd been expecting at all. A thin plume of smoke rose from the chimney. Someone was home. Where was the door? Rod walked onto the deck, ducking under the washing, and wondered around, looking for an entrance. There was movement behind the net curtains and a noise at the top end of the deck. Ben's head appeared, a worried expression on his face, and then he emerged from the cabin. His blue eyes lit up.

'Dad,' he said. 'Hi, how you doing? Good to see you. Come on in.'

Rod flung an arm around Ben's shoulder. 'Good to see you, too, son.' He followed Ben down the stairs and into a narrow room. He didn't know quite what he'd been expecting, but certainly nothing as nice as the well-furnished lounge area. Everywhere looked clean and tidy and the smell of something cooking wafted his way. 'Somebody's been busy.'

'It's stew for tea,' Ben said. 'Sit down. I'll put the kettle on.' He gestured to an upholstered L-shaped bench seat set around a small table. 'You look shocked. Mum's told you I'm living in a hovel I suppose? Not looking after myself. Well I've a cold and a bit of a cough, but we've all had one. It wouldn't do Mum any harm to visit us and see how we live for herself instead of making assumptions. The thing is, this is cheaper than renting bricks and mortar and a much nicer environment. We're close to the park and the shops. It's peaceful. It's what we want. We've dumped Tanya's druggy mates. To be honest, I thought it was one of them when I heard you on the deck. We're trying to live a decent life for Charlie's sake.' He nodded in the direction of a framed picture, of a blonde-haired child, on a nearby shelf.

'Charlie?' Rod frowned. 'Ah, Tanya's son. Thought you looked a bit concerned earlier. Are the ex mates giving you a hard time?'

'Nothing I can't handle,' Ben replied. 'Tanya and Charlie are out with her mum at the moment. Coffee or tea?'

'Err, tea please. I'm on caffeine cutbacks.'

'We've got caffeine free coffee, Dad. Tan prefers it.'

'I'll have a coffee then.' Rod stroked his chin and looked around. Ben was at the bottom end of the boat in the neat galley kitchen. The whole place was sparkling. It certainly didn't look like the home of a couple of junkies, nor was there a smell of damp like Jenny had implied. Ben looked well enough, a bit pale, hardly surprising if he had a cold. But there was something about him. He seemed nervous. Rod wondered what he was up to. Pointless asking him though. He'd never get a straight answer.

'Are you managing okay for money?' he asked as Ben handed him a mug.

'Yeah. I'm working as a barman at The Navigation. I do four nights. Started a couple of weeks ago. Tanya cleans there in the mornings. We're doing fine. They do meals and we get veg and meat off Chef if there's anything left over. That's what's in the pot. A free tea.'

Rod nodded. 'The job's better than nothing, then?'

'It's hardly the career Mum would have chosen for me, but there's not much work about that fits in with us looking after Charlie. Also,' Ben continued, 'I'm playing guitar on Saturday and Sunday nights with a band.'

'Oh, well done, mate,' Rod said. 'Now that pleases me no end.'

'The money will go towards the rent. Like I said, this is cheaper than a flat. It'll do us for a while until we get on our feet.'

Rod sipped his coffee. A boat like this would be ideal for him and Mandy. Somewhere cosy and cheap until things got sorted. Although he couldn't see Mandy agreeing to that idea somehow. She was used to a few of life's little luxuries and a big, spacious home. He was asking her to give up an awful lot to be with him.

'I'll show you around when you've finished your coffee,' Ben said, breaking his thoughts.

'Thanks, I'd like that. I'll stay for a while. I need to pop into town before I head back home. I'll leave about five, if that's okay?' He might as well relax here with Ben before he paid his visit to Mandy. 'Get your guitar out. Let's have a bit of a jam,' he said, watching an anxious expression cross Ben's face. 'What's up? Are you worried Tanya won't like your Dad hanging around?'

*

CHAPTER TWELVE

Mandy felt her jaw dropping as Dee outlined her surprise proposition. She put her mug down on the coffee table and tried to concentrate, hardly able to take it all in. Dee was explaining that David and she were now an item and he was planning to move in with her at the weekend. Mandy felt thrilled for her friend and could see the excitement in Dee's blue eyes. There was a contented glow about her that was new. But the best bit of all was that David was spending the next few months finishing the renovations on his own cottage and intended to rent it out. It would probably be ready in time for Christmas.

'His long term plan is that we sell both cottages and emigrate to Australia,' Dee said. 'But that won't be for a few years yet. Sally's far too young to abandon and she won't want to come with us because of her boyfriend. So anyway, we thought you and Rod might be ready to move in together by the time the cottage is ready. What do you think? It would do you for a couple of years until you get sorted out properly. David will do a good deal on the rent too and he won't want a deposit up front.'

'I don't know what to say.' Mandy's eyes filled for the umpteenth time that day. 'Your own news is wonderful, of course, and I'm so happy for you. But the cottage - wow - that takes some beating. I can't believe it. Oh, I wish I could call Rod and tell him.'

'Why don't you?'

Mandy looked at her watch and shook her head. 'Jenny will be home by now, no doubt. He might nip out later and call me. I'll have to wait and see.'

'Would you like to take a look at the cottage? I've got the key. David said to show you around if you like. He's working away for a few days.'

Mandy jumped up. 'I'd love to,' she said, flinging her arms around Dee.

'I'll warn you now it's a bit of a building site. But you'll be able to see beyond that with your eye for décor and stuff. Come on.'

*

Bags of cement, radiators and half constructed kitchen units littered the floor of the lounge. But Mandy could only stare at the stripped oak ceiling beams and brick inglenook fireplace. Her mind conjured up cosy nights with Rod in front of a log fire, sipping glasses of wine. Bliss. The kitchen was partly finished with a staircase leading directly off. Mandy went to the French doors and looked outside at the small yard. She could picture the tall brick walls painted white, like Dee's, with tubs of colourful flowers, a picnic table and maybe a little barbecue for the summer.

They wandered upstairs and looked in the two bedrooms. A small one at the back, where Rod could store his drums and stuff, and a huge main bedroom at the front with long distance views over the rooftops towards Lyme Park. David had built stripped pine wardrobes down one side, painted the walls cream and sanded and varnished the floor boards. It was the only room in the house that was habitable and seemed to be the one he was currently living in. Boxes of books and records vied for space alongside a big brass bed and a TV and video machine on a stand under the window. The bathroom across the landing was in the process of being tiled. Mandy liked the neat white suite with a shower above. The matching white tiles with an occasional dark blue inset created a nautical theme in her mind's eye.

'I can see your mind working overtime, planning colour schemes,' Dee said with a laugh. 'What do you think?'

'It's perfect. I love it.'

'There's an attic like mine up those little stairs.' Dee pointed to a narrow staircase between the two bedrooms. 'You could use it as a workroom if you ever bring jobs home to finish. These used to be weavers cottages. They were built for the workers employed by the mill down the road. The men used to work at the mill and their wives and kids in the attics. What a bloody life!'

Mandy smiled, followed Dee up the staircase and stepped into a huge room with two Velux windows that flooded the area with light.

'David's going to put a couple of radiators up here, so it will be nice and warm.'

'This could be the spare bedroom so the girls can stay over - if they want to - of course.' Mandy bit her lip as her voice wavered. Tears flowed freely. Her girls might not speak to her again, never mind stay over.

'Oh, Mandy.' Dee put her arms around her. 'Told you it wouldn't be easy. You'll cry buckets before you're done, believe me. You look so tired. You need to get as much sleep as you can. Try and keep your strength up. And make sure you eat properly, too. You've lost loads of weight. Not that you don't look good on it. But it's too much too soon.'

Mandy nodded. 'My nerves are on edge all the time. I'm sure Mike knows more than he's letting on and he's biding his time before he says anything. He's hardly spoken to me since I got back from Brighton. Then there's Rod's op, and I need to call Sue's son to see how she is. I feel like I'm coming down with flu, I'm really tired and there's always something to worry about.' She told Dee about Rod's missing phone bill. 'It's all so stressful and I'm finding it harder to cope with than I thought I would. When I'm alone with Rod it all disappears, but as soon as he leaves me I start getting scary thoughts crashing around in my head and I feel panicky.'

'I know what you mean.' Dee squeezed her arm. 'Get yourself a tonic from Boots. If you're not eating you won't be getting any vitamins and you'll feel drained. Come on, let's have another coffee at mine before you go home.'

*

Rod lay wide awake, staring at the ceiling. He'd spoken to Mandy earlier on her way home from Dee's. She'd sounded really excited as she told him that Dee's bloke David was willing to rent them his cottage later this year when it was ready. That would fit in quite well with their plans. Give him time to get over his operation and get back on track with work. The girls' exams would be out of the way and they'd have time to save a few quid towards furniture and stuff.

If his op was done in the next couple of weeks, as Jenny seemed to think it would be, from talking to others in the health care scheme at work, then the next obstacle would be the Malta trip and how to get out of it. If he was back working within a week or two of the op, then he could hardly use the excuse of not feeling well enough, to cancel. But he needed to be working as soon as he could. He wanted to try and leave home with a clean financial slate and make sure Jenny had some money to live off, before he got involved with solicitors and divorce, and was ordered to pay whatever they thought he should. Jenny would want her pound of flesh; he'd no doubts about that. With only Beth still at home to support, he hoped he wouldn't get ripped off too much. Even if Ben came back he was old enough to look after himself financially. He had a feeling that the love on a canal boat thing would end in disaster soon enough. But what the hell, Ben would just have to learn to cope the hard way. Something was far from right there, but he had enough problems of his own to worry about. Ben wasn't a little kid and he'd made his own bed. Still, the caring dad side of him couldn't help but be concerned. As he'd left the boat earlier a shady looking character had passed him on the towpath and made his way onto Ben's boat. He'd been tempted to go back, but didn't want to keep Mandy waiting around all alone in the shop.

He drew a deep breath and popped a Polo mint into his mouth. He was desperate for a fag, more so than ever at the moment. He hadn't a clue how to go about things. Maybe Jed would be able to give him a few pointers, himself being twice divorced. He turned onto his side and hoped he'd dream about Mandy. They'd arranged to meet tomorrow lunchtime on the Devonshire Arms car park after she'd finished the fitting she was booked to do. She'd told him she didn't want to have lunch in the pub as he'd suggested, in case they were seen by anyone they knew, but that they should leave one of the cars and find somewhere private to park up. Before that he planned to take his old drum kit to Johnny Roadhouse and hopefully raise enough to pay that bloody phone bill.

*

'Four-hundred-and-fifty quid! Wow! That's brilliant.' Mandy stared into the envelope Rod had given her. 'I'll pay your phone bill and put the rest away towards our future.'

'Well that's what it's for,' Rod said. 'I knew I'd get a decent amount because vintage Rogers's kits are quite sought after. Before that bloody bill arrived my plan was to sell or part ex the kit for a fancy does-it-all keyboard. I'm sure I could earn more money as a self-contained act. If I did that I could still drum a couple of nights a week and then do some solo gigs in pubs and social clubs, while I get the act off the ground.'

'Would you have the confidence to do that?' Mandy stroked his cheek.

'Yeah, I think so. I could do sixties stuff and Eagles and a bit of country rock. Build up a few sets and I'd be good to go. I'm certainly gonna give it a try anyway. Once we get on our feet I'll get the keyboard and a PA and book some rehearsal time. I won't need to work away as much. I'll try and get a Manchester agent so the gigs won't be too far to travel. That'll save on digs and food. You can always come with me if I'm further away; in fact you can come to all the gigs if you want.' He drew her into his arms and kissed her.

Mandy snuggled closer. They were parked in an old farm gateway on a deserted road in the Goyt Valley. It was raining heavily and the windows of Rod's car had steamed up quickly.

'Let's climb in the back,' he whispered and helped her over the seats.

They kissed and caressed and Mandy felt herself relaxing for the first time that day. They were half undressed under the old travel rug Rod used to cover his drum kit, when she felt a thud against the side of the car. Rod groaned as she sat up. 'What was that,' she whispered as another thud came, this time heavier, and then another. She was conscious of the sound of sheep baaing. A sharp rap on the windscreen had Rod leaping up and fastening his jeans.

'What the fuck,' he began, rubbing at the misted up window. He jumped as a big weather-beaten face appeared. The owner flashed him a gappy grin, indicating he move the car back. 'Shit, we're surrounded by bloody sheep and that old guy wants to put them in the field,' he said, clambering into the front and starting up the engine. 'Thought we were safe here, doesn't look like this gate's been open for years. Stay under the rug, Mand, while I find somewhere else to park.' Mouthing sorry to the old farmer, Rod switched on the fan to clear the windows and backed slowly out of the gateway.

Mandy started to giggle as he tried to avoid the sheep that were all over the road. She couldn't stop and was hysterical as Rod pulled into another gateway further down the lane. He turned to look at her and joined in with her laughter. 'Come into the back for a few more minutes,' she said. 'But I don't think we should get up to too much, just in case.'

'I'm glad you think it's funny, 'he said, grinning. 'Almost at the point of no return and accosted by sheep. Bloody hell!'

*

'What time are you leaving tomorrow,' Mandy asked as Rod pulled up beside her car. 'I do wish you didn't have to go.'

'So do I. But I'll be back soon for the op. Might even be the end of next week. At least I'll get a few nights work in the meantime. I feel better now I don't have to worry about that bloody bill. I'll be here for about a couple of weeks after the op. That should take us through to July. Try and think of an excuse to come to Brighton again for a few days before my stint down there finishes. You've got a while to come up with something.'

'I'll try,' Mandy said. 'I need to get on top of everything at the shop in the next few weeks. And then it'll be September…'

'Malta?'

She nodded. 'How the hell are we going to get out of that?'

'No idea. But we've got time to think about it. I'll call you later before you finish work and I'll see you on my next trip home.'

She held him close and felt the tears well. 'I'll miss you.'

'And I'll miss you. Just keep thinking about the future. That'll keep you going. Give Sue my love when you visit her tonight. Look after one another. She needs you.'

*

Sue rooted in her sponge bag and then pressed a door key into Mandy's hand.

'What's that for?' Mandy frowned.

'I'm staying with my brother and his wife for a few weeks when I leave here.' She indicated the hospital ward with a wave of her hand. 'The doctor said I could go home on Friday. But I've to rest and I know I won't if I go back to my place. Not only that, our Steve won't let Pete visit me at his house. I don't want to see Pete at the moment. I couldn't stand to see him pitying me or worse, rejecting me. I don't feel strong enough to cope with that. I can't even speak to him without getting upset, so a break is best until I decide what to do for the future.'

Mandy nodded. 'Can you manage without any contact though?' She knew she wouldn't be able to cope without speaking to Rod, especially if she was as ill as Sue. 'You're being very brave.'

Sue shrugged. 'I'm not really. I'm trying to get through this the best I can. Anyway, the key is for you to water my plants. Also, if Rod manages to get home anytime soon, there's a spare room you can use when you get the chance to see him. After that tale you've just told me about sheep and angry farmers, I think you'll need it! Don't hug me,' she finished as Mandy jumped to her feet. 'I'm all sutured up and very sore.' She caught Mandy's hand and squeezed it. 'You'll come and see me at Steve's, won't you?'

'Of course I will. And thank you so much. Rod'll be home soon enough to have his op. We might have a bit of time to be alone before it.' She shook her head. 'I don't know; what a pair you are.'

'We'll both be fine in a few weeks. I'll be starting chemotherapy very soon, so it's best I'm being looked after for a while. Our Steve's wife's a good one. It was her idea they take care of me,' Sue finished as a bell rang, signalling the end of visiting hour.

Mandy stood up and wafted a hand in front of her face. 'Is it warm in here or is it me?'

Sue smiled. 'Perhaps you're getting a hot flush. You're coming up to that funny age.'

'I'm not even forty-six yet,' Mandy protested. 'It'll be a few more years before I get menopausal, I hope.'

'Some of the women I work with started in their mid-forties,' Sue said. 'But if you're still regular then you've nothing to worry about.'

'Oh I am, regular as clockwork,' Mandy said, smiling. 'Always have been.' She put on her jacket and leant to kiss Sue on the cheek. 'Call me if you want anything bringing in tomorrow night. I'll see you then. Get some sleep now. You look tired.'

'So do you. You've got really dark circles under your eyes. Stop worrying about everybody and look after yourself. I'll see you tomorrow. And, Mand, it's great news about David's cottage. At least you know you'll have a nice roof over your heads.'

*

Mandy looked up as Mike came into the room. He smiled and sat down beside her.

'How was Sue?'

'She was cheerful enough. Putting on a brave face as always. I'll go and see her again tomorrow night.'

'Jenny called while you were out.'

'Oh, right. What did she want?'

'Rod's ill. He's got to have some sort of heart operation. He's been home to see the doc. He collapsed in Brighton after a gig and was rushed to hospital. Anyway, Jen's arranging it all under private health care. I'd like to have caught up with him but he's driving back to Brighton tomorrow until an appointment can be made for him at the hospital.'

'Well I hope he's going to be okay,' Mandy said, praying her face wasn't giving anything away. 'Is Jenny alright? I bet she's flapping, as usual.'

'That's a bit unkind. She's very worried,' Mike said, the tone of his voice changing slightly. 'It's normal for a wife to be concerned when her husband's ill. I hope you'd be the same about me.'

Mandy chewed her lip. 'I didn't mean anything by that. It's just that Jenny always flaps over the least little thing. You know she does.'

'I'd hardly call being worried about the health of the man she loves a little thing. Sometimes, Mandy you should think before you open your mouth.' He got up and poured himself a whisky. 'Do you want anything to drink?'

‘No thanks.’ She stared at his back, hating him for reminding her that Jenny loved Rod very much. She could block it from her mind when she was with him. Never even giving it a thought that he belonged to someone else, because together they felt so very right and no one else mattered. ‘I’m going to bed. I’m tired and I’ve got a really busy next few weeks coming up.’

He sat back down again. ‘You’ll have to stop gallivanting away on trips then. Save your time off now for Malta.’

‘Err, will Rod be able to fly if he’s having this op? Bit risky, isn’t it? Maybe we should cancel. I’m not really bothered to be honest.’ She hoped she sounded casual enough.

‘He should be fine by then,’ Mike replied. ‘And I’m bothered and so is Jenny. She’s really looking forward to it. She’ll have spent nearly all summer on her own so the trip will be great for her and Rod to catch up with each other. It’s not all about you, you know. We can’t let them down.’

Mandy got to her feet. He was in an argumentative mood and she wasn’t being drawn in. ‘Whatever. I’m going for a shower. See you later.’ He didn’t look up as she left the room. She closed the door behind her. The dogs followed her up the stairs and crowded into the bathroom with her, vying for space on the fluffy bathmat. Max tried to push Poppy off as she lay sprawled on her back, a happy expression in her eyes. Mandy smiled and reached into the airing cupboard. She shook another bath mat onto the floor and Max lay down with a contented grunt. ‘What will you do without me?’ she muttered. ‘I don’t suppose David will let me have two big dogs in the cottage. It wouldn’t be fair. You’ll probably wreck the place while I’m at work. I'll have to come and visit you here. If Mike'll let me in, that is.' She bent to tickle their ears.

*

'What?' Mandy said, miles away as she measured fabric on the cutting table.

'I said call for you,' Sarah repeated, looking in a meaningful way at Carol's back. 'It's Rod,' she mouthed.

Mandy nodded. 'Err, Carol, would you pop to Greggs and get me a tuna sandwich before you go home please?' She fished in her pocket for a five pound note. 'I'll have a cake as well but nothing heavy and creamy. My stomach's feeling a bit queasy today.'

'Of course. Are you okay for milk for coffees?'

'Get us a pint while you're out. Thanks, Carol.'

Carol put on her coat and lumbered away.

Mandy grabbed the phone from Sarah who made herself scarce. 'Sorry about that, Rod. We had to get rid of Carol first. She was sitting right under the phone. Have you heard anything?'

'I'm coming home on Thursday,' he said. *'Seeing the specialist Friday at Manchester Royal and it's looking likely that I'll be having the op the following week. So I'll be home for about three weeks in total. Not good, because I won't earn a penny all that time, but there's not much I can do about it. I'll see if I can get some sick pay to tide me over.'*

'If you need it there's the money left over from your drum kit,' Mandy said.

'No, that's for us. Jen thinks Johnny Roadhouse are trying to sell it for me and that's why it's no longer in the garage. I can spin that one out for a few months, hopefully. Any chance of me seeing you on Thursday, after you finish work, and before I go home? I'll time the journey to get there for five.'

'Yes, perfect. Meet me at Sue's house. I've got the key to water her plants. She said we could use the spare room if we wanted to. I completely forgot to tell you.'

'Really? Oh she's a sweetheart, that girl. Tell her thanks so much when you next see her. Are you still really busy?'

'We are. It's a nightmare. I'm trying to keep on top, but it's not easy.'

'How are things with Mike?'

'Much the same. We go through the motions of being pleasant to each other when the kids are around. But even the dogs are picking up on the atmosphere.'

'Well, chin up. It won't be for much longer. Let me get over this op and then we'll talk some more. Maybe we can get something on a short term let until David's place is ready.'

'We haven't got the money to do that. We'll have to put up with things for now. I can handle it okay; it's just Malta I can't get my head around.'

'Leave it with me. Let me have a real good think about what we can do to get out of it. I'd better go now; we're rehearsing a few new songs. I'll call you later. Love you.'

'Love you, too.' Mandy hung up and sat down on the armchair.

'Coffee?' Sarah popped her head around the door.

'Can I have tea instead? I don't fancy a coffee and I didn't enjoy that one this morning either.'

'Well it's the same brand we always have.' Sarah waved a jar of Gold Blend at her.

'Hmm, it just didn't taste right somehow. It's probably just me and this dickey tummy thing. I'll be alright when I've had something to eat.'

'You're very pale lately. Are you okay, I mean apart from feeling a bit grim?'

Mandy screwed up her face. ‘I think I’m just totally stressed out, Sarah. Worrying about Sue and Rod and how the hell I’m going to get out of going to Malta. No wonder I feel so ropey… what?’ she said as Sarah stared at her for a long moment.

‘Nothing.’ Sarah turned back towards the kitchen.

‘Sarah, what is it?’

Sarah spun round and faced her. ‘Is there any chance you could be pregnant? When my sister was expecting she went right off coffee and she looked like you do now. Pale with dark circles under her eyes.’

‘Pregnant! No, I don’t think so,’ Mandy broke off as the shop bell rang and Carol came back in.

‘Right, I’ll get my bag and be off,’ Carol announced, putting Greggs bags and Mandy’s change on the cutting table. She handed Sarah the bottle of milk. ‘See you tomorrow.’

‘You will, ‘ Mandy said. ‘Bye.’

‘Just a thought,’ Sarah continued, as Carol left.

Mandy ran her hands though her hair. ‘Oh my God, I hope I’m not. Christ, I’ve got enough things to worry about, without that. Bloody hell. Pass me my diary from that shelf.’ She unlocked it and turned to last month. Only the other night she’d told Sue she was regular as clockwork, but at the moment she couldn’t even remember when the last one had been. And wouldn’t you just know it; she hadn’t made her usual note. She thought back. When had she told Mike she couldn’t sleep with him because of her period? Think, think. It was the week he’d invited his mother to Sunday lunch and that was the anniversary of his dad’s death. So it would have been the third week of April and now it was the end of May. She did a quick calculation and worked out that she was fourteen days late, going off her twenty-eight day cycle. She stared at Sarah in horror.

‘How late are you?’ Sarah asked.

‘Fourteen days,’ she cried. ‘Shit, Sarah. I can’t be, I just can’t be. I’m forty-five for crying out loud. Must be the menopause kicking in. I thought I had a hot flush the other night.’

‘Mum had me when she was forty-seven,’ Sarah said. ‘Sorry, Mandy, but it looks like you might be. Shall I go to Boots and get you a testing kit? Then at least you’ll know for sure.’

Mandy nodded. ‘Take the money out of the till. I can’t believe this. Why the hell didn’t I realise? I’ve had three flipping kids; I should have recognised the signs. I’ve felt rough for days. I thought I was coming down with flu or something. Drop the catch as you go out. I can’t face customers at the moment. Just hammer on the door when you come back.’

Mandy sat with her head in her hands as Sarah left. She felt stunned, to say the least. She thought back to the Birmingham hotel and the chocolate condoms. That must have been it. They’d been really careful since, as far as she could recall. She felt churned up. There was no way she could eat lunch now. If it wasn’t one thing it was another. Prior to Rod, life had been bearable, just about, predictable almost. Since Rod her world had turned on its head. And now this. What the hell was she going to do?

Sarah was rapping at the door. Mandy let her in and dropped the catch again.

‘Right, let’s have a look at the instructions.’ Mandy opened the packet and took out the white plastic stick. ‘Do I just wee on it?’

Sarah nodded. ‘Then you wait for a blue line to appear. If it doesn’t then you’re not.’

The toilet was round the back and they shared it with the hairdresser next door. Thankfully it was vacant and Mandy hurried inside. She couldn't believe she was doing this. She dragged herself back indoors and placed the stick on the sink. Sarah was looking anxious, pacing up and down the work room.

'It's on the sink.' Mandy sat down on the chair and waited for what felt like hours. 'Will you go and look?' she said eventually.

Mandy didn't even need Sarah to tell her, she just knew.

Sarah came back and nodded. 'The line's blue.'

'Oh God,' Mandy wailed. 'What the hell am I going to do now?' She burst into tears and Sarah put her arms around her.

'It's Rod's, I guess,' she whispered.

'Oh yes,' Mandy sobbed. 'It's definitely Rod's.'

*

CHAPTER THIRTEEN

Mandy drove straight to Dee's after leaving work, her thoughts in a whirl. She couldn't face seeing Mike and the girls at the moment. Not until she'd got her head into gear anyway. She hadn't even called Dee to check she was home and breathed a sigh of relief when she saw her car parked outside the cottage. She swung in behind. Dee was in the front garden dead-heading flowers. She looked up and smiled as Mandy got out of the car.

'Hello. Wasn't expecting you tonight. You okay?'

Mandy shook her head and burst into tears.

Dee put her arms around her and took her indoors. 'What's wrong? Is it Rod? Is he alright?' She led Mandy to the sofa and sat her down.

Mandy choked on sobs as she told Dee the events of the afternoon.

'Oh my God!' Dee clapped a hand to her mouth. 'Mandy! That's all you need.'

'I know,' Mandy cried. 'I don't know what to do. I can't tell Rod before his operation. He might have a heart attack with the shock.'

Dee nodded her agreement. 'I suppose it's a daft question, but do you want it?'

Mandy shrugged. 'I haven't even thought that far. It's just a nightmare. It's the last thing I expected.'

'You need a bit of time to get your head around things. Let Rod get the op done before you say anything. Keep out of Mike's way as much as you can. Your girls aren't daft, they'll be asking questions if you start throwing up all over the place.'

'Fortunately I'm hardly ever sick when I'm pregnant. Just queasy, pale and can't stand the smell of bacon and coffee. I'll have to pretend I've got an upset stomach for now.'

'Well don't bury your head in the sand. I know it's early days, but this isn't going to go away. It's serious stuff. Have you any idea when it happened? You can work out how many weeks you actually are, rather than going off your dates. Then you know roughly how long you've got to decide if you want to keep it or have a termination.'

Mandy chewed her lip. 'Think it must have been when I met Rod in Birmingham. It was the only time we didn't use anything last month. Just over four weeks, I guess.'

'Okay, well that buys you a bit of time. Rod should be on the mend by the end of June. Then you'll need to talk and make a decision.'

'We can't afford a child,' Mandy said. 'We'll be struggling as it is. I need to work. I wouldn't be able to run up ladders and lift heavy rolls of fabric. Jenny'll go spare, so will Mike. This changes everything. Telling them we're leaving because we want to be together is one thing. But this, oh Christ, Dee! What have we done?'

Dee shook her head, seemingly lost for words. 'I just don't know what to say. Are you going to see Sue later?'

'I was. I'll have to. I can't let her down. There's no way I can talk to her about this. You know what she's like. She'll say I should have it.'

'Only because she's Catholic. At the end of the day you have to do what's right for you - and Rod. Have you eaten today?'

'No, I did the test at lunchtime and couldn't face my sandwich.'

'Right, come through to the kitchen and I'll make you eggs on toast. You need something inside you or you'll pass out. You look really ill.'

Mandy took a seat at the table while Dee busied herself poaching eggs and brewing tea. She felt a bit hungry now and the smell of the toast made her mouth water. Dee placed a plate in front of her and sat down opposite, hands wrapped around a mug.

'It's not the end of the world, Mandy. It might be the best thing for you and Rod.'

Mandy looked up from her plate. 'How? If I was twenty years younger and single I might just agree with you. But not now, at our age. It should never have happened. We shouldn't have started the affair in the first place. What on earth were we thinking? I can't keep it, can I? There's no way.'

Dee patted her hand. 'Your mind's all over the place. Like I said, you need a bit of time to come to terms with it. Then you have to tell Rod when he's back on his feet.'

'I've no spare money to pay for a termination. The next quarter's rent's due on the shop at the end of this month, I've got a huge shop phone bill from calling Rod's mobile. I can't go NHS. It'd be on my medical records and that nosy receptionist at our doctor's might see them.'

'I can lend you a bit of money if you go privately. Try and find out how much it will cost.'

'I will. Thanks, Dee.' Mandy sniffed and dashed her hand across her eyes. 'I feel a right heartless cow talking like this. I would have loved a family with Rod if things had been different. But not now, and not like this.'

Dee nodded. 'I know. Finish your tea and go and see Sue. Try and put it out of your mind for a while or she'll pick up that something's wrong. Ring me later if you want to talk. I'm always here for you.'

*

Mandy smiled as she swung onto the drive of her home. Her eldest daughter Becky's car was also parked up. She hadn't seen her for over a week so it would be lovely to catch up, and ask how her little grandsons were doing. She must make some time to take them out for a treat very soon. Focusing on family life would take her mind off her problems for a while. She grabbed her handbag and the small holdall of clothes Sue had given her to wash.

The girls were in the lounge, all three talking at once; Becky, the image of herself with long dark hair and blue eyes, taking centre stage. Louise and Nicole looked up to her. Although similar in appearance, their younger daughters had more of Mike's features than Becky did. In spite of being a busy mum Becky always had time for her sisters and sorted out their little problems. Mandy watched from the doorway. They hadn't spotted her yet. Mike was sprawled on one of the sofas, a big smile plastered across his face. She really couldn't fault him as a dad. The girls loved him to bits when they weren't arguing with him about bills. She was so lucky in that she had the perfect family - almost. Guilt washed over her as she thought how she would destroy their close-knit unity later this year. How could she do that to them, ruin their Christmas and everything they were secure and comfortable with. The dogs were in the midst, vying for attention as usual. She felt like an outsider for a moment. She couldn't bear the thoughts that she might lose them, banished from her own home, all because she'd fallen in love with Rod.

Nicole looked over and smiled. 'Mum, hi. Come and sit down. You look whacked.'

'How was Sue?' Mike asked, moving over to make room. He gave her a peck on the cheek. 'Want a glass of something?'

'Oh, err, no thanks. And Sue's doing fine. She'll be out of hospital in the next day or two. She's going to stay with her brother and his wife for a few weeks.'

'That's good,' Becky said. 'I know you've been really worried about her, Mum. Sure you won't have a drink? We've been waiting for you.'

'Becky's got some news, haven't you, love?' Mike said, turning to smile at his eldest. 'You might want to raise a toast!'

'No drink, thanks. Bit of an upset tummy. So, Becky, come on, what's your news? Have you found a job at last that fits in with the boys and school?'

'You could say that,' Becky said with a laugh. 'It's an unpaid job though. I'll let Nicole tell you. She's bursting to say something.'

Nicole jumped to her feet. 'Thanks Beck!' She turned to Mandy, her face alight with excitement. 'Becky's pregnant, again. Isn't that wonderful, Mum? You might get a granddaughter this time!'

Mandy felt the room spinning and then Mike was patting her cheeks and the girls were crowding round with anxious expressions. Even the dogs looked worried.

'You okay, Mand?' Mike asked, as though from a distant planet, his voice echoing.

'God, Mum, sorry if it was such a shock,' Becky said. 'I thought you'd be really pleased.'

Mandy struggled to focus and forced a smile. She drew a deep breath. 'Becky, love, I'm thrilled to bits. I'm not feeling too good and I think the smell and the heat at the hospital got to me. Come here; let me give you a hug. Congratulations, sweetheart. When are you due?' she asked as Becky moved into her arms.

'I'm six weeks by my dates, but probably only about four. Andy didn't want to tell anyone until we're past three months, but I couldn't wait that long. I'm due January 30th.'

Mandy nodded. By a rough guesstimate, so was she. There was no way she could jump ship now. The last thing she wanted was to cause upset for Becky. Could things really get any more complicated? She fixed on a smile. 'Get me a glass of ginger ale with ice please, Nic. Then I can toast Becky's good news.' She leant back against the cushions and wondered how the hell her life had become so screwed up.

*

'You do understand, don't you?' Mandy stared at Rod, willing him to. She was trying so hard not to cry again. Her eyes felt sore and gritty from constant tears. They'd met at Sue's place and were ensconced in the spare room. She'd just told him that Becky was pregnant, the baby was due late January, and she couldn't leave home until after the birth.

Rod sighed and rolled onto his back. 'So, what if David decides to let the cottage to someone else if we can't move in?'

She shrugged. 'We could still sign the lease and pay him rent until we're ready. We'll have somewhere private to go then. I can't leave until after Becky has the baby, Rod. I'd never forgive myself if she got all stressed and lost it. I can't have that on my conscience. They're all going to be devastated as it is. Please try and understand.'

He stared at her in silence for a long moment. 'Okay. Whatever you say. But that's it, Mandy. That's the deadline. We either do it then, or not at all. I can't handle not being with you for much longer. If you don't want to be with me, just say so. I'm still leaving Jenny. I'll go and work away for the winter, cruise ships or something.'

Mandy sat up and stared at him. 'So - you'd be quite happy to leave me, too. It's okay for you. You've only got yourself to think about. You've always done as you pleased, Rod; lived the life of a single man. Jenny's been a saint to put up with it for all these years.' She swallowed hard. They shouldn't be arguing. It was the last time they'd get a chance to be together, certainly for a few more days and then Rod would be in hospital. But he was being selfish. It wouldn't hurt to postpone their plans a few extra weeks. They could get Christmas out of the way, Becky's baby and then…

He reached for her and pulled her back down beside him. 'I don't want to leave you. But I'm not staying around when I leave Jenny. I couldn't handle it unless I was with you. I'd rather be working away.'

'And then you'd meet someone else and forget about me.'

'It doesn't even enter the equation, Mandy. Why are you saying that? I love you, you know I do. This is for life for me. I thought you felt the same.'

She nodded and stroked his cheek, wanting to share her problem with him, but terrified the shock would trigger a heart attack. All the worry she carried on her shoulders made her moody and snappy. After a sleepless night she'd made up her mind to terminate her pregnancy. There was no choice. One half of her felt she should keep it a secret from Rod forever, but the other half knew he had a right to know. Not only that, she'd need some financial contribution from him. There was the money left over from the drums, but she couldn't just help herself without asking him first.

That night in the Majestic Club in Brighton, when he'd first sung Fast Movin' Train, he'd told Jed's girl they were looking forward to enjoying a child-free zone. She doubted very much that he'd want her to go ahead and have the baby. Then there was her age…what if there was something wrong with it? They'd be fifty before it even started school. Pensioners by the time it hit sixteen. So many things to consider. She'd found the address of a clinic in the Yellow Pages this morning. It was out of town but not too far to travel. Maybe Dee would go with her. She'd made a note of the number and even got as far as dialing to enquire about the cost, but hung up when Carol had barged in. Still, she had a few weeks grace to sort things out and to get some money together, but the sooner the better really, before she had a change of heart.

'You're miles away,' Rod said, interrupting her jumbled thoughts. 'Not yourself at all. It's worrying me, Mandy. Am I losing you?'

'Of course not,' she reassured, seeing the concerned expression on his face. 'I've a lot going on in my head. I'm scared to death about you, this op and our future.'

'It'll all be fine. Can we put everything out of our minds for now?' He smoothed her hair back and kissed her. 'Let's just enjoy the next hour. It might be ages before we get another chance to make love. I need something to keep me going over the next couple of weeks. Something to think about while I'm lying all alone in my hospital bed.'

She smiled as his eyes twinkled, and she kissed him back, relaxing in his arms.

*

'Good luck for tomorrow. Call me as soon as you can,' Mandy said as Rod held her close on Sue's doorstep.

'I will. Jen will want to come to the hospital with me. Not a lot I can do about that, I'm afraid. As soon as I'm alone I'll speak to you. I'd love to see you over the weekend, but I doubt she'll leave my side and I need to find time to visit my dad. I haven't seen him in weeks. He'll probably want to go out for a family meal. I'll have to play things by ear, babe.'

'It's okay. I understand. I'll talk to you soon.'

'You will. I love you. Thanks for making me feel better.'

'Love you too.' Mandy watched as he got into his car and waved until he was out of sight.

Back inside she watered Sue's plants, made herself a cup of tea and sat down on the sofa in the neat and tidy lounge, bracing herself to go home and don her happy family hat.

*

Rod drove home, his heart heavy. He couldn't believe the news that Becky was pregnant and Mandy didn't want to leave her family until after the baby was born. He wondered if she'd even given a thought to the Malta trip as there was no way they'd get out of it now. His plan had been to get over the op, tell Jenny he was leaving her, and why, and hopefully Mandy would have followed suit with Mike. David's cottage wouldn't be ready for a while but he'd even consider renting a caravan for a couple of months. Anything to get the ball rolling. He had a feeling that Mandy was keeping something from him. She had a troubled air about her - had been distant - almost. It bothered him. Was she regretting things? Maybe she'd changed her mind, wanted to stay with Mike and was stalling telling him because of his op. But no, she wouldn't let him down, would she? Her eyes, her very actions, told him she cared and she was always telling him that she loved him. He couldn't be without her now. She was his world and he was being stupid, letting his imagination run away. She was a good mother and had every right to be concerned about her daughter. His phone rang in his pocket. It was Mandy. He smiled and answered the call.

'Just a quick I love you before you get home,' she said.

'Oh, Mand, I love you too. That's cheered me up. I'm busy convincing myself here that you don't want me anymore.'

'Rod, you idiot! Of course I do. You've no idea how much. I'll talk to you soon. Goodnight.'

'G'night, sweetheart, take care.'

*

Mandy grabbed the phone. She'd been waiting on tenterhooks all day and it was now almost closing time.

'It's me,' Rod told her. *'Sorry to take so long. Jenny's only just left me alone. She's nipped to the shop on the corner so I can't talk for long. I'm being done Wednesday.'*

'That soon?' Mandy drew a deep breath. 'How long will you be in?'

'No longer than forty-eight hours, they said. That's if there's no complication. Come and see me at home next weekend with Mike. No doubt Jen will call you when I've had the op done. At least you'll know that I'm okay.'

'I wish I could visit you at the hospital,' Mandy said. 'I hate the thought of not seeing you for ages. But I suppose Jen will be there all the time and your kids and I don't feel I can face them in that sort of situation.' The thought of Jenny sitting by Rod's bed, fussing and holding his hand made her feel ill. She couldn't bear to see any affection between them at all, no matter how slight.

'I understand. Anyway, having you close will send my blood pressure through the roof,' he said with a laugh. *'I'll have to leave my mobile phone at home. I won't be able to use it in there. If I get the opportunity I'll call you from a payphone.'*

'Okay. Don't forget to remove all the text messages I sent you. Jenny might have a snoop around on your phone.'

'Already done,' he said. *'Not something I wanted to do, but not much choice. You should delete the ones I sent to you, just in case Mike finds them anytime.'*

'I will. Call me when you can before you go in.'

'Of course. If I get a minute I'll pop in and see you. If not, I'll see you next Saturday, hopefully. But I'll definitely speak to you before Wednesday.'

*

'Why have you got those flowers?' Mike asked as Mandy clambered into his car, carrying a huge bunch of white lilies she'd retrieved from her boot. 'They're the sort they use for funerals. We're supposed to be cheering Rod up.'

'They're for Jenny,' she replied. 'Lilies are her favourites. Got grapes for Rod! More as a joke than anything.' She smiled, trying hard to fight the jittery feelings in her stomach. Her hands were clammy and she felt sick again. All Friday and today she'd fought off the nausea. It was getting worse as the days went by. She really should get her arse into gear and call that clinic. She shouldn't keep putting it off. But she couldn't face it until she knew that Rod was okay and going back to finish his stint in Brighton. Worrying about him was enough to cope with at the moment. His operation had been successful. He'd called her the morning after the op while she was driving to work. She'd almost cried with relief to hear him sounding so upbeat and cheerful. She'd tossed and turned most of the previous night with Mike snoring beside her. In the end she'd got up and made herself a mug of chamomile tea, eventually dozing off on the sofa with the dogs squashed either side of her.

'Sorry,' she looked at Mike. 'Did you say something?' They were at the temporary traffic lights for the road works, close to the off license.

'I said shall I grab a couple of bottles of wine?'

'Err, yes if you want. Rod might not be allowed alcohol and I don't feel too great, so I'll pass. But you and Jen can have a few drinks. I'll drive home.'

He pulled over and turned to look at her. 'You still feel rough? You should see the doc.'

She nodded. 'It's that tummy bug. It'll pass soon. No need for the doctor.'

He shrugged. 'Won't be a minute.' She sat back as he got out of the car. Had he looked at her a bit funny just then? She pulled the sleeves of her jacket down over her hands. Sarah had got her some wrist bands from Boots that were supposed to stop nausea, and some herby tablets with stem ginger in them. Nothing seemed to be helping though. She hadn't felt this bad with the girls. Her previous pregnancies had been text book perfect; identical in fact. Once she'd had Becky she knew immediately that the others were also girls, and she'd been right. But this pregnancy was very different. In the shower earlier she'd noticed her tummy was already slightly rounded and her breasts felt fuller. More noticeable because of the weight she'd lost since starting the affair probably. It was only just over a week since Rod had last seen her naked and she felt sure he'd spot the changes right away. She wondered, for a fleeting moment, if the baby might be a boy and then dismissed the thought as a sob caught in her throat. She couldn't even allow herself to think of it as a baby.

Mike got back in the car and handed her a carrier bag. 'Got some nibbly things too, just in case Jen hasn't had time to shop.'

Mandy peered in the bag and smiled at the large bar of Galaxy, nestling amongst the packets of crisps and nuts. Now she might just manage a bit of chocolate. That was something she hadn't gone off.

'Thought it might make you smile,' Mike said. 'Not much else does these days.'

'That's a bit mean. You know I've had a lot on my plate lately. The shop's dead busy and I'm worrying about Sue, she's starting chemotherapy on Monday. And then I worry about Becky too and hope things will be alright there.'

'Becky'll be fine. She's blooming. She popped in before you got home from work. She had a bag of baby clothes she'd just bought and all three girls were oohing and aahing over them.'

Mandy nodded, glad she hadn't been home. She'd get her head around baby things eventually. All she had to do now was get through the next few hours in caring friend mode rather than anxious lover. With a bit of luck she might get a minute alone with Rod while Mike and Jen sorted out the drinks and nibbles in the kitchen. Knowing Jen's penchant for putting everything in fancy dishes, that was a possibility.

*

Rod reached for Mandy's hand and squeezed it gently. 'You okay? You look really pale.'

'Still a bit off colour with that tummy bug,' she said. 'But I feel better now I've seen you. You look brighter than I thought you would. Are you very sore? I noticed you limping when you walked in the room.'

Jenny had gone to get ice from the freezer in the garage. Mike had insisted on carrying the ice bucket for her.

'I am a bit,' he said. 'Wanna see my war wound while they're outside?' He yanked down his joggers.

Mandy gasped. His groin was black and blue. No wonder he limped.

'It looks worse than it is,' he reassured her. 'They must have used some brute force to put that suture in. That's why I can't stand my jeans on.' He smiled and pulled his jogging pants back up. 'I'm used to your delicate touch in that area!'

She smiled and shook her head. 'It'll fade eventually. It's so good to see you again. I've really missed you. Even just speaking to you.'

'I know. I've missed you too. Jenny's going back to work on Monday. Maybe we can meet at Sue's sometime in the afternoon?'

'But will you be okay? I mean, how long did they say it would be before…?'

'Before I can drive?' he teased. 'Forty-eight hours, that all.'

Mandy tutted. 'You know full well what I mean.'

'I can have sex whenever I feel ready,' he said, on a more serious note. 'And no, I didn't ask them while Jen was in the room.'

'Thank goodness for that,' Mandy said. 'I mean, that Jen wasn't in the room.' She grinned as he opened his mouth. 'I'm teasing too. Just let me know what time. I'll arrange a few hours off.'

*

'So he'll be fine for flying,' Jenny was saying as Mandy came back into the room. She'd just been standing by the open bathroom window taking a few deep breaths and worrying about Rod seeing her naked next week. She'd have to get to Sue's before he arrived and draw the curtains. Trouble was, Rod liked to look at her in the light. Oh bugger, she'd just have to say she'd put a bit of weight back on if he noticed anything.

'Well that's good news, mate,' Mike said. 'Excellent. We don't need to cancel our trip, Mand. Rod's going to be okay to travel.'

'Oh, lovely,' Mandy said, looking at Rod whose cheeks were flushed. 'You okay, Rod? You're looking a bit hot and bothered.' He could at least have warned her that flying had also been discussed when he'd mentioned sex and driving.

'Yeah, I'm fine.' He wafted a hand in front of his face. 'It's a bit hot in here. Where's that fan, Jen?'

'It's upstairs. I'll go and get it. You look a bit feverish. I hope you're not getting an infection in that wound.'

Jenny left the room and Rod turned to Mike. 'Look, I've been told, I might be okay to fly. But I won't know for certain until after my check up and they've run a few more tests. Jen's getting ahead of herself as usual. To be honest, Mike, I'd rather the trip was put on hold or cancelled even. I need to get back to work. I've already lost a lot of money with this heart problem and Malta is something we can ill afford at the moment. I could actually do with getting our money back to get us out of a bit of a mess. But I don't want to be the one to ruin it for her. Is there any way you can call it off? Tell her you've gotta work abroad or anything else you can think of that might sound feasible. You'd be doing me a massive favour, mate. And you'll help keep my blood pressure under control.'

Mandy held her breath, waiting for Mike's reply. He looked disappointed, his eyes dark and unfathomable. 'Well, if you're sure, Rod. I'll see what I can do. Didn't realise things were so tight on the financial front. I know you only get paid when you work so it should have dawned on me. Perhaps we could lend you the money?'

'I'd never be able to pay you back, Mike. But thanks for the offer.'

'Okay,' Mike nodded. 'Leave it with me.'

Mandy leant back on the sofa, feeling faint with relief as Jenny came back in carrying the fan.

'Mike, can you lean over that little table and plug this in for me?' she asked. 'You'll need to unplug the lamp first.'

'Sure.'

As Mike and Jenny fussed with the fan, Mandy looked at Rod who put two fingers to his lips and blew her a secret kiss. He smiled. She nodded and smiled back. He too looked relieved and his high colour was fading now, his blood pressure returning to normal.

*

CHAPTER FOURTEEN

JULY 1994

Mandy sat back and fastened her seat belt. She wasn't too keen on flying, but today was special. Today she was going to surprise Rod. He'd no idea she was on her way to see him. The return flight to Gatwick was Sue's treat. Sue had insisted she go. From Gatwick she could pick up a train direct to Brighton then a taxi to the house. By Sue's reckoning, the trip from Manchester to Rod's door should take less than two hours. Mike thought she was visiting Lesley for a few days. It was a while since she'd seen Lesley, so he hadn't even questioned her plans. She'd stayed at Dee's last night and David had run her to the airport this morning. It was early; just gone eight. Rod had been working last night and would probably still be in bed when she arrived. She was planning to tell him about her pregnancy. Decisions needed to be made and quick. On a daily basis she swung from wanting to keep the baby, knowing it wasn't even an option, to having a termination. She really couldn't go on with the dithering around; at this rate it would be too late. Rod should have his say then they could decide together. Neither could then apportion blame on the other, later. She was now almost ten weeks pregnant, still feeling so very queasy and Sue had guessed. That's why she'd insisted on this trip. What surprised Mandy was that Sue hadn't tried to talk her into making any decisions. She just said she needed to talk to Rod and as soon as possible.

*

Mandy flagged down a taxi outside Brighton Station. Ten minutes later they pulled up outside the house and she gathered up her bags, paid the driver and told him to keep the change. Seagulls were making a racket. She took a deep breath and could smell the sea. It made her feel strangely at peace and surprisingly hungry.

She pressed the doorbell and stepped back, suddenly nervous. Maybe she should have let him know she was coming. But then it wouldn't have been a surprise. The door opened a crack and then wider as a bare chested Jed, wearing black jeans and nothing on his feet, smiled and held out his arms.

'Didn't know you were coming, Mandy,' he said, kissing her cheek. 'Rod didn't say. Come on in.' He took her bags and she followed him into the kitchen where Jim the keyboard player, clad in boxers and a faded Rolling Stones tour T shirt, his unruly grey curls standing on end, was making toast.

'Morning, Mandy,' he greeted. 'Want a slice and a coffee?'

'I'd love some toast, please, Jim. But can I have tea instead of coffee?'

'Sure. I've just brewed a pot. Take a seat.' He lifted a pile of laundry off a chair and bundled it into a basket by the back door. 'Ironing! This morning's chore,' he said with a grin.

'Rather you than me,' Mandy said, and sat down. 'Rod still sleeping?'

'Think so.' Jed put the teapot on the table. 'Not seen or heard him yet anyway. Shall I call him?'

'Let him rest. He doesn't know I'm coming. I'll have some breakfast and then go and surprise him.'

'Have you driven down?' Jed asked, pouring her a mug of tea. He passed a milk bottle across and she helped herself.

‘I flew to Gatwick and took a train and taxi,’ she replied, buttering a slice of toast. ‘It was so quick. I can’t believe I’m here.’

‘Best way to do it,’ Jed said. ‘Expensive, but okay for a one-off. Is it a special occasion? Not his birthday, is it?’

‘No, I just want to spend a bit of time with him. Make sure he’s looking after himself properly. How’s he been?’ She frowned as she saw a furtive look pass between Jed and Jim. For a fleeting moment she wondered if Rod had another woman, but no, he wouldn’t do that to her, would he? Why should she even think it? She realised how vulnerable and insecure she was feeling with her life. Probably her hormones. They were all over the place. She swallowed hard. ‘What?’

‘Nothing,’ Jed said. ‘He’s doing his best. Remembering to take his pills and stuff.’

‘But?’ Mandy prompted, and then had a light-bulb moment. ‘He’s smoking again, isn’t he? I just know it. Oh, god, he’s a pain. I knew once he got back down here he wouldn’t last long.’

‘He’s not having as many as he used to,’ Jed said. ‘About half. He was a bit low when he came back and he’s surrounded by us lot smoking. Don’t suppose he stood much of a chance really. Think he’s missing you. Pity you can’t be here all the time to take care of him.’

‘I know.’ Mandy sighed. ‘But it’s not possible.’ She finished her toast and drank her tea. ‘I’ll go up and see him now.’

*

She could hear water running as she tapped on Rod’s door. No reply; he was obviously in the shower. She went into the room. The window was open but the smell of a freshly smoked cigarette lingered, the tell-tale butt end in the ashtray. The noise from the seagulls was even louder up here. The shower room door was ajar and she could hear Rod singing, but she couldn't make out what the song was. She smiled, stripped off her clothes, desperate to be with him now. The look on his face when she drew back the shower curtain was one of shock and then pure joy. He grabbed hold of her and pulled her to him.

'I'm dreaming, right? How - where…? Oh my God, Mandy, I can't believe it!' He pulled her closer and kissed her.

She clung to him, kissing him back as he ran his hands up and down her spine, grabbing her buttocks and grinding against her.

'You feel real enough to me,' he whispered.

'Good.' She took a deep breath and held her stomach in as tight as she could. It wasn't so bad when she was lying down as it went flat and she could still get into her normal clothes. He was squeezing her breasts now, tweaking her nipples but seemed unaware of their increased size. Mind you, he hadn't noticed at Sue's the last time they made love, after his operation. Maybe they didn't look much different to him, but they certainly felt different to her.

He turned the water off and grabbed a couple of towels. He wrapped one around her and, fastening the other around his middle, led her to the bed. 'If I'm gonna wake up soon and find this is all a dream, I want to make love to you right away, before I do.'

*

Mandy sighed blissfully as Rod rolled off and pulled her into his arms. He lay with his mouth against her ear, telling her over and over that he loved her and nibbling her lobes. She felt relaxed for the first time in ages.

'Still can't believe you're here,' he whispered.

'Well it's all thanks to Sue,' she said and told him how their kind friend had treated her. 'I said I'd try and get here one last time before you finish your stint. And with Sarah and Carol taking their holidays in the next few weeks, it's now or never. Mike thinks I'm at Lesley's.'

'How's it going with him?'

She shrugged. 'I'm coping. He's out a lot and I've been doing a few fittings at night, so our paths don't cross that much. I told you Louise moved in with her boyfriend last week, didn't I? Well we had Becky's kids to stay on Saturday night to give her a break. They slept on camp beds in our room. They both had snotty colds and what with them, snuffling and Mike snoring, I couldn't sleep. So I went and slept in Louise's room and I've stayed there since. Mike doesn't seem bothered. He's not even asked me to go back and I'm not offering.'

Rod smiled and squeezed her tight. 'That makes me feel better.'

'Thought it would. The gulf's widening between me and Mike. When he's around he seems to be watching me, studying me almost, as though he's waiting to say something, but never does. It might just be my guilty conscience, but it freaks me out.' She stared up at the ceiling, bracing herself to tell him about the baby. She felt very mellow and he had that loved-up look on his face that told her he felt the same. It was probably the best opportunity she'd get today. 'Rod…'

'Yeah? Oh fuck, look at the time!' He was staring past her at the bedside clock. 'I need to get dressed, babe. We've got a full blown rehearsal this afternoon. Do you want to stay here and chill? I won't have room in the car for you. I need to pick up my drums from last night's venue and take them to the new club in Hove.

Jed's car's off the road so I've got to squeeze him and his gear in, too.'

'It's okay. I don't want to disrupt your plans. You didn't know I was gonna land on you today. I'll find something to do to keep myself occupied. It's a gorgeous day. I'll have a stroll around The Lanes and then go and sit on the beach for an hour or two. I'll buy a book to read.'

'Okay, I'll be back around five. We'll grab something to eat and then drive up to Hove. How long are you staying?'

'Just tonight and tomorrow,' she replied as he slid out of bed and pulled on some clothes. 'And, Rod?'

'Yeah?'

'Don't have too many cigarettes, please.'

He blushed slightly. 'I'm sorry. I did try; I really did, but…'

'I know - it's hard and I'm not going to nag you. Maybe next year, when we're living together, eh?' Her news would have to wait until later now. The moment had passed. He bent to kiss her. She wound her arms around his neck and whispered, 'I love you so, so much.'

'I love you, too, babe.' He stroked her hair. 'I'll call you when we're leaving the club. Enjoy your wander around town and take care.' He handed her a front door key and blew her a kiss as he left the room.

*

Mandy was glad she'd brought a sundress with her. She popped into a chemist on The Lanes and bought some sun cream. It was scorching and the last thing she needed was to go home with sunburn or Mike would be suspicious. It might be raining in Shrewsbury. She must remember to call Lesley to find out. But whatever, she planned to enjoy a bit of sun on her skin for one day at least. She found a secondhand bookshop, had a browse around, and bought a copy of Georgia by Lesley Pearce for two pounds. She'd read a first issue last year, but lent it to someone who hadn't returned it. It was a lovely story about a sixties soul band and a mixed-race girl singer. Right up her street and one to lose herself in for a few hours. She read the first chapter sat at a table outside a café and enjoyed a tuna salad and an orange juice.

A shop opposite caught her eye. A Vespa scooter was parked outside, all decked out with fur and mirrors, just like the ones the Mods had rode years ago. She decided to have a wander around the shop before going to the beach. The window was decked out with sixties memorabilia, a Dansette record player, loaded with forty-fives. A Midwinter, leaf-sprigged tea set, like the one Mike's mum had used years ago when he'd first taken her to meet his parents, arranged on a tray, and to the side, a mannequin wearing a black and white Mary Quant mini dress, just like she and Jenny used to wear to go dancing. She felt a little pang as she thought of Jenny and how much she would have loved to root around in a shop like this. She pushed the thought away and went inside.

A seventies Afghan coat hung directly in front of her. She smiled, remembering the one Lesley had got for her twenty-first birthday and how, when it got wet in the rain one night, had stunk to high heaven so that no one would sit next to her on the bus going home. This one also had a certain odour and it wasn't even wet. She moved further into the shop, looking at clothes that brought back a million memories, and teak furniture similar to the stuff she and Mike had bought for their first modest little home. Parkas like Mike and Rod had worn when they were teenagers.

Guitars and an old sparkly drum kit, similar to the one Rod had recently sold, filled the back room of the shop. Posters of The Small Faces, The Stones and The Who plastered the walls. A young man asked if he could help. She told him she was just browsing and enjoying the trip down memory lane. She felt overcome with nostalgia and almost close to tears, wishing she could turn back the clock to the day Rod had first asked her out. There was a basket of magazines near the window display, Beatle and Elvis monthlies; Oh Boy; Honey and Petticoat. So many memories; she should write them down while she still had the thoughts in her head. Before he died her granddad had been able to vividly recall war stories, but not what happened to him yesterday. That might happen to her one day. She'd always kept a diary, but her earlier ones had been chucked away when her mum cleared out her room after she left home to marry Mike. But she could still recall so many things from her teens. Music scene stuff. Groups she'd seen performing and who frequented the record shop she'd worked in until she had Becky. She said goodbye to the young man and strolled down the lane towards the beach. She popped into the newsagent's on the corner and bought a bottle of water, a reporter's notepad and pen.

*

The next couple of hours flew by as Mandy scribbled page after page of thoughts and ideas. She was totally immersed in her own little world and almost missed Rod's call. He was back earlier than he thought he'd be and said he'd join her for a while on the beach.

She watched for him and waved as she saw him running down the steps towards her. He dropped down, kissed her and took a swig of water from the bottle.

'Whatcha doing?' he asked, pointing to her notepad.

‘Just writing some thoughts down about the sixties.’ She told him about the shop and all the memories it had triggered. ‘I thought I might do a sort of article and send it to a music mag, Mojo or something.’

He scanned the pages and nodded. ‘Sounds quite good. You’ve got a better memory than me. I’d forgotten half this stuff. Perhaps you could do a series of articles or a book or something, you know; facts about the local music scene, sort of like Brian Matthews, Sounds of the Sixties, but, Thoughts of the Sixties. Get someone to illustrate it or better still try and get your hands on some photos. You could even talk to some of the guys from the old bands, get some input from them. Most of them are still around. I keep in touch with a few. I can fix that up for you.’

‘Hmm, I like the idea of that. I feel quite excited, thinking about it.’ She looked around. ‘I need the loo and to stretch my legs. Shall we walk up to The Source?’

He pulled her to her feet and slipped his arm around her waist. She drew a deep breath and held her stomach in. His hand was on her hip, caressing her through the cotton fabric of her sundress. At least the dress was loose and didn’t cling to her rounded stomach. She bent to pick up her bag and grabbed his hand as he moved his arm, and held on tight, safer than having his arm around her middle. Maybe tonight after the gig, she’d tell him then, she decided, as they made their way to the beachside bar.

*

The Grosvenor Club was as crowded as The Majestic in Brighton had been. The audience was an older crowd, more her and Rod’s age, Mandy thought as she glanced around. The club was nicely set out, like an old style cabaret club, with two tier seating, lamps on all the tables and the stage at the far end.

'Think you're the youngest in here,' she said to Jed's girl.

Penny giggled and looked around. 'Think you're right, Mandy. They're a nice crowd though. They loved the sixties stuff, all singing along.'

Mandy nodded. She was looking forward to Rod doing his solo stuff in the second half. She moved up as he and Jed came back from the bar with drinks. Rod sat down next to her and placed a glass of red wine in front of her as the club compere put a Drifters CD on, turning up the volume full blast.

'Oh - I err - wanted a soft drink, juice or…,' she tailed off as Rod frowned. 'That last drink's given me a bit of a headache. Must be too much sitting in the sun.' Truth was, she'd got horrendous heartburn. The one glass of red wine she'd allowed herself was now crippling her and she had no Tums in her bag to relieve it. Not only that, she shouldn't really be drinking, just in case.

'I'll have it for later,' Penny said. 'Shame to let a decent glass of wine go to waste.'

Jed got to his feet. 'I'll go and get Mandy a soft drink in exchange. Coke?'

'Err, can you get me a dry ginger with ice in a tall glass, please, Jed. Thanks.'

Rod slipped his arm around her waist. 'You okay, love? You look a bit tired.'

'I'm fine. It's been a long day. I was at the airport really early to check in.' She felt so tired, she could fall asleep right now, leaning against his shoulder.

'I can hear a phone ringing,' Penny said. 'It's not my ring tone. Is it yours, Mandy?'

Mandy reached for her handbag and took her phone out. She stared at the screen. 'It's Lesley,' she said to Rod. 'Shit, I wonder what she wants.'

'Answer it then,' he said. 'Might be urgent.'

Mandy answered and screwed up her face. 'She can't hear me properly, it's too noisy. Hang on Lesley,' she yelled. She hurried to the club entrance and dashed out to the street, Rod, looking anxious, on her heels. She'd spoken to Lesley before they left for the club, just to make sure Mike hadn't called for any reason. 'Can you hear me now? Good. What's wrong? Oh shit, has he? Just now? Oh you did. Okay, thanks, I'll call him back.'

She ended the call and turned to Rod. 'Mike called. She told him I'm in the bath and she'll get me to call him back as soon as possible.'

'Why didn't he call your mobile?' Rod asked.

'He did, apparently. I didn't hear it ring. But if it hadn't been for Penny I'd have missed Lesley's call too.' She looked at the caller display and nodded. 'One missed call. God, I hope there's nothing wrong at home. I can hardly dash back in a hurry from here.'

'Call him then. See what he wants.'

'I can't call him from the street. The bloody seagulls are so noisy tonight. He's not daft. They don't have gulls at Lesley's. It's busy in the club and the music's so loud. What shall I do?' A feeling of panic washed over her. Mike wouldn't ring her unless it was important. He never did. What if it was Becky? Please God, don't let anything be wrong.

'The dressing room,' Rod said. 'It's upstairs. It's quieter than the rest of the club. Come on.' He grabbed her hand and pulled her back inside.

She sat down on a chair in the small dressing room where every surface was piled high with changes of clothes for the band. Rod said he'd wait on the stairs outside to make sure no one walked in on her. She pressed her home number and Mike answered after a few rings. 'Hi, it's me. Sorry, I was in the bath. I can't talk for long, Mike cos I've got hardly any credit left and Lesley's Jack's using the landline and I thought it might be urgent as you never call me so I didn't want to wait until he'd finished.' She realised she was babbling and fell quiet while he spoke.

'Not really urgent. I can't remember when you said you'd be home. I have to fly to Germany on Thursday morning for work and it means leaving Nicole alone with the dogs. Louise is away for a couple of days so she can't stay. Just wondered if you'll be back in time. Nic can't remember when you said you'd be home either.'

'I'll be back on Wednesday night,' she said, relieved. 'In plenty of time. Just glad to know nothing's wrong.'

'Sorry to worry you. How are you feeling? Hope the rest's doing you some good.'

'I'm fine,' she replied, surprised at his concern. 'Just tired. Nice to have a break with nothing to do. Are the girls okay and the dogs?'

'Yep. All fine. Jenny rang earlier. Asked for you. Told her you're at Lesley's.'

'Oh, did she? I'll call her when I get back to work.'

'Yeah, she was frantic. She'd been trying to get hold of Rod for a couple of hours. His dad's been rushed to hospital. He's had a stroke and he's in a bad way. Anyway, I'm sure she'll have managed to get in touch by now. She thought she might have to call the police so that they could let him know.'

Mandy could hardly breathe let alone speak. She swallowed hard. 'Well why did she call me?'

'Just to let us know and she probably needed someone to talk to. She was very upset.'

'God, hope he's alright and I hope she gets hold of Rod soon. Got to go now before this runs out. See you Wednesday.' She ended the call, feeling sick. She opened the door. Rod was sitting on the stairs with his back to her. 'Rod, come in here, please.'

He got to his feet and looked at her. 'Fuck, he knows, doesn't he? Shit. Is he coming down to get you?'

She shook her head. 'Where's your phone?'

He pointed to the little dressing table. 'Over there. Why?'

'Turn it on. Jen's been trying to get hold of you urgently for the last few hours. That's not why Mike called. He wanted to know when I was coming home 'cos he's got to away on Thursday. He just happened to mention that she'd talked to him earlier.'

He sighed. 'I spoke to her this morning. What the fuck's wrong now?' He picked up his phone and switched it on. 'Missed calls and messages,' he said, raising his eyebrows. 'It had better be important.'

'Rod.' She put her hand on his arm. She should tell him rather than he hears it from a voice message. 'Sit down, darling. Something's happened.'

He sat on the chair and she knelt in front of him and took his hands. 'What sort of something?' he began. 'Is it Ben? Has something bad happened to him?' He was white-faced now and trembling.

She shook her head. 'It's not Ben or any of your other kids. It's your dad, Rod. He's had a stroke and he's in hospital. You'd better call Jenny right away.'

He stared at her, his mouth open. 'No. Not my dad. He's fine. I spoke to him yesterday.'

She held him close. ‘Just call Jen,’ she whispered. ‘I’ll go and tell Jed. We need to drive home tonight.’

*

She left Rod calling home and went in search of Jed. A hurried explanation later, Jed was calling the stand-in drummer who conveniently lived in Hove and was free to finish the gig tonight.

‘Don’t worry, Mandy,’ Jed said. ‘Just get yourselves off home. Mitch can take Rod’s drums back to his place tomorrow and we’ll sort ourselves out. Tell him not to worry.’

‘It never rains but it pours for us lately,’ Mandy said. ‘Rod so badly needs to work. He’s already lost a lot of earnings this summer.’

‘It can’t be helped.’ Jed put his arm around her shoulders. ‘Here he is now. We’ll see you again soon, no doubt.’

‘I’m so sorry, mate,’ Rod began.

‘Hey, no worries. We’re sorted. Mitch’ll help us out. You only get one dad. Go home and see him. Fingers crossed he’ll make a good recovery.’

*

‘What did Jenny say?’ Mandy asked as Rod drove them back to Brighton to get Mandy’s bags and for him to pack a case.

‘That he’s in a bad way. He’s paralyzed down the left side and his speech has gone. He was on the bowling green when it happened. Fortunately one of the old chaps does first aid, recognised the signs and called an ambulance right away. That’s probably saved his life.’

‘I can’t believe it,’ Mandy said. ‘It’s a good job Mike called Lesley or we’d have been none the wiser until the police turned up. That would have been awful.’

‘The police?’

‘Yeah, that’s what Jenny told Mike. That she was going to ask the police to get in touch with you. You really should keep your phone turned on, Rod. There always seems to be an emergency when you switch it off and always when I’m with you!’

‘Sorry, Mand.’ He reached for her hand. ‘Here we are again. You get a trip down here and something happens to fuck it up. Were fated, me and you. At least that’s what it feels like sometimes. Like we’re not meant to be.’

‘I know,’ she sighed. ‘But this isn’t something we could have predicted. Your poor old dad. I bet Sheila’s beside herself with worry,’ she said referring to Rod’s dad’s partner.

‘She’ll be out of her mind. She loves the old devil to bits. Jenny told me not to drive home tonight. She’s worried about my heart and she said there’s nothing I can do anyway. But I’d rather get there in case he takes a turn for the worse. I said I’ll take it easy and have a couple of stops on the way. I’ll take you to Dee’s and you’ll have to stay holed up there until Wednesday or Mike will wonder why you’ve arrived home early. Especially with me getting back at the same time. Don’t want him putting two and two together.’

Mandy nodded. She’d better get her head into gear for a long night. And there was no way she could say anything to him about the baby right now. He’d got enough to cope with. Jesus, she was going to have to forget telling him and just get it sorted herself. Dee had promised to help her financially and the only other way she could do it was to borrow some from the quarter’s rent money and pay the rest next month. Screw the shop for once. There were more important things to deal with.

*

CHAPTER FIFTEEN

Mandy chewed her nails as she waited to be called. Dee gave her arm a comforting squeeze. Friday morning, they should both be working, but the clinic had had a cancellation and she'd grabbed it. After talking things over with Dee yesterday she'd decided there was no further time to waste. Between them they'd scraped together the £250 she'd been quoted. If the clinic agreed, the termination would be one day next week. She'd no idea how she was going to cope. Sarah was away from Saturday, Carol could only work part-time, and there was a mountain of curtains and blinds needing completion and fitting. Dee said she could take a couple more days off work and help out, for which she was grateful.

She'd only spoken to Rod three times since he'd dropped her off Tuesday morning. His dad was in a bad way, he'd told her, and unable to do anything for himself. He planned to spend as much time at the hospital with him as he could. He said he'd try and pop in the shop to see her as soon as possible. She'd told him not to worry, that his dad's needs must come first. Then she'd tentatively asked if Jenny was at the hospital with him. 'Well yeah' he'd replied. 'Dad thinks the world of Jen and her being around is good for him.'

Mandy knew Rod's dad thought a lot of Jenny and it was right and proper that she should be there. But a selfish part of her hated the thought of her and Rod spending so much time together. Things like this brought people closer, patched up failing relationships. Since Rod had said - We're fated, me and you - Like we're not meant to be - she had this feeling that maybe he was right and it was time to end things before they did any further damage to their marriages. But then she thought about the nights they'd spent together, all the magical times they'd made love. She couldn't bear to think that there might not be more. Rod had ended his last call to her with I love you, babe, as he always did. But maybe he was saying it out of habit. He'd have so much time just to sit and think now. Perhaps he'd decide that what he was doing was wrong. She felt tears welling and choked back a sob.

'Mrs Radcliffe,' the receptionist called.

'Good luck,' Dee said. 'I'll wait here for you.'

Mandy's legs felt like jellies as she followed a navy-suited woman down a plush carpeted corridor to a small room, furnished with a single leather arm chair and a table with a selection of glossy magazines. She felt ready to pass out as she sat down. A tray with a jug of iced water and a glass was placed in front of her.

'Drink as much as you can,' the woman said. 'You need a full bladder for the scan.'

'Scan?'

'Yes, we need to be certain how advanced the pregnancy is before you see our counsellor.'

'Oh!' No one had told her, and it hadn't even dawned on her that she'd need a scan, never mind counselling. 'I didn't realise…' She'd assumed she'd just see a doctor, who'd agree to the termination and that would be it. What if they tried to talk her out of it? It wouldn't take much doing. She didn't really want to go ahead, but knew she had no choice. It would be best all round.

'I'll be back in ten minutes. Don't go to the toilet meantime.' The woman left the room.

Mandy poured a glass of water. She sipped it slowly. How the hell could she drink the whole jug without needing the loo? She was never off the damn thing lately. By the time the woman came back she was on the last glassful and at bursting point.

'Ready?'

She nodded.

'Follow me.'

In the scan room she was handed a blue cotton gown and told to undress behind a screen. A horrible thought occurred and she hoped to god they wouldn't give her an internal before they let her use the loo. How the hell had she got herself into this bloody mess at her age? Why on earth had she got involved with Rod in the first place? Why hadn't she just said no to the affair? She'd totally screwed up big time and she only had herself to blame. The sonographer called her name. She walked towards the bed and sat down while the lady took some details. She must have seen the pained expression on her face for she smiled reassuringly.

'Won't be too long and then you can use the bathroom. Swing your legs up onto the bed and lie flat on your back.' The sonographer pulled the gown up and squeezed gel onto Mandy's stomach. In spite of the warmth of the day it felt cold, made her shiver. 'I'm just going to run the Doppler over your tummy and check on the screen to see where we're at. Try and relax.'

Relax! Mandy screwed her eyes shut and took a deep breath. She'd never felt so un-relaxed in her life. She didn't want to look at the screen. Because if she did, it would be all too real. She could feel the Doppler running round and round and over her tummy, pressing down near her bladder, making her flinch. The woman was silent as she worked. Mandy was aware of her breathing and a clock ticking somewhere in the otherwise quiet room.

'Mrs Radcliffe,' the sonographer said, still pressing hard on her stomach.

'Yes.' Mandy opened her eyes and squinted at the woman. She tried so hard not to look at the screen, so hard, but could not stop herself. There'd been no such thing as scans when she'd had her girls. Becky had scan pictures of her boys and they looked like little aliens, waving their arms around. Her eyes widened. The screen showed a perfectly formed tiny human, lying deadly still.

'Your estimate of ten weeks is correct,' the sonographer said. 'But the foetus stopped growing about two weeks ago, although your body has continued to maintain the pregnancy. It sometimes happens. Within the next few days you'll start to miscarry.'

'Oh!' Mandy stared at the screen. It was all she could say. Tears ran sideways, down her face, dripping into her ears. 'I didn't want to look,' she sobbed. 'I didn't want to see him. Poor little thing. He must have known I couldn't have him.' She could feel herself getting hysterical, could hardly breathe but knew she had to get to the loo urgently. And she'd called it him. There was no way of knowing now, but she was certain it was a boy.

The sonographer helped her off the bed and into the nearby toilet, closing the door discreetly behind her.

Mandy sat on the loo and cried until she could cry no more. She got to her feet, feeling numb. Back in the room the sonographer was writing up notes. She looked up and gestured to a seat by the desk.

'What do I do now?' Mandy asked. 'I mean, I still feel pregnant. Heartburn, queasy and stuff. Are you sure he's not just sleeping?' Maybe the sonographer had made a mistake. If she had, she was walking out of there right now and keeping her baby.

The sonographer nodded. 'I'm sure. You can see the consultant now. I've spoken to him and he's waiting for you. If you get dressed I'll take you to his room.'

Mandy shuffled behind the screen and pulled on her clothes. She couldn't get the picture out of her head; the tiny little human, lying so still. It would be with her forever. She wanted Rod right now more than she'd ever wanted him in her life. She needed him to hold her and tell her everything would be alright. She was desperate to talk to him, to share her grief. She couldn't even call him because his phone would be turned off and she had to wait until he called her. Never before had she felt so alone. This week could have been a turning point. Deep down she'd been hoping Rod would tell her to have the baby; that everything would be okay. They'd get through it somehow. It had been a turning point alright, but not in the way she'd expected.

*

Mandy rolled onto her side and drew her knees up, thanking God she was in Louise's old bedroom. Mike was back from Germany and had gone out for his usual Friday night pint. Nicole was sleeping at her friend's house with Beth. When Beth arrived to collect Nicole, Mandy had asked how her granddad was.

'He's very poorly,' Beth said. 'Mum and Dad are at the hospital all the time. Dad's really upset. I don't like seeing him so sad. It's hard for him, having no brothers and sisters.'

'I'm sure,' Mandy said, giving Beth a hug. 'Tell your parents I'm thinking about them.'

'I will. I'll get Mum to call you when she has time.'

Mandy saw the girls out. She'd come straight up to bed with a hot water bottle and pain killers. She was in agony now and cried out. The dogs snuffled anxiously, trying to climb up onto the bed but she pushed them away. She couldn't bear their weight at the moment. The consultant said he'd prescribe something to make the foetus come away quickly, or she could wait for a miscarriage to occur naturally, which, he'd assured her, would most certainly happen in the next few days.

'Why did it die?' she asked. 'Was it something I did?'

He shook his head. 'We often don't know why a baby dies in the womb. It can be due to a number of reasons, like chromosomal abnormalities.'

'I should have seen a doctor earlier. I've been putting it off and letting everyone else's problems and feelings come first. I'm totally to blame. Maybe something could have been done to save it. You must think I'm mad saying that when I came here for a termination. But as soon as I saw him, I couldn't have gone ahead.'

'That's why we insist a patient has counselling first. People do indeed change their minds.'

She told him she just wanted it over now as quickly as possible. They'd inserted a pessary, told her it would soften her cervix, and given her pills to take at intervals over the next few hours. They still charged her £250. No surgery would be necessary, which she was relieved about. How the heck would she explain away a hospital stay to Mike and the girls? Only if complications arose would she need to go into hospital. Fingers crossed they wouldn't, but right now she wished she could go to sleep until it was all over.

*

Rod lit a cigarette and leant back against the car park wall. He took a long drag and stared up at the moonlit sky. What a week. It had started so full of promise too. He'd popped out to put another ticket on the car. It was just after ten-thirty and the hospital had told him he could stay with his dad until midnight. Jenny had taken Sheila home an hour ago. They were both exhausted. Jenny had been a rock this week. It hadn't been easy, sitting side by side with nothing much to say and him fighting feelings of guilt. But she'd been good with Dad and that's what this was all about. Every now and then Dad mumbled words that were fairly coherent and at other times jumbled. But one thing that stuck in Rod's mind was something Dad had said last night after Jenny and Sheila left. It had taken him ages to decipher the words but they eventually made some sort of sense. Dad had said, "Look after Jenny, son. Stop messing her around!" When he'd asked Dad what he meant, he'd closed his eyes and fallen asleep. Now Rod was wondering if his dad knew about the affair. Or more likely he meant that he should quit working away and spend more time at home with Jen.

He desperately needed to speak to Mandy. He was missing her so much and needed her support. He should arrange to meet her at Sue's, but it didn't seem right to be enjoying himself while his dad was lying so ill. Mandy was really busy at the shop and seemed to be mithered whenever he'd called her. He supposed Mike would have gone out for his usual drink, it was Friday after all. He rooted for change in his pocket, did the parking ticket before he forgot and sat in the car for a few minutes. Should he call her, chance Mike being out? He might have stayed in, seeing as he'd been away and would have only got back early evening. But Mike was a creature of habit and if a pint had his name on it…

He pressed redial and waited and waited. He was about to hang up when Mandy answered. She'd been crying, he could tell. 'What's wrong, babe? Why are you upset?'

'Oh, Rod. I'm okay,' she replied. *'Just feeling sorry for myself. I'm missing you.'*

'Not half as much as I'm missing you,' he said. 'This is a nightmare. I don't know what's going to happen. They keep saying they'll transfer Dad to a rehabilitation unit and try and get him back on his feet, but he's developed a chest infection now. So he's got to stay put for the time being. I'm worried about my bloody job. Jenny's got special leave, she still gets paid, but me - well - you know my situation. It's shite. I just don't know what to do. I'm contracted for another seven weeks down south. I'm wondering if I can get out of it and find something with a local band. Trouble is the money's nowhere near as good as it is down there. I'm in despair, Mand. Thank God Mike got us that Malta money back. At least we can pay the mortgage this month.'

'Do you want the drum kit money?'

'No. That's for us and David's place. It stays where it is. I need to see you, I really do. Can we meet at Sue's sometime next week?'

'*Err.*' She hesitated, and he wondered why. *'I've no cover in the shop, except for Carol and it's not fair to leave her on her own when we're so busy.'*

'Well I could come to the shop one lunchtime. You can send her out and we can lock up. I need you desperately, babe.' She didn't reply. 'Mandy, what is it? Don't you want to see me?'

'Of course I do. I'm just very busy, that's all.'

He heard her take a deep breath. ‘I know you are, but I need to see you. I’ll be there Monday at one. I have to go back inside now. I love you, babe.’ He ended the call before she had a chance to respond.

*

Rod got a coffee from the vending machine and went back to the ward. Dad was sleeping. They’d given him oxygen and his breathing was laboured. Rod sat by the bed, twiddling his thumbs. He wondered why Mandy had been funny with him. It was like she didn’t want to see him. He guessed she was upset that he was spending a lot of time with Jenny and not her, but for fuck’s sake, there wasn’t much choice and he knew where he’d rather be. He wished he’d brought a book or magazine with him. Ben and James had called in earlier and Beth popped in after college. He’d been glad to see his kids, even though Ben had a shifty air about him again and constantly checked his phone. Beth cheered her granddad up with her big smile and bright chatter. She’d almost finished college now. A-level results would be out soon. She was excited. God alone knew how they’d afford for her to go to Uni. Jenny said Beth might get a grant and if he wasn’t earning she’d stand a better chance. But not earning would bring more problems. Jenny had suggested earlier in the year that they ask his dad for a loan. Well he couldn’t do that now. And what if, when Dad recovered, they sent him home? He couldn’t go back to Sheila’s place. The flat was far too small for someone who’d probably be in a wheelchair and he was a bulky man. Sheila was too tiny and frail to look after him properly. They’d have to have him at their place. But who’d look after him there? It was unfair to expect Jenny to do it and he was hardly ever around. And what about moving in with Mandy? He could hardly take his dad as well. The only other option would be a nursing home. Rod felt choked, thinking how his dad had always looked after him, given him everything he needed and wanted as a kid. How could he pack him off to a nursing home? Life was so fucking cruel at times.

*

Mandy heard Mike come in and say hello to the dogs. She'd put them out on the landing when she'd got up to use the loo. Nothing much had happened yet except the pains and she'd passed a few clots. But the pains were stronger than ever now and moving lower down. One thing she'd noticed, but only in the last couple of hours, she wasn't feeling nauseous anymore. Dee had offered to help her on Monday and Tuesday. If she felt too rough to go into work, Dee would open up and take charge. She'd have to text Rod and ask him to meet her at Sue's instead. It would be easier to talk there. And they needed to. She felt the need to grieve, but not on her own.

She'd no idea how long everything would take. It might be twenty-four hours, it could be more. They hadn't been specific at the clinic. Just gave her a pamphlet that told her what to expect. There was no way she could work tomorrow. The shop would have to remain closed. Dee would go in first thing and put a notice of apology in the window. It would have to suffice. If customers complained, well it was tough. The world wouldn't end if they didn't get their curtains on time. She'd have to tell Mike she felt too ill to work. Play the tummy bug game again or a dose of summer flu. She hoped he'd be out of the house for most of the day. He took it in turns with his brother to take their mum weekend shopping. Fortunately it was Mike's turn tomorrow and there'd been mention of her choosing some new bedroom furniture. Knowing her mother-in-law, it would take ages. And if Nic went out with Beth, then she could get on with things on her own. Dee said she'd keep calling her to make sure she was okay. She closed her eyes and prayed for sleep.

*

Rod tossed and turned all night. He got up at five, wandered downstairs, made a mug of coffee and lit a fag. Jenny would give him earache for smoking in the house, but what the hell. She'd already given him enough for smoking again anyway. A complete contrast to Mandy's, I won't nag you, attitude. He couldn't face another full day of sitting in the hospital with Jenny and Sheila. He'd call the ward about eight and if they told him there was no further deterioration in his dad's condition, he'd take a break this morning and go into town. Call in Johnny Roadhouse or Dawson's and look at keyboards. Not that he was in a position to buy one, but looking was a start. He might pop in and see Mandy first. Surprise her. He needed to know things were okay between them. Her reluctance to see him bothered him. Part of the reason he couldn't sleep. She usually worked alone on Saturday if Sarah was away, so it would be a good time to visit. He didn't want to wait until Monday and spend all weekend worrying that something was wrong. He finished his fag and went to take a shower.

*

Mandy listened for the door closing and slid out of bed. She tweaked the curtains to one side to make sure Mike was leaving. He was backing off the drive. He'd brought her a mug of tea up an hour ago. It still sat on the bedside table, cold now with a milky skin. He'd come in to wake her, thinking her alarm had failed to go off. She told him she felt really ill, not up to working today and that Sarah would take care of things. She didn't dare tell him that Sarah was on holiday and the shop would remain closed. Hopefully he'd never find out. He'd call it bad planning; she'd lose money, no way to run a business, etcetera. At the moment she couldn't care less if she never set foot in the shop again. She wanted to curl up and die. She felt exhausted, had been awake for most of the night. It was all over by five. She'd crawled back to bed and cried into her pillow. She'd been sufficiently flushed, snotty and headachy enough to convince Mike she was suffering from a heavy summer cold. He said maybe she'd caught it from their grandsons. She agreed.

She shuffled to the bathroom and ran a bath. The dogs were hovering, worried expressions as usual. While the bath filled she rang Dee and cried down the phone. Dee told her she'd stuck the notice on the shop window and that while she was there a customer came in to collect some curtains. Fortunately it was a completed order and bagged ready to go and the cheque was in the till.

'Thanks so much, Dee. Once it's cashed I'll give you your hundred quid back.'

'No rush for that,' Dee assured. *'Have you heard from Rod? How's his dad?'*

'He called me last night while I was in agony. I could hardly speak to him and I think he thought I was being funny. His dad's really poorly. Rod said he's got a chest infection now. He's insisting on seeing me Monday. He said he'd come to the shop. But I'll ask him to meet me at Sue's instead.'

'You're going to tell him, aren't you?'

'I need to. It's a loss and I want to share it with him. This weekend is going to be so hard to get through. Thank God the girls are out for most of it. Mike will be with his mum for hours today and he's got a gig tonight. I'm going to have a soak and wash my hair now. Brighten myself up a bit. I've sweated buckets and I ache from top to toe.'

'Hardly surprising. Do you want some company? I've got a bit of shopping to do first. But I'm free after that. David's gone fishing with his mate. He'll be out all day. I'll get us something nice for lunch.'

'Dee, that'll be lovely. Thank you. See you in a bit then.'

*

Rod stared at the sign on the window.

CLOSED DUE TO UNFORESEEN CIRCUMSTANCES.

WE APOLOGISE FOR ANY INCONVENIENCE.

THE SHOP WILL RE-OPEN MONDAY AT 10.00.

He rattled the locked door and peered through the window. All in darkness. Very odd. Mandy hadn't said anything about being closed today. He scratched his chin, wondering what to do now. Dare he call her? He hoped she wasn't ill. She didn't sound too good last night, but he'd put that down to her crying. He set off back to his car on the Co-op car park around the corner and spotted Dee coming out of the store with a laden trolley. He leant against the car, waited until she drew almost level and wolf-whistled to get her attention. She looked up with a frown.

'Oh, Rod, it's you. I was about to tell you to sod off!'

'Nice to see you, too. Do you know where Mandy is? The shop's closed.'

'Err, she's not too good. She's having a day off.'

'That's not like her. Especially when she's got no cover. She'd work if she was dying rather than lose customers.'

'Yes, well, she can't today.' Dee looked away, fiddling with something in her shopping trolley.

Rod stared at her. 'So, what's wrong with her? She seemed okay when I spoke to her last night. Bit weepy, but it's been a difficult week for us both...' he tailed off. Why was Dee looking at him as though he'd crawled from under a stone?

'It's been a difficult week alright,' she muttered.

'Do you know if Mike's home today?'

'Not sure. How's your dad?' She seemed eager to change the subject.

'No change. I'm going in to see him later. I err; think I'll chance calling Mandy. I need to see her, or at least to speak to her.'

Dee shrugged. 'I'm seeing her later for lunch. I can pass on a message.'

'No thanks. I'll call her.'

'Suit yourself. I'd better get this shopping home. See you again. Hope your dad gets well soon.'

'Thanks.' Rod stared after her and got into his car. Weird. Dee was usually chatty and jokey with him. He wondered if he'd done something to offend her. He shook his head and pressed Mandy's number.

*

Mandy lay on the bed wrapped in a bath towel. The effort of drying herself had further exhausted her. She felt a bit peckish and fancied tea and toast but hadn't the energy to get up and make it. She'd have to wait until Dee arrived with lunch. She pulled the duvet over and closed her eyes, thinking an hour's sleep would do her good.

Her phone rang out on the bedside table. She grabbed it. Rod! She really didn't feel like talking, but his dad might have taken a turn for the worse.

'Mandy, hi. Why is the shop closed? What's wrong? Are you ill?' His questions tumbled over one another.

She took a deep breath and tried to sound bright and breezy. 'Hi yourself. I felt a bit off colour, that's all. How's your dad?'

'Bout the same. You're a bit off colour? Enough to lose a whole day's business? Especially Saturday. That's not like you, babe.'

'God, you sound like Mike. I can be ill. It is allowed, you know!'

'Well, yeah, but you never are.'

'Well I am today. Why aren't you at the hospital?'

'I needed a break. I'm going later. I presume Mike's out?'

'He is.'

'Can I come and see you then? Just for a few minutes. Please.'

She was silent for a long moment. 'Not sure that's a good idea, Rod.'

'Why? I'm a family friend. It wouldn't be odd for a friend to pop in for a coffee whether Mike was there or not. Would it?'

'I suppose not. But Nic and your Beth may come back anytime and Dee's coming for lunch.'

'Yeah, I know. I saw her on the Co-op car park. She was a bit odd with me. What do you know about that?'

'Nothing. You're probably imagining it.'

'She was definitely odd and that's not like Dee. Is something wrong, Mandy? I err,' he hesitated, 'I have this feeling you might be dumping me. I'd rather know than have you string it out because my dad's ill and you don't want to upset me. I can't stand not knowing. It's doing my head in. I feel stressed enough as it is.'

'Where are you now?'

'Still on the Co-op car park. Why?'

'Give me ten minutes and then come over. I have to warn you that I don't look or feel my best.'

'You always look good to me, babe. See you in ten. Love you.'

'Love you too.' She ended the call and took a deep breath. Might as well tell him now. Fancy him thinking she wanted to dump him. It was the last thing on her mind. She needed him more than ever, but so did his family at the moment.

*

Rod drove to Mandy's convinced she would tell him they had to finish. He couldn't bear it. Without Mandy in his life he had nothing. Okay, not strictly true, he had a wife and kids. But Mandy was his soul mate. She made waking up in the morning something to look forward to. Even though he couldn't see her most days, that first phone call, usually when she'd just arrived at work, made it all worthwhile. Afterwards he'd lie in bed thinking about her and dreaming of the day they could move into David's place. He parked the car outside the house and looked up at the bedroom window. It was Louise's old room. The one Mandy had told him she now slept in. She was pulling back the curtains and waving to him.

Next thing he was in her arms in the hall, kissing her for all he was worth. He carried her through into the lounge and put her gently down on the sofa.

'Babe, you look pale.' He held her close. She wore a pair of loose, black linen pants and a baggy black T-shirt, no makeup and her long hair was scraped into a damp pony tail. The black clothes drained what bit of colour she had. Her eyes were red-rimmed as though she'd cried buckets, but she still felt good in his arms and he didn't want to let her go.

'I'm sorry I look so scruffy,' she began. 'I've not even dried my hair, just shoved it up.'

'You still look beautiful to me. You always do. What's wrong? Please tell me.'

'Okay.' She pulled away from him and shut the lounge door. 'Just in case anyone comes in while we're talking. If Nic and Beth come back, we'll tell them you dropped in to tell us how your dad is.'

He nodded and took both her hands. 'I have a feeling that what you're going to tell me won't be good.'

'It's not.' She took a deep breath. 'I, err, I lost our baby this morning.' A sob caught in her throat and she looked down at her hands in his.

He stared at her. 'Our baby? You were pregnant? My God, Mandy why didn't you tell me?'

'I tried. I really did, but there were so many things going on. Your heart operation; I didn't want to stress you. Then your dad was rushed to hospital when I came down to Brighton to tell you. I thought you had enough to cope with.' Tears ran down her cheeks as she looked at him.

Rod felt stunned. This was the last thing he expected. She looked so lost and vulnerable. He enveloped her in his arms. 'I'm so sorry. How far were you?'

'Ten weeks,' she cried. 'It happened the night we were in Birmingham. I didn't know what to do. Part of me wanted it. But you told Penny you wanted a child-free-zone and I knew you wouldn't want me to have it.'

'Oh, babe.' He felt lost for words. 'If you'd told me we could have talked about it. You shouldn't have had to worry all alone. Does Dee know? Is that why she was funny with me earlier?'

She nodded. 'She's been very supportive. When your dad took ill I had to make a decision. I couldn't tell you then and getting hold of you since has been difficult. I went to a clinic, Dee came with me. We scraped the money together between us.'

'You had an abortion - without telling me?' He let go of her and sat back. 'Mandy, how could you do that? After everything we've been to one another.'

'No,' she sobbed. 'I didn't. I went to the clinic for a consultation. When they did a scan I wasn't going to look, because I knew I couldn't keep him. But I did look and he was there, but so still and tiny. He died about two weeks ago, they said. It's all my fault for keeping it a secret. I should have seen a doctor earlier. I just kept putting it off.'

Rod put his head in his hands. To say he was shocked was an understatement. He couldn't believe it. Mandy was hysterical now and he grabbed her and pulled her close. 'It's not your fault. Don't say that. These things happen. So, what did the clinic do?'

'They gave me something to make it come away,' she sniffed, rubbing her hand across her eyes. 'I lay in bed all night in agony, with Mike in the next bedroom. I was in terrible pain when you called me and I could hardly speak. Then this morning it all just happened. It was awful.'

'You shouldn't have had to go through that on your own. If you'd told me last night I would have come over right away.'

'How? Mike was only round the corner at the pub. I coped the best I could.'

'I should have been there for you. I feel terrible. - You said "he". Was it a boy then?'

She smiled lightly through her tears. 'I don't know. It was too soon to tell. But I had a feeling it might have been. I always wanted a boy.'

He hugged her so tight she squealed. 'If you want a baby we can have one next year.'

‘I couldn’t go through that again. There might be all sorts of reasons why it happened. Probably my age. Whatever it was, he wasn’t meant to make it. Poor little scrap. I felt so ill the whole time. I should have realised something was wrong.’

He nodded. ‘You’ve been pale and off colour for weeks. No wonder. Oh, babe, I can’t believe you went through all that with Mike in the next room. He doesn’t know, does he?’

‘Are you serious? I’d be dead by now! You too, probably. No one knows except Sarah and my close girl friends. I was due around the same time as Becky’s due. I don’t know how I’m going to cope when the time comes.’

‘I’ll be right there waiting for you. You know that don’t you? As soon as you say the word, we’re off. And, Mandy, please don’t keep anything like this from me again.’

She raised an eyebrow. ‘There won’t be anything like this again. We’re taking no more chances. To think it happened on the very night you suggested having a vasectomy, too.’

‘Bloody ironical,’ he said. ‘But that’s it now. I’ll see about getting the snip if you’re absolutely sure you don’t want to try again.’

‘I don’t. I couldn’t handle it if something went wrong.’

He kissed her and held her close. ‘We’ve had a right few months, haven’t we? Let’s hope things get better soon.’

The doorbell rang. Mandy went to answer and let in Dee.

Rod looked up as Dee followed Mandy back into the lounge. ‘Thank you for looking after her in my absence,’ he said.

Dee nodded. ‘It’s what friends are for. But I can’t go through that again, Rod.’

‘You won’t have to,’ he said. ‘I’ll leave you two to chat and go and see Dad. God knows what’s going to happen there, but it ain’t looking good.’

Mandy walked him to the door and kissed him goodbye. ‘I’ll call you later,’ he said. ‘Is Mike playing tonight?’

‘He is.’

‘Good. I’ll call you as often as I can then. Get some rest now. I love you, babe.’

‘Love you too, Rod.’

*

CHAPTER SIXTEEN

Rod spotted Jenny marching down the hospital corridor towards him. She wore a peeved expression. Now what had he done? 'Hi, Jen, how's it going?'

'Where've you been? I've called you a few times but your phone just rang out.'

'Sorry, left it in the car while I tried some keyboards. Why, what's up? Is Dad worse?' He really couldn't handle a run in with Jenny. His head was full of what Mandy had just told him. He felt torn in two. He wanted to be there for her but was needed here. Mandy should be his number one priority right now. She needed him and he wanted to look after her. Although he'd only heard about the baby two hours ago, he felt a sense of loss and a need to sit somewhere on his own for a while to take it all in.

'There's no real change in him.' Jenny replied. 'But it's Sheila. She doesn't feel well now and wants me to take her home.' She rolled her eyes heavenward. 'If it's not one thing it's another.'

'Do you want me to take her?' Rod offered. 'Then I'll come back and you can get off. You've done enough this week.'

'Would you?' Jenny's face softened. 'Thanks, Rod. I could do with getting some housework done and I want to do a big shop.'

He nodded. He could sit quietly and contemplate while his dad slept. At least he wouldn't have to make small talk all afternoon. 'Why are you out here, by the way?'

'Just popping to the shop. I fancied some chocolate. I'll get a paper. You can read the sports page to Dad. He'll like that.'

'Will he? Alright then. I'll go up to the ward and get Sheila sorted. We'll wait until you come back before we leave.'

*

Dad was awake, propped up on pillows. He looked grey, drawn and still wore the oxygen mask. Rod dropped a kiss on top of his head and squeezed his hand. He gave Sheila a hug. She looked washed out, eyes red-rimmed. In spite of the warm day she wore a brown speckled cardigan and reminded Rod of a little sparrow.

'Jen won't be a minute, Sheila and then I'll take you home.'

'Thank you, love. I'm feeling very tired.' Sheila smiled wearily. 'I think it's telling on all of us, this sitting around. Are you okay, Rod? You look a bit pale.'

'Yeah, I'm fine. Like you, a bit tired. Be glad when we know what they intend doing with Dad.'

'I don't think they'll let him home. I couldn't look after him. He's too heavy. They told Jenny they'll get a physiotherapist in to help him clear his chest. He rattles. Doesn't sound right to me.'

'Hmm.' Rod leant closer and listened. 'You're right. He shouldn't be doing that, surely. I'll get a nurse.'

He went to the nurses' station at the end of the ward. A pleasant-faced nurse greeted him with a smile. He smiled back. She was nicer looking than the sour-faced battle-axe who'd thrown him out at midnight. 'Err, it's my dad. He's making a funny noise when he breathes in. I haven't noticed him doing it before. Can you come and look at him please?'

‘Of course.’ She followed Rod. ‘Now then, Mr Davis,’ she addressed Rod’s dad. ‘Let’s pop you up the bed a bit. Make you more comfortable.’ She adjusted the back rest and pillows and turned to Rod. ‘I’m going to call a doctor. He sounds very congested.’

Rod stared after her as she left. She came back within minutes. ‘Doctor’s on his way,’ she said and drew the curtains around the bed. She adjusted Dad’s oxygen mask and wiped his mouth as Jenny popped her head around.

‘You gave me a bit of a scare then when I saw the curtains pulled,’ she said, ducking inside. ‘What’s going on?’

Rod explained. ‘Will you take Sheila? I want to be here when the doc comes.’

‘Of course. Shall I come back? Do you need me?’

He shook his head. ‘I’ll call you if I do. Thanks, Jen. See you tonight.’ He helped Sheila to her feet. ‘You go home and take a rest. I’ll see you tomorrow.’ He gave Sheila a hug and Jenny a quick peck on the cheek as they left.

The nurse was changing Dad’s pyjama jacket now. Rod watched as she pulled the sleeve up his lifeless left arm. He felt tears welling and blinked them away. He couldn’t be a wimp in front of a complete stranger. She tucked the bed covers around and tenderly swept Dad’s hair from his face. Tears did fall then. That simple gesture did it. He was feeling wobbly today, hardly surprising.

‘It’s okay to cry, you know,’ the nurse said. ‘It’s hard to see the man who brought you up, so helpless. I’ve been there myself.’ She patted his arm. ‘Doctor will be here soon. I’ll bring you a cup of tea.’

Rod sat down next to the bed and took his dad’s hand. Dad squeezed it. Rod squeezed back and smiled.

'She was nice, wasn't she, Dad. Pity they're not all like her.' Dad squeezed his hand again. Rod swallowed hard. Was this how it would be from now on? All their father son conversations about football, Formula One and which pub served the best pint in Pickford conveyed with the squeeze of a hand.

The nurse brought tea for them both; Dad's in a beaker with a lid, similar to the ones the kids used as babies. Rod lifted it to Dad's lips and fought back tears as he sipped with difficulty, tea dribbling from his mouth. Rod mopped him up with a handful of tissues and cursed fucking God under his breath for letting things like this happen. But then, he wasn't one for religion, so there'd be no chance of God hearing and taking much notice anyway. Dad turned his head away to indicate he'd had enough and Rod put the oxygen mask back into place. He sat down and drank his tea, head whirling. What had he done to deserve a year like this? Apart from his whirlwind romance with Mandy, it had been shite so far. He looked up as the doctor parted the curtains and swept in, accompanied by the nice nurse.

*

Mandy saw Dee out and went upstairs to lie down. She still felt exhausted. Mike hadn't arrived back from his trip out with his mum. He'd be in a rush when he got home to load his gear and dash back out for the gig. Rod had called her half an hour ago. He'd sounded upset and she wished she could put her arms around him and hold him. His dad's chest infection had developed into pneumonia and he'd been moved to a side room on his own. He told her he'd try and call her again, but that Jenny was on her way back to the hospital, so it might be difficult. He said he'd see if he could nip out for a fag later and call her then. She rolled onto her side and closed her eyes. She awoke later to loud bangs and thuds and the dogs barking.

'Get out of the bloody way!' Mike was shouting as she peered over the banisters. The bag carrying his stage clothes lay in the hall and he was sitting on a stair halfway down, rubbing his ankle. He shook his fist at Max.

'What happened?' She went to sit on the stair behind him.

'He bloody tripped me up! Jesus, what a fucking day! I'm on the last minute as it is.'

'Can you stand?'

He got to his feet, wincing as he put weight on his right foot. 'Just about. I'll be okay.' He hobbled down the last few stairs, glaring at Max who skulked away down the hall.

'Are you sure. Would you like me to drive you?'

'No, you don't look well at all and the gig's in Preston. It's too far. Sorry for waking you. I peeped in to say bye but you were flat out. How are you feeling now?'

'Still a bit grim,' she said, feeling guilty that he was actually showing concern. She changed the subject. 'Did your mum get her furniture?'

He rolled his eyes.' Did she fuck! All that bloody time wasted. But at least I got lunch out of her, which is as well because I've had no time to eat anything since I got home.'

'Get a sandwich or a pie at the club. Don't have too much beer on an empty stomach. You've got to drive home, remember.'

He nodded. 'See you tomorrow. Hope you feel better later.' He pecked her cheek, grabbed his clothes bag and left the house.

Mandy shut the door after him and leant against it.

*

Mandy took the call from Jenny late Sunday evening. Rod's dad had passed away just after five.

'The end seemed to come very quickly,' Jenny said. 'I'll let you know when the funeral is. It'll be a cremation. We're trying to arrange it for this week so Rod can go back to work as soon as possible.'

Mandy chewed her lip before replying, trying to be tactful in her choice of words. 'I'm so sorry. Thanks for letting us know, Jen. But maybe Rod won't want to dash back to work. He'll need time to get his head around things. I know Mike did when his dad passed away. What I'm trying to say, is don't rush him.'

There was silence for a moment, then, 'I think I know what's best for Rod. He copes better when he doesn't have too much time on his hands.'

'Sorry,' Mandy began, 'I didn't mean to interfere. Pass on our condolences to Rod. We're here if you need us.' She said goodbye and hung up. Bloody hell, Jenny sounded a bit narked then. Perhaps she should have kept her mouth shut. She went into the lounge where Mike and Nicole were relaxing after Sunday lunch, cooked by the pair of them. They'd insisted she rest. 'That was Jen. Rod's dad passed away at teatime.'

'Oh, that's bad news,' Mike said. 'Is Rod okay?'

'I didn't get to speak to him. Maybe you should call him later when they've finished letting people know.'

'I will. It'll be tough for Rod, being an only child and his mum already gone. At least I had our kid and Mum to help with the arrangements when Dad died.'

'I know. But no doubt Jenny will do her bit,' Mandy said, wishing with all her heart that she could call Rod or go to see him, just to hold him.

Nicole jumped up. 'I'll go and see Beth. She'll be dead upset. She was close to her granddad. Do you want me to nip to the garage, Mum and get you a card.'

'It's okay, love. I'll get one tomorrow. They don't have much choice at the garage.' She wanted to choose something appropriate, something with words that would convey to Rod how she was feeling, so he'd know her thoughts were with him. When he'd called her late last night, after escaping from Jenny for a cigarette, he'd told he couldn't get her news out of his head. He'd thought about nothing else while his dad had drifted in and out of a restless sleep.

'Try not to dwell on it too much,' she'd told him. 'It will drive you crazy thinking about, what if. It's with me all the time. One of us needs to stay strong and you've got all that going on, too. Don't get too stressed and remember to keep up with your medication. I'll see you soon, hopefully.'

*

Mandy stood stiffly by the chapel wall with Nicole as Mike slipped his arm around her shoulders. She hated funerals at the best of times, but this one was going to be hard to get through. Who was it once said arrange neither a funeral nor a house move for a Friday? She couldn't remember, but they were right. The traffic had been horrendous on the A6. The hearse was already ten minutes late. She'd bet Jenny was blowing a gasket by now. She nodded at someone she vaguely recognised. Probably one of Rod and Jenny's neighbours. There wouldn't be many mourners. There was hardly any family; just Rod, Jenny, their kids and Sheila. Jenny's parents were long dead and she hadn't spoken to her brother for years.

Half a dozen elderly people made their way towards the chapel. Mandy supposed they were friends of Sheila and Rod's dad. Maybe from the same retirement flats. They were somberly dressed in black. She half smiled. It was funny how the elderly still stuck to wearing all black for funerals. She looked down at her own outfit. Black drained her, but she'd succumbed to black trousers, as a mark of respect, with a purple silk loose top and her shades, no jacket. The day was too warm. They were going back to Rod and Jenny's later for a buffet. She'd rather go straight home, but Jenny had insisted.

'Here they come,' Mike whispered as the hearse came into view.

Mandy gave an involuntary shiver. The vehicle behind carried the whole family. Rod was out first and helped Jenny, and then Sheila who clung to his arm, crying. Jenny linked her arm through James's and Ben slipped his arm around Beth's shoulders. There was no sign of Tanya, Ben's girlfriend. Perhaps as well, Mandy thought, given that Jenny didn't like the girl. They followed the family inside the chapel after the coffin. Mandy led Mike and Nicole into a pew halfway down. She didn't want to be too close. It didn't feel right, with her and Rod being lovers. Rod caught her eye as he looked around and she gave a slight nod and glanced away. His look told her all she needed to know. It was enough for now.

*

Mandy's hands shook as she filled a glass with water at the kitchen sink. She rooted in her handbag for paracetamol and popped a couple in her mouth. She took a swig of water and sat down on a stool at the breakfast bar, looking out of the window. The funeral party was outside in the garden. Jenny, sitting quietly with Sheila, under a tree on the stone bench that came from Rod's old family home. Mike, in animated conversation with James about jobs. Beth and Nicole were up in Beth's bedroom. Ben was talking to neighbours and swigging from a bottle of beer. She couldn't see Rod anywhere. She finished her water and went into the lounge. It was nice and cool with a slight breeze blowing in through the open window. She felt tired and still not a hundred percent and hoped people wouldn't think she was being rude if she sat quietly on her own for a few minutes. She shut her eyes. She heard the front door open and close. She assumed it might be Ben taking off. He'd looked bored, checking his watch from time to time and fiddling with his phone.

'Mind if I join you?'

She opened her eyes. Rod stood in front of her, looking good in a dark grey suit and white shirt. He'd removed his black tie from earlier. Her heart thudded loud in her ears. She never saw him in formal dress. In fact, she couldn't even recall seeing him in a suit since his wedding day. He closed the door to the hall. 'Please do,' she said and sat upright. 'How are you?' She hadn't had a chance to speak to him properly yet.

'Better for seeing you,' he said. 'I nipped out to get some fags. I'm back on twenty a day. I will give it up though, when the time's right. I promise.'

She nodded. 'Whenever you're ready I'll support you. I've so missed you. It's been a week when I've really needed you.'

'Me too,' he said. He took her in his arms and kissed her, sighing into her hair. 'It's been such a very long week. Can I see you tomorrow? I'll come to the shop.'

'Of course. I'll lock up at one for an hour. I'm on my own tomorrow.'

'I'll be there.' He rubbed her tummy gently through her silky top, bending to plant a kiss on it. 'How are you feeling?'

'So, so. Still getting a few cramps. But that could go on for another week or two, apparently. I'm getting there.'

'Well as long as we can have a kiss and a cuddle tomorrow, that'll do me,' he said, holding her close. 'I'm not going back to Brighton until next Saturday. Got a lot of sorting out to do for Sheila next week. Dad left a will. I'm booked to see the solicitor on Monday. Hopefully I'll be able to see you before the weekend.'

'That'll be great,' she said. 'You'd better go back to the garden before Jenny comes looking for you. I'll follow in a few minutes. I love you.'

'I love you too, babe.' He gave her a lingering kiss and left the room.

*

'One night next week then,' Mike was saying as Mandy went to join him in the garden.

'Wednesday or Thursday'll be best for me,' Rod said. 'I'll need an early night Friday. I'm off back to Brighton. I'm working Saturday night.'

'So, what's this?' Mandy asked, frowning. 'You two planning a lad's night out?' Surely they weren't.

'Mike's asked us over,' Jenny said.

'Oh, okay.' She breathed a relieved sigh. 'It'll have to be a takeaway. I'm working both those days. Too busy to cook anything. Decide which night and then I won't book fittings in.'

'Wednesday,' Rod said. 'Will that suit you, Mand?'

'Suits me fine. Why don't we ask a few others over?' she directed at Mike. 'Ian and Elaine and Steve and Karen. We haven't seen them for ages. Bet Rod and Jenny haven't either. Make a nice night of it.' There was no way she was entertaining with just the four of them. The other couples were fun and lord knows they all needed cheering up.

'Sounds good to me,' Mike said. Rod and Jenny nodded. 'Right, are we ready for off? I'll give Nicole a shout.'

Jenny wandered back to sit with Sheila. Mandy looked at Rod and shook her head. 'Bloody hell. Whose bright idea was that?'

'Jenny's. She said it would be nice to spend a bit of time together before I go back to Brighton. Mike suggested coming to your place.'

She nodded. 'We'll have to grin and bear it then.'

'Smart move to think of asking the others.'

'Yeah. Let's hope they're free mid-week.'

'Fingers crossed. See you tomorrow.'

'You will.' She turned as Mike, Nicole and Beth came outside.

'Can I stay the night, Mum? Please. Beth wants me to.'

'If Jenny and Rod says it's okay, then it's fine by me. Come and get a change of clothes and Dad'll run you back.' She caught a gleam in Rod's eye and knew he'd call her if he thought Mike was out of the way. She gave a slight nod to show it was okay.

'You can stay with pleasure, Nic,' Rod said, slipping his arm around Beth's shoulders. 'Beth could use your company. I'll order pizzas later. How does that sound?'

Nicole smiled. 'Thanks, Uncle Rod.'

*

Rod sat in front of his dad's solicitor, mouth agape. The guy had just told him Dad had left him nearly twenty grand. 'I honestly didn't think Dad had any money left from the sale of our family home.'

‘He invested wisely,’ the solicitor said.

Rod took a deep breath. The end of his money worries. But he could see another set cropping up in their place. Jen would push for a holiday and want to spend some on the house. He could take his time finding another contract after Brighton finished. But most of all he had the money to walk away and set up home with Mandy. Except they couldn’t do that, because of Becky’s expected baby. Why was life never simple?

The solicitor asked him to sign several forms and handed him a cheque. He left the office with lightness to his step and a smile on his face. ‘Bless you, Dad and thank you,’ he muttered. They’d already cashed several policies, taken out ages ago by his mum. They’d paid out more than enough for the funeral and he’d offered Sheila what was left but she’d turned him down. Her late husband left her very comfortable, she’d told him. He’d put the money away to help with Beth’s Uni fees. Jenny’s eyes had lit up as no doubt they would when he showed her the paying in slip today. Pity he didn’t have a bank account of his own, other than his business account, he thought as he made his way to Nat West. He waited ages in the queue and then turned and walked out. The Cheshire Building Society beckoned. Dare he open an account of his own? Tell Jen the money from Dad’s will would take a while to come through while he decided what to do. Sod it. He crossed over and went inside.

‘Yes, Sir, can I help?’ A young, bespectacled girl behind the glass screen smiled at him.

‘Err, yes, I’d like to open an account please.’ Rod felt nervous and a bit guilty. He didn’t know why. Well yeah, he did, but it was his money when all’s said and done. The last time he’d opened a bank account was with Jenny the week they got married. He hardly ever used it. He always got paid in cash. He didn't even use a cheque book. Jenny dealt with the financial side of things. She did his books, paid his tax and national insurance and gave him a handful of paying in slips each month so he could make his contribution to both accounts. On the odd occasion he ran out of money he used a credit card.

The girl behind the glass invited him into a little office at the back of the building. She made him a coffee and took his details down on a form. 'Have you any ID with you, Mr Davis? Ideally a driving license or a passport and a gas, phone, or electricity bill with your address.'

Rod shook his head. 'I've got my license on me, but nothing else. The address on my license is not the one I want correspondence sending to. I just want to pay a cheque in, that's all.' He didn't want Jenny getting wind of what he was doing. Shit, why was nothing straight forward?

'I can't complete the transaction without recording all your details and proof of your home address.' The girl looked at him patiently. 'If you'll bring them in later, I'll get your account up and running, complete with your correspondence address.'

He got to his feet. 'I'll leave it, thanks.' Might as well pay it into bloody Nat West. It wouldn't clear for few days anyway, so Jenny couldn't get her mitts on it for a while. He got his phone out and called Mandy. He hadn't spoken to her since Saturday when he'd seen her in the shop at lunchtime. She said she might be able to see him today because Sarah was back at work. Fingers crossed she could.

*

‘I know it might seem like a good idea, Rod, but you can’t hide all that money away. Jenny’ll have a fit.’

They were sitting in Mandy’s car on a deserted car park near The Roman Lakes. Rod had just told her about his inheritance and how he felt reluctant to put it in the joint account.

‘I know. But she’s such a spendthrift if there’s spare money. This is my chance of getting the keyboard and a new PA. Making sure there’s something to put towards Beth’s Uni fees. And, I want some for us. I could pay David six months rent in advance. Then we can sit back for a while until the dust settles and take it from there. It would make our first few months that much easier until I get sorted with my solo plans.’

Mandy nodded. ‘It would. So ask Jenny to speak to you before she spends any lump sums. If she doesn’t like it, tell her you’ll put the money in another account in case you can’t work anytime.’

‘Mrs Sensible,’ he teased. ‘That might work for you and Mike, but not for me and Jen. I guess I’ll have to chance it and see.’

‘There is another way,’ she said. ‘That’s if you trust me, of course.’

‘With my life.’

‘I’ve got a Cheshire account. There’s not a lot in it, but I keep it open in case I ever want to save for anything. Not that there’s much left from the shop money lately to save. You could stash a bit of it away in there once the cheque clears.’

He smiled and pulled her to him. ‘Brilliant! Aw, thanks, Mand. I’ll pay it in Nat West when we get back. Think I’ll pop in and surprise Ben later. I’m not happy about him at all. Did you notice how shifty he was at Dad’s funeral? Looking at his watch, checking his bloody phone all the time. He was like that on his visit to the hospital too. I think he's dealing. If he's not, he's certainly mixed up in something illegal. All that bullshit about starting a new life and dropping Tanya's druggy mates. Load of bollocks. Don't think he's touching the hard stuff himself, he doesn't look as though he is. Probably just does weed. But something's not right.'

'It must be a worry. I'd be frantic if he was mine. Doesn't Jenny say anything?'

'Not really. Jenny likes things clean and tidy in her head. She would never admit to having a drug-dealing son! She prefers to bury her head in the sand. Anyway, enough about them. Give me a kiss while we've got the chance. I doubt whether I'll get time to see you again now before Wednesday night. I promised to help Sheila sort Dad's clothes and take them to the charity shop tomorrow.'

'Ah yes, Wednesday. Should be fun. Huh! Could do without it to be honest. I still feel a bit under the weather.'

Rod held her close. 'I'm sure you do. It'll take a while to get your head around it. I had a "what if" moment last night while I was lying in bed.'

'Did you? I have a lot of those. I picture this little boy, and us, on Brighton beach. I still feel it was a boy.' She sighed. 'But I guess that's just me being fanciful.'

'If it helps, we'll always think of him in that way.' He smiled. 'I don't do religion and stuff, but if there's anything beyond this life, then maybe Dad's looking after him, playing footy, sailing boats, like he used to with me.'

'Oh, Rod.' Mandy's eyes filled. 'That's lovely. It makes me feel so much better.'

'And me. I do wish you'd told me earlier, but I understand why you felt you couldn't. What are we like?' he finished as she took a tissue from her pocket and wiped his eyes and her own.

*

Mandy opened two bottles of red wine and stood them on the worktop to breathe. She put two bottles of white in the fridge alongside cans of lager and went to open the patio doors. The dining room felt like an oven. It had been such a warm week but overcast tonight, like thunder might be in the air later. She set the table and popped napkins by the side of each plate. Mike came into the room, carrying a box. He was dressed casually in pale blue T-shirt and jeans.

'Thought we might have a game of Trivial Pursuit after we've eaten,' he said. 'Don't suppose anyone will want a very late night. Most of us are working tomorrow.'

Mandy smiled. 'Good idea. We've not played Triv for ages. I know Jenny enjoys a game. Right, I'm going up to dry my hair and get dressed. Listen for the door.'

Mike nodded and helped himself to a lager.

'I've only just put those in the fridge. They won't be very cold.'

'It'll do,' he said. 'I'll put some music on.'

The sound of Jackson Browne's Running on Empty followed her up the stairs. She dried her hair, applied light makeup; anything more would slide off in this heat, slicked her lips with dusky pink gloss, tipped her head upside down and ran her fingers through her hair. She flicked her head back and shook it. Her hair fell in a tousled cloud around her shoulders, just how Rod said he liked it. She lifted a white Indian cotton dress from the wardrobe and slipped it on over white lacey underwear. The narrow shoulder straps and close fitting bodice, trimmed with gold braid, gave way to a gently flaring knee-length skirt. She always felt good in the dress but hadn't worn it this summer. Now she'd lost her baby tummy it fitted perfectly again. Gold strappy sandals set off her lightly tanned legs.

Pity she and Rod couldn't slope off alone tonight. She was desperate to spend time with him before he went back to work. The doorbell rang and she heard Mike greeting Rod and Jenny. Her stomach did a flip as she heard Rod saying Hi and should he put the beer in the fridge. A generous spray of perfume, a forced friendly smile and she tripped lightly down the stairs. Mike was in the kitchen fixing a white wine spritzer for Jenny who was by his side chatting to him.

'Same for you, Mandy?'

'Please.'

She went into the lounge where Rod was swigging from a can of Stella. His eyes widened as he looked at her.

'Fucking hell, Mand,' he whispered. 'You look amazing. How the hell am I supposed to keep my hands off you tonight?'

She smiled. Exactly the response she'd hoped for. 'I could say the same to you,' she whispered back, eyeing his faded Levis, tight black T-shirt and breathing in the scent of the woody aftershave that drove her crazy. She flopped down on a sofa and he sat down opposite.

'I daren't sit next to you,' he said with a smirk.

'I know. You can sit next to Jen instead.' She stopped as Mike and Jenny came in. Mike handed her a drink and she sat back, smiling.

'You look lovely, Mandy,' Jenny said. 'New dress?'

'I bought it last year. Only worn it a couple of times.'

'Is it Monsoon?'

Mandy nodded. Jenny was wearing the floaty outfit she'd worn on her birthday.

‘I thought I’d give this another airing,’ Jenny said. ‘I haven’t worn it since my birthday. Mind you, I haven’t been out anywhere. I think we’re due for a girls’ night out soon, don’t you? Maybe we could do something next week when Rod’s away.’

The doorbell rang again and Mike went to let the guests in. Mandy silently thanked God. Saved by the bell before Jenny started mithering further about going out.

‘Come and sit down,’ Mandy invited as Ian, Elaine, Steve and Karen crowded in. ‘Nice to see you all. Mike, drinks all round, please. Spritzer for you girls okay? Lager for the boys?’ She got to her feet and went to help Mike in the kitchen.

He smiled and pulled her to him as she stood beside him, popping ice into tall glasses. She stiffened slightly and moved away.

‘You look lovely,’ he said. ‘I’d like you back in our bed tonight. You said you’re feeling better now and we’ve spent quite enough time apart.’

She stared at him, lost for words. ‘Err, now’s not really the time to be having this conversation, Mike.’

‘We’ll have it later then, when everyone’s gone home.’

He was looking at her closely, his face creased in a slight frown. She could feel her cheeks heating and reached for two cans of lager and made her way back to the lounge, leaving Mike to follow with the spritzers.

‘I’ll get the menus and then you can all choose what you want. Sorry I haven’t been able to cook us anything, but I’m so busy at work at the moment.’

‘Hey, no worries, Mandy,’ Ian said. ‘Good of you to invite us round on a weekday. We promise not to overstay our welcome.’

Mandy smiled. She'd known the foursome since her teens. They were part of the old sixties crowd. Ian had always been a heart-throb. Over six-feet tall, he'd had the looks of Scott Walker in his youth, but unfortunately not the voice. Now almost bald and twice the size of his teenage self, he and Elaine were proud parents of four sons. Steve and Karen had no family. Whether through choice or fate, Mandy had no idea and the diminutive couple never discussed their childless state. She handed out menus. 'Right, what's everyone having?'

*

'Have you had enough to eat?' Mandy asked. 'Okay,' she continued as they all nodded. 'Mike, top everyone up while I clear the table.'

'I'll help you.' Jenny got to her feet and carried dishes through to the kitchen.

'You sit down, Jenny. I'll do it. You're a guest. Go and relax.' Mandy flicked her hair back and started to load the dishwasher.

'Actually,' Jenny said, lowering her voice. 'I just wanted to say congratulations.'

Mandy looked up and frowned. 'For what?'

'The baby.'

'What?' Mandy dropped a glass and it shattered on the tiled floor. 'Shit!'

'Becky. The new baby.'

'Oh, Becky! Yes, thank you.' Mandy reached under the sink for the dustpan and brush and swept up the shards while Jenny wittered on.

'Nicole told our Beth. I haven't had the time to talk to you properly what with Rod's dad and things. I bet you're really thrilled. I can't wait for me and Rod to have grandkids.' She smiled; a dreamy expression on her face. 'That's what it's all about, isn't it? Family.'

She lowered her voice. 'That's why I always feel sorry for Karen and Steve. No kids. It wouldn't do for me.'

'Oh, I don't know. They seem happy enough.'

'Yes, but I mean, well, I think they just put on a brave face.'

'Jenny, you have no idea why they don't have kids.' Mandy kicked the kitchen door closed. She wished Jenny would just bugger off and leave her to get on with things. 'It's probably their choice. But really, it's none of your business.'

'I didn't mean anything by it, ' Jenny said, her cheeks flushing. 'But you can't help feeling a bit sorry for them, can you?'

'Yes, I can. Now if you'll excuse me, I need the loo.' Mandy rushed out of the kitchen and up the stairs. She locked herself in the bathroom and sat down on the side of the bath. She felt slightly pissed and knew she should have stuck to soft drinks. She took a few deep breaths and went back downstairs.

Mike had got the Trivial Pursuits out and organized two teams. He'd shuffled everyone around into different seats. Mandy found herself next to Rod.

'Right, Jenny, Ian, Mandy and Rod against us lot.' Mike gestured with his hand. 'Everybody got a drink? Yeah, okay, I'll start.'

As Mike read out the first question, Mandy felt Rod's hand on her knee. The tablecloth provided a good screen. She smiled and pressed her leg against his as Ian shouted out the answer. Rod knocked back his glass of wine and helped himself to another. He gestured the bottle at her. She shook her head. 'Are you driving?' she muttered. She'd seen him down three cans of lager and three large glasses of red.

'James dropped us off. We'll get a cab back. I fancied getting pissed for once in my life. Been a shit last few weeks.'

'Looks like Jenny does too.' Mandy raised an eyebrow as Jenny batted her lashes at Ian, giggling as he got the second question wrong. Rod's hand was caressing her thigh now. 'Be careful,' she mouthed. He had the devil in him tonight. She could see it in his eyes. His hand crept under her skirt, inching right to the top of her thigh. She caught her breath and tried to move her leg, but Rod held on fast. Mike looked at her and said, 'Mandy's turn.'

She'd bet her cheeks were as pink as Elaine's top and tried to concentrate on the question Mike was asking. It was in the entertainment category and she got it right.

'Rod, are you ready?' Mike looked down the table; everyone's eyes turned to Rod.

'Rod, stop it,' Mandy mouthed as he smiled drunkenly at her. She pushed at his hand but he still wouldn't move it. He looked at Mike, waiting for the question as Mike seemed to flick the card to the floor. Mandy couldn't tell whether it was a deliberate move or a genuine accident. He dropped to his knees. When he got up, clutching the card, his face white, her stomach turned over. 'Rod, stop it,' she whispered again, 'Mike saw you.' She was conscious of Elaine and Steve looking curiously at her.

'Stop what?' Rod looked at her wide-eyed.

'Mandy,' Mike said, throwing the card onto the table. 'Lounge, now. You too, Rod!'

Mandy got to her feet as Jenny said, 'What's going on? Why do you want Rod and Mandy in the lounge?'

‘Just wait here a minute, Jen,’ Mike said as Rod got unsteadily to his feet and followed Mandy out of the room.

Mandy could hear the others all talking at once. Their voices were echoing in her head and she felt she might pass out at any minute. She sat down on the sofa. Rod stood opposite the window, leaning against the radiator, an expression of mutiny in his eyes.

‘So!’ Mike closed the lounge door. ‘Who’s gonna tell me what’s going on?’

‘What do you mean?’’ Mandy said, chewing her lip. ‘There’s nothing going on.’

‘Don’t take me for a fool, Mandy. I’ve had my suspicions for weeks, but I was hoping I was wrong. Rod?’

Rod stared at the floor and shrugged. ‘Like Mandy said, there’s nothing going on.’

‘Nothing?’ Mike said calmly, his cheek twitching. ‘You call having your hand up my wife’s skirt, nothing?’

‘He didn’t,’ Mandy protested, knowing it was pointless. ‘He, err…’ she fell silent as Jenny popped her head around the door.

‘Can I come in now? What’s going on? Rod?’ She looked at him, her lips quivering. ‘Mike?’

‘He’s fucking my wife!’ Mike yelled, pulling her in by the arm and slamming the door shut.

‘What?’ Jenny’s face drained and she sat down heavily on the sofa. ‘Don’t be ridiculous, Mike. He wouldn’t. You can’t accuse him of that without any proof.’

‘Mike,’ Mandy said. ‘You’ve got it all wrong. We were mucking about. We’ve had too much to drink. Rod was only tickling my leg, that’s all.’

'Tickling your fucking leg! He was almost in your knickers! And if it's proof you want, Jenny, wait there.' Mike dashed out of the room. Mandy heard him running upstairs, drawers opening and cupboard doors banging. Then he was back, thrusting handfuls of stuff at Jenny. 'There's your proof. His phone number's all over that bill. Train tickets to Brighton. Why would she go down there if it wasn't to be with him? Bet you didn't know I'd got those, Mandy, eh?' he directed at her. 'Shouldn't leave your handbag lying around.'

Mandy stared at the other things Mike had thrown onto Jenny's lap. A packet of condoms; she'd missed them but thought she'd left them at Sue's. His diary, the one she'd found in his briefcase. He grabbed it back and waved it in the air.

'Dates,' he said, flicking through it. 'Loads of dates when I know they've been together.'

Mandy looked at Rod. He seemed shocked into silence and continued to stare at the floor.

'Rod. Tell me it's not true?' Jenny whispered. 'Please.'

He looked up then. 'It's true,' he muttered.

'But why? I thought you loved me. We always said we had the perfect marriage.'

'No, Jen. It was you who always said that. I just agreed to keep the peace.'

'You bastard!' She picked up a bottle that someone had left on a side table. It was half full of lager. She threw it at Rod who ducked. The bottle hit a framed print and smashed the glass, the lager dripping down the wall and behind the radiator. Mandy leapt up and ran to Rod who put his arm around her. He had a small cut on his ear; blood dripping onto his shoulder.

'Jenny, you've hurt him,' she yelled. She reached a tissue from the coffee table and held it to Rod's ear.

'I intended to,' Jenny shouted back. 'How could you, Mandy? How could you do this? I thought you were my friend. You're nothing but a slag!'

'Don't you dare call Mandy names,' Rod said. 'And as for the perfect marriage, you hardly even notice when I'm in the room, never mind anything else. I think the same goes for Mike. You've always taken Mandy for granted,' he directed at Mike. 'She deserves better.'

'Don't tell me how to treat my wife,' Mike said, too calmly. He clenched and unclenched his fists.

Jenny started to cry and retch at the same time. 'I'm going to be sick.' She put her hands to her mouth.

Mike flew out of the room and brought a bowl back with him. He held it as Jenny threw up, and then wiped her face with a tissue. 'Look what you've done to her,' he yelled at Rod. 'She deserves better than she's had from you. You're never there for her. Always swanning off somewhere. And I bet Mandy's not your only bit on the side. I know you of old, remember!' He stopped as someone tapped lightly on the door and opened it slightly.

Ian called out, 'Sorry to intrude, but we're off now. Just letting you know. We'll see ourselves out.'

'Sorry, Ian,' Mike apologised. 'We've a bit of a problem. See you again.'

'A bit of a problem! How embarrassing,' Jenny cried. 'Now everyone will know about this.'

Mandy shook her head. 'Not everybody gossips, Jenny.' She turned to Rod. 'So, this is it. What do we do now?'

'I want to go home,' Jenny cried her face all blotchy and her nose snotty. Tears streamed down her cheeks. 'Tell her it's a mistake, Rod. That you love me and won't be seeing her again.'

Rod shook his head. 'I can't do that, Jenny. I love Mandy. I want to be with her.'

'But the children, what about the children?'

'James and Ben are adults and Beth's not a little girl anymore.'

'But we need you, Rod, please. Don't do this to me.' She got up and clung to his arm. 'Please, let's go home. We can sort it out. We'll talk. I can forgive you. I don't want you to leave me. I couldn't bear it.'

'Jenny,' Mike touched her arm. 'Aren't you the least bit angry with him? Why are you so willing to forgive him?'

'Because he's all I've got,' she cried. 'I bet it was you made a play for him, Mandy. Didn't you? You encouraged him all along.'

'For fuck's sake, Jenny,' Mike said, clearly frustrated. 'The sun doesn't shine out of his arse. Show a bit of dignity. We should tell them both to get lost. They're welcome to each other. How long's it been going on?' he directed at Mandy.

'Since March,' she whispered, feeling so sick inside.

'I thought so.'

'March?' Jenny's mouth hung open. 'But it can't have. I'd have known if Rod was seeing her all that time. And he's been ill, remember. You're lying, Mandy.'

Mandy sighed and shook her head.

Rod nodded. 'March is right.'

Jenny flew at him and smacked him across the face. She ran her nails down his cheek and drew blood. She hauled herself at Mandy and grabbed her hair. Mandy screamed and Rod yanked Jenny off. He wrestled her to the sofa and pulled her into his arms where she cried heartbrokenly against his shoulder.

'Call a cab for us,' he yelled at Mike. 'I need to get her home.' He looked at Mandy, white-faced as Mike left the room. 'Fucking hell! I'll call you tomorrow,' he mouthed.

She nodded, too stunned to speak. What had she been expecting? That Mike and Jenny would give their blessing and wave them off as they skipped down the garden path to their happy new life? She'd no idea. But Jenny's hysterics had shocked her. Mike's calmness also scared the shit out of her. She was dreading being alone with him. She looked up as he came back into the room, his face pale, high colour spots on his cheeks and he looked totally defeated.

'Ten minutes,' he muttered. 'Go and wait in the hall. You can sit on the stairs. And you,' he pointed at Mandy. 'Get out of here. Go upstairs. I don't want you anywhere near him ever again.'

'But,' Mandy stuttered.

'Just go, Mand,' Rod said. 'I'll speak to you tomorrow.'

'You fucking won't,' Mike growled.

'But we have to sort things out,' Mandy cried. 'You can't tell me what to do. Who do you think you are?'

'The man you married! Now go.'

Jenny looked up, rubbing her face with her hand. 'There's nothing to sort out, Mandy. You had a fling, it's over. Rod's coming home with me. We love each other.'

'It was more than just a fling,' Mandy yelled. 'We planned a future. I love Rod more than anything. He loves me. Don't you?'

Rod nodded. 'You know I do. But I've got to get Jenny home. We need to talk. So do you and Mike. And I *will* call you tomorrow, no matter what he says. You can flatten me if you want to, Mike. I don't give a flying fuck to be honest.'

'Don't tempt me,' Mike yelled as a horn tooted outside. 'Now get out of my house. I don't want to see you or speak to you again. All those years of friendship, and you've wiped them out, Rod. I hope you're fucking proud of yourself.'

*

CHAPTER SEVENTEEN

Mandy ran upstairs and into the bedroom, tears streaming down her face. The dogs had been shut in here all night as Karen was terrified of them. They leapt up at her, whimpering, but she pushed them away, slammed the door and dashed to the window. Rod was helping Jenny into the back of the cab. Mandy opened the window and called his name. He turned, a look of despair on his face, and raised his hand.

'Tomorrow,' he mouthed and got in beside Jenny.

The cab pulled away. Mandy closed the window and drew the curtains. She felt sick; her legs like jellies. Her hands shook uncontrollably and she could hardly breathe. She couldn't believe what had happened. She flung herself onto the bed and cried into the duvet. Never in her wildest dreams did she think they'd ever get caught out. She'd imagined various scenarios, in which they told Mike and Jenny they were leaving, but only when they were ready, and not before David's cozy cottage awaited their arrival. She recalled Sue's words that Jenny and Mike wouldn't let them go easily. She heard footsteps on the stairs. Mike. She curled into a ball, dreading him opening the door.

He came into the room and sat down on the bed. 'Mandy,' he said quietly. 'Look at me, please.'

She rolled onto her back and wiped her eyes.

'Why, Mandy?'

No point in lying or sugar-coating the truth. He wasn't like Jenny and he wouldn't appreciate it. She shrugged. 'I'm sorry, Mike. I didn't mean to hurt you, but I fell in love with Rod. I am in love with him.'

‘And you honestly think he loves you? Forget it, Rod loves himself. I know him only too well. We go back to school days. He was my closest mate, and that’s what hurts like hell. No wonder the pair of you didn’t want to go to Malta. Looking for bloody excuses to get out of it all the time.’

‘I couldn’t face it, Mike. But Rod’s reason wasn’t just an excuse. He’d had his heart op…’ she stopped. He was shaking his head as though pitying her. ‘You don’t know him the way I do,’ she carried on. ‘He does love me.’ She choked on sobs. ‘We want to be together. We’ve just …’ She stopped before she blurted out something best kept to herself. ‘We’ve been through such a lot these last few months.’

‘And so have we. Do the last twenty-five years count for nothing?’

‘Of course they do. But we’ve grown apart. You know we have. You’ve never shown me that you wanted to make it right. We’ve been living almost separate lives for ages. The only time you bother to put on a caring show is when the girls are around or we’re entertaining. Other than that I might just as well be invisible.’

‘I never know what you expect from me,’ he said. ‘When I’ve shown you any affection you’ve rejected me. I can only take so much.’ He looked down at his hands. ‘I hate what you’ve done with him. I knew it was happening, well I had a feeling it was, but I can’t get my head around it.’ He reached out and touched her arm, but she moved away. ‘I still love you, Mandy. I think I’ll be able to forgive you in time. We’ll put this fling behind us. Patch things up. Move on.’

She stared at him, shaking her head. He simply didn’t get it. ‘My God, Mike, you’re turning into Jenny. I’d rather you rant and rave at me than tell me you’ll forgive me. It wasn't a fling. I don't want to patch things up, or put it behind us. It wouldn't work. It didn't work before. It'd be even worse now. You'd be constantly throwing the fact I've slept with Rod at me every time we have a row, you know you would.'

'I wouldn't. And don't say his name. I don't ever want to hear it in this house again. We can make it work if you'd put some effort in. We've a lot going for us, Mandy. The girls, Becky's boys, the new baby to look forward to. A lovely home. No money worries. I change your car for you every three years. You don't know when you're well off. You'd have nothing with him. He'd never be there for you. Look how Jenny's always alone. She's practically brought their kids up single handed.'

'That's not fair. He has to work away for better money. He works bloody hard. And apart from our family, everything else you mention's material stuff. I don't ask you to change my car. I can live without a new one. That's just you being snobby. Thinking people will look down on you if your car's over three years old. I'll manage with what I've got. I work hard myself, don't forget. I've put money into this place; it's mine as much as it's yours. But I can't stay here, Mike. You repress me; make me feel worthless at times. I've given up on trying to make you care. When Rod comes for me tomorrow I'm going with him.'

'Huh. You honestly think he'll turn up like a bloody knight on a white charger? Get real, Mandy. You won't see him again. He's had his fun, he's been found out. That's it. It's over. He'll be patching things up with Jenny now, begging her forgiveness. Then he'll piss off back to Brighton, leaving the poor cow at home, you in bits, and he'll move on to the next conquest. You're not his first affair and you won't be his last. The sooner you get your bloody head around that, the better for all of us.' He got to his feet and turned at the door. 'I'm right you know, you'll see. I'll speak to you tomorrow when you've had time to reconsider.'

As Mike closed the door Mandy lay back and stared at the ceiling, blinking back tears. She couldn't believe he'd been calm. But he might not be tomorrow. He'd probably tell her to leave. Throw her out on the streets. She recalled Jenny saying she suspected Rod of straying, but she could forgive him, as long as he didn't bring trouble home. Rod had sworn that he hadn't strayed for a long time and she believed him. The way he touched her, spoke to her, putting her on a pedestal, singing their song for her, always with such love in his eyes. They weren't the actions of a man just out for a bit of fun. He'd been foolish tonight, but that was down to alcohol. She shouldn't have sat next to him. Too much temptation. Rod didn't drink a lot. The amount he'd had tonight made him careless. When he called her tomorrow she would be ready to go with him. She didn't know when, she didn't know where, and at the moment she didn't care.

She'd need to pack a bag, enough things for a few days. She could come back for the rest of her stuff another time. Thank goodness Nicole was out for the night. At least she'd been spared that horrible scene. She'd have to speak to her girls tomorrow, explain what had gone on and hope to god it wouldn't stress Becky too much. She rubbed her head where Jenny had pulled her hair. It bloody well hurt. It was a wonder she hadn't yanked it out by the roots. But it was no more than she deserved. Rod's poor face had looked a mess as he left. She hoped the gouges from Jenny's nails wouldn't leave scars. What if she went crazy when he got her home? She might stick a knife in his back. He'd half joked that she'd do that if she found out about them. But what if she did? Anything could happen. She closed her eyes, but knew sleep would be impossible.

*

Rod handed Jenny a glass of water and sat down on the arm of the sofa opposite. She was quiet now, chewing her thumb, deadly pale but had a look on her face he couldn't fathom.

'Want to talk?' he ventured after several silent minutes ticked by. He lit a cigarette. She didn't even tell him to go outside and smoke it. It was almost like she'd shut down. Her eyes looked blank. He felt terrible, so guilty. With his dad's ramblings, about looking after her, buzzing around in his head, he tried to feel anything other than pity, but he couldn't, and certainly not love. He couldn't spend the rest of his life with the wrong woman; it would end up killing him. And it wouldn't be fair on her. She could be free to find someone who would love her as much as he loved Mandy. He took a deep breath. His chest felt tight for the first time in ages.

'Nothing to say is there?' she said quietly, startling him out of his thoughts. 'You made a silly mistake. But it's all over now.'

'Jen,' he began, 'it's not all over and it wasn't a mistake. I love Mandy. I want to be with her. I'm so sorry I've hurt you. I don't know what else to say.'

She shrugged and got to her feet. 'I'm sorry I scratched your face. Be sure to clean it and put some Savlon on. I'm going to bed now. Beth will be home soon. I don't want her to see me like this. You go to bed too. Sleep on it. You'll feel better by morning. You'll realise what a lucky escape you've had. Mandy could never love you like I do.'

'Sit down, Jen. I have to talk to you.' He pushed her gently back onto the sofa and sat beside her.

She looked expectantly at him, her eyes less blank now. He cleared his throat. 'I'm, err, going back to Brighton tomorrow. I know it's a day early, but there's no point in me sticking around. Dad left me a bit of money. I'll make sure you're okay. You can stay in the house. I don't want you to worry about having to sell it or anything.'

She frowned. 'Why on earth would we sell the house?'

'Jen, have you listened to anything I've said? I'm leaving you. Our marriage is over. I'll see you're okay for money and I'll talk to Beth before I go. Tell her what's happening.'

'Okay, Rod.' She got to her feet. 'Goodnight.'

He stared after her as she left the room. For fuck's sake, had she taken anything in? Now what? Maybe it would sink in overnight. Who knew? He wished he could call Mandy. Tell her to be ready to go with him tomorrow. With a bit of luck she would be. No matter what happened here, he had no choice other than to go back. He couldn't let the band down again. He'd like the option to work with them next summer and have Mandy join him for as long as she could leave the shop. It was better he was out of the way while Jenny got her head around things. Staying here wouldn't help her at all. He took his angina spray from his pocket and gave a quick blast under his tongue.

*

Mandy sat in the lounge, hugging a mug of tea. She stared at the stain on the wallpaper and the smashed glass on the framed print. The only physical signs of last night's nightmare. It was five am and she couldn't sleep. She'd tossed and turned until she could stand it no longer and got up, took a shower and came downstairs with the dogs, both now snoring on the rug. She'd thrown clothes and toiletries into a bag in case Rod wanted her to go with him. It was in the hall waiting. She'd half expected him to call her during the night. When he didn't she'd tormented herself with thoughts of him and Jenny making up in a frenzied passion. He wouldn't, surely? But she couldn't quite dismiss the thought. It insisted on lingering, tormenting her, and drove her to despair. She heard a door opening upstairs and then the shower running. Mike? Nicole? She'd have to face them soon enough. She needed to tell Nicole that she was leaving. Her phone rang out in her dressing gown pocket. It made her jump and she slopped tea on her leg. Her heart leapt. Rod!

'Mandy, are you okay, babe? What a nightmare! I've been desperate to call but I didn't want to make things any worse for you.'

'I'm okay. Same here, I've been dying to hear from you. What's happening?'

'I'm leaving her. Going back to Brighton as soon as I've spoken to Beth. Are you coming with me? I mean, do you want to, or have you decided to stay with Mike?'

Mandy's eyes filled with tears. Sobs filled her throat as she tried to speak. 'I'm coming with you, of course.'

'Thank, God. I'll be there as soon as I can.'

'I'll be waiting. I love you.'

'Love you too, babe.'

A movement by the door caught her eye. Mike.

'So, that's it? You're going with him? You're throwing everything away to be with a penniless womanizer? You'll regret it, Mandy.'

'I don't think I will.' Her voice was almost a whisper. 'Money doesn't matter to Rod and me and he isn't a womanizer. You're only saying that to hurt me.'

He shrugged. 'Suit yourself.' He came into the room and sat down. 'I'm giving work a miss today. Wait until he comes round. Then I can wish you both well.'

His voice was heavy with sarcasm. She shook her head. 'And you wonder why I'm going, why I don't want to stay with you. Being with Rod's like a breath of fresh air compared to…' she stopped as Nicole popped her head around the door.

'Mum, what do you mean? Where are you going?'

'Nicole, come here, love. I need to talk to you,' Mandy held out her arms.

Nicole came to sit beside her and Mandy held her close. 'I'm going away for a while,' she began. 'To Brighton with Rod. We, err, we want to be together. I'm leaving your dad, but I'm not leaving you girls. I want you to understand that.'

Nicole pulled back and stared at her as though she were mad. 'But you can't do that, Mum. Please, you can't leave Dad. I don't want to stay here without you. And you can't take Beth's dad away. What will Aunty Jen do?' Tears ran down Nicole's cheeks. 'Mum, please, you can't do it.'

'You satisfied now?' Mike said, getting up and pulling his sobbing daughter into his arms. 'And bear in mind, this is only the tip of the iceberg.'

Mandy felt sick. She put her head in her hands and cried.

*

'But, Dad,' Beth said, her lips trembling. 'Why are you doing this? Me and Mum, we need you.'

Rod lit his umpteenth cigarette since he got up. 'I can't stay here, Beth. Me and your mum, it doesn't work anymore. It hasn't for a long time. I'll be back to see you as often as I can. You won't even notice the difference. I'm hardly ever here anyway.'

‘But Nic’s mum. How could you, Dad? Nic’s my best mate. She’ll probably never speak to me again.’

‘Don’t cry, Beth,’ Jenny said, walking into the lounge. ‘Your dad’s only going back to work, love. He’ll be home in a few weeks.’

Beth stared at her mother. ‘He’s going off with Aunt Mandy, Mum. He’s going to be living with her. Dad, doesn’t she know? Haven’t you told her?’

Rod sighed. ‘Of course she knows. Don’t you, Jen? She’s in denial. Thinks all it takes is a good night’s sleep and everything will be fine. Well it’s not fine. I’m going to Brighton and I’m taking Mandy with me. In a few months we’ll be moving into a cottage together. It’s all arranged. Jen, you’ve got to get your head around this. Our marriage hasn’t worked for a long time.’

Jenny stared at him. Her face crumpled and she started to cry. It was a strange cry. A high-pitched keening sound that seemed to come from deep within.

‘Jenny.’ He put his arm out and she clung to him.

‘Don’t leave me, please don’t leave me. I can’t bear it, Rod. I love you.’

Rod extricated himself from her grasp. ‘I have to go. It’s best all round.’ He went into the hall and picked up his car keys and leather jacket. His bags were already in the car. ‘Beth, I’ll call you later. Bye.’ As he tried to open the front door, Jenny threw herself onto the floor and grabbed his legs. She was screaming and crying and clawing at him, begging him not to leave her. He looked at Beth in despair. ‘Help me.’

‘Mum, please, come on,’ Beth said, trying to get Jenny to her feet. ‘Let him go.’

Jenny turned and clung to Beth, sobbing wildly.

‘Just go, Dad. And don’t come back. I don’t want to see you again.’ Beth pushed him out of the door and slammed it.

*

Rod sat in his car on the drive, shaking. Why had he ever thought it would be easy? Just tell them it was over and he and Mandy would drive away into the sunset to their lovely new lives. Shit, it was a nightmare and had only just begun. What the fuck would James and Ben say? He'd have to call them tonight. He hoped Mandy was ready and then they could just get away. He lit another cigarette and drove to Mandy's place. Fuck! Mike was still home. He usually went to work earlier than this. Mind you, after last night, he probably couldn't face work today. And no doubt they'd had the same scenario here with Nicole as he'd had with Beth. He didn't fancy seeing Mike again, but he wasn't such a wimp that he'd just toot his horn and wait for Mandy to come out to him.

He rang the bell. Mandy let him in and told him to wait in the hall for a minute with her bag. She went into the lounge and closed the door. He picked up the bag as the dogs sniffed curiously at his feet. He could hear raised voices. The lounge door opened and Mike came to stand in front of him. Rod looked away from his piercing gaze. He could hear Mandy speaking quietly to Nicole. She was crying when she eventually came out of the room.

Mike was still staring. Rod felt uncomfortable.

'We're off now, Mike,' Mandy said. 'I'll call Nicole later. And I'll speak to Becky and Louise later too and tell them what's happened.'

'Not before I speak to them, you won't,' he said, still staring at Rod. 'I'll tell them what sort of a mother they've got. You'll be lucky if they speak to you again.'

'Mike, please. Don't use the girls like that. I love my daughters, but I also love Rod. I'm entitled to be happy, you know.'

‘Yeah, sure. Both of you are. At the expense of everybody else’s happiness. Oh, but I mustn’t forget, you two have got the monopoly on love, haven’t you? Well go on; piss off, the pair of you. I don’t ever want to see you again. See how long your love lasts when all your problems come home to roost. If you think I’ll make it easy for you to get a divorce, you can think again.’

Rod gritted his teeth. He’d heard enough. He just wanted to get Mandy out of there before he was tempted to punch Mike in his sneering gob. ‘Come on, love.’ He took her hand. ‘Let’s go.’

*

‘Fucking hell!’ Rod started the engine. He turned to kiss Mandy, but could see Mike glaring at them from the doorstep. He drove around the corner, pulled up and took her in his arms. He kissed her and she clung to him. ‘It can only get better now,’ he said. ‘That’s the worst bit out of the way. Them knowing and the actual leaving.’

She shook her head. ‘No, Rod. I think the worst is yet to come. I hope we’re strong enough to deal with it. Have you told James and Ben?’

‘I’ll call them later. Although no doubt Beth will be on the job now.’

‘I have to tell Becky and Louise. I’m dreading it. Nic was in bits.’

‘So was Beth. If I didn’t have to go back down south it would have been easier all round.’

‘We’d have had to leave home today though. At least we’ll have a roof over our heads for a while until we sort out what we’re going to do. I mean, there’s the shop to think about, too. I’ll lose loads of business at this rate. I’ll need to speak to Sarah later. Tell her not to take any more orders for now until I get back. Her and

Carol can finish what's already on the go. That'll bring enough in to pay their wages.'

'I'll need to pay the lads what I owe them in back rent when we get down there. But at least we can use Dad's money to live off for a while. Would you rather not come with me? Maybe stay at Sue's or Dee's for now?'

'No, the shop can wait. I need to be with you, Rod. I can't bear the thought of you down there on your own.'

'Let's get going then. We'll stop for breakfast in an hour or so.'

*

Rod's phone rang out as they sat in the services, sharing a plate of toast and pot of coffee. Neither had much appetite, but he insisted they'd feel better after a bite to eat.

'Beth,' he said, looking at the screen. 'I'd better take it.'

Mandy nodded. 'Of course.'

Beth was yelling and crying. He struggled to understand what she was saying, but he got the gist. Jenny had locked herself in the bathroom with her sleeping tablets and a bottle of vodka. Beth couldn't get the door open and her mum was no longer crying, just silent. 'Shit! Have you called your brothers and an ambulance?' He felt himself shaking and looked across at Mandy whose face drained as he spoke. 'Okay, Beth, calm down sweetheart. I'm on my way.'

'What?' Mandy said as he jumped to his feet. 'Who's hurt? What's happened?'

He quickly explained. 'We've gotta go back. I can't believe she'd try anything like this. Jen's always so sensible. I didn't even know that she took sleeping tablets. My God, Mandy, what the fuck have we started?'

Mandy took his keys. 'You're in no fit state to drive. Call Beth and keep her on the line. I'll get us home.'

*

Rod sat in the hospital waiting room, his arms around a sobbing Beth. They were joined by James and Ben who demanded to know what had happened. Rod explained as Beth sobbed even louder.

'You were leaving her?' James shook his head, an incredulous expression on his pale face. 'Hell, Dad, she can't handle life without you. She needs you.'

'I know,' Rod said quietly. 'But it's not right. We live like strangers. I don't make her happy. I'm no good for her.'

'But she loves you,' Ben said. 'Dad, you can't walk out on her.'

'I came back, didn't I?' Rod snapped and then relented when he saw Ben's hurt expression. 'I'm sorry, son. My head's all over the place. Let's just hope she'll be okay. We'll talk about what's gonna happen later.' He looked at his watch. 'They've had her in there for ages. She was unconscious. God knows what they're doing.'

'I'll go and ask someone,' James said and disappeared down the corridor, Ben on his heels.

'Dad?' Beth pulled on his arm. 'You are staying with us now, yeah? I know you have to go away to work, but you could take Mum to Brighton with you. I don't want her left on her own. What if she does it again?'

Rod's heart sank to his feet. Beth was right. Jenny topping herself was the last thing he needed on his conscience. He felt anger rise inside as well as pity for her. She seemed determined to trap him again, like she'd done just over twenty-five years ago when she'd lied and told him she was on the pill. He felt sorry for her, but at the moment, apart from hoping she'd make a full recovery, he felt nothing but hatred towards her. He knew he shouldn't feel like this. She could have died, she was the mother of his kids, but he couldn't help himself. He needed to call Mandy. She'd dropped him at the hospital and told him she'd go to Sue's until she heard from him.

'I'll be back in a minute,' he told Beth. 'I need a fag. Come and get me if they say we can see her.'

*

'I've put a spoonful of sugar in,' Sue said. 'It's good for shock.'

'Thanks, Sue.' Mandy took the proffered mug and grimaced at the sweetness of the coffee. 'I'm sorry to land on you, but I've nowhere else to go. I didn't even know if you'd be here or still at your brother's.' She'd given Sue a quick explanation as to why she was here and driving Rod's car. 'How are you feeling?'

'Not too bad. I felt ready to come home for a while. So what exactly happened last night? How did Mike find out about you and Rod?'

Mandy could feel her cheeks heating as she went into detail about last night's fiasco. 'It shouldn't have happened. If only I'd sat somewhere else, out of Rod's way. If only he hadn't had too much to drink. I suppose I could go on and on.'

'Do you think Mike planned the seating deliberately, so that you ended up next to Rod, just to see if anything untoward went on?'

'I wouldn't put it past him. It was the only seat left when I went back into the room. I don't know what's going to happen now. I hope to God Jenny pulls through. Rod stayed on the phone with Beth until the ambulance arrived and that was the last update. I presume Jenny was unconscious. Beth couldn't get a response from the bathroom.' She felt tears welling. 'Rod's gonna have to stay with her now. She might try it again. We couldn't have that on our conscience.'

Sue shook her head. 'Oh, Mandy. I feel a bit sorry for her, but what a bloody manipulator she is. Should you call Mike? Let him know.'

'Nic might have spoken to Beth. I'm sure he will know by now. Do you think I should call him?'

Sue nodded and passed the house phone over. She left the room while Mandy spoke to a clip-toned Mike.

'I already know about Jen,' he said. *'I hope the pair of you are satisfied now. The damage you've done to our families is unbelievable. If Jenny doesn't pull through, how are you going to live with it?*

'I don't know,' she mumbled. 'But if you're trying to make me feel worse than I already do, you're succeeding, Mike.'

'Good. No more than you deserve. Where are you now?'

'At Sue's. Rod's at the hospital.'

'And so he should be. No doubt he'll go back home when they discharge Jen.'

'Maybe.'

'Well don't get the notion you can come back here. I don't want you back. You'll have to stay at Sue's.'

'You can't stop me coming back. It's my home.'

'You didn't think that this morning when you were swanning off to your Brighton love-nest.''

He hung up, leaving Mandy with tears streaming down her face. She'd wanted to ask if Becky and Louise had been told.

'Sue, I've finished. He hung up on me, said I can't go back to the house,' she sobbed, as Sue came back into the room. 'I wanted to see the girls, or at least to ask if they're okay. He'll have been poisoning their minds against me.'

Sue slipped an arm around her shoulders. 'I'll call the girls and ask them to come here later. You can talk to them properly then without him interfering. And you can stay here with me tonight and for as long as you need to. Until you speak to Rod, you're in limbo. You're still a bit fragile as well. It's not even two weeks since your miscarriage.'

Mandy nodded. 'Thank you. What would I do without you?'

Sue smiled. 'The same goes for you. I need your support too.'

Mandy's phone rang. She grabbed it from the coffee table. 'It's Rod. How is she?' Her voice wavered as she spoke.

'No idea,' he said. *'We still haven't been allowed in to see her. Christ knows what they're actually doing. It's been ages.'*

'But she's still alive?'

'Yes, thank God. The kids are all here. Are you okay? I'm so sorry, babe. Never in my wildest dreams could I have imagined this happening. Beth assumes I'll be going home with them and that'll be it. I don't wanna do that. But what if she tries it again? I tell you, Mandy, I feel so bloody stressed. I had to use my angina spray again when I came out to talk to you. That's twice now in the last few hours.'

Mandy swallowed hard, fighting back tears. 'Rod, if you feel for one moment that Jenny will try it again, then there's no choice. You have to go home. We'd never be able to live with the guilt. It would destroy our relationship. I'd rather we part as friends now and try and get on with our lives.'

'Whatever happens, Mandy, I'll never stop loving you. You'll always be the one for me. You know that, don't you?'

'Yes,' she whispered, tears falling down her cheeks. 'The same goes for me. I'll never stop loving you, Rod.'

He was silent for a moment. *'I suppose I'd better go back inside. Maybe they'll let us see her now. I'll get James to drop me at Sue's later to collect my car. Will you still be there?'*

'Yes. I'm staying with Sue for a while. Mike told me not to come home.'

'Oh, babe, I'm so sorry. This is my fault. All because I couldn't hold my bloody drink.'

'See you later, Rod. Good luck.' She couldn't bear to hear him finish with, "I love you, babe," and ended the call.

*

Rod followed Beth and his sons into the small room where Jenny was propped up on pillows, her face pale and her hair lank on her shoulders. A faint smell of vomit and disinfectant lingered and turned his stomach. She was attached to an IV drip. Her face lit up as she looked at him and there was a momentary smug glint in her eyes, but it vanished as quickly as it had come.

'Rod, I knew you'd come back to me.' Her lips quivered and her eyes filled with tears as the kids crowded around the bed, hugging and kissing her.

He stood back, feeling repulsed and sick. She held out her hand. He took it and squeezed it gently. She felt cold and he had to remind himself that she could have died and that was his fault. He forced a smiled, tried to make an effort. 'How are you feeling?'

She put her hand up to her neck. 'My throat feels really sore. They pumped my stomach and I've been very sick. But I'm okay. Err, kids, would you leave me and your dad alone for a few minutes, please.'

James shepherded Ben and Beth out and closed the door.

'Why did you do it, Jen?' Rod felt anger rising again. 'What the fuck did you think you were playing at? Beth was beside herself.'

'I didn't want you to leave me,' she cried. 'I couldn't cope, thinking of you with Mandy.'

'So you thought taking the selfish way out was the answer? You honestly think that we've got a cat in hell's chance of patching things up now?'

'But you must care.' She stared at him. The smug glint was back. 'Why else would you come back?'

'For the kids. I thought their mother had killed herself. How did you think that would make me feel? Or them?'

'I didn't think,' she said quietly. 'I was distraught. I just wanted to sleep until it was all over and you came back.'

He shook his head. 'I haven't got a choice, have I? You've got me well and truly by the balls!'

Before she could respond a doctor came into the room. 'Mrs Davies. How are you feeling now?' He turned to Rod without waiting for a reply. 'We'll keep your wife in overnight as a precaution. She'll be discharged in the morning. An appointment will be made for her to see a psychiatrist who'll assess her needs.'

Jenny looked aghast. 'I'm not going mad you know. He was leaving me. I couldn't stand it.'

The doctor nodded. 'Even so, Mrs Davies, you tried to take your own life. We take that sort of thing very seriously. You obviously need help.'

'Rod, tell him I won't do it again. I'll go and see my own doctor when I get home. I don't want to stay here.' She tried to get out of bed and the drip stand wobbled. Rod caught hold of it. 'Take me home, Rod, please. I'll be fine.'

He held up his hands. 'You stay here until they say you're okay to leave. I don't want the responsibility of you at home tonight.'

The doctor nodded. 'Your husband's right. You'll feel groggy for a few hours and may end up falling. You're dehydrated and we need to get fluids back into you.'

Rod sat down on a chair next to the bed as the doctor left. What he was about to say made him want to run screaming from the room. But say it, he had to. 'Now listen to me, Jen. I'll come and collect you tomorrow as soon as they say it's okay. I'll need to get straight off to Brighton and you'll be coming with me then you can't pull another stunt like this. Make sure you get a shower and wash your hair later. You don't smell too great. Don't take it as an insult,' he said as she frowned. 'I'm not sitting for hours in a car with you stinking of puke!'

Her face lit up. 'Am I really going with you? Oh, Rod, that'll be great. I'll need clothes and toiletries. It'll be like a nice little holiday for us.'

'Beth will sort stuff out for you and bring it tonight. And Jen, you're coming with me because we need to talk very seriously. It's not a holiday. Don't get any ideas. I'll be working most of the time. I'll go and find the kids now and grab a taxi. I need to go and get my car.'

'Where is your car?'

'Mandy's got it. She's at Sue's waiting for me. She dropped me off, but didn't feel it was right to hang around here.'

'But it's over with Mandy now. Isn't it? We're back together again.'

He stared at her. Was she deliberately playing dumb? Or did she genuinely not get it? 'I'll see you later.' He left the room feeling like he could punch someone. Instead he went to find his kids. They were in the café. He told them what he was doing.

'I'll run you for your car, Dad,' James offered.

'It's okay, son. I was going to ask you. But I need some space; a bit of time to get my head around things. I'll walk down to the taxi rank in town and grab a cab from there. I'll see you all back here later.'

*

Mandy stared down at the floor, trying hard not to cry again as Rod sat beside her and told her of his plans for the next few days. Plans that were so different to the ones they'd made early this morning.

'I understand,' she said, reaching for his hand. 'It's not going to be easy for you.'

He raised an eyebrow. 'That's an understatement. Jed and the lads think that you're my wife. I don't know what the fuck I'm going to say to them. Whatever, it'll have to be when she's out of earshot. Not only that, she thinks I'm sharing a flat and a bedroom, not a bloody big house.'

'Tangled webs,' Mandy whispered. 'I can't bear the thoughts of her in our room - all the wonderful times we've had up there. It'll taint your memories.'

'I know. I don't want it either. But I've got no choice. I'll sleep on the floor or downstairs on a sofa. I'm only working four days and off Wednesday and Thursday so I'll bring her home and then go back on my own. Hopefully she won't pull another stunt like that. I know she's devastated and I feel terrible about that, but even so… I'll have to get Ben to stay with Beth. I don't want to leave her alone. She's really shocked by what Jenny did.'

'Poor Beth. My girls are coming over late afternoon. I need to talk to them. They'll want answers and I don't really have any.'

'Do you want to go back to Mike?'

She shrugged. 'No, but like you, I haven't really got a choice. I can't stay here for ever. Oh, Rod, why has it come to this? I so want to be with you.'

Rod pulled her into his arms and cried with her. 'We'll be together one day. I promise you. It's a big ask, but will you wait for me?'

She nodded through her tears. 'I'm not going anywhere without you.'

*

CHAPTER EIGHTEEN

'Wait in the car for a few minutes,' Rod said, pulling up outside the Brighton house. 'I need to check with the lads that it's okay for you to stay. We're a bit pushed for space and it'll mean having to swap rooms. I'll see if Jed will let us have his big bedroom for a few nights.'

Jenny stared at him. 'Well you obviously didn't have trouble with rooms when she came to stay. So why is it such a problem when you bring your wife?'

'Shut it, Jen.' He got out of the car and let himself in. No way was he prepared to talk about Mandy with her. During the journey she'd gone on and on, desperate for details. Wanting to know how many times they'd slept together, where they'd planned to live. From her initial denial she'd gone into overdrive and it was doing his head in. They'd stopped twice at the services and both times he'd called Mandy from the safe confines of the gents. Speaking to her and hearing the sadness in her voice, he really felt as though his heart had been ripped out. He also had to remind himself that Jenny must be feeling similar pain, but it was hard to remain tolerant.

Jed greeted him from the kitchen. 'Hi, mate. How you doing? Glad to have you back. We've missed you. How's your lovely missus?'

Rod sighed. He sat down at the table and accepted a mug of coffee. He told Jed what had happened, his voice wavering as he explained how he'd had to leave Mandy behind and bring his real wife instead. 'So will you cover for me and pretend the top room is yours and then she won't give me too much earache? I'll say I was sharing with Jim.'

Jed patted his shoulder. 'Bloody hell, Rod, all that on top of losing your old man! You poor sod. I hope Mandy's okay and that you get it sorted soon. Leave it with me, I'll explain to the others.'

'You'd better tell Penny, too,' Rod said. 'Because Jenny will have to come to the gigs. Can't leave her alone at the moment. And, Jed, I can't possibly sing Fast Movin' Train, I couldn't bear it.'

'I understand. We'll sub it.' Jed gave a wry grin. 'What about Lyin' Eyes instead.'

Rod half smiled. 'Very droll. I'll dump our bags in the hall and take her for a quick walk around The Lanes so that it looks as though you're getting the room ready. I'd put clean bedding on the week I left. It'll do. Will you whiz up and open the window.'

'Go on, bugger off, I'll see to it.'

*

Jenny stared after Jed's girl as she sashayed across the room to the bar. Rod knew that look. It was one of disapproval. She'd turned her nose up as they walked into the Majestic Club, complained about sitting alone while he set up his drums that Mitch had dropped off. He was so thrilled to be reunited with his kit that Jenny's moans couldn't dampen his few moments of pleasure. They'd had a strange day today. He'd tried talking to her about the future, told her he wanted a divorce. She was back in denial mode again and refused to discuss it, said she'd never agree and that he'd soon realise he'd made a mistake. Last night he'd slept on the landing on a camp bed Jed had found in the hall cupboard. He'd told Jenny he wasn't sharing the double bed. He couldn't handle it. There'd been tears and recriminations. He'd stayed firm and determined and checked on her every hour, but she'd slept soundly.

'She's young enough to be his daughter!' Jenny said, breaking his thoughts.

'She is. But so what? He's besotted with her, and she loves him. It works for them and it's nothing to do with you.'

'I know. But it's not very nice. How would you feel if Beth went out with someone your age?'

'Penny's a bit older than Beth, but if a guy made Beth happy and took care of her, his age wouldn't bother me. You need to change your outlook on things. You're far too narrow. I see everything in this job, couples from all walks of life. Anyway, quit criticising others and try and enjoy yourself tonight. How long is it since you've seen me play?'

She shrugged. 'Years. You haven't played local for a long time.'

'Would it have made a difference? You hardly ever came to gigs anyway. Now you can watch me earn that money you spend so easily!' He shouldn't dig at her, but couldn't seem to help himself. She was still pale and had told him she was tired and would rather stay at the house than come out. But he was taking no chances. Nor was she having any alcohol. The hospital had said not to after prescribing anti-depressants on her discharge. They'd also told him an appointment would be made for her to have counselling. He knew she was fragile, but she felt like a rope around his neck that was strangling the life out of him.

'I'm going up to the dressing room,' he said as Penny arrived back with a tray of drinks. 'Pen'll look after you.' He took a glass of orange juice from the tray and placed it in front of Jenny. He winked at Penny who gave him a slight nod of understanding and a sympathetic smile. 'Just need to put my clothes on hangers.' His stage clothes were a bit crumpled as they'd been in the bag since he'd dumped them at the house the night his dad took ill. They could have done with a wash, or at least an iron running over them, but they'd have to do

Upstairs he called Mandy. She told him that she and Sue were watching a video of a Queen concert. Sue had taped it ages ago but never got round to watching.

'Have you been drinking?' he asked, smiling. It was good to hear her sounding more relaxed than the last time he spoke to her. 'You sound a bit squiffy.'

'Yes, we've had a bottle of wine with a pizza. I needed to chill. I'm missing you. The girls have been to see me again.'

'How are they?'

'Okay. At least they still want to know me. They've talked to each other and told me they understand how I feel. They've agreed their dad could have made more effort in the past. Nic said he wants me home now he's calmed down. He promised to change and said we need to talk again. I'm going tomorrow for Sunday lunch. I don't want to go back to him, Rod. But I can't stay at Sue's forever and there's nowhere else to go.'

'I'm so sorry for this mess. It's agony for both of us. I'm missing you like crazy. She's sitting downstairs with Penny. They all know, by the way and they're covering for me.'

'That's good of them.' She was silent for a moment. *'Err, I've been thinking today and I've come up with a plan. See if you like it. When you come home it's only for short spells, so you can handle that for a bit longer. I know you said you might do something more local but that was for us, not her. So try and get another contract out of the area, maybe even renew with Timeless, for a*

while anyway, until you get going solo. I'll move into David's on my own when it's ready. Then I'll be free to come away with you whenever possible and you can spend some nights with me at the cottage when you've got time off. You could tell her you weren't coming home for whatever reason. But the thing is, *she* can *stay married, because knowing Jen she'll be more bothered about what people will say than anything else. She'll hate being the dumped one. She can keep her status until it dawns on her that you really do want out.'*

He was quiet while he took in what she was suggesting. 'Bloody hell, Mand, you've thought it out well. I'll pay half the rent and bills. Hopefully there'll come a time when she'll tell me to piss off. That way it'll be her choice and she can hold her head up and tell everyone she chucked me out. Is that what you're trying to say?'

'Yeah. She might cope better that way. I'll go back home for the time being. But I'll tell Mike that I want a divorce, not because of you, but because I've had enough.'

'He'll still blame me.'

'No doubt. But he needs to look to himself for some of the blame. I'll tell him that too, but whatever, he won't make divorce an easy option.'

'Neither will Jen. But we don't need it to be together, only if we want to marry sometime in the future. I'd better go back now and make sure she's okay. She was pulling her Mary Whitehouse face at Jed and Pen's relationship. I feel so much better for talking to you. I'm actually looking forward to playing now. I'll close my eyes and imagine you sitting out there, watching me.'

'I'll be there in spirit, Rod. I love you.'

‘Love you too, babe. I’ll call you before the second spot.’

*

‘I’m not giving you a divorce, Mandy. I’m willing to try and make our marriage work. If you want a divorce you’ll have to wait for as long as it takes.’ Mike sat back on the sofa, clutching a tumbler of whisky.

Mandy shrugged. It was exactly what she expected. Well she was quite prepared to walk out with nothing when she was ready. She hadn’t the energy to argue. They’d had quite a pleasant family lunch. Becky and her partner had taken the children home now. Louise and Nicole had gone out, so it was just the two of them. She’d told him coming home was temporary and that in time she’d be looking for somewhere else to live.

‘You admitted to the girls that you’ve not treated me very nice and that you’ll change. But both you and I know that isn’t going to happen, Mike. Okay, you might for a week or two, and then you’ll be back to your old ways.’

‘Suit yourself,’ he said. ‘You won’t know unless you give it a try. What’s the score with lover boy? Beth told Nic he’s taken Jen to Brighton. She also said that Jen was hoping they’d patch things up and start afresh. Told you he’d let you down, didn’t I?’

‘You did, ‘ Mandy said, gritting her teeth. She was so tempted to smack him across his smug face. ‘Seems you were right after all. Good luck to them. One thing though, I know we can’t patch things up. Jenny would forgive Rod anything, but you wouldn’t forgive me. She’ll sweep it under the carpet and pretend it never happened. But you’d never let me forget.’

She felt brave enough to argue her corner because Rod had spoken to her earlier and told her to hang in. He’d be seeing her on Wednesday when he brought

Jenny home. She told him she'd stay at the shop after closing time if he could make it. She couldn't wait. She got to her feet and gave Mike what she hoped was a determined smile. 'Right, I'm off. I'll stay at Sue's again tonight but I'll be back here after work tomorrow. Will you want anything to eat? I'll need to shop if you do. Or maybe we can grab a takeaway when you get home.'

'I'm going out straight from work tomorrow,' he said. 'Curry with the lads from the office.'

'Fine, I'll go and see Dee and have something to eat with her then. Catch up with you soon.'

*

'So, when do you think it will be ready?' Mandy asked. She and Dee were sitting in the lounge, relaxing after enormous portions of tuna pasta bake, washed down with a nice glass of red. David had gone out to play snooker.

'David reckons it'll be another couple of months,' Dee replied. 'Are you sure you can stand living alone?'

'Well you did it for years and Sue does. I'll be fine. I'll make it my own cosy little nest. I need the space to get myself together, Dee. My head's completely mashed. I'm dreading going back home, but if I can fix a date in my mind for leaving, it'll help me cope better.'

'And how will things work with Rod? She's going to be watching his every move.'

'I know, but I'm sure he'll manage to spend some time with me. He's agreed to pay half the rent and bills. I'll be free to join him wherever he's working without me having to keep making excuses about where I'm going. It's the best of a bad job for now.'

*

'What the fuck's been going on here?' Rod demanded as he and Jenny arrived home on Wednesday afternoon.

The lounge looked like a doss house. Lager cans and overflowing ashtrays littered the coffee table. CD's lay scattered all over the floor and filthy sleeping bags adorned the sofa. The smell of unwashed bodies and cannabis hung heavily in the air. Rod opened both sides of the bay window to let in air as Jenny wrinkled her nose and gagged. There was no sign of life. Beth would be at college no doubt. But this mess wouldn't be down to her. This was Ben's shit.

Jenny's face fell as she surveyed her normally immaculate lounge. 'What a mess. Looks like Ben's had a party. He's so thoughtless. He knew we were due home today. He could at least have cleaned up.'

'Ben!' Rod roared up the stairs. Silence. 'Bet he's working,' he said, walking back into the lounge. 'Probably thought he'd get his pub shift over and clean up when he got back. Lazy little sod! You sit down, Jen. I'll get a bin bag.'

'I'll get one,' Jenny said as the front door opened and Ben strolled in, looking as though he hadn't a care in the world.

'Hi,' he greeted them. 'How's things? You feeling better now, Mum?'

'Yes, thank you. What's been going on here?'

'Ah, yeah, didn't think you'd be back this early. Had a couple of mates over for a few drinks. Sorry 'bout the mess. I'll clean it up now.'

'The place stinks,' Rod said. 'Get those filthy sleeping bags out of here. Shove 'em in the garage for now. They're bloody rancid. Where was Beth while you and your manky mates were getting pissed and stoned?'

'In her room,' Ben said. 'We had a fight; she was giving me earache about having people in.'

'And she was right,' Rod yelled. 'Do you ever think about anybody other than yourself, Ben? What if things had got out of hand? Beth's a vulnerable young girl. Anything could have happened. I leave you in charge for a few days and you turn the place into a dump. Clean this lot up and then you can clear off back to Tanya.'

Ben shuffled his feet and looked down at the floor. 'Err, we split up. I've moved back in here. Nowhere else to go. Sorry, Mum, been sleeping in your fancy guest room 'cos I let my mates kip down here. I was hoping you'd say I could stay and have my old room back.'

Rod rolled his eyes. Fuck. The one thing he'd been looking forward to was a couple of good night's sleep in his own room before the long drive back to Brighton.

Jenny's cheeks flushed pink. 'Erm, that's your dad's room now. You'll have to make things up with Tanya or find a flat. There's no room here for you.'

'Yeah, but you and Dad are sorted now. He'll be sleeping in your room, surely? And I can't go back to Tan, her ex is out of nick and she's back with him. I've been warned not to go near her.'

'Oh well, that's just fucking great!' Rod exclaimed. 'The local thug gets out and everybody else's life is tipped upside down. Have you asked James if you can flat share with him?'

'He won't want me in his poncey flat,' Ben smirked. 'Anyway, his bird stays over most nights. I'd cramp his style.'

Rod held up his hands. 'Right, get this shit tip sorted. You can sleep on the sofa for a week and then I want you out. That should give you time to find a flat. And don't bring any of your mates back here again. Do you hear me?'

'Yeah, loud and clear.'

'Right, I'm off to town to drop my prescription in at Boots,' Rod said. 'Make your mother a cup of tea after you've slung the sleeping bags outside. Jesus, I've slept in some bloody flea pits when I've been on the road in my younger days, but I don't think I've ever smelt anything as bad as those.'

'I'll come into town with you,' Jenny said, moving swiftly towards the door.

Rod shook his head. 'No, you won't.' He couldn't handle another minute of her wittering down his ear. 'I need some peace. I'll see you later.'

Jenny's lips trembled. 'Promise you won't go and see Mandy.'

'She'll be working,' he snapped. 'Give me some fucking space, Jen. I can't take much more.' He stormed out of the house and slammed the door. He sat in the car for a few minutes to compose himself and lit a cigarette. Jesus, he'd just about had enough. Mandy would be locking up in half an hour. He couldn't wait to hold her again. He started the car, drove around the corner and called her.

*

Mandy curled herself tightly around Rod as he sat in the old armchair. She breathed in the scent of him, ran her hands over his body, kissed him and held him as tight as she could while he did likewise. She wished they could make love properly but she was still suffering the after effects of her miscarriage and didn't feel quite ready yet. It was agonizing to know he had to go back to Brighton soon and she couldn't go with him. She had to keep thinking positively about their future, making her plans to move into the cottage. That would keep her going for the next few months. Dee had kindly lent her a word processor. She hadn't a clue how to type, but she was determined to give it a try.

‘You know those notes I made in Brighton, about the sixties?’ she began. ‘Well until we can be together, that’s going to be my project. Dee’s going to teach me how to type and I’ll have a bash at writing that article. It’ll give me something to do. I can shut myself away from Mike and just get cracking. This place isn’t doing too well. I’ve lost customers with taking such a lot of time out this year. I’m only just scraping by at the moment. To be honest Rod, I’ve lost all interest. I might close it down soon. I can still take on commissions and use the big loft room at David’s to work in. That way I’ll have no shop rent and rates to pay and no staff wages. So I’ll still be able to earn a living, but what I thought was, if I learn to type I could maybe get another job in an estate agents or something.’

‘Hmm, you could, but then you’d be a lot more tied than you are now and you wouldn’t be able to come away with me as often.’

‘Oh God, yes, I never thought of that. But I think I’ll definitely close the shop down, or sublet it. If I do that then the landlords won’t hold me to the end of the lease for the rent. Every penny I earn will be mine to live off then. I’ll still learn to type though, so I can do my article properly. That thing prints pages out as well.’

Rod smiled. ‘Good idea. Keep you out of trouble. I thought what you’d written was very informed. You should seriously think about doing something on the local music scene. Try making it into a book like I suggested and I’ll get you some interviews with the old band members.’

‘I’ll see. I need to walk before I can run.’ Mandy smiled and ran her hand down his cheek. ‘Your scratches are healing. Don’t think you’ll have scars.’

'Good. Vicious so and so, wasn't she? I suppose it was no more than I deserved.' He looked at his watch. 'Shit, it's gone seven. I'd better head back. She'll think I've got lost. I told her I was dropping my prescription into Boots. She asked me to promise not to come and see you.'

'And?'

'I told her to give me some space. She'll guess I'm here. But she'll pretend I'm not. I have a feeling she may call you soon or even come in here. Ignore her calls, get the others to answer and tell her you're out. If she comes in, well I don't know what to suggest, babe.'

'Don't worry. I'll tell her I haven't seen you or spoken to you. You'd better go now in case she's out looking for you.'

'Can I see you tomorrow?'

'It'll have to be lunchtime. I've got a busy day and a fitting after work.'

'I'll do my best. I'll call you one way or the other. Love you, babe.'

'Love you too, Rod.'

*

Rod woke startled from a deep sleep. What the hell was that bang? He sat up as the noise came again. What the fuck was Ben up to now? Crashing and banging around. Why couldn't he come in from work quietly and show a bit of consideration? He glanced at the clock on the bedside table. 3 AM. He frowned. Bit late for him finishing his pub shift. Must have gone on somewhere else. The sound of breaking glass had him leaping up and pulling on his dressing gown over T-shirt and boxers. He went out onto the landing and was met by a worried looking Beth and Jenny.

'What's going on?' he asked.

‘I think someone’s trying to break in,’ Jenny whispered, pulling the belt of her silky robe tight. She grabbed his arm as he made to run down the stairs. ‘They’ve put a brick through the front door glass. Be careful, Rod. Please,’ she begged as he shook her off and rushed down the stairs.’

‘You two stay there,’ he shouted over his shoulder. ‘Call the police, Jenny. My phone’s by the bed. Tell them to be quick.’

‘What number do I dial,’ she cried.

‘999, Mum,’ he heard Beth say.

Ben came wandering out of the lounge, hair standing on end and a puzzled look on his face. ‘What’s that racket?’

A large hand was poking through the broken glass trying to unfasten the lock. Ben’s face went pale. Rod looked at him. ‘Do you know who it is?’ The outline of the intruder, against what was left of the stained glass panel, was tall and well built. Rod knew he’d be no match for him and neither would Ben.

Ben nodded. ‘Tanya’s bloke.’

As he spoke a man’s voice said, ‘He’s in there. I heard him speak.’

‘I’ll kill the little bastard for you when I get my hands on him,’ a second man’s voice said.

The hand continued to fumble with the lock but struggled to turn it. Rod looked around for something to whack it with as the first man said. ‘Smash the rest of the fucking window.’

‘I’m trying not to waken the whole family. Robbo said he’ll be sleeping on the sofa. All we need to do is get in there, finish him off and get out quick.’

‘Granddad’s golf clubs,’ Ben whispered. ‘Mum put them in the hall cupboard.’

Rod nodded, quickly reached in and grabbed a club as the catch on the front door gave way and the big man fell into the hall. Rod swung the club into the air and smashed it down on the front of the man's head, taking him by surprise. He yelled as blood spurted from his nose and as he raised the club again Rod heard Jenny and Beth screaming for him to stop. The other man took one look and ran off down the drive as a police car came into view. Ben ran to the door and shouted at the officers that the man was getting away.

Rod dropped the club onto the hall carpet and sat down on the bottom stair his head in his hands. The man was quiet now, crumpled in a heap. What if he'd killed him? He'd do time. Life. He'd die in prison and never get to be with Mandy. Beth sat beside him, sobbing. He put his arm around her and held her tight. He didn't even notice that Jenny had gone back upstairs. The man groaned and stirred. Rod thanked God as he opened his eyes and looked straight at him.

'I'll get you for this,' the man threatened.

'You won't,' the policeman bending over the man said. 'He's on parole,' he told Rod. 'And he's broken just about every last condition. We'll get him patched up and sent straight back down. I'll call an ambulance. I'll need to take a statement when we've got shut of him. Are you okay, sir? You look really shaken.'

Rod took a deep breath. 'I'm getting a chest pain,' he told the officer. 'I need my angina spray.' He excused himself and went back upstairs. Jenny was sitting on the bed with his phone in her hands. Her eyes wide in her pale face.

'You rang her today and every day while we were away,' she said. 'There's a list of calls to her number. You promised you wouldn't contact her.'

'No, I didn't,' he said, picking up his spray and blasting it under his tongue. The minty hit took his breath away momentarily. 'You asked me to promise and I didn't reply. We'll talk about this later. The officer wants to take a statement. I nearly killed that guy tonight, Jen and all you can do is mither about if I've spoken to Mandy. That fucker was after our Ben. That's what he came here for. He's Tanya's fella. Or he was. He'll be going straight back inside. We'd better go down. I'll get Beth to make some tea.'

'So, have you seen her?'

'Later,' he said and grabbed her by the arm. 'Downstairs, now.'

*

Rod sat back on the sofa and gave a statement to the officer who also tried to take one from an extremely shaken Ben. The officer suggested hot sweet tea and Beth took her brother into the kitchen and made him some. He followed her back into the lounge as she brought a tray of mugs through.

'I thought we were being burgled at first,' Rod said. 'Until Ben realised who they were and we heard them threatening to get in and finish him off. Ben's been seeing the big fella's girl while he was inside. In fact they were living together on a houseboat until recently.'

'The officer consulted his notes. 'Tanya? She's been beaten up tonight, I'm afraid. Her boyfriend is a very unforgiving piece of work. One of his parole conditions was to stay away from Tanya and the little lad. She's terrified of him.'

Ben looked up. 'Is she okay? And Charlie? Is he alright? She told me to clear off because he wanted her back. She said it was what she wanted too.'

'She'll be okay in a day or two. It's nothing too serious. Charlie's with her mother for now. I'm afraid

Tanya was too scared to go against her boyfriend's orders. She's in the hospital up the road. I reckon she could use a friend, Ben.'

Ben nodded. 'I'll go and see her tomorrow.'

'Will he be pressing charges against me for smashing his face with a golf club?' Rod asked.

'He might try, but he'll be advised that it's not in his best interests, Mr Davies. It didn't look like there'd be any lasting damage. More's the pity, but you didn't hear me say that! He was breaking into your property with the intentions of causing ABH to your son, maybe even attempted murder. You might be asked to come into the station to make a further statement, but we'll contact you if that's the case.'

'I'll be out of the area after tomorrow for a good few weeks,' Rod said. 'I work in Brighton.'

'Not to worry. I'll leave you all in peace for now.' He got to his feet and followed Rod into the hall. 'Have you got a piece of wood to cover that broken glass with until you can get a glazier in? If you give the crime reference number to your insurer, you'll be able to put in a claim. Not cheap that stained glass.'

'I'll find something,' Rod said. 'Thanks very much.'

Back in the lounge Ben was still shaking. 'Dad, I'm so sorry. My God you could have been facing a murder charge now.'

'Don't dwell on it, son. I'm sorry about Tanya. What a bleeding thug. I hope he didn't hurt the little lad.'

'I'll call at Tanya's mum's tomorrow before I go and see her. We were doing fine and then suddenly she tells me it's over, doesn't love me anymore, wants me out and she's back with him. I'd no idea he was threatening her.'

Rod looked at Beth and Jenny, pale and tired, although Jenny was still giving him the evil eye. Well it could wait because he was knackered and he still had to board up the broken door. 'Go to bed, you two. Go on, I want to talk to Ben in private.'

'What about?' Jenny said, frowning at him. 'If it's about what I found on your phone…'

'For fuck's sake, Jen, just go to bed. We'll talk about that later. Don't you think I've had enough for one night?'

Beth took her mother's arm, kissed her dad and Ben goodnight and led her out of the room.

'Thank God for that,' Rod said, flopping back against the cushions. 'You can come out to the garage with me while we look for a piece of wood in a minute. But first I want you to be honest with me.'

Ben nodded. 'I know what you're gonna ask, Dad.'

'You do?'

'Yeah. Was I dealing on his patch? I was. I thought it wouldn't matter. He wasn't around, although a few of his sidekicks threatened me, but mainly about me seeing Tanya. I thought I was smart enough to carry it off. I only dealt in weed and E. No hard stuff. I always listened to what you told me there.' Ben grinned sheepishly. 'I need a fresh start, Dad. To get away from here. I need to be free of Tanya. I thought I loved her once. I feel sorry for her, but it's time to move on. I'll make sure she's okay first though.'

'Thanks for being honest with me, Ben. How's that mate of yours doing that went up to Edinburgh? The one that asked you to join his band ages ago but you wouldn't leave home.'

'Rory? I don't know. Maybe I'll give him a call and go and visit. But don't you need me here for now to see to Mum?'

Rod shook his head. 'Mum's got to get used to dealing with life. We can't mollycoddle her forever. Right, let's get this door sorted and try and get a few hours kip.'

*

Mandy stared, shocked, as Rod related the events of the previous night. They were on the deserted car park by the Roman Lakes again. She felt sick and horrified that someone should threaten Ben's life. Things like this didn't happen to families like theirs.

'Thank God you were home,' she said.

'Yes, for once in my life it was a blessing,' Rod agreed. 'I'm just a bit worried about leaving Jen and Beth alone now. But the officer who took my statement phoned this morning to ask if we're okay and I told him my concerns. He's given me a phone number they can call direct if they've any problems. I've got a guy coming round later to fit a burglar alarm. So hopefully they'll be alright.'

'And Ben? What will he do now?'

'Get himself sorted, I hope. He's gonna get in touch with an old mate and visit him. I'll give him a few quid to get his new life started. Oh, talking of a few quid.' He dug in his pocket and pulled out an envelope. 'There's five grand in there. Stick it in your Cheshire account. It's for when you move into David's place.'

'Mandy stared into the envelope. 'Five thousand pounds? Oh my God! Rod, what will Jenny say?'

He shrugged. 'No idea. But leave me to deal with that. I got cash rather than give you a personal cheque. She won't be able to trace it back then. It's for us, to get us started.'

Tears filled her eyes and she hugged him. 'Thank you so much. That's a big weight off my mind. I can pay a couple of months rent in advance and set up the workroom upstairs. There's a woman who might be interested in taking on the shop lease. She's one of my customers. She fancies opening an antique shop, which is good, because I'm taking the business with me. She's been looking for suitable premises for ages. I might give her a call later.'

'That's great. I'm gonna get off now, babe. I want to be home when that guy comes to fit the alarm. Jen won't take it all in when he explains how it works. I'll have to repeat myself 'til I'm blue in the face! I'll call you later when I can get a bit of time alone and tomorrow I can call you as often as I like.'

'Drive safely tomorrow. I'll see you in September. It seems ages away.'

'It does. But it'll fly by. We both need to keep busy and you can plod on with your plans for that article and our new place.'

*

CHAPTER NINTEEN

FEBRUARY 1995

Mandy looked down at the crumpled little face. Deep blue eyes stared back at her, unblinking. Chubby fists pushed their way into an impatient mouth, accompanied by grunts and snuffles. Her new grandson was hungry. He was less than two hours old but those eyes told her he'd been here before. She smiled and stroked him under his chin. He was the spit of Becky's partner Andy, and looked nothing like her mental picture of the baby she'd lost. She was glad. The heartache was back though, along with the thoughts that she might have shared a moment like this with Rod. Best not to dwell on it. Today was a happy day. She looked across at her daughter who had a proud smile on her face.

'Ten pounds, Mum!' Becky said. 'No wonder I looked like the side of a house. He's bloody huge. And he's two weeks early. Good job I didn't go full term, it doesn't bear thinking about. Sorry you didn't get your granddaughter again though. You'll have to wait now until Louise and Nic produce. He's definitely my last. It felt like giving birth to a baby elephant.'

Mandy smiled. 'He'll do just fine, Becky. He's beautiful. The image of Andy, and I think he's going to be blonde like your others. His eyebrows and what bit of hair he's got are fair.' She ran a finger over the soft downy head. 'So, has he got a name yet?'

'Harry,' Becky said. 'Harry Michael - after Dad. Thought it might cheer him up a bit. He's a right Victor Meldrew at the moment. That woman he's been seeing from work doesn't seem to be doing him much good.'

‘Hmm, probably because she won’t let him have all his own way,’ Mandy muttered. ‘He’ll soon realise he can’t treat every woman like he treated me and get away with it. But he’ll be really pleased about the name,’ she added.

She’d been surprised, after all his bluster, how badly Mike seemed to be affected by her leaving him. She’d told him she planned to move into David’s cottage as soon as it was ready. That she needed space to get her head around things, space that she couldn’t get at the family home. He appeared to accept it at first, probably because he thought she’d change her mind, and he even suggested she take some of the furniture. But as the day drew closer he’d sulked, picked fights and in the end walked out of the house while the man with a van she’d hired loaded her things. She guessed he was hurting more than he’d let on. They’d agreed to remain amicable for the girls and their grandchildren. How he would react when he discovered she was still seeing Rod remained to be seen. Saying goodbye to the dogs had been agony. Their anxious faces had followed her every move and when the van man shouted he was ready to roll, she’d dropped to her knees and sobbed into their fur, promising to visit as soon as she could.

David had finished the cottage at the beginning of November, a bit later than anticipated, but in good time for Rod to spend her birthday with her. They’d had a wonderful day. He’d cooked a meal for them, fussed over her, ran her a bubble bath, lit scented candles, and then brought two glasses of chilled white wine upstairs and climbed in the bath with her. Afterwards they made love on the rug in front of the wood-burning stove and then he sung her a couple of songs using his new keyboard. He was so romantic and she loved it. She didn’t think she could feel any happier than she’d felt that night. She'd also spent a couple of nights away with him in the Midlands on the run up to Christmas, but the shop had been too busy with seasonal orders to leave for too long. The woman who wanted to start an antiques business had been eager to take on the lease. A fifty-per-cent-off sale in January, coupled with the Christmas takings, had brought in enough money to cover the business debts, leaving her with a clean slate to begin working from home. It felt less stressful, having only one set of rent and bills to find.

'Come back to earth, Mother!' Becky waved a hand in front of her eyes.

'Sorry, love, I was miles away.'

'I could tell,' Becky said a look of amusement in her eyes. 'You were in a trance. I bet I know who you were thinking about.'

'You do?'

'Uncle Rod! It's been months since it all blew up. But I think you're finding it hard to forget. Are you still in love with him?'

Mandy could feel her cheeks heating. 'No,' she fibbed. 'Well, I miss him, of course. We were friends for over thirty years. You can't wipe that out overnight.'

Becky nodded. 'If it's any consolation Beth told Nic that she doesn't think her dad's coming home for good again. He only pops in on the odd day to see them. Aunty Jen's still refusing to accept it's over. Beth's tried to talk to her about letting him go and starting a new life. But Aunty Jen says she knows it's not really what he wants. She's so blinkered, isn't she, Mum? At least you've moved on. You'll meet someone else soon enough.'

Mandy smiled. 'I'm in no rush. Your dad still won't agree to a divorce. I've got to wait a full two years from the day I left him.'

Becky frowned. 'Surely he can't stop you seeing a new man if you meet someone you fancy.'

'No, he can't. But I don't wish to antagonize him. I want what I'm entitled to out of the house. He's stalling on buying me out and he won't put it up for sale while Nic's still at home. If he thought I was seeing someone he might get even more awkward.'

'That doesn't seem fair when he's taking that woman out occasionally. Nic said he stayed over at her place last Saturday night.'

'Did he now? Interesting.' She made a mental note of the date to write in her diary. During a drunken rant this week, when she'd popped in to see the dogs, Mike threatened that if he decided to divorce her, it would be for adultery with Rod and not because their marriage had irreconcilably broken down. In an earlier discussion he'd promised not to do that as it may cause Jenny further upset. He was forever changing his mind to wind her up. It would be handy to have the name of the other woman and the dates Mike had presumably slept with her, just in case. Well at least she'd got a start now.

'Are you going shopping when you leave here, Mum?'

'Yes, do you want me to get something for you?'

'A Valentine's card for Andy, please. You don't have to choose a pressie, Harry's his gift this year.' Becky smiled and looked at her watch. 'He should be back soon with the boys. He's picking them up from school. I hope Tommy won't be too disappointed. He told me to make sure he got a sister this time. Young

Andy's not bothered what we have. He's not that interested in babies.'

'Typical six-year-old!' Mandy grinned. 'I'll go to the shops then and see you tonight.' She gave baby Harry back to Becky and dropped a kiss on her head. 'See you later, sweetheart and well done.'

*

Tomorrow was Valentine's Day. Rod was driving back to spend a couple of days with her. He'd promised to be here by early evening after dropping his kit off at the group's next venue. He'd extended his contract with Timeless, although the seaside gigs, out of season, were few and far between. He spent a lot of time in the Midlands, South Wales, Portsmouth and Southampton, doing the odd solo gig in between working with the band. Mandy had watched him play a solo gig during her visit to the Midlands. She'd felt so proud as he'd bantered with the audience, telling near-the-knuckle jokes as well as singing. His act had gone down really well. Between them they'd picked out several songs they both liked. Rod had amazed her with his ability to learn them so quickly. Whenever she heard something on the radio that she felt would suit his voice and style she made a note and told him. She couldn't wait for them to be together permanently and have him working local, then she could go to all the gigs.

She unpacked her shopping and put Becky's card for Andy on the dresser. She'd bought a black silk shirt for Rod and hung it on a hanger over the lounge door. It would look nice on stage. His brown hair had developed a lot more silver steaks over the last few months, hardly surprising, she thought, but it suited him and he always looked good in black. She'd made a card and stuck a photograph of the two of them, that Dee had taken the other week, on the front. Inside she'd made up her own verse. It was a poem she'd written especially for Rod called Soulmates. She'd surprised herself lately with her writing capers and after a few false starts, felt quite proud of the poem. Dee had given her lessons on how to use the word processor. She was a quick learner and decided, as Rod had suggested, that writing a factual book rather than an article was a good idea. But a couple of weeks ago David had brought a book round to show her called "It Happened in Manchester" and it was very similar to what she had in mind. She felt it was pointless to continue in the same vein, but she enjoyed writing and her ideas soon developed into a fictional story. Characters began to take shape in her mind. A young band, their girls and the antics they got up to in an effort to become famous. Each night she spent a couple of hours jotting down further ideas. Scenes played out in her head. It would probably never come to anything, but it certainly gave her something to do and made her feel closer to Rod as she picked his brains for tales about his bands and their time on the road.

In the kitchen she put the kettle on. There was a knock at the door as it boiled and she let in Sue, who kicked off her shoes and flopped down on the sofa. Mandy gave her a mug of tea and a Danish pastry.

'It's freezing out there,' Sue said. 'Lovely and warm in here though. So, how was the baby? And Becky?'

'He's lovely. Enormous! Ten pounds! Sorry if I sounded a bit frantic when I called you, but she'd just given birth. I had to go straight to the hospital. I was trying to catch you before you left to come here.'

'Don't worry about it. I went into Pickford instead and bought some baby things. I'll wrap them here and you can take them in tonight. Ten pounds, eh? Good job I got the next size up from newborn.'

'Makes your eyes water, doesn't it?'

'Ouch!' Sue grimaced. 'Certainly does. Bet she's glad it's over. How did you feel when you saw him?'

Mandy was quiet for a moment. 'Sad, but I put on a brave face. I was fine after a few minutes. I'd been dreading it, but I was okay.' She got up to throw a log into the stove and blinked away a tear.

Sue stretched out her legs on the sofa and sighed. 'It's so cozy in here. I love it and you've got it really nice, it's not at all twee.'

'Thanks.' Mandy looked proudly around the lounge. Some of Rod's dad's money had gone towards a pair of cream sofas, which sat either side of the fireplace, two stripped pine side tables and the matching Welsh dresser. She'd painted the walls a rich cream with the chimney breast a contrasting dark plum that she'd had specially mixed. Rod had hung a huge pine framed mirror above the stove. It looked good against the strong colour. David had stripped and varnished the floorboards and a beige wool Chinese rug sat in front of the fire in between the sofas. Mandy had made the curtains and matching cushions from a bold beige and plum Sanderson print.

'I'm very happy here, I feel so comfortable. From the first day I moved in, had tea at Dee's and she and David got me plastered on vodka and Coke, I've felt right at home.' She grinned as she recalled how the pair had helped her home, popped her into bed fully clothed, minus her boots, locked up and put the keys through the letterbox. She'd slept until Rod had called her Sunday lunchtime. She'd never felt strange living alone and certainly didn't feel lonely. Instead there was an enormous sense of relief and freedom. No more pussyfooting around and walking on eggshells. It was pure bliss to come and go as she pleased. Because she spent time writing late into the night she developed a routine of a sleep in, breakfast at ten, followed by a shower and then lying on the bed to call Rod. It set the pattern of her mornings before beginning work in the big loft room at eleven.

'I love that.' Sue pointed to the black silk shirt. 'For Rod, I presume?'

'Yep. For Valentine's Day. He's coming home for a couple of days.'

'Ah, right,' Sue said. 'And when you say home, you mean he's coming here?'

Mandy nodded. 'Jen thinks he's down south all week.'

'So, he's not seeing her at all tomorrow?'

'No, he's coming straight here. Why do you ask?'

'She was in the coffee shop in town on Saturday,' Sue began. 'I didn't see her at first because she had her back to me, talking to a woman I don't know. I sat at the table behind them; the only one free. I dropped my handbag on the floor. The woman saw me struggling with my shopping and picked it up. Jenny turned, saw it was me and turned back without letting on. Then she starts talking in a really loud voice. She asked the woman if she was doing anything special for Valentine's Day. The woman said her and her hubby don't bother anymore. Jenny said Rod was coming home especially and they were having a romantic night away in a hotel, but she didn't know where as it was a surprise. She said he always makes Valentine's Day really special because they see so little of each other the rest of the year and he always gave her red roses. It was obviously said for my benefit so that I'd overhear, report back, and then you're supposed to think everything's hunky dory.'

Mandy shook her head. ‘Rod told me he’s really looking forward to tomorrow. He and Jen haven’t bothered with Valentine’s for years. But strangely enough, last year we actually did do something, pure coincidence it was Valentine’s Day though. We all went for a curry. A guy came into the restaurant, selling red roses for the ladies. Rod just looked away. Mike ended up buying two, one each for me and Jen! She told Mike it was the first time she’d had a red rose for years! So, you’re right, Sue, that performance would have been for your benefit, so you could pass it on to me.’

‘Well, she was "Rod this, Rod that, Rod the other",’ Sue said. ‘You’ve got to feel a bit sorry for her I suppose. But it’s time she woke up and smelt the bloody coffee. Quite honestly, if I had a husband who’d cheated on me, only dropped in occasionally, slept in the spare room and then buggered off again the next day, I’d tell him to piss off for good!’

‘Me too. Hopefully she will this year. Rod’s getting fed up of working away all the time. James had a right go at him recently when Rod told him he’d soon be leaving for good. James said if he did, then he wants nothing more to do with him and he said he’d get Ben and Beth on side too. He told Rod that if he doesn’t do right by their mum and stay with her, then he can forget he’s got kids. It’s so unfair. Rod does his best; he works hard, pays all the bills. He gave her some of his dad’s money to get some new stuff for the house. She’s still on the sick ‘cos she says she can’t cope. She’s had counselling and medication, but it’s obviously not working if she’s still pretending things are fine.

‘Rod gets really depressed himself when he’s been home. He even suggested we pack up and move abroad to get away from it all and he’ll try and get work playing in bars. But I don’t want to run away. I’ve done my leaving and got myself sorted. Besides, the girls need me, especially Becky now she's had the new baby. He's going to have to be really firm with Jen, or we might as well forget our plans and he stays with her and let's me go. I don't want to do this hiding away thing forever. We can't go out when he's here. We have to stay holed up in case anyone sees us. He has to park a few streets away so his car isn't seen outside. We can only carry on like this for so long.'

'I know, it's hard, but you wouldn't want it to end. And if he did move in with you properly Mike would be a real arse about things. You might lose out money-wise. Don't think there's an easy answer, Mand. You're both just going to have to be patient. But at least you get a clear idea of what's going on in that fuddled head of hers now.'

Mandy nodded. 'I won't let it spoil tomorrow. It's only a month to our first anniversary too. Almost a year since we went to Hartshead Moor. Can't believe everything that's happened since.'

*

Rod pulled up outside the cottage and leapt out of the car. He grabbed his holdall and a bouquet of flowers from the back seat. He glanced around to make sure he wasn't being watched and let himself in at the front door. Mandy hurried through from the kitchen to greet him. He kissed her as she flung her arms around him.

'You're early,' she said. 'Thanks for your lovely card. It came this morning.'

'Good. I wanted you to have it first thing rather than wait for me getting here. I made good time, beat the rush hour. These are for you.' He gave her the hand tied bouquet of early spring flowers and red roses. 'The woman in the flower shop let me pick my own.

Thought the colours would look nice in here. Did I do well?'

'You did.' She planted a kiss on his lips. 'They're gorgeous. Thank you.'

'I've got a surprise for you. I'll get it and then move the car.'

'Okay. Mysterious!' She stood by the front door as he wrestled a large flat box from the back of the car. She sidestepped as he struggled indoors. 'What on earth is it?'

'A pine desk,' he said, smiling. 'I'll put it together tomorrow.'

'Oh, Rod, that's really thoughtful of you,' she said, hugging him. 'I take up the whole of the kitchen table when I'm writing. I've had to clear everything away so we can eat. It'll be so nice to be organized with a desk.'

'I was thinking maybe we could get you a computer and a proper printer.'

'A computer?' Mandy looked worried. 'I wouldn't have a clue what to do with it. I'm just getting to grips with the processor.'

'Dee uses one at work. She'll be able to help you. And the college is just down the hill. You could go to a class and learn. I'll pay.'

'Would you? Really? I suppose I could give it a go then. Thank you.'

He smiled and ruffled her hair. 'I'll shift the car. Back in a minute.'

He parked two roads away and lit a cigarette as he walked back to the cottage. He had something else to give Mandy later, but it could wait for the right moment. In the kitchen she was putting the finishing touches to the table. Little red candles in dainty glass holders, red and gold napkins. She turned to smile as he stood watching her. Her black velvet skirt fitted snugly over her hips and the red of her silky top added a glow to her face. He felt the blood rush to his groin as she bent to take vases from the cupboard under the sink. He couldn't wait for later, it was two weeks since his last trip home and he was desperate to make love to her.

'I'll arrange the flowers,' she said.

'I'll leave you to it while I take a shower.' He picked up his holdall. 'What's for dinner, by the way? It smells lovely.'

'Rosemary chicken, roast potatoes and lots of fancy veggies. And for dessert I got out-of-season strawberries and home made dairy ice cream from that little farm shop down the road.'

'Yum! Sounds good. I'm starving.'

'By the time you've had your shower it'll be nearly ready to serve up.'

*

Mandy arranged the flowers in the vases and placed a small one, with some of the red roses, in the middle of the table. She took two vases into the lounge and placed one on the windowsill and the other on the floor beside the fireplace, threw a log into the wood-burner and drew the curtains against the chilly night. She could hear Rod singing as he showered and her stomach did a little loop as she thought about the wonderful night she knew they were going to have. On one of the side tables was a fancy black and gold bag containing the silk shirt wrapped in black tissue paper. She'd had a devil of a job finding black, but she liked to wrap her parcels just so and had tracked some down in a craft shop along with a shiny gold envelope for her home-made card. She hoped Rod would like the poem.

She sat down on the sofa and waited for him to join her. He was with her in a few minutes, dressed in clean jeans and black T-shirt, his hair wet and spiky. He flopped down beside her and she gave him his gift.

He unwrapped it and held the shirt against him. 'It's perfect. I'll wear it on stage. Thank you, babe.'

'You're welcome. I thought it would look good when you're performing.' She handed him the gold envelope.

He slid the card out and smiled at the picture of the two of them, arms around each other on Dee's sofa, looking deep into one another's eyes. He read the poem and looked at her, shaking his head. 'Did you write this?'

She nodded. 'Don't you like it?'

'Like it? I love it. It's bloody wonderful.' He pulled her into his arms, held her tight and kissed her. 'Nobody has ever done anything like that for me. It's so special, so personal. I can't believe you wrote it. I tell you what; I've got a load of half-finished songs lying around. We could have a look at them; see if you can help me. What do you think?'

'Rod, I'd love to. I want to be really involved in whatever you do when we're together.'

'And you will be. I've got something else I want to give you. I was saving it for the right time and that'll be now. Won't be a minute.'

Mandy sat back and smiled as he shot off up the stairs. He hurried back, carrying a small black velvet pouch. He tipped two gold bands onto her palm. 'My parents' rings,' he said as she looked puzzled. 'I'd like to have them made into a ring for you. I thought we could get a jeweller to fashion them into something you'd like and you can choose whatever stone you fancied.'

Her eyes filled with tears as she looked at the rings. Both worn, one much thinner; his mother's ring. Rod's mum and dad had been happy for years. Hopefully that would be a good omen. 'I don't know what to say,' she whispered. 'This means so much to me. Are you sure you don't want them to go to Beth?'

'She wouldn't appreciate them. Not trendy enough. I want you to have them. I know we can't get married or engaged yet, but this would mean a lot to me. I've thought about it for weeks since Dad died, but obviously I couldn't do anything while you were living with Mike. So I thought I'd save them for today. Have a think about what stone you'd like, a diamond or something, and I'll get it sorted.'

'Don't need to think. I know exactly what I'd like. I'm not a diamond sort of girl. I just love opals, fiery opals.'

'An opal it is then.' He laughed and pulled her to him. 'I'll take them into town tomorrow and get it organised. Hopefully next time I'm home the ring will be ready and we'll have another celebration. Shall we eat now? I'm nearly passing out.'

Mandy smiled. 'It's all the excitement. Come through and light the candles while I dish up. I got pink champagne too.'

*

Mandy asked for a window seat in Brambles. Sue was joining her for lunch. Her stomach churned as the door opened. It wasn't Sue, but a trendy young couple who were shown to a seat near the back of the restaurant. The door opened again and Sue walked in. The smile on her friend's face was a mile wide. Mandy knew the news must be good.

'Well?' she prompted as the waiter showed Sue to her seat.

'All clear!' Sue exclaimed. 'It's bloody well gone, Mand. I can't believe it.'

‘Oh my God! Fantastic. Oh come here, let me give you a hug.’ Mandy nearly knocked Sue off her seat in her enthusiasm.

‘Mind my wig,’ Sue said, grinning. She straightened the blonde bob that looked so like her own hair. ‘I still need regular checkups and blood tests. The first lot’s in three months. I might book a holiday if those come back okay. Do you fancy going away somewhere in the summer? It’ll have to be school hols because I’ll be going back to work after the Easter break.’

Mandy nodded. ‘I’d love to, but I’ll have to see what happens in the next few weeks.’

‘Well we’ve plenty of time to think about it. Shall we order? Then you can tell me your latest news. A drink first I think, to celebrate. A carafe of house red please,’ she said to the young waiter. ‘Better bring us some bread too.’ She turned back to Mandy. ‘Wine goes straight to my head at lunchtime. I’ve had nothing to eat all day. Couldn’t face it before going to the hospital.’

‘Same here,’ Mandy said. ‘Been on tenterhooks all morning. Haven’t even done any work. I couldn’t concentrate.’

‘Are you still enjoying working from home again?’

‘Yes, it’s much easier this time around because I’ve got no kids under my feet. I’m doing okay. Jen’s going back to work too, apparently. Next week, I think. That’ll make things easier for Rod. He said the other day his dad’s money’s going down quickly. He transferred what was left to a new account, but he needs to keep dipping in it to give to Jenny. God knows what she spends it all on, considering she claims to hardly leave the house. Rod’s coming home on Wednesday. It’s his duty visit time. He’s gonna call in and see me first, but he’ll be staying there overnight.’

‘That’s a pity,’ Sue said. ‘Can’t he just pop in and see her and then spend the night with you?’

Mandy laughed. ‘If only. It doesn’t work like that, I’m afraid. Can you imagine? Hi, Jen, nice to see you. Don’t bother cooking for me; I’ll be sleeping at Mandy’s tonight! He’s staying at mine the second night. He’ll tell her he’s got to go back early.’

‘She knows you’ve left Mike though and got your own place. I’m surprised she hasn’t tried to find you yet.’

‘I’m surprised, too. Nic said my name never crops up when she goes round to see Beth. But Beth told Jenny I’d left Mike the week I did it. It must go round and round in her head, wondering if Rod comes to see me. It would mine.’

‘Mine too,’ Sue said as the waiter brought the wine and a basket of bread to the table. ‘She’ll know that he does, believe me. But she’ll never admit it to herself and she won’t ask Rod because that would mean saying your name and planting it in his head.’ Sue poured them each a glass of wine. She raised hers to Mandy’s. ‘I’m giving my fella the elbow this week. I’ve got through the treatment without missing him; it’s time to say get lost. So here’s to our futures, Mandy. May they be a bit better than the past!’

*

Rod pulled up outside his house. He no longer thought of it as home. It was almost four in the afternoon, but the lounge and bedroom curtains were still closed. Jenny was up because he’d spoken to her when he stopped for a coffee and a pee at Knutsford. He’d been at Mandy’s for a couple of hours, so Jen would have had plenty of time to get her arse into gear. Maybe she was lying down, rehearsing her woe is me act in readiness. He lit a cigarette and sat in the car for a few minutes. Tearing himself away from Mandy had been hard. He could quite happily have stayed in bed with her for his whole two day break. Instead he had to leave her and come here, to play the usual game of unhappy families. He stubbed out the end of his fag, chucked it out the car window and braced himself.

He let himself into the house, walked past the lounge door that was slightly ajar, dumped his bag in the hall and went into the kitchen. A bottle of red wine stood open on the worktop. He picked it up; half empty. 'Jen, I'm back. Where are you?'

'In here,' she called from the lounge.

He pushed open the door but couldn't see her at first. 'Why are the bloody curtains closed?' He yanked them back and turned to look at her. She was lying on the sofa; glass in hand, a towel wrapped around her middle. She got to her feet and moved towards him.

'I closed the curtains because it's more private,' she said.

He stared at her. 'For what?'

She let the towel slip to the floor and stood naked in front of him.

'We've got the place to ourselves,' she whispered. 'It's been so long, Rod.' She reached for him and he backed away, recoiling from her touch.

'For fuck's sake! What do you think you're playing at? Get upstairs and put some bloody clothes on.'

Her lips quivered as he picked the towel up and threw it to her. He felt repulsed. She burst into tears and ran from the room. He rummaged in the drinks cupboard and poured himself a whisky. What the hell had got into her? Where on earth had she got the notion he'd want to make love to her? Certainly not from him. He sat down on the sofa she'd vacated and let his head fall back against the cushions. Christ, this was a good start.

He left it ten minutes and then called up the stairs. 'Are you dressed now? I'm coming up.'

She was fully clothed, lying on the bed, staring up at the ceiling. 'Why did you do that, Jen? All the years we've been married, you've never once met me naked when I've walked into the house. Why start now when it's all over?'

She ignored his questions. 'You're seeing Mandy again, aren't you? Is that where you've been today? I was expecting you home ages ago. It doesn't take three hours to drive from Knutsford Services.'

Shit, had he told her he was at Knutsford? He'd meant to say the services and not give a name. He just got so mithered with everything. He felt under pressure when he was here. He knew he couldn't go on like this. It had to stop. But if he told her now that he was going to Mandy she'd be straight on the phone to Mike and that would screw up Mandy's entitlement from the house. Fuck, why was everything about money? Peace of mind, happiness, you couldn't buy those things and at the moment Rod knew he'd settle for being skint forever if he could just walk out of the trap Jenny had got him in.

'I nipped into Pickford Music Exchange,' he lied. 'Got talking to a guy I worked with in a band years ago. Lot to catch up with.'

'Why didn't you tell me you'd be doing that then?'

'Why should I? We live separate lives now. I don't need to tell you my every move. I don't ask you yours.'

'I don't believe you. You were with Mandy. I know you're seeing her again. In fact, you probably never stopped.'

He shrugged. 'Whatever. You don't believe a word I say anyway. Have it your own way.'

'So you are seeing her?'

'If you say so.' He got up, walked out of the room and went downstairs. He called Beth and asked her what time she was coming home.

'Mum said to stay out of the way all afternoon, Dad. She wanted to see you on her own. But I'm cold and I've got no money to hang around in town.'

'Get the bus home, sweetheart. I need to talk to you.' He ended the call and rang Mandy. 'Can I stay tonight? I'll explain when I get there.'

'You're going to her?' Jenny was standing in the doorway. 'Does Mike know you're seeing her again?'

'No, but I'll leave you to tell him after I've gone. Come and sit down.'

She sat opposite him, staring unblinkingly.

'Are you taking your medication?' he asked. 'You shouldn't be drinking.' At least she wasn't screaming and shouting at him. She seemed to be very calm. He hoped to God it wasn't the one before the storm again. His chest felt tight. He used his spray.

'You got a pain?' she asked, a worried frown crossing her face. 'Is that my fault?'

'Well, put it this way, I only ever use it when I'm here. I never get pains when I'm away. This can't go on, Jenny. We need to make the split official. Like I told you before, you can have the house and while I'm able, I'll continue to pay the mortgage and help with the bills. But you have to go back to work and help me. If you can't do that then we'll need to sell the house and get you and Beth a little flat.'

She looked horrified, as he knew she would. 'I'm not giving up my home just because you can't keep it in your pants!' she spat.

'Fine, then you'll be happy to help me keep the roof over your head by going back to work. Otherwise, there's no choice. I'll pack what bit of stuff I've got here and put it in the car. Beth's on her way home. I need to talk with her. I'll take my dad's golf clubs with me. I don't want them ending up at the tip. Did the police return the one they took as evidence? There was no case so I presume they've finished with it now.'

'Yes, but I'll get them.'

She made to get up off the sofa, but Rod beat her to the door. He didn't quite trust her not to whack him with a club and she'd seemed a bit agitated as she made her move.

She stood back chewing her lip as he rummaged in the cupboard under the stairs.

'What the fuck's all this lot?' He pulled out two boxed kettles and two toasters and delved back in for more. By the time he'd finished the hall floor was littered with small electrical appliances. Hairdryers, irons, sandwich makers, more kettles and toasters. He reckoned there was several hundred pounds worth. Each box had a store receipt stuck to the lid. He scratched his head and looked at Jenny who stood with tears running down her cheeks. 'I don't get this. What's going on, Jen?'

'I paid for them all. I didn't steal anything.'

'I can see that. They've all got receipts. But why?'

She shrugged. 'I just like buying things for the house.'

'I'm sure you do. But this isn't normal. Is this where all the extra money I gave you went?'

She nodded. 'Sorry. I didn't want you to see them. I'll take them back tomorrow.'

'You can go and see the doctor. Are you sure you went for all the counselling sessions?'

'No, I didn't. I stopped taking my pills too.'

'Right, well tomorrow you can go to the doctors and Beth will go with you.'

'Can't you take me?'

'No. You have to stand on your own two feet now, Jenny. It's not good for you that I keep coming home.'

'But I live for your visits, you know I do.'

'Yes, I do know. And that's the problem. You're not getting on with your life in the weeks in-between. You have to let go.'

'I still won't divorce you,' she said. 'You'll have to wait. And if you ever marry her, I'll kill myself.' She sat down on the bottom stair, looking like Beth when she'd been told off.

He sighed. It was so hard to remain calm and in control and not bawl and shout at her. But he wasn't backing down now. 'Don't be ridiculous. Stop trying to control me. It's not gonna work anymore. I don't need to be married to be happy. It's not the be all and end all, you know. It didn't do us much good, did it? Nor Mike and Mandy. Right, I'll load this lot into my car. You can help me carry them out. The bloody neighbours'll think we've robbed Curry's or something.'

She grabbed his arm as he bent to pick up some toasters. 'Rod, can we still be friends.'

'That'll be up to you and how things go. But you have to put some effort in and take responsibility for your own life now, Jen. I can't do it for you anymore. The stress will finish me off.'

*

'I can't believe it,' Mandy said, staring at the pile of boxes lined up by the back wall of the lounge. 'It kind of beggar's belief. Why not clothes or perfume, something more feminine, at least? Is it a form of kleptomania?'

'Maybe.' Rod sighed. 'It's weird. Never heard anything like it. Anyway, I'll try and get the money back tomorrow.'

'She knows you're here now?'

'She does. But she doesn't have the address. We'll let a bit of water flow under the bridge first. I guess you need to put Mike in the picture. I'll have to speak to Ben and James later too. Beth was fine. I think Ben will be okay, but if James chooses not to call me Dad anymore that's up to him. It hurts, but I can't live my life under their rules. I've done it for long enough.'

Mandy nodded and looked at her watch. 'I'll see if Mike's home from work now. Catch him before Jenny spills the beans. You go and make us a coffee and unpack your clothes. Help yourself to wardrobe space.'

He took her hands. 'Mand?'

'What?'

'We've done it! We're living together.'

She smiled. 'Yeah, we are! But we're not quite out of the woods yet.'

Rod nodded and left her alone while she called her old home.

'Nic, hi, darling. Is your dad home yet?'

'Err, he is, but he's waiting for a taxi to the airport. Hang on; I'll get him for you.' Mandy heard Nic yelling "Dad" then Mike picked up, sounding mellow. Obviously had a drink, or three.

'Mandy, what can I do for you? Have to be quick, I'm going away.'

'With work? What about the dogs and Nic? Hope Louise is going to be staying over.'

'Err, no, not work, pleasure. Off to Turkey for a week with a friend from the office. Last minute booking. Louise is staying with Nic and the dogs.'

‘Right, I see. I heard you weren’t getting on too well with your erm, friend from the office.’

He was quiet for a long moment. ‘Not really anything to do with you, but things have improved.’

‘Good. I’m happy for you. You sound relaxed right now. Well - I’m glad I caught you before you go swanning off. I want to tell you something.’ She took a deep breath and could hardly keep the smile out of her voice. ‘Rod’s moved in with me. So when you get back, we’ll discuss our divorce and you buying me out of the house. I’m serious, Mike,’ she said before he had a chance to say anything. ‘You going away with another woman must mean that our marriage has well and truly, irreconcilably broken down. Wouldn’t you say?’ He was quiet again and she heard the doorbell ringing. ‘Sounds like your taxi’s here. Have a good time.’ She hung up and sat back on the sofa, hugging the phone.

‘What’s happening?’ Rod came in with the coffees and put them on the side table. ‘Why are you grinning like an idiot? What did he say?’

‘Not a lot! He hasn’t a blooming leg to stand on. He’s only off to Turkey with a woman from work. I caught him as the taxi arrived.’

‘No way? Bloody hell. The old hypocrite. I wonder if he was already giving her one and that’s why he was such a bastard with you.’

‘Who knows,’ Mandy said, snuggling up to him. ‘If he was I couldn’t give a damn. Well, that’s him and Jen dealt with to a point. Just my girls now. But to be honest, I don’t think they’ll be that surprised.’

‘No more hiding away,’ Rod said. ‘We can actually go into Pickford quite openly tomorrow and pick your ring up. You can try it to make sure it fits you. They took the measurement from your old wedding ring like you suggested, so it should be fine.’

‘Can’t wait. It feels odd not having a ring on after all the years I’ve worn one.’

‘I know it’s not the same as a wedding ring, but to me it means so much to know you’ll be wearing it,’ he said, squeezing her.

‘It will mean the world to me too, Rod. It’s just as important as a wedding ring, if not more. You do realise it’s a year next week since Hartshead Moor? I’ll try the ring tomorrow for size, but why don’t we save you giving it to me until our first anniversary?’

‘Okay, that’s perfect. We’ll have a little celebration. Can’t believe we’ve made it.’ He shook his head in wonder. ‘Just shows that when the time’s right, it’s right.’

‘When you suggested *Fast Movin’ Train* for our song, you couldn’t have picked anything more appropriate,’ she said, smiling ‘Those first few months were just like being on a speeding train. Now we’re off it, I feel I can relax at last.’

‘Me too. I’m going to spend the rest of my life loving you, Mandy. Is that okay?’

She smiled and held him close. ‘Totally.’

***

SOULMATES
Mandy's Valentine's poem for Rod

There are no legal ties to bind us
You give me the space to be free
In our head and our hearts we are never apart
We're Soulmates for life, you and me
You always know what I'm thinking
Our wavelengths are almost the same
We're two of a kind, in tune but not blind
To the problems that come with the game
We've known each other forever
But our paths only criss-crossed before
Then your twinkling blue eyes sent a signal
With the promise that there would be more
When I see you on stage dressed in black
I get such a thrill, you're my man
As your voice fills my head with sweet music
I know I'm your number one fan
Our love is immeasurable pleasure
Without it we're lonely and blue
It's something to nurture and treasure
We're Soulmates for life, me and you

BY THE SAME AUTHOR

THE ROCK'N'ROLL YEARS SERIES:
Three Steps to Heaven #1
'Til I Kissed You #2
Always On My Mind #3
Not Fade Away: #4
That'll Be The Day: #5 The prequel to Three Steps To Heaven. Set in the late 50's early 60's.

THE FAIRGROUND/BIKER ROMANCE SERIES:
Cathy's Clown: #1

Ruby Tuesday #2. The sequel to Cathy's Clown coming soon.

It's Only Words: An Anthology of romantic short stories

Pam Howes can be found on Twitter @PamHowes1

Facebook **http://www.facebook.com/pages/Pam-Howes-Author/260328010709267**

Lightning Source UK Ltd.
Milton Keynes UK
UKHW011902030323
418007UK00001B/65

9 781786 973931